THE CURSED MELODIES

CONNIE GLYNN

PENGUIN BOOKS

PENGUIN BOOKS

UK | USA | Canada | Ireland | Australia
India | New Zealand | South Africa

Penguin Books is part of the Penguin Random House group of companies
whose addresses can be found at global.penguinrandomhouse.com

www.penguin.co.uk   www.puffin.co.uk   www.ladybird.co.uk

First published 2025
This edition published 2026

002

Set in 12/15pt Goudy Oldstyle Std
Typeset by Jouve (UK), Milton Keynes
Printed and bound in Great Britain by Clays Ltd, Elcograf S.p.A.

The authorized representative in the EEA is Penguin Random House Ireland,
Morrison Chambers, 32 Nassau Street, Dublin D02 YH68

A CIP catalogue record for this book is available from the British Library

ISBN: 978-0-241-64616-8

All correspondence to:
Penguin Books
Penguin Random House Children's
One Embassy Gardens, 8 Viaduct Gardens, London SW11 7BW

For all the oddballs. You'll find where you belong.

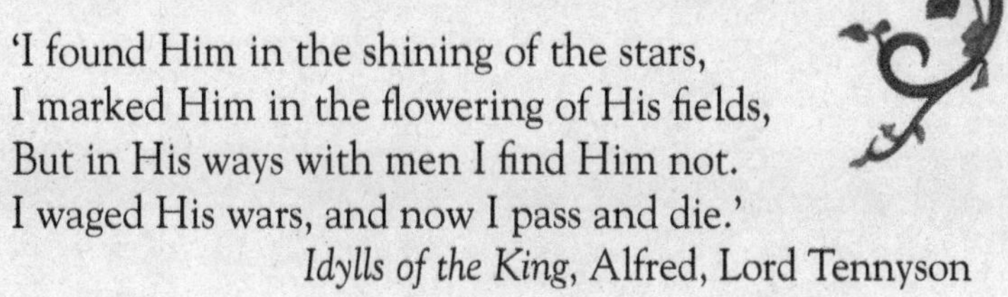

'I found Him in the shining of the stars,
I marked Him in the flowering of His fields,
But in His ways with men I find Him not.
I waged His wars, and now I pass and die.'
Idylls of the King, Alfred, Lord Tennyson

'We only go around once . . . I hope.'
Daria Morgendorffer

Before Our Story Began

In the not-too-distant past, one you might almost recognize, a very important book was burning alive.

A young man stood over the pages, encouraging the purple and blue fire with his voice like a shepherd leading his flock. Never mind that it would not scorch through. The purpose of the spell was not to burn, not really, but to undo. To do what fire does best, and transform. You see, this fire was not made from heat, or sparked by flint; it came from the source of all magic itself – music.

As the charm played, the notes in the melody hummed and soared, a conjuring so ancient it might change the very course of history. At least, that is what the man hoped it might do.

Downstairs, there was a ruckus, the clatter of wood on wood, of furniture squeaking across floorboards. Voices shouted up the stairs.

They had arrived.

The man peered through the gap in the curtains where a single sliver of moonlight tore a line across the room. The book kept burning.

In the distance, purple-robed figures approached from the wooded path with light singing in their palms. They moved slowly and deliberately, like the shadows cast by clouds. He knew whom they were here for – *what* they were here for. Attendants from the Shadow Library, come to take them to their king, to the Magisters themselves.

It was time for the man and his companions to answer for their crimes.

But first, before the lot of them were whisked away to meet their fate within the Shadow Library – that keeper of lost knowledge, spells and stories – before they would stand before the Grand Coterie for judgement, he must finish the spell.

The fate of the world depended on it.

There was a knock on the door just as the fire sighed into oblivion. With one last hiss, the contents of the book vanished. The whispering ink of the pages turning to nothing but a dark memory. A memory from long ago, when Rupert Faymore had pored over those withered symbols – monsters, dragons and magic beyond his wildest dreams. All that time ago, when he'd asked himself that dreaded question:

What's the worst that could happen from reading a book?

1

The Twins

Forty years later . . .

Astrid and Jonas entered society in much the way they meant to carry on. Together, and with as much peculiarity as possible.

Back then, Sister Theresa had not found a single baby on the convent doorstep. No . . . She'd found two.

Twins.

They weren't swaddled in blankets or crying in a woven basket. When Astrid and Jonas were discovered on that bitterly cold February night, they each had a crown of yellow duckling-feather hair and matching shards of a bone-white coin tucked beside them. They were clasping hands, they were fast asleep and they were protected by nothing more than a bed of moss.

What would become of such infants? What would society do with them? The same as it always did when confronted with the strange and unusual.

Put them in confinement.

And so it was that their worse-than-ordinary upbringing led them to this particular moment in time, where their story really begins – when, sitting in a stuffy classroom,

Astrid had the sudden and undeniable tingle up her spine, the one that told her she was about to do something she was definitely not supposed to.

At the opposite end of the room, three girls giggled and shrieked.

'A ghost?' a fourth girl scoffed. 'Don't be ridiculous.'

Astrid squinted down at her hand of cards, unable to stop eavesdropping on her schoolmates' voices.

Not even ten minutes since the teacher had left them alone in the dingy classroom, and already the room was fighting back against the throbbing monotony of after-school detention.

For Astrid and two of the boys, that involved a game of cards and a pile of trinkets for the winner. A tall boy from the year above, Greg, was her current mark, the poor thing foolishly raising the stakes with the very item they were after. A matte black, heart-shaped lighter – a Vivienne Westwood knock-off. As Jonas had explained in great detail, this was a perfect copy of the one Prince Theodore had been seen wearing round his neck in an interview recently, so half the kingdom's teenage population now coveted it.

Astrid couldn't understand her brother's (and the entire world's, for that matter) obsession with the prince; to Astrid, the royal family were no more than glorified reality stars. Nevertheless, she remained determined to get her brother that lighter before a teacher came to collect them. It was them against the world, and they would do anything to keep the other happy.

'Are you joking?' This came from a girl Astrid recognized – Esther. After yet another expulsion, the twins had only been at Priory Park Secondary School for a few weeks, but had already learned that Esther and her gang were common faces in detention. They were always in trouble for skipping class and breaking uniform codes. The other girls usually spoke in hushed whispers, but Esther's voice had a nasal chord that was impossible to tune out. 'Have you seriously not heard about it?'

Astrid bit her tongue. Of course the girl had heard about it – hadn't everyone in the entire school district?

Monsters, mysteries.

Ghosts.

And the unlucky girl who claimed she'd seen it with her own eyes.

Astrid reminded herself she should not be listening to this story, that it was precisely one of those things she and her brother were *not supposed to do*.

'Well, duh,' the other girl grumbled. 'I just don't believe it.'

Absently fiddling with the fractured medallion round her neck, Astrid surveyed the room. Despite summer coming to an end and the weather turning grey, it was stuffy in the room. There were eight students in total, all sat at PVC desks as rain steamed up the only window. The plastic smiley-face clock at the end of the room slowly counted down their hour of after-school imprisonment. Her brother Jonas was sprawled on the floor, eyes directed towards the grey cloudscape in the window, nibbling on a pencil, seemingly pondering his maths homework. It was a ruse, of course; he was actually using the window's reflection to see Greg's cards, tapping his pocket once for truth and twice for cheat.

Since the term had started two weeks ago, this was only the second time the twins had found themselves in detention. The first had been for a paid homework service they'd organized (which was apparently frowned upon), and this time they were booked for stealing communion wafers. ('But the campus squirrels were hungry . . .' Jonas had protested to the headmaster, to no avail.)

A collection of motivational posters hung on the walls, trembling slightly in the breeze from the faulty air filter:

'*Say I can more than I can't.*'

'*Picture yourself a winner.*'

Someone had crossed out half of one that urged '*Trust yourself*' and replaced it with '*Kill*'.

'It's true,' Esther insisted. 'Lizzy saw it. That's why she's been off school. She said it lured her down to the abandoned station, where that girl died in the nineties. You know, the one who drowned?' She was getting into it now, the story reaching a higher pitch as her excitement spilled over. 'She said the sound is like a dying animal, but sometimes it has this creepy melody that makes your eyes water and your teeth ache.'

Out of the corner of her eye, Astrid saw her brother's nostrils twitch, picking up on the same tantalizing scent of something strange and otherworldly. But *they shouldn't*, not ever, and especially not today. The mother superior had reminded them over and over that they 'must be back quick sharp' to the group home because tonight they had a meeting with their social worker. If they were late, or if they were caught talking about anything 'worrying', it could land them a meeting with Doctor Harris. And a meeting with Doctor Harris could mean separation, bare rooms and the good doctor's particular brand of isolation 'treatment'.

So, they did their best to block out the pull they felt in their gut, telling them to *pay attention*, and instead tried to focus on playing cards.

'Worst of all are the creature's teeth,' Esther continued. 'It doesn't want to eat you. No, its goal is to leave a mark so that a curse will stay with you forever.' Grinning, Esther traced a mark over one of the indents on her palm. 'Two curved lines of teeth, almost human, only razor-sharp – sharp enough to bite through the football the girls' team was practising with.'

'Well, I don't believe it,' the sceptic huffed. The twins couldn't remember her name, but recognized her by her trademark heavy make-up and dyed black hair – another detention regular.

'Are you calling Lizzy a liar?' Esther demanded.

'Well, yeah? Like, how did she get away if whatever it is got close enough to steal her football? Plus, she said she barely remembered anything.' She crossed her arms. 'Either you or Lizzy are making it up.'

'Two queens.' Astrid laid the queen and ten face down on the table in front of Greg. The debate around Lizzy's and Esther's honour would have to wait. She had all four queens herself, but it was better to keep hold of them, to lure someone into calling her out later when the stakes were higher.

'One queen.'

Bingo.

Astrid grinned. 'Cheat!'

Greg stood up and slammed his hands on the table.

'*You two* are cheating!' he roared. A regular in detention, Greg had beautiful blue eyes, perfect chestnut hair and a red-hot temper.

'Well, yes, that is the premise of the game,' Jonas said from the floor, snickering.

'No, you're not tricking us again. You're *cheating* cheating!' he replied.

Suddenly, Astrid could feel the weight of the room watching them.

'I'm not gonna let you make me look like an idiot.'

'Oh, come now, *Gregory*, I would never do such a thing,' she assured him.

Jonas nodded, a smirk teasing his lips as he got up to stand next to his sister. 'You have no trouble doing that all on your own.'

With a grunt, Greg grabbed all the cards on the table and threw them wildly across the room.

Astrid held her ground.

'The winnings are ours.'

'I think the hell not,' Greg growled.

'I know how you can settle this,' the sceptical girl in the corner said, staring up at them through shimmery eye shadow.

Everyone paused, including the twins. They could have just taken the prize, but there was something about the words, about the rain growing at the window, about the itch under their skin; Astrid and Jonas knew something was different about that day.

'We're listening.' The twins spoke in unison.

'We meet at Priory Park after detention by the gap in the fence,' mystery-name girl announced. 'Whoever goes into the abandoned station and finds Lizzy's football first is the winner. Simple.'

In seconds, the room erupted into excited *oohs* and *aahs*, the enthusiasm making it clear Greg would be greatly disappointing everyone if he said no.

'Oh, I like that idea,' Greg lied. Both twins saw how his fingers fidgeted nervously. 'But if I win, I want something just as good.'

The twins shared a quick glance.

'Go on.'

A menacing grin stretched over Greg's face. 'I want one of your necklaces.'

Astrid resisted the urge to clutch her pendant. This was a battle of wills and she refused to show any weakness. She thought of the things Doctor Harris had written about their medallions in his file. During their time in his care, they'd snuck into his office one night and read each venomous line.

The twins are in possession of medallion shards that they keep on strings round their necks. The surface is covered in what appear to be spiral etchings and some sort of sword. They believe the substance to be white gold, but the jagged tearing is proof that the item is not any kind of rare metal. They are under the illusion that the symbol must belong to their family's coat of arms, or perhaps a secret society, but all appraisals of the item have shown it to be an entirely made-up emblem with no historical match. Despite the twins being told these hard facts, they continue to have an unhealthy attachment to the shards and their obsession with the medallion's significance suggests severe delusions of grandeur. Although we are legally not allowed to take any items away from the patients unless they pose a serious risk to their health and safety, it is my professional opinion that the items should be removed.

It was clear what Greg was trying to do. He was trying to get them to back down. Little did he know, there was more to this now than simply winning. There was that sweet taste of the unknown, and the tantalizing scent of something they were not supposed to do.

'So, do you agree?' mystery-name girl asked.

There was only one problem . . .

'The Cuckoos aren't allowed near nature unsupervised,' Esther announced with a chewing-gum smile. 'All of those kids from The Sisters of Mercy Group Home are a little strange but the Cuckoos, they're like . . . *weird*. They're allergic to grass, or something. Makes them confused. That's why they can never hang around after school. Strict curfew.'

'What the hell are "the Cuckoos"?' the other girl groused, and from the way she glared at Esther, Astrid was starting to suspect there was a long-standing rivalry between the two.

'Well, *Steph* –' that was it – 'that's what they call them in that old horror movie with the creepy kids. I mean . . . look at them.'

Despite Esther's tactless language, the twins had to admit, with their stark blonde hair and doll-like faces, it was a rather accurate observation.

The rest of the classroom looked at the twins expectantly, taking in their oddly pale skin and hair, the frightening precision with which they wore their grey school blazers and white shirts, and the matching shards that hung round their necks. They thought they were weird, everyone did, but they didn't know the half of it.

Esther was, in fact, half right about their 'strict curfew', but it wasn't an allergy at fault; it was something far more alarming. Something they certainly wouldn't be telling their peers.

The thing about Astrid and Jonas that you need to understand is that they were strange – stranger even than anyone in that classroom could comprehend. It was not their ethereal appearance or their unnerving wisdom that had had them locked away as children, it was what they could hear. You see, Astrid and Jonas, ever since they were small, claimed that the universe – every plant, tree and creature – was always singing.

Only they could hear it. Messages and secrets just for them. An endless sea of melodies they could float in.

After a number of 'incidents' when they were small, Astrid and Jonas had spent years under the care of Doctor Harris, a man who seemed to have dedicated his life to fixing the twins and their broken minds. Even now they could hear him. '*Remember, it's all in your head,*' he'd say, even as the trees beckoned them closer.

This, missing their curfew, breaking into an abandoned station, hunting *ghosts*? It was everything they were *not* supposed to do. And that was before they even set foot on a single blade of glorious grass.

Astrid clutched the shard at her neck, feeling each jagged indent like she was tracing her own skin. When she looked to Jonas, he was doing the very same.

They could have pushed for the spoils of the card game. They'd won them fair and square, but neither of them cared about the black-heart lighter any more. This was about so much more. A golden opportunity had presented itself, to follow the lure, the whispers of the earth, and to be able to claim they simply gave in to peer pressure. How could they resist?

Astrid felt the smile stretch over her brother's face just as her own did.

'We'll do it,' Jonas said.

'What?' Greg stuttered, clearly not expecting them to agree.

Their social worker would have to wait, for the twins had mischief to attend to.

Astrid grinned, holding her hand out for Greg to shake. 'We'll meet you at the abandoned station at five o'clock after detention. First one out with the ball wins.'

By the time Astrid and Jonas made it to the park near the school, it was clear word had spread of their little competition. A crowd of students had gathered by the bushes along the fenced-off area at the edge of Priory Park. Beyond the jagged gap in the wire fence, past the brambles and buddleia, they'd find the blocked-off old station. Excited murmurs followed the twins as they made their way through the excitable students.

Esther held her phone out as a stopwatch. Greg was showing off, running on the spot and stretching – incorrectly, Jonas noted, murmuring to Astrid: 'He's going to give himself an injury before we even start.'

Astrid tossed her bag in the pile forming by one of the overgrown bushes.

'I mean, how can someone so hot be so stupid?'

'I fear, Jonas, that it's his stupidity that makes him so attractive to you.'

Jonas strolled towards the fence, pulling his sleeves over his palms to carefully lift the barbed wire to allow Greg to squeeze through into the bushes on the other side. Ever the gentleman. 'Don't want you to hurt your pretty face,' he said.

Greg did not take the compliment well.

'Freak,' he grumbled, getting down on his knees to crawl through.

'I'll stay behind and keep note of the winner,' Esther announced, scribbling notes in the back of a schoolbook, then placing the pencil behind her ear.

Now all the twins had to do was follow Greg and the race could begin – except that involved getting through those thick, spiky bushes. Bushes they shouldn't be anywhere near, let alone *touch*. Astrid realized her palms were sweating.

Turning to Astrid, Jonas shrugged. 'I'm sure it'll be fine.'

He most certainly did *not* think it would be fine, and Astrid could feel the prickle of the lie along her shoulder blades as if she'd just told it herself. Nevertheless, they got on their knees and into the bush.

With autumn creeping up on them, the breeze had a pleasant chill, coming from the London docks. The twins' sad grey uniforms did little to stave off the cold, their knees soaked with mud. Despite this, both calmed as they crawled through. Thorns avoided their skin, nettles seemed to dampen at their touch. The earth was welcoming them.

'It's happening again,' Jonas whispered, turning to look at his sister.

Astrid hummed in agreement. They could smell the soil, sweet and *alive*, and it was singing, so quietly they could almost believe it was a trick, the purr of the cool earth like balm on a wound.

When they emerged on the other side of the bush, they were in a grotto. Mossy rock and forget-me-nots dotted the cracked slabs. Hawthorn and alder swayed and whispered in the breeze.

Everything felt slow and hazy, like opening their eyes underwater. The wind was gentler, a steady *hush hush*, the scent of the ground was more potent and the tree cover drenched them in shadow. They could scarcely see the sky beyond.

This place was strange. Strange like them.

'Can you hear that?' Jonas whispered.

She could. All around them there was shining dust in the air, and it was singing to them, now clear as a bell. A melody so delicate and rare they wanted to catch it in a bottle.

'*It's all in your head.*' Astrid heard the doctor's words like an alarm. She wondered if Jonas did too, but then they looked at each other, and laughed.

Wanting to hear more, both twins edged forward, only for Astrid's foot to catch on something: a broken ornament – a face, in fact – made of clay and composed of leaves and vines, set into the soil, its indented eyes staring back up at them.

'Curious,' Jonas mused, leaning down to inspect the cracked face.

'What is it?'

'Hey!' Greg's voice abruptly pulled them away.

The moment they turned, the trees began to shake, a fresh gust blowing the leaves into the big, dark hole behind Greg – the gaping entrance to the abandoned underground station. Creeping vines looped around the steps, and stubborn flora and red-cap mushrooms filled cracks in the stone steps that descended into the darkness.

A fairy ring? To the twins, it felt more like a portal, and they were sure it hummed a melancholic, low drone.

'Oh!' Astrid smiled in delight, dusting herself off. She wanted to examine this place up close, run her fingers through the dust and hold her ear to each leaf so it could tell her the truth of this extraordinary, gloomy grotto.

'Are we all ready then?' Jonas asked.

From the gap in the bushes, Esther's face appeared. She held her hand out in a thumbs-up. 'Countdown incoming.'

'Let's get this over with,' Greg muttered, shivering. 'This place gives me the creeps.'

The twins lined themselves up beside Greg at the steps and waited, rabbit-hearted, as Esther shouted a countdown.

'Three!'

When Astrid and Jonas were found fifteen years ago on that bitterly cold February night on the doorstep of Saint Joan's Convent, they had been holding hands, fast asleep, wrapped in a bed of moss.

'Two!'

Growing up, they were in possession of three things: matching shards of medallion clasped round each of their necks, an unwavering bond between them and a deep, inexorable yearning to find where they came from.

'One . . .'

Jonas's hand sought out Astrid's and they held on to each other. Then they stared right into the singing abyss – and ran.

2
Strange Teeth

Hidden within the darkness, flood waters lay stagnant, mottled jade and pungent like mould. Now three teenagers splashed through, sending ripples along the surface.

'Mother Mary!' Greg screeched as the cold consumed his body.

The twins, only a few paces ahead, could see that the tunnel split in two, both escapes filled with more putrid water.

Unfortunately for the twins, they couldn't swim. They'd never been taught.

'If it gets too deep –' Jonas gasped.

'We turn back,' Astrid finished, even as their hearts pummelled in their chests.

The light in the ruined ticket office was scarce. The further they explored, the deeper the darkness and water.

And yet, their feet kept moving.

'Left,' Jonas muttered.

Astrid trusted her brother implicitly. He was about the only person in the world she trusted at all.

'Wait! Where are you going?' Greg's voice echoed against the damp walls as Astrid and Jonas rounded the corner. 'The football's not gonna have gone that far.'

The twins paused where the tunnel went further down,

huffing clouds of breath that they could scarcely see in the dwindling light.

'Look,' Astrid whispered.

Dim as a dying ember, the walls were coming alive with glowing moss. Going further down, it spread like a chant, the glow passing from one clump of moss to another, blue and gold dust lighting a path.

Like flexing an old, unused muscle, they could hear it clearly now, chiming like the memory of laughter, or an ancient song.

'I feel strange,' Jonas murmured, and Astrid nodded.

Her teeth were aching.

Limited as these crumbs of light were, the twins had to squint, but with the glow, they could make out the faint blue of each other's eyes, and the frenzied black holes of their dilated pupils.

'Come back!' Greg called from behind them, distant and nervous.

The twins suspected he sensed something too, even if he couldn't hear the songs. Ignoring him to focus on the new sensation, they turned back to the luminous trail and kept on, slower now, the freezing water coming up and up to their thighs.

'It's too dark down there, come back!' Greg sounded truly afraid now, his voice desperate and far away, and that fear crystallized into anger when they heard him shout one last fraught plea. 'This isn't funny!'

He's right about that, Astrid thought. But she couldn't stop herself being drawn on by the song.

'This better be worth it,' she grumbled aloud. She was shivering, and her teeth had begun to chatter. They were now nearly up to their hips in bone-freezing water.

This wasn't about finding the football, or winning. This was more than they could possibly explain. A secret, waiting in the water, meant only for them to find.

'Here.' Jonas pulled at Astrid's hand, stopping her from going any further. Gently, the two of them came together, limbs trembling as they protected each other from the cold.

Around them the cavern was deathly silent, other than the slow drips of water from the damp ceiling.

'Are you scared?' Jonas asked, feeling Astrid's pulse with his thumb.

'Not yet.'

Curious, the twins raised their palms to the mossy walls. The blue light burned brighter under their fingertips, spurred to life by their touch. Here, the melody was sweet and bright – welcoming like a fanfare.

It reminded Astrid of that same comfort she got from holding the shard round her neck. Right then, leaning into the sounds of this strange cavern, she felt vindicated – this was fate; they were meant to be here, she was sure of it.

This wasn't a delusion or delirium. It couldn't be.

Together, the twins tried to make out the message of the tune, the secrets of this place. There were no words – there never were – yet they understood it like their own private language. And down here, the music was stronger than they had ever heard it before.

They could have spent hours untangling the sounds, basking in that giddy melody, trying to make sense of what they were hearing. All of it so real, not a trick in their heads. Real, and so close . . . Except, there was something sour at the edges, seeping into the song like an infection. No, a warning.

Something was wrong.

Look out!

Both twins pulled away from the wall hard just as something splashed nearby. They could make out a rippling sound in the distance. Something approaching.

Astrid thought of the girl who had died in these waters years ago only to become a ghost story kids tell in school. She wondered what she must have felt in that moment. The moment she knew she was going to die.

The something came closer.

Now the prickles of fear were taking root at the base of Astrid's spine, and to squash them she stepped towards the movement, and asked quite sensibly: 'What are you?'

A rat.

The creature, quite peculiarly, stared back at them, whiskers flicking as she made a series of curious little squeaks, before turning away and swimming off into the dark.

'Is it just me, or did that rat just mock us?' Jonas asked.

As absurd as the encounter had been, Astrid still couldn't ignore the bad feeling in her stomach, the kind she got when she knew the weather was about to turn. But then something snapped in their minds, a sudden clang of discord.

It was awful, a low drone of a sickly melody, each chord warped, but even as they covered their ears it would not cease, the song turning into a wail.

Their breaths came out shaky.

'Is that real?' Astrid whispered. 'Or in our heads?'

Before Jonas could answer, something erupted from the water with a great splash that sent them both backwards.

'Jonas!' Astrid called, wading back to find his hand again as the *thing* bobbed on the surface.

They clambered against the nearest moss-lit wall, hearts hammering in their chests.

Clutching each other, they took in the object below.

'*Oh.*' Astrid laughed. The football gently floated into her grasp. 'We've been looking for you,' she whispered, her voice echoing off the damp bricks.

She turned the ball over, taking in its deflated state. There were two curved lines sliced into it. Were they . . . *bite* marks?

And it must have been thrown towards them from somewhere . . . but where?

Jonas had turned entirely still.

'What's wrong?' Astrid asked.

'Well, if that's the ball . . .' Jonas gulped, steadily pointing to the darkness ahead. 'Then what's that?'

Following the direction of his finger, Astrid felt her blood turn to ice.

Obscured in shadow, two cold round eyes glared back at them.

And beneath the yellowing sockets, a wide mouth grinned.

Long black tendrils like tar crawled from the smiling head, floating menacingly on the water's surface. Worst of all, Astrid could hear the twisted melody, a pitch so discordant that it made her eyes sting. It had become a single panicked sound, the meaning clear:

Run!

Shaking themselves out of their panic, the twins did precisely as they were told.

Furiously, Astrid tugged at Jonas, pulling him back just as the *thing* shrieked, preparing to strike.

Bolting back the way they'd come, the water around them churned, splashing and surrounding them until they were drenched.

Behind them, the screeching followed, echoing off the subterranean walls like a haunted lullaby. It sounded like laughter, and then like a scream, and as they got further away, more like a woman crying.

'What in the queen's crown *is* that thing?' Jonas huffed, the two of them finally reaching water shallow enough for them to be able to properly run.

'I don't know, but don't look back!' Astrid cried, yanking again at Jonas to hurry.

They sprinted, hand in hand, back to the steps. When they emerged, wet and filthy as drowned rats, they could hear voices beyond the bushes.

'There they are!' someone shouted from the other side of the fence.

Leaves rustling, a face appeared from the bush – Greg – and he looked relieved?

More hands appeared, clearing a path, and both twins dived through, covered from head to toe in mud, twigs sticking to their hair.

'What the hell happened?' a disembodied voice asked as they scrambled back to the park. Finally they paused for a moment to listen. There was no music, no monster.

Their hearts still racing in their chests, it took a moment for Astrid and Jonas to convince themselves the danger was gone.

They were safe.

And they'd won.

Astrid threw the football down with a thud.

'We win,' Jonas gasped.

Both twins fell to the ground, as hot and relieved as foxes who'd just survived a hunt.

Despite their gasping, they watched, smug, as their fellow students took in the deflated ball.

But something was off, looking up at the faces gazing down at them. For one thing, there weren't as many of them as before: just Greg, Esther, Steph and two other kids.

'Where is everyone?' Jonas panted, turning himself over.

'Are you kidding?' Steph cried. 'You guys have been down there for over two hours. We nearly called someone!'

Astrid faltered; surely that couldn't be true. And yet, looking around, the light was dwindling. It shouldn't have been past five thirty, but the sun was clearly setting.

'Did you see it?' Jonas looked at Greg.

'See what?' Greg asked. 'I turned back when you two started doing that creepy singing. Very funny,' he added sarcastically.

Astrid looked at her twin. Neither of them had been singing. Which meant Greg had heard it too – the monstrous thing lurking down there. Which meant it was real. It was *really* real.

Astrid's eyes went wide as she stared at Jonas, the two of them suddenly aware of just how serious this was. She felt giddy with it, bubbles of laughter creeping up her stomach.

But before they could open their mouths to respond, Greg pointed across the field. 'Who's that?'

Everyone turned to stare at two silhouetted figures heading towards them from across the park.

'Oh dear,' Astrid sighed. She helped Jonas to his feet.

They dusted themselves off, Jonas helping his sister wring out grimy water from her soaking hair. Clearing his throat, he held out his hand to receive the black-heart lighter, only for Greg to shake his head, distraught.

'I . . . I lost it down there,' he admitted, putting his head in his hands as if despairing. 'I tried to use it for a light and dropped it in the water.'

'Queen's mercy,' Jonas grumbled, scowling at the boy. 'You're lucky we have other things to worry about right now.'

Astrid nodded, the same grim realization setting into her bones. She couldn't decide whether the individuals striding towards them were worse than any evil hiding in the abandoned station.

It was their social worker, and at her side was their arch-nemesis.

Doctor Harris.

3
Gwen

A few hours earlier . . .

Gwen was restless, and she was determined to make it everyone else's problem.

'Now, let's try this again,' she said, huffing as she placed a small white feather atop a stack of books as delicately as she was able to in such a bad mood.

Alone in her room, Gwen had been attempting to do the very thing she shouldn't – she was trying to teach herself a spell. Scattered along the purple bedspread were the remnants of her activities – pages, feathers, flowers and, of course, her violin.

Pinned to the wall above the headboard was the Circle of Fifths, and the hand-scrawled spell in question. It was a page from her sister's old academy book, every note elegant and curved and dripping with lacy daintiness. That was the kind of patience one needed for instrumentation. But Gwen found no serenity in spellcraft.

Magnus Faymore always said, '*Listen to the Bloom.*' It was the first lesson Pledges learned. Gwen was not a Pledge; in fact, she was not studying at any magical school at all.

There was great power inside her; she knew it, she could *feel* it. Like water ready to boil over, it was always simmering . . . If only Gwen could overcome her little problem.

Picking up her violin, Gwen's fingers twitched over the bow. After one has mastered the melodies of magic, they can conjure them at will. Until then, she needed her instrument.

'OK, I can do this.'

She breathed out long and slow, and tried once again.

Meandering, yet sure as a gust, the melody of Wind was one of the first of the Twelve Spells you were to learn as a Pledge, right at the start of your magical education.

For a musician as skilled as Gwen, the tune remained easy enough to play, each correct note lighting up inside her in recognition.

Magic was all about composure and intention, or so her sister would say. Master the spells, and you can do anything your heart desires – and for Gwen, she desired simply to call the wind to blow the feather up above her.

Simple, surely, and most certainly not scary. Not at all.

In response to the melody and meditation, her Bloom began to come alive in her throat and her fingers.

'OK, stay calm,' she willed herself, keeping her breath steady.

As the magic lit up along her skin, she was sure, this time, *this time*, it was going to be all right.

Except, of course, it was never all right.

This was the part where the spell should have taken form. Instead, Gwen broke out in a cold sweat, her fingers trembling.

It was happening again.

She felt it, as familiar as a recurring nightmare – spiky shadows of fear creeping over to snuff out the light of her Bloom. Then the memories.

The storm.

The screaming.

The sensation left her shaking, so real she was sure she could feel something dark and terrible whispering in her ear. *Useless, terrible, cursed.*

Flustered, she threw the violin down, the melody screeching to a halt. Reacting to her fears, the spell had formed into something chaotic, a sudden frantic wind that whipped Gwen's two dark plaits around and smacked her in the face.

They called it a magical phobia, one no one could cure. Ever since her parents had died, she had become terrified of her own magic.

'Hey!' she barked at the wind, and was rather startled when, in response, there came a knocking at her door.

In a panic, she quickly hid her lessons under the bed, squirelling the borrowed spellbook pages away like a dirty secret.

The polite rapping at her door was soon accompanied by a courteous voice.

'Gwen, dear, are you there?'

Marching over, Gwen swung the door open so fast that the man on the other side almost fell backwards in shock.

'What is it, Elijah?'

Now, Gwen knew very well that her tone of voice was entirely uncalled-for, but she'd set a precedent for her temperament now and meant to carry on.

'Could we have a little chat?'

'I'm busy,' Gwen spat, crossing her arms over her chest for good measure.

'Ah, well, I can see you're not in the most hospitable mood.' As Elijah backed away, she noted a fresh scone sparkling upon the tray in his hands. Her traitorous mouth filled with saliva. 'I'll just take this back downstairs –'

'Wait!' Gwen called after him. 'I'll come too.' Marching past him to the creaky old staircase, she grumbled under her breath, 'I was about to get a drink.'

Elijah made a noise somewhere between a laugh and a hum, his big cheeks rounding in a smile. 'Excellent, I just put the kettle on.'

Long before Gwen's parents had joined the Faymore Cluster, back when Clusters were still common amongst Bloom Blooded folk, the Faymores themselves had moved into Windyside Cottage, a charming building that sat a little further up the woodland path. Faymore Manor itself was intended to house the other families in the Cluster, so that the children and Pledges would have plenty of space to study magic. Now mostly unoccupied, it had eleven bedrooms, two parlours, a practice room, a library, an apothecary in the basement, a study, a dining room, and – the very heart of the household – the kitchen.

A low rumble came from the kettle as they wandered in, and Elijah began to busy himself with preparing pots and cups and plates, getting ready for Jan and Thomas after their Apprentice work ended.

Outside, Gwen could hear the end of a spell, followed by a boom that made dust dance from the corners of the room, the dangling pots and pans clanking as they tried to jump ship from their hooks – a regular occurrence in the Faymore household.

Elijah frantically skipped about the terracotta tiles to rescue his falling kitchenware, while Gwen made herself acquainted with the buttery warmth of his baking, mentally preparing herself for whatever pep talk he had planned.

Elijah Ackerman, now Elijah Faymore, had married Magnus Faymore decades ago. Now nearly seventy, he didn't look a day over forty to a Red Blood, and was only just starting to show small flecks of red in his brown eyes – the first sign of ageing in Bloom Bloods. He always reminded Gwen of ginger cake: round and sturdy in stature, with a sweet but frantic temperament, and hair and fluffy beard the colour of late-autumn leaves.

Mouth still full, Gwen muttered sullenly, 'Hwat are 'ay 'orking on 'oday?'

'One of these days you're going to choke if you don't chew your food properly.' Elijah tutted, reaching for the kettle as it began to scream on the stove.

Rolling her eyes, Gwen swallowed hard, thumping her chest to get the dregs down.

'I *said*, what are they working on today?'

Suddenly something big collided with the building, rattling the wall and sending a teacup bouncing off the granite counter. Elijah narrowly caught it with his foot.

'They're with Lorelei. She's brought them a grunt troll so they can practise using their Savonnettes to store and rehabilitate magical creatures.' Elijah placed the teacup back down and began filling it with the bubbling water. 'Although I do wish they would do it away from the house.'

Ah yes, their Savonnettes – specially charmed pocket watches. Jan and Thomas had received silver ones after graduating from Pledges to Apprentices, and next year, when they became Custodians, they'd upgrade to gold.

Then everyone in the whole of Faymore Manor would have gold ones . . . when Gwen didn't even have a bronze one yet.

'Where's Magnus?' Gwen asked, reaching greedily for the hot cup.

'He's gone to see the queen –' Cutting himself off, Elijah reoriented himself. 'Excuse me, *the Magister*, to discuss the list of duties that need fulfilling, which, mind you, he's going to have mighty trouble doing, seeing as he's left the notes in his office.'

Gwen paused where she was blowing on her tea, the words tugging her in the direction of the cottage, where the unprotected office was waiting.

'Did he now?' she mused, trying to hide her smile behind the cup.

With a self-soothing groan, Elijah lowered himself into the seat opposite Gwen, and Gwen watched, envious, as he began to absent-mindedly hum the spell of Fire, his voice deep and warm as he sent the Bloom up through his palms to heat the underside of the teacup.

These easy and trivial uses of the Twelve Spells were second nature to any Custodian of the Order – to reheat a drink with Fire, to cool it with Ice. All things that Gwen could scarcely dream of being able to do without panicking.

She was a lion frightened of its own roar, the biggest embarrassment magical society had ever seen.

'Listen, Gwen dear,' Elijah began, taking his glasses off to wipe a small smudge away. 'We know your heart is still set on taking your Pledge and studying at Fountains Abbey Academy, and we promise we're doing everything we can to find an agreement with them concerning your . . . special circumstances . . .'

Huffing, Gwen tried to tune out the speech. She'd heard it a million times. The facts were still the same. Fountains Abbey was the only Order academy in Western Europe, and if she couldn't get in, she was doomed.

'We were wondering, though, if you might reconsider library training. There's more to the Order than magic and adventure, you know? They always need new archivists and librarians. Why, you could even end up working at the Shadow Library itself.'

As Elijah babbled on, his body became more animated, hands waving in the air, an action that caused the gold pocket watch at his breast to wink alluringly in Gwen's direction.

She wanted to reach out and snatch the teasing Savonnette; surely it was intentionally provoking her?

'I don't want to be an archivist,' she lamented, feeling pathetic when the words made her sinuses sting. 'I want to take my Pledge at Fountains Abbey and travel the world just like my parents did. And I want to study with other Bloom Bloods.' It was all Gwen wanted, to be cured. Then she would be useful, and normal.

Anyway, the life of an archivist seemed lonely to her, and she was sick of being alone.

Elijah gave her a sorry look, one that immediately had Gwen wanting to hide inside her shirt and scream.

'You could always study here, Gwen; you don't need to take the Pledge. You know, not even two hundred years ago it was very normal for people to just study within their Cluster. That's what Magnus's parents did, and mine.'

Gwen sighed. She didn't have the energy to hear the whole bit about 'the old times' again. While the rest of Bloom Blooded society lived amongst each other in hidden

Order-protected settlements, the Faymores remained on the outskirts, committed to the old ways of 'Clusters' and seclusion. It's like they were still living in the magical dark age. If Gwen didn't find a way to solve her problem or prove herself, she'd be stuck at Faymore Manor studying spells she couldn't use and sorting potions she couldn't make for the rest of her life. Totally isolated.

'You're right, I feel much better now,' she lied through a thick smile, cutting off Elijah as she launched herself from the table. ''Hanks for 'ea,' she mumbled, shoving the last bite of scone into her mouth.

From behind, Gwen could hear Elijah's chair screeching against the tile, drowning out his own stumbling response of '*Chew your food, Gwen!*' as she marched through the kitchen doorway and down the hall.

Slipping into her well-loved pair of army boots, Gwen paused on the way out, where she found herself eye to eye with her sister's spare potion bag.

With only a split second of deliberation, she grabbed it too before running out of the back door.

'Thanks, Jan,' she muttered.

Holding steady near the cliff's edge along the Valley of Rocks in North Devon, Faymore Manor had – on a clear day and from the right vantage point – a view of Wales across the channel. This day was not a clear day, and Gwen would've been lucky to see the shore below with how low the clouds were hanging.

Health and safety had never been much of a concern on the Faymore Estate, and there was a perilous path down the crag that led to an isolated beach, a place where she and her sister had often run amok – before Jan had gone away to Fountains Abbey to study and come back so terribly *responsible.* To Gwen, it often seemed that everyone who graduated from their Pledge immediately became no fun at all.

She took the route through the graveyard. This hidden place, between the manor and Windyside Cottage, was home to the many past generations of the Faymore Cluster. Gravestones cropped up from the ground as wilfully and commonly as wildflowers, while the twisted trees creaked like the murmurs of old souls. They were all ghosts now, from a time when Faymore Manor was full of life.

Gwen read a few of them as she passed.

Rupert Faymore. Mary Faymore. Edgar Faymore.

And there, under the willow, her mother and father.

Rani Chatterjee. Samir Chatterjee.

Slowing her ascent, Gwen whispered a blessing to her parents under her breath. Slinking round the side of the cottage, she made her way over to the large oak tree whose thick old branches cradled the office window on the second floor. With a quick jump, she latched on to a lower branch to haul herself up with ease. It felt natural to her, having spent so many of her days traipsing by herself through the acres of land, kicking rocks, squishing berries, washing her feet in rain-bloated streams and, of course, climbing trees.

Gwen patted the sturdy tree branch in gratitude for it not letting her fall to her death.

In response, little green and brown faces appeared in the corners of her vision, tiny spirits with leaf wings and petal hats, proof that this place was filled to the brim with Bloom. Magic was safe on the estate.

From her vantage point on the branch, Gwen could see the cloth lampshade through the window; someone – most likely Magnus – had left the lights on. Determined, she reached up to the ledge, and hauled herself up and over. Unfortunately, the weakness of the plan came at her floor-first as she tumbled through.

'Ouch!' she grumbled, rubbing her forehead, and feeling rather pathetic.

Scowling at no one in particular, Gwen righted herself, to find she was directly in front of Magnus's desk.

The whole room practically screamed Magnus Faymore, from the scent of sandalwood and piles of dusty books to the showy crimson walls and velvet furniture.

Rolling up her shirt sleeves, Gwen trawled haphazardly through the drawers of his desk until she found her spoils – a cracked-leather book with a frazzled red ribbon dangling from its spine. The thing looked old as sin itself and the victim of numerous catastrophes. Inside, the pages were crinkled with water damage.

Gwen had never much concerned herself with the odd jobs assigned to the Faymore Cluster by the Order, so, flicking through, she ignored all the spellwork and jargon she didn't understand until – aha!

Recent magical anomalies that require our attention:

It was the most recent page, and Magnus had even kindly drawn a map and directions to go with each mission.

The first was a case up in Scotland, in which rumours of a scaly beast had been spreading around a small loch.

But it was the second mission that caught Gwen's attention, not just because of the words, but because of the peculiar yet pleasant feeling that spread through her chest as she read it over:

Following the ley lines up through the east of London, a rumour has begun to emerge of a strange entity in an abandoned underground station. Students from the local schools speak of a ghost that lives in the flood waters, saying it 'sings' to them through a tear in the fencing of Priory Park.

It is likely a weeping woman of some kind – possibly a bolotnitsa or rusalka, based on the descriptions – but there is a small possibility that the creature may be valuable to our research, and therefore it requires further investigation before a Custodian is assigned to deliver it to an appropriate habitat.

If the coast is clear, I would request using this mission as a shadowing opportunity for our soon-to-be-graduating Apprentices (Thomas Murphy and Jananki Chatterjee) to practise calming magical creatures and, at their discretion, move the creature to our local Enchanted Quarter.

She could all but smell it, the London air, and the sound of the Bloom, twinkling, singing: *This way, this way.*

Fairies of the weeping woman variety were scarcely ever dangerous. She could talk to it, show that she wasn't afraid and that she could even be helpful . . .

Before she could finish the thought, a shout came from outside, and Gwen started, shoving the notebook back in the drawer. Calming herself, she clambered over to peek out of the window to find Thomas and her sister outside with Lorelei.

'Quickly, get it!' Thomas called, narrowly dodging the snout of a little troll as the creature nearly crashed straight into his legs.

Their lesson, it seemed, had moved into the woods.

The grunt troll – a gluttonous, moody beast that resembled a small boar on two legs – was held in place with spells, its tusks glinting with intent as Thomas conjured melodies of magic to whip it this way and that. On the other side, Jan threw potions, each of them thrumming with a mixture of songs to lull the creature into a sleepy daze.

Once it was subdued, its slimy, bulbous skin shining like oil in the sunlight, Jan pulled out her silver Savonnette, holding it like a prayer at her chest, ready to perform Deliverance. The spell would hold the beast safely until they took it back to a large Enchanted Quarter, hidden away from the Red Blooded world.

Gwen had seen the deceptive thing in use before, had seen its power: to hold a magical being. If your magic was strong enough, and your Savonnette powerful enough, you could subdue even the greatest of monsters, and contain them.

This was one of the many duties of Bloom Bloods who joined the Order: to devote their lives to the protection and research of the magical world, from ancient traditions and studies, to magical creatures and habitats. Gwen was all but dying to be included.

'I'm going,' Gwen said to no one in particular, opening the drawer again to grab the notebook. She knew it was a reckless, terrible idea. But if she couldn't cure her magical phobia, she needed to prove she could still be useful in the field, spells or no spells.

Mischief and adventure now running rampant through her mind, Gwen pulled at the desk with a little too much force, freezing in her tracks as she heard the telltale crack of something breaking.

'Shoot.' Quickly leaning down, she checked the underside of the table to find a small split. Then, as she was gazing up at the break, trying to figure out how to hide it, the entire panel of wood came loose and proceeded to smack her in the face, swiftly followed by a rainfall of paper.

Furious, she sat up, only to find herself surrounded by a mess of faded photographs, sepia faces everywhere.

'What the –'

It appeared the desk had not broken at all. No – Gwen had discovered a secret compartment.

Her anger dwindling into confusion, she took in each of the faces in the photos. A few of them she could just about recognize as Magnus and Elijah, although much younger. There was one in particular that caught her eye – a whole group, eight in total, but she recognized Magnus and Elijah again, and a woman, right at the end, who had the exact same features as Gwen herself. Same curved nose, same honey-brown skin and inky-black hair, and the same pout plastered on her face, which stared out at her now, perfectly still and in focus while the figure next to her was unrecognizable, blurred by movement. Gwen knew her name, Rani, but she had called this woman by a different title.

'Mum?' she whispered down at the photo.

Turning it over, she found a date and location on the back. It was decades old and taken at a place called the Fairy Pools in the Isle of Skye.

'*The Rapscallions' first mission to hunt for Ancient Magic.*' Gwen read the handwriting on the back like it was a fairy tale.

Ancient Magic – she'd heard of it before, formidable spellwork that had been long lost in the magical dark age. There were whole departments within the Order dedicated to its study, yet still it remained mythic in nature. The tales told of beings who could talk to animals, move the seas, or command the very earth. And darker practices, cursed songs that were better left buried. And apparently, Magnus, Elijah and her mother had once been looking for it.

Gwen knew her mother had been friends with the Faymores at school, but she'd never heard anything about her studying Ancient Magic.

Without a second thought, she stole the photo away in her pocket.

Flitting over the collection, Gwen was considering what to do with the rest of it, when something golden winked at her from under one of the piles of photos.

'No way . . .' She nearly gasped.

Because there it was, glittering under the light.

A golden Savonnette.

No, not gold . . . this was something else, almost white, like bone. And it was not like any Savonnette she'd seen before. There was no clock inside; instead it was hollow, like a locket, and the outside pattern was far more intricate, covered in spirals like twisting roots that overlapped beneath the usual Pendragon sigil of a sword in the waves.

Something terrible must have happened to the owner, for the lid of the thing was torn violently down the middle, the sigil split in half.

What had happened to it?

Looking at the thing gave her a terribly uneasy feeling, yet she couldn't pull her eyes away. The hard ridges of the indents along her fingers, the weight of it, like holding the world in her hands. And the sound, whispers of Bloom, coaxing, like it recognized her.

Entranced, she knew she should put it down, but at the thought, her fingers curled tighter. She couldn't let it go. Like it was meant for her. Like it was *speaking* to her.

Take me . . .

Gwen blinked at the broken thing. She couldn't put it down.

So, swallowing, she hid it away in her pocket. Shaking her head free of any trepidation she might have over the blatant theft, Gwen meticulously placed everything else back in the hidden compartment. Part of her had been tempted to search through the rest of the items, but she had a mission, and, she told herself, she could always come back for them another time.

Mind made up, she reached for the notebook again (carefully this time) and looked over the little map, sounding out the destination in her head:

Priory Park.

With a smile tugging at her lips, she set off back out of the window towards a fate she could not even dream of.

4

The Doctor

'Now, I want you to tell me: what is this plant feeling?'

Wrapped up in blankets, the twins sat side by side in the barren office of the convent group home. Denise, their social worker, was standing outside in the corridor with the Reverend Mother.

Waiting for a verdict.

Under the blankets the twins were still soaked, and Astrid felt clumps of mud sticking to her hair. Glancing over, she saw how Jonas too was carrying some debris in his. They matched, as usual.

'What is the plant saying? Or is it being quiet right now?'

Neither twin spoke.

Doctor Harris held a single potted tiger jaws, all prickly green leaves and yellow flowers. He placed it on the desk between them, alongside the deflated football.

Unfortunately for the twins, Doctor Harris had been a consistent figure in their life ever since primary school. It started with one incident involving the release of the class hamster. Then there was the time a boy stamped on a daffodil the twins were attempting to converse with; he'd soon come down with a non-lethal case of Ruta poisoning. And then there was the teacher – a terrible woman, always telling them off, keeping them detained and shouting in her awful, shrill voice. One evening she'd put her hat on after class and was promptly stung.

Nettles. Sewn into the lining.

Then one day, Doctor Harris had been called in.

'*What made you do that?*' he'd asked.

'*The plants spoke to us,*' the twins had explained, as though it all made the most sense in the world.

And their fate was sealed.

Carted off to the Saint Peter Institute for Troubled Children, the twins spent years under the doctor's care, getting to know him intimately, while he, in turn, attempted to dissect their brilliant but 'broken' minds.

Many of the things the twins had found unpleasant about the doctor the last time they saw him were still present, in abundance – his cartoony voice, the whistle of his hairy nose. But worst of all was the thick artificial lemon scent that followed him around, the kind you would find in a public toilet or hospital ward. The kind that makes you think it must be covering up something awful.

'Are either of you going to answer me?' he asked now, glancing between them, 'Or am I getting the silent treatment again?'

On the table the plant practically throbbed.

'Won't you look at it, at least?' the doctor tried. He sighed. 'Are you at least sorry for frightening that nice young man?'

'I don't know about any *nice young man*, but Greg certainly seemed to frighten himself.'

The doctor did not react to Jonas's response, and the silence was so taut, Astrid could almost see the doctor's heart beating through his sweater.

Saint Joan's Convent was an old nineteenth-century building, but the area that housed the foster children had long ago been converted with cheap, institutional carpet tiles and PVC bunk beds in rooms that surrounded a large communal space lined with second-hand furniture. Spartan. Utilitarian. Hateful.

The office was one of the newer additions, but already it almost looked like a storage room, stuffed with miscellaneous items from years gone by, including a plastic Christmas tree that sagged against the wall behind the doctor.

'Really, you two . . .' The doctor took off his glasses to rub the lenses on the corner of his shirt – an entirely futile endeavour, as they steamed up as soon as he placed them back on his nose. 'You're so clever. Your test scores alone could put you at a university level. Why do you insist on all this misbehaviour? Are you trying to get expelled again? Because they're running out of schools that will take you. Or is this all a cry for attention?'

Here we go, Astrid thought.

'After what you did today, how can I think anything other than that you've had a relapse in your deliria?' His smile emerged, false and disdainful. 'You need my help.'

'We're fine,' Astrid burst out. 'It was a prank, that's all!'

'You were in that dangerous old station for two hours,' Doctor Harris cut in, smile dropping like a lead weight. 'You could have been seriously injured. Or worse. And I'm told it was once again all this fuss made over your little necklaces.'

There it is. Astrid could have sensed it a mile away. Beside her, Jonas's fingers began to tap on his trouser leg.

'Be honest with me, you two. I think our relationship warrants at least that level of respect. Did you not think that the bite on the ball could have been from a rat, or a fox? Why would your thoughts go to monsters? Doesn't that seem ridiculous to you?'

'It wasn't a rat.' Astrid could feel her temper rising.

Doctor Harris began to tut. Then he came out from behind his desk, closer to the twins, until he stood at Astrid's back, his shadow like spilled ink falling over her.

All the while, the tiger jaws throbbed. It wanted them to do something, but what? If they could just concentrate.

'This thing!'

Jonas's eyes went wide as the doctor reached over Astrid's shoulder and touched the pendant resting on her chest.

'Why don't you let me take it off you? See how it feels?'

The room began to spin, lights glowing bright, and the plant on the table practically screeching. There were no words, but if there were, it would be screaming, a single warning that she could not let the pendant be removed under any circumstances.

'Maybe it would be a relief?'

At the nape of her neck, the doctor's cold, clammy fingers fiddled with the knot.

'Hey!' Jonas leapt up to snatch the doctor's hand away, but it was too late.

The room lit up as though it was on fire, and the throbbing song of the tiger jaws crystallized into one clear, wordless instruction.

Bite him!

Turning sharply, Astrid clutched the doctor's wrist between both her hands, stretched her jaw wide, and bit down hard. The iron tang of blood burst across her lips as the doctor cried out in pain.

'Get off me! Get off!'

In his alarm, Doctor Harris scrabbled back, falling down against the desk, the tiger jaws glittering above his head.

'We know it wasn't a rat,' Jonas hissed, coming to stand by his sister, 'because the mark looks bigger than that one.' He pointed to the doctor's bleeding arm.

'You two are out of control!' Doctor Harris howled, and in his frantic attempt to get behind the desk to safety, he knocked the plant so that its pot smashed to pieces across the floor. 'You need help! Serious help!'

The noise must have alerted the abbess, because a great commotion came bustling down the hall and sent the door flying open.

'What in Mary and Joseph's name have you two done now?'

The Reverend Mother's face looked so red that Astrid imagined steam might start shooting out of her habit at any moment.

'She *bit* me!' Doctor Harris wailed.

Denise, their social worker, took in the scene, and sighed. She'd seen it all before.

'Lord's mercy!' The Reverend Mother clasped her chest, looking about ready to faint.

Denise cut her eyes sharply at the twins. 'I'm sure they know the damage they've done.'

Having been on their case since they were first found on the convent doorstep, Denise was a hardened woman with eyebrows as thick as her resolve. She was one of the few people who seemed not to lose their cool from prolonged exposure to the twins – a feat that should not be taken lightly.

'Little devils, the two of you!' The Reverend Mother's voice reached an unholy pitch. 'Changelings here to bring me to an early grave!'

'Will everyone settle down, *please*!' Denise implored, but the twins weren't doing anything now.

'He tried to take our pendant!' Astrid and Jonas spoke in unison.

Doctor Harris marched towards his briefcase.

'I'll have my verdict on your desk tomorrow, Denise. But I think it's clear that these two need separating if they are to have any hope of successful treatment.' Storming past, the doctor gave the twins a wide berth. 'Goodnight.'

It took Astrid a moment to feel the weight of the doctor's words.

Separating.

'He can't,' Jonas said, but even Astrid could hear that his voice was frayed.

They wouldn't survive it.

Denise gave them a grave look, as though this was all inevitable.

Their 'caretakers' had the ammunition now. The ammunition to tear the siblings apart and lock them away.

Dinner that night was a peculiar affair. Rumours of the twins' 'demonic possession' had spread amongst the few kids residing in the group home.

Most of them were significantly younger than the twins, mere hatchlings. They watched them cautiously from the TV room during dinner, whispering their theories, safe from Astrid and Jonas's domain in the mess room – an appropriate name, with its hazy light and the indelible tomato stains decorating the carpet.

Fluffy from their shower, and sporting fresh pyjamas, the twins sat at their rickety plastic table. Their senses had settled, the melody of the *thing* in the station now a murky memory.

But it had happened.

It was real.

So it was unfortunate that they'd shot themselves in the foot with Doctor Harris. Again.

In retrospect, Jonas had to acknowledge that Astrid biting the doctor was, perhaps, if he was being very honest with himself, an unwise decision. But he'd heard it too, the tiger jaws, and if Astrid hadn't got him herself, Jonas would surely have done something worse after seeing that muppet of a doctor touch his sister with his sticky sausage fingers.

At Astrid's neck, the medallion shard still dangled merrily, oblivious to the kidnapping attempt it had so narrowly evaded.

'This food is a little lacking for a last supper.' Jonas flipped over a piece of grey mystery meat with his plastic spoon. As soon as he spoke, he saw the look in his sister's eye, the sapphires iced over. He knew that look. She was deep in thought.

Tomorrow they'd receive an updated treatment plan, and if the doctor got his way – which he would – the two of them would likely be back at the Saint Peter Institute by the end of the week.

'I can't do confinement again, not without you,' he admitted.

The two of them glanced at the window on the opposite side of the mess room.

It had rained unrelentingly since the doctor had left, and Jonas imagined what the earth might smell like. Sweet, fresh and vibrant. The smell of freedom. Dread crept down his throat like ash.

It was too late now. They'd made their bed, and they'd have to lie in it.

From the living room, shouting erupted. Jenny – an older student – demanded that everyone quieten down so she could adjust the dials on the boxy TV.

'Put it back and turn it up!' another kid shouted, and Jonas couldn't help leaning to the side to see what had everyone's attention.

Through the archway that separated the mess room from the lounge, the screen flickered to life with an image of Queen Beatrice. Her wife and son came into view, a headline scrolling along the bottom of the screen, announcing how the prince had been seen going for dinner with some popular teen starlet.

'Queen's mercy!' Jenny exclaimed. 'Lots of people will be crying about this at school tomorrow.'

Jonas understood that the royal family, born into wealth and fame, was frankly ridiculous. Yet he couldn't stop himself; he'd always been fascinated by the prince.

Perhaps because they were about the same age, or maybe it was simply because Jonas, like everyone else in the world, was keenly aware of how abnormally good-looking the prince was.

There he was, glowing on the screen like some shiny New Age deity, his trademark black-heart lighter resting at his chest on a chain. Seeing this boy raised by two loving parents, adored by society, knowing exactly where he came from, and with the power and agency to do anything he wanted . . .

Right then, it was enough to infuriate him.

Jonas leaned even further over to get a better look at the TV screen. Prince Theodore Doria had many nicknames: the Adorable Doria, the Pretty Prince and, most often, as he was affectionately called in the press, Prince Teddy. The cutesy name appeared along the screen, the prince above pictured in riding gear, his warm tawny complexion in stark contrast to the cold blue sash draped over his shoulder. He was smiling, the proud, expectant smile of a pampered and pure-bred dog.

What was it like, Jonas wondered, to be so adored? All their lives, the twins had only ever been looked at like they were dirt.

'Jonas,' Astrid said softly. But there was a weight to his name. 'It's time for us to leave.'

There were lots of things Jonas and his sister simply knew.

They knew the power or poison of every leaf and herb, and the precise moment it would rain on any given day. They knew the time by looking at a shadow, and a person's intentions by how they treated the smallest flower.

And right then, hearing Astrid say those words, he also knew they were true.

'When?' he asked, a smile creeping over his face in sudden understanding.

'Tonight,' she said. 'We're going back to the station, and we're going to catch that monster.'

5

What We've Been Looking For

'Lights out now, you two,' Sister Agnes announced, poking her head round their bedroom door.

The twins turned over in their bunks and blinked sleepily at the nun, until she switched the light off.

'Thank you,' Astrid said, with artificial sweetness.

'Don't make a habit of it,' Sister Agnes cautioned.

The moment the door clicked shut, Jonas slid out from his covers and swung himself down into Astrid's bunk.

'Well, she sure made a habit of it. Habit, nuns?' he whispered. 'Get it?'

Astrid's lips twitched into a smile and Jonas felt a tickle of laughter deep in his belly.

'Come on,' Astrid said, grabbing some clothes from their closet. 'We need to fluff up these beds so it looks like we're still sleeping.'

The two began their silent work, collecting garments to shape into the form of bodies beneath the covers.

Even with the lights out, it was never truly dark or quiet in the home. There was always movement, footsteps creaking along the corridors, the hum of electricity.

A glimmer of light crept beneath their door, so Astrid could see what she was doing; it lit up their plastic desk and the stack of cardboard boxes that held their few dismal belongings. They'd never settled like the other kids.

Peering down from his bunk, Jonas noticed that his sister's fingers were trembling.

'We're not supposed to be here,' Astrid whispered. 'Dirt is only dirt when it's in the wrong place.'

Jonas could feel an uncomfortable prickle across his chest. 'What are you saying?'

Hunching her shoulders, Astrid hesitated, sighing with defeat over an argument she hadn't even started yet. 'If this doesn't work, Jonas, if we can't find that monster and prove our sanity . . . or if they catch us and drag us back . . . I want you to tell them it was all my idea, and all this time you were just playing along to keep me happy.'

Satisfied with his dummy-body, Jonas climbed down again to stand behind his sister.

'Maybe,' he whispered into the night.

Astrid turned from her work, lifting a brow.

'If I wasn't about to suggest you do the very same thing.'

Astrid huffed, her hands momentarily tightening round the bedding.

'If we are to be separated, then what's more appealing?' she asked, turning with her hands on her hips. 'A content life, where you can flex your mind and discover all the secrets this world has to offer, or one in which you're locked away?'

Sighing, Jonas reached for her hand. That familiar cool touch of her creamy skin was a mirror of his own.

'I can never be content with my life if you aren't in it,' he said honestly.

Astrid sighed and sat back, looking at the person she held dearest in the world. 'Such is our dilemma.'

'And if Doctor Harris should happen to succumb to some arsenic in his tea . . .'

'*Arsenic?*' Astrid scolded, before a sly glint entered her eyes. 'We both know hemlock is far more efficient and available.'

Jonas grinned, but there was an ache in his chest.

'We can't be separated,' he said. 'It would be like tearing my spirit in two.'

Astrid's head sank in agreement. This was the truth.

It was them, forever. Only them. Against the world.

'We'll find whatever is in that ghastly hole, and we'll prove once and for all that we're not making things up.'

Jonas hummed in agreement. 'And then maybe . . .' His voice trailed off, reluctant to say such hopeful words aloud.

Understanding, Astrid reached up to touch her piece of the split medallion at her neck, the white gold winking in the dim light as though it held a great secret. The twins would not rest until it was uncovered.

Somewhere, out there in the world, was the truth of where they came from. And perhaps . . .

'We'll find it,' Astrid whispered. 'We'll find out what we are.' She smiled up at him, that sweet, earnest look they only shared with each other. 'Now come on, let's get out of here and find that monster.'

Jonas tiptoed to the window and cautiously drew back the curtains.

Every window was installed with restrictors to avoid any possibility of an accident – or escapees.

The frames refused to open much wider than a palm's width. Unless, of course, you'd long since broken off the window jammer and stuck it back down with a gummy adhesive – which, as luck would have it, Jonas had done to every single bedroom they'd been placed in since they were six. Just for emergencies, of course.

In one satisfying snap, the entire section of the jammer attached to the window came loose and fell against the wall.

'See?' Jonas grinned, feeling very pleased with himself. 'Not just a pretty face.'

Astrid levelled him with a wilting look, stepping past to place her hands on the cool glass.

The latch squawked from lack of use as she pushed on the panel.

The twins froze, waiting. But there was no sound of feet down the hallway, no alarms set to announce their escape. It was just the two of them, and the dark, cool night beckoning beyond, calling them out. Wanting them to escape.

'After you,' Astrid offered, kneeling down for Jonas to use her as a step.

As if they'd rehearsed it a million times, Jonas hauled himself up and out through the window with the precision of a master escapologist. He found his footing and settled, birdlike, on the ledge, reaching out a hand to help his sister.

The night air was thick with fog, a crescent moon shining only dimly. It was the kind of night that promised mystery and magic. The twins trusted in that promise and leapt into the air. For a moment, it felt as though their souls flew free. Whatever happened from here on in, it had to be better than the past.

They landed in a tumble of limbs, the gravel biting back. But the twins, ever prepared, had a trump card up their pyjama sleeves, and hidden in the bins under their dorm window were two backpacks that had previously suffered the indignity of being squeezed through the crack in the window.

'Catch!' Astrid called, tossing one of the backpacks to Jonas.

With disgust, he picked off some apple peel and a handful of used tissues. Best not to look too closely.

Huddled behind the building opposite, the two made quick work of changing into the backpack's secret stash – their spare school uniforms and matching grey sweaters. Unfortunately, they had to make do with a set of hideous plimsolls, as their regular shoes were still drying by the main entrance. They couldn't go back for them now. They couldn't go back for anything.

'Good?' Astrid asked, picking off some muck from Jonas's shoulder.

He nodded, and without another word, they grabbed each other's hand and ran into the night to find whatever mystery was calling to them.

At this time of night the docks were empty, the loaders and shipmen resting before their early call. Flitting through the dense haze, the twins were entirely unheard and unseen, little creepers squeezing through tight crevices and broken fences.

Until, at last, they could smell it: the grass in the small park by the school, a single patch of fresh green amongst all the concrete.

Retracing their steps through the park, they found the overgrown bush, submitting themselves once more to the prickly brambles. And there it was again, that melody, a distant hum in the back of their heads. As welcoming as the line of red-cap mushrooms alongside.

Emerging on the other side of the same broken fence from that morning, all was still. No leaf shook, or blade of grass swayed. It was only them, and that distant tune they didn't yet understand.

'Now what?' Jonas whispered, scared his own voice might break the spell.

The twins peered down into the void of the stairwell, the darkness stretching endlessly.

Earlier, when they'd first been summoned to this isolated place, the sunlight shining through the leaves had set strands of dust dancing, summoning a petal-soft melody that only the twins could hear. Now there was not even a breeze, the murky moonlight held captive in the mist. And the airborne dust, which had coalesced into thick pillars of blue and gold, did not move at all.

Astrid dared to swipe her hand through a column.

Flickering at her touch, the dust began to strobe, gold flecks blinking blue, the melody turning sharp. 'What do you think it is?'

Jonas started, looking back into the brambles where, only a moment ago, there had been the line of mushrooms.

'Did you see that?'

Astrid stared at the empty space. 'The mushrooms moved.'

Both twins froze to the spot, looking at each other. There was no logical answer.

Astrid wandered around, noticing things that they had missed before.

Piles of seeds, and were those acorn hats? And petal dresses? Many of the flowers and mushrooms appeared to have changed location. But how? And, more importantly, why?

In her wandering, Astrid came upon something strange, right by the station entrance, something that only sparked more questions.

A twig snapped in half on the ground, and beside it, a fresh muddy boot print.

A print that went right in the direction of the station.

'Was this here before?' she asked Jonas, who was now staring down at it as well, the two of them oddly mesmerized by the boot print's lacy pattern. 'I couldn't say . . . Come on,' he finally managed, pulling himself away. 'We have a monster to catch.'

The twins paused at the lip of the stairwell, and then ran down into the bleeding darkness. Once more they splashed through the ticket hall, the water leaking into their shoes and rising up and up as they continued on.

Starting as a distant whispering, it was a hush nearly indistinguishable from the *swish swish* of their own bodies wading through the icy water. The further they went on, turning left again at the same tunnel, the more the noise began to rise with the water. It was wordless music, yet they understood it as clearly as any spoken language.

This way. This way.

Hurry!

'Oh, wait a second,' Jonas suddenly announced, stopping them abruptly. He reached down until his arms were submerged all the way up to the elbows. 'It's got to be here somewhere,' he muttered, even as the gentle song around them began to grow impatient.

'What in the queen's crown are you doing?' Astrid wheezed through the cold, her teeth chattering.

Shaking his head, Jonas squinted at the water, annoyed.

'The black-heart lighter,' he said. 'Greg must have dropped it around here somewhere.'

With a well-practised eye roll, Astrid pulled him back out of the water, and onward. 'We can look for it later, right now we –'

The words dried up on Astrid's tongue. The melody around them had shifted.

They both stood still, ready, listening.

What had at first just been the moss, that murmuring melody that told them where to go, that promised to light a path, was changing into something . . . odd. Along the wall, other foliage began to reveal itself – vines and roots that seemed to move like snakes. It would have been frightening, except the music that came from it was exhilarating.

Jonas focused on that new melody, a sound that seemed to come from inside his head, frantic, a great crescendo building to something unknown. He felt it in his throat, burning like a scream unspoken.

'Astrid,' he breathed, the two of them wading as slowly as drifting leaves in the hip-deep water. 'Something is coming.'

At this, a shriek echoed down the tunnel, piercing through the moss murmurs, a single bloody sound getting closer and closer.

They stopped in their tracks.

The moss fell silent, a silence of anticipation.

This was it, they were sure, whatever they were looking for, the thing that they had been searching for all this time. And it was coming right towards them. All they had to do was catch it, somehow, and they would be free.

And yet neither twin could move, and when Jonas looked over at his sister, she was hardly distinguishable from a statue, her eyes glowing icily in the limited light of the moss.

'I'm not afraid,' she said.

Then a fast-moving figure began to emerge in the bioluminescent light. There was a shape now – human?

'Most unusual . . .' Jonas blinked in the darkness. It looked like a girl.

Maybe this was the ghost that lived in the flooded station? Maybe the rumours were true? But then she spoke – no, screamed, her arms beating the water as she charged towards them:

'Get out of the way!'

But it was too late, and in one great splash that sent the water crashing around them, the girl barrelled through their interlocked fingers.

And it was the strangest thing, because as she tore between them, Jonas and Astrid saw so clearly her two brown eyes, like simmering embers ready to set the world on fire. It ignited something inside them.

Falling into the river, time seemed to speed back to a normal pace, and Jonas grappled rather pathetically in search of Astrid.

Instead of his sister, small fingers wrapped round his arm, and with near inhuman strength, pulled him to the surface and, rather rudely, shoved him back, just in time for him to catch the blood-curdling screech of something dreadful. They could hear the discord it wrought, how the moss on the walls recoiled at the upset of sounds.

'Oh god, oh god, oh god!' the mysterious girl let out in a panic, her fingers fumbling in her bag.

Jonas glanced past her at the dreadful some*thing* that was coming.

The twins saw only a flash of it before their vision turned green at the edges – a fat serpent tail, knots of oily hair, and a jaw split open by rows of too-large human teeth.

As the wicked thing lunged at them, the twins felt their eyes glaze over, their bodies moving precisely as if controlled by strings. But it was not puppet strings that compelled them: it was the growing call of the melodies, the moss and roots and vines screaming at them to do something – anything!

Something their bodies already knew how to do.

Starting in their throats, it was a pleasant sort of burning, words still unspoken. They chased the feeling, the ancient vibrations of a long-lost song.

This girl, the earth told them, *cannot come to any harm.*

And then they began to sing.

A seed breaking through the soil. The haunting harmony of trees creaking in a hurricane. Earthen. Alive.

The monster screamed as it was violently pummelled by the flora around them, but the twins did not stop, the melody spilling from their lips soothing that deep burn of yearning they'd always been plagued by.

Wide-eyed and euphoric, Astrid and Jonas came to stand by the girl, their power near bursting out of their skin. All this time, the two of them had been searching.

But this, the twins realized, *this* is what they'd been looking for.

6

Shadows in the Water

Earlier . . .

Rattling into Paddington Station just after sunset, the steam train from Barnstaple into the city had been an insufferable affair. Gwen had got into a fight with the ticket machine, only to be rained on at her stopover, causing her to arrive damp and in a foul mood. She scowled at anyone who dared ask if she was lost – which she most certainly was not.

Gwen had spent most of her life in the company of magic-wielding Bloom Bloods and was accustomed to the sprawling meadows and salty air of the Devonshire landscape. By contrast, the city streets of the Red Blood world, where those without magic lived their oblivious lives, were filthy and frustrating. They stank of fumes, and were full of angry people in suits and ties.

At the bus stop, as she searched for the correct change in her parka, a woman yelled from behind her in the queue, 'Either buy a ticket or get out of the way!'

Gwen gestured rudely in response, then climbed to the upper level of the big red bus where she could get a better view of the strange city on the way to her target.

In this place, everything green was contained. Trees in cages, parks in their fences. She wondered how any Bloom was able to survive at all.

Yet she knew that magic could thrive in any environment. Weeds pierced through slabs of pavement tiles, widening a crack. Magical spaces could still be born – even here – and from them, any manner of magical things could come to life.

With a wheeze of brakes, the bus came to a stop, announcing Priory Park. Gwen's stop. She alighted along with a gaggle of girls around her own age who clutched drenched umbrellas and laughed and fluttered about like crows, squawking jokes with punchlines Gwen didn't understand.

Avoiding the puddles along the pavement, Gwen followed them down the road with only her own shadow for company.

'When in Mother Mary's name did it get so misty?' one of the girls asked, clutching at her coat.

'Maybe it's . . . the GHOST!' Another girl jumped on her friend's back, causing a riot of screaming as the group bolted away from the park entrance.

Gwen was alone again.

This was the very nature of the Order. To flit about unnoticed, protecting humanity with quiet dignity from things that were best kept in the dark. And it was with this thought in her head – of herself as a great and revered Custodian – that a car drove past, its wheels hissing through a puddle on the roadside, and soaked Gwen from head to toe.

Gasping, Gwen froze in place. 'You have to be kidding me!' she cried after the car as it disappeared round a corner, sending up more rainbows of rain.

Shoulders sagging, she waddled into the park in a freshly foul mood.

Lamplight revealed the path's course, in places flickering or failing entirely. The park was scarcely occupied, its banks of grass muddy and freckled by fallen leaves, with only a lone biker who whizzed by and vanished into the gloom.

Gwen marched through the fog in the direction of her target, a gap where the fencing hung loose, glowing like a neon sign. She squeezed through and crawled on her hands and knees into the bushes beyond, muttering at the mud caking her corduroys, swatting at the twigs pinching her plaits. Stumbling out the other side, Gwen promptly tripped on another tuft of wet grass, tumbling forward into thick mud.

'That's IT!' Gwen growled, pulling violently at her trapped leg, until it came loose from the mud with a thick *schlock*.

Her other foot went down hard on an unfortunate twig that snapped, and she stomped into the weathered concrete with the footprint staring back up at her accusingly. She now understood why those with Red Blood preferred to cut up and cut out the natural world, because right then it was enough to make her scream.

'I swear, I . . .'

Gwen found she wasn't able to remember her next words as her gaze settled ahead and a chill ran through her. The station entrance receded into a vast gaping darkness. She felt that same creeping fear she experienced whenever she tried to use her Bloom, because right then, she was sure, the darkness was looking back at her.

I'm not scared, I'm not scared, I'm not scared. She repeated the words to herself, refusing to give up so quickly.

She shuddered, the chill from the damp clothes seeping into her bones. She glanced around, unnerved by the sense that something was watching her.

'Right,' Gwen announced, ignoring the warning alarm of fear. She marched down into the station, reminding herself that her first order of business was to –

'Gross!' she cried, her boots sinking into the water below.

She allowed herself a momentary whimper, then continued charging on. Her first order of business was to track down this monster. Pulling out her torch, Gwen set a beam of light to break through the darkness, and she saw that the entire station was nothing more than a cold and muddy lake.

Just her luck.

With a well-practised groan, she continued wading through.

Gwen knew a few key facts about frightened magical creatures: they were excellent at hiding, they were most likely watching you, and, most importantly, you must never ever hurt them.

'*The Order does not deal in death*,' Magnus always told them.

No matter how scary or aggressive a creature became, no matter its nature, Bloom Bloods were there to conserve and study, not harm. Lucky for Gwen, a weeping woman would likely be easy to soothe, even without using spells; they could sing together, and she could calm her. There were other ways to subdue magical creatures without using magic, and Gwen was going to prove it. Then she would return home with a smug grin and shove the evidence in everyone's face. Ha!

'OK!' Gwen breathed, reaching back behind her for the comfort of the wall, her fingers connecting with the soft, fleshy mass of moss that grew there. The sensation shocked her as if she'd touched a spark, a single gasp escaping her lips as her other hand dropped the torch, plunging her into darkness.

Only – it wasn't darkness at all. With the artificial light extinguished, this underground world's true heart began to beat. A glowing system of moss throbbed to life, its blue and emerald lights as vast as any galaxy.

Magic, she realized, awakening.

Then the water surrounding her limbs began to ripple. From that glowing reflection, a face was formed – and it was not her own. Gwen watched as a shadow stared back up at her, a black abyss, eyeless, yet looking back at her nonetheless.

Strangest of all, she *knew* this shadow, she was sure of it . . . She felt it whenever she tried to use her Bloom.

With her breath still caught in her throat, she heard a terrible noise, not through her ears, but from inside her body, as if the sound were vibrating up from the moss through her fingers, through her veins, and piercing her heart. It was awful, discordant, like a melody turned rotten and foul, and not at all what Bloom should sound like.

Gradually, then all at once, the sound grew, although 'sound' was not quite the right word, for what Gwen heard in that cavern was a very clear, very real voice.

'I've found you.'

Gasping, Gwen looked up and around, sure she would see something, but the water had gone back to being just that, only water. The horrifying reflection had rippled into nothing, and with it, the words too had melted away. All that remained was the undeniable sense that she was being watched.

'Hello?' Gwen called, her voice squeaky with fear. If there was a weeping woman, Gwen needed to show that she was friendly, and safe. Even if in that moment Gwen was the one who needed reassurance.

Then, not more than twenty metres away, the water began to ripple again, creating a serpentine line along the surface. Gwen blinked, and in that split second, a creature emerged.

Immobilized in her shock, Gwen could do nothing but stare as a smiling face appeared from the shadows, a sharp glint of teeth that tore a white streak across the darkness. This was no rusalka, nor was it any type of weeping woman she recognized from her books of magical creatures. It was huge, with hair like tangled roots and its skin like rot, and eyes weeping water black as oil. And behind its face, slithering back and forth, was the rippling body of a snake.

A discordant clang of Bloom sounded, so awful it made Gwen's eyes sting. Her heart thudded near painfully in her chest as she realized this beast was – inexplicably – a creature from a distant sea: a serpent woman known as the Nure-onna. She was extremely dangerous, and Gwen was very much out of her league.

'Damn.'

Gwen had barely a moment to process the realization when the creature shrieked, a miserable wailing of a sound that cut at Gwen's heart like a burning knife, and the monster revealed two huge rows of human teeth.

You will be pleased to know that in that moment Gwen crushed her reckless need to prove herself and instead did the sensible thing. She screamed, and ran.

Splashing a course back the way she'd come, Gwen was a stampede of one, beating the water into white bubbles where she cut through the muck. As she charged onwards, she saw a beacon in the distance – pale blue light glinting off crowns of golden angel hair.

One thought pierced her mind while her legs splashed ever forward: *Have I died?*

The figures, growing closer with each step, were not angels at all, but tall, dainty humans – teens like her – delicate as sugar dust, their pale skin almost like porcelain. Who *were* these reckless teens? Who in their right mind would come down here?

Who indeed.

'Get out of the way!' she screamed.

She had hardly a moment to catch the utter bewilderment on their faces – icy eyes, pink cheeks, pretty. She went barrelling into their interlocked hands, sending all three of them crashing down into the water.

Gwen clambered desperately at the water for purchase, finding only a bony arm to cling on to.

A fresh, monstrous shriek kick-started Gwen's brain back into gear, and she had just enough sense to pull and shove the strangers behind her, ignoring their cries of indignation as she grabbed for a freezing potion and popped the lid with her thumb.

'Oh god, oh god, oh god,' Gwen mumbled, desperately trying to summon even a crumb of her Bloom to throw the potion, but her body was screaming in fear, her Bloom locked behind a wall of shadow.

There was no time. The beast was upon them.

She braced herself for the imminent pain – teeth crushing her neck, or for her heart to be swiftly detached from her chest . . .

And yet, the moment didn't come.

Instead, all she heard was singing. The sound echoed off the glowing moss on the walls, an intricate duet of a spell.

In a flash, the creature in front of her was consumed. Coming from every angle, from hidden places beneath the water and above them, hundreds of roots, leaves and stems grew rapidly – impossibly – and swarmed the serpent woman. The beast let out screeches of protest as its body bashed against the roof where it was stuck firmly in place, no matter how much it wriggled and snapped its jaws.

Gwen had never in her magical life seen a power like it.

'Well, that's new,' the boy remarked, also staring up.

Gwen looked over at him and saw an emerald glow fading from his eyes, so fast Gwen wondered if she'd imagined it. Still huffing and dazed, it took her a moment to convince herself the beast was indeed securely restrained (and that she hadn't died). And once she was sure, she turned in a fresh blaze of fury to the intruders on her mission.

'You're Bloom Blooded!' she all but roared. 'Are you from Fountains Abbey?' Then, putting two and two together, Gwen deflated. 'Someone sent you after me, didn't they? Who was it?'

Gwen's two intruders stood silent, soaked from head to toe and glistening blue and green in the moss light, their hair slicked down to the pale, goose-egg pallor of their faces. Gwen wanted to touch their skin, to see if it would crack.

To see if they were human.

They glanced at one another, and the shift in reflected light gave their irises a sharp spark, like catching a glint on the edge of a knife.

Twins, she realized. With terrifying powers.

'What in the Twelve Spells even *was* that?' Gwen spluttered, trying to make sense of what she'd seen them do.

'Was that Ancient Magic? I've never heard anything like it.' She gestured to the moss above – the magic that should be impossible.

Or perhaps, she feared, it was only impossible for her.

'Ancient what?' The twins blinked at her in response, as though they really didn't know what she was talking about. Gwen wasn't buying it.

Entirely ignoring her, much to Gwen's irritation, they both waded past, and, as if they'd never known fear in their lives, approached the now suspended monster.

'Extraordinary,' the girl said, and her voice was a harp chord, every note of it plucking at something deep in the marrow of Gwen's soul. She didn't like that.

Gwen was growing irate, not just at what she believed to be two formidable students from Fountains Abbey interfering with her shot at redemption, but also because the serpent woman had deeply disturbed her. The discordant melody of something evil and wrong, the hollow gape of its eyes, its rotten body, the fact it was even there at all . . . It all sat entirely outside her understanding of magical creatures.

And then there were these twins, wielding unknown magic with such terrifying precision. They were almost as frightening as the beast itself.

'Don't,' she demanded, shoving the boy with her shoulder, stopping him from poking the creature. 'Are you quite well?'

In response, the trapped creature let out a shriek, rot spitting from its lips, which had them all jumping in alarm.

Something was definitely not right.

Trying to ignore the terrible discordant Bloom coming from the beast, Gwen assessed the vines, and realized they would not hold for much longer. So, scowling at the twins, she turned on her heel and began marching out of that god-forsaken hole in the ground.

'Hey now!' the boy called out.

'We have questions for you!' the girl joined in, splish-splashing after her.

Gwen ignored them, stomping through the muck until she was at last reunited with the night sky.

'Goodness, you can walk fast for someone with such little legs,' the girl said as she huffed behind her, climbing up the steps. 'Won't you please stop and tell us about that creature and what we did?'

'We're only curious,' the boy added. 'What is the Bloom you speak of?'

'Do you hear plants singing too?' the girl added.

A twig snapped under Gwen's foot, and she turned on the twins abruptly.

There they were, standing at the cusp of the station entrance, pale skin practically glittering in the silver moonlight – so perfect and shiny and talented, just as Pledges should be, and right then, to Gwen, they were everything that was wrong. You see, just as Gwen had wrongly assumed the twins to be prodigy students of Fountains Abbey, she had also assumed that they must be making fun of her.

'You think you're so special with your strange magic, don't you?' she said, puffing out her chest as she quickly scrambled to think of something that would put them in their place. 'But have you even got Savonnettes?'

The twins tilted their heads to the side, confused, and Gwen took the moment to reach into her pocket and pull out the broken pocket watch.

'Well, I do, and it's a special one,' she said, terribly pleased with herself. 'So there.'

Like fool's gold in her palm, the useless item glittered between them, the etched sword rising from the sea on the torn lid.

But the twins did not give her the look of shock and awe she had hoped for; instead they stared down as if Gwen had presented them with a beating heart.

The girl reached out her hand, eyes wide like she'd seen a ghost, and traced the broken sigil with her finger, with all the care one might give a small, helpless animal.

'Hey, don't –'

Gwen stopped short, taken aback by the severity of this girl's stare, how it trapped her in place and stole the words right out of her mouth. Though Gwen was loath to admit it, this girl was beautiful – they both were – and, having seen what they could do with their magic, it was diabolically unfair.

That's when Gwen finally saw them, dangling round both of their necks on strings, violent tears down the middle – two shards from the lid of an old Savonnette. No, not just any Savonnette. Swirling etchings, entirely unique. The very one Gwen now held in her palm.

'Where did you get those?' Gwen breathed, hardly believing what she was seeing.

'We've had these since we were babies,' the girl explained, a minute quiver to her voice. 'And you –' her eyes widened, excited – 'you know what it is, don't you? Where did you get this? Where's it from? What is it?'

'Um, you know, a Savonnette? Everyone has one in the Order of Pendragon,' Gwen prompted, yet she was growing nervous. 'Society of Magical Study and Conservation? I . . . I lied, this isn't mine, I found it this morning.'

'Where?' the boy demanded, staring intensely.

Swallowing, Gwen's fingers tightened round the Savonnette.

'Queen's mercy . . . You really don't know? But . . . that doesn't make any sense. How did you do that with the moss and vines? Why would you have *those shards*? I don't –' Gwen tried to reason with herself, yet it was abundantly clear the impossible had happened. She'd stumbled across not one but *two* exceptional Bloom Bloods who'd gone undetected by the Order. And somehow they had the missing parts of the Savonnette she'd stolen.

'Oh Mary. I'm gonna have to take you to Magnus Faymore . . .' She was mumbling to herself now, practically blowing steam from her ears as she paced around the enchanted glade. 'Why did I steal this? What was I thinking? . . . Oh god, I'm going to be in so much trouble.'

Mortified by her own foolishness, Gwen continued to spiral, until the girl reached out and grabbed her shoulders, giving her a little shake. 'Calm down,' she told her. 'Tell us about this Magnus.'

But before Gwen could crystallize her thoughts into an answer, they were interrupted by the sound of a siren. A police siren, to be precise, and the sound of it, getting closer until it whizzed by, froze the twins on the spot as if they'd picked up a very bad scent.

Putting two and two together, Gwen gasped. 'You're runaways!'

They nodded, and Gwen could not help but become flustered by the way the girl looked at her with that serious expression, like their very lives were in the balance.

Gwen had wanted to prove she was useful, and now she finally had that chance.

'I'm taking you to Magnus,' she declared, biting back her worries. 'I don't know who you are, or why this has happened, but that's the only way we're going to get any answers about this.' She looked past them into the gloomy station entrance. 'And someone with a really fancy Savonnette needs to come and collect that thing before it breaks loose.'

The twins looked up and down at Gwen in her soaked and muddy clothes, as she stood shivering in the breeze. Then they leaned into each other like trees in the wind, whispers carrying like leaves. The boy eventually scowled at his sister, then turned back to face Gwen.

'We'll come with you. Maybe.'

The girl also looked Gwen straight in the face. The fog had cleared and now the moon shone strong and bright, lighting up the glint in her eyes. 'But first, tell us who you are.'

7

The Order of Pendragon

Her name was Gwen. A dreamy name, almost a sigh. Astrid pondered on it on the train from Paddington, the way it lit up like a question, one they must find an answer to, no matter where it took them.

She'd looked so funny to the twins in the bright red phone box by the station, yelling into the receiver, fierce as a cornered dog as she explained the situation to their mysterious soon-to-be hosts. There had been a lot of back and forth. This monster, it seemed, was not where it was supposed to be, and someone was going to have to deal with it.

It was late now, long past midnight, and they watched her, this small fiery girl, scowling in her sleep as the train rocked her to and fro. In the grey night light, her bronze skin was almost blue, and her black plaits silver. She was small in a way that could have been cute, but with her lips in a permanent pout and her thick brows always furrowed, her prettiness was barbed, like the thorn on the stem of a rose.

In Gwen's pocket, the Savonnette, as she had called it, was safely away again. Just out of sight.

'The Order of Pendragon,' Astrid hummed.

'Society of Magical Study and Conservation,' Jonas responded, rubbing his chin thoughtfully as he too stared at their dozing companion. 'I'm certainly curious about this Magnus Faymore.'

There was a twinge in his chest. He was nervous. Astrid felt it too.

Outside, the endless, rolling world of grass and sea seemed to shake as the train rumbled along the track. London was far behind them now, replaced by glimpses of sleeping towns, silent waters and acres of shadowy fields in the darkness.

'We'll get our answers,' Astrid murmured. 'Then *we* will decide what to do.'

Tilting his head, Jonas held out his hand until Astrid leaned forward, and the two shook their pinkies in a childish promise.

'It's us against the world,' Jonas whispered. 'Forever.'

Despite herself, Astrid looked over Gwen once more, still fascinated by the sleeping girl.

Something undeniable had happened in that abandoned tunnel: the moss hadn't simply communicated with them, it had followed their will. A simmering power that they had always held in the darkest corridors of their mortal bodies, but had never found the key to unlock, until now. Until Gwen.

'Forever,' she said, just as the train screeched to a halt.

'What?' Gwen grumbled, blinking back into reality.

'This appears to be our stop,' Jonas explained before she could make a fuss over being so rudely awakened.

A drizzle of rain greeted them at the old brick station, with one dozing ticket inspector snoring in his sleep as the twins jumped the barrier.

'Hey,' Gwen called to them. 'Don't umm . . .' She hesitated, scrunching up her nose. 'Don't do any of that Ancient Magic stuff until we speak to Magnus, OK? It's – how do I say this – it's not normal.'

Astrid glanced at her brother, both narrowing their eyes. They knew better than most that not being normal led to tests, and doctors, and other such unpleasantness.

'I'm not entirely sure we could even if we wanted to.'

Gwen nodded at this, satisfied, but the twins were left with an uneasy feeling.

Astrid leaned over to reassure her brother. 'We'll be OK.'

Jonas nodded, and the pair followed Gwen out into the darkness.

Beneath the banks of grass outside the station, a single vehicle squeaked to a stop – a beat-up old Morris Minor the colour of mustard, its engine rumbling.

Gwen and the twins made their way to the stuttering car, holding their arms over their heads as makeshift umbrellas while the driver's-side window slowly rolled down.

'You have no idea how much trouble you're in.'

The owner of the voice had a face far too cherubic for his tone. Perfect ringlets of soft black hair framed rounded cheeks, and a most remarkable flurry of vitiligo left clouds of pink over his dewy brown skin.

'Yeah, yeah,' Gwen grumbled.

Pushing aside a selection of instrument cases, the twins squeezed into the back, with Gwen squished between them.

'Belts on,' the boy called back, and with no warning, the engine roared beneath them, the wheels violently shrieking as the car revved away.

A girl in the front passenger seat turned to Gwen, long hair in a single silky plait flicking about like a cat's tail with each bump they went over. She had a thin, elongated face and was so tall her head nearly hit the roof of the car.

'I'm very upset with you. You know Magnus was trawling the beach? They thought you might have drowned. Are you listening to me?' she all but squawked while Gwen nodded sombrely. 'How could you run off like that when you know you can't use magic properly?'

Astrid cut a glance at Jonas, the two immediately curious about what precisely was wrong with Gwen's magic. It seemed they were not the only ones with abnormal powers.

'Stop it – don't talk about that.' Shrinking in on herself, Gwen glared at the twins, clearly embarrassed, then stared daggers at her sister. 'I could handle myself just fine.'

The tall girl turned to the twins, a smile spreading across her face like honey on toast. 'Thank you for rescuing my sister,' she trilled. 'I'm Jan.'

'And I'm Thomas,' the boy added, glancing back at them in the rear-view mirror. 'You must be Astrid and Jonas, the mysterious lost Bloom Bloods.'

Bloom Bloods. The very same term Gwen had used to describe them. Astrid found herself staring down into her own palm, made curious by the insinuation that there was something fundamentally different about their blood – something strange and magical.

'I suppose we are,' Jonas said, and Astrid noted that he too was analysing his own skin.

'Well,' Thomas continued, glancing at Jan, 'whatever you are, you've caused quite a stir.'

Gwen perked up at this, listening intently.

'How so?' the twins asked, wary.

'It was a little scandalous, actually,' Jan said. 'After Gwen called, they had to write all these letters, and we heard

Magnus on a call with *the* Beatrice Doria. Then off he went to the study at the cove, saying he'd be back later and for us to take care of you in the meantime.'

The twins froze, glancing at one another. Jonas had suddenly lost his voice, so Astrid asked the question for them: 'I'm sorry, did you just say Beatrice Doria? As in, the Queen of England?'

The other three in the car looked at each other as if they were trying to communicate with aliens.

'Wow,' Thomas spluttered, 'you guys really don't know anything, huh?'

'*Thomas*,' Jan warned.

'I told you,' Gwen said with a smirk.

'*Gwen*.' Jan tutted before turning to the twins again. 'Sorry about them. I'm sure this is all very confusing for you.' She smiled that sweet honey smile again. 'You might know her as the queen, but to us she's the Magister of the entire Western European Faction, which includes our humble little Faymore Cluster . . . or how would the Red Bloods say it? Oh yes – a coven.'

The twins hung on each word like a cliff they might fall from.

'Her bloodline has held the position since the Order of Pendragon was formed nearly five hundred years ago. Every faction has a Magister and five Ambassadors for each area of study. All together, they form the Grand Coterie, who have protected and reinvigorated Bloom Blooded society, pulling us out of the magical dark age.'

It sounded like she was reading off a prompt, and the twins, of course, had a million questions. Like, how many people knew about magic and Bloom Bloods? What kind of hold did they have on the world? And from the way Jonas's pupils dilated, Astrid guessed he had some very specific questions about Prince Teddy's involvement.

But this new knowledge delivered a fresh wave of jitters. The magical Order was powerful, perhaps more so than they could comprehend, and yet somehow the twins had been kept out of its sight. But why? Astrid absent-mindedly twisted the pendant at her neck.

When they arrived at the mud-slick drive, the rain was slowing to a drizzle, the darkness thick. Through the wet sheen, they could barely make out a landscape of dense forest sprawling beyond – green, and wild, and *singing*.

The twins could smell it; it was almost overwhelming, great lungfuls of air so clean it was as if they were taking their very first breaths.

'The doctor would simply die if he saw us right now,' Astrid chuckled.

A wicked smirk spread across her brother's face as he replied, 'One can only dream.'

'Come on,' Thomas called to them. 'It's a bit of a walk.'

Out of the car, the twins could see Jan and Thomas entirely – or more so, their clothes. All tweed and ruffles and delicate lace, as if everyone in this *Faymore Cluster* had stepped out of an old painting. But their clothes were not the most surprising thing. With a short whistle, Thomas held out his hand, and the twins watched, fascinated, as a small fire ignited in his open palm. The flame flickered and hummed, beaming a clean light for them to follow.

They walked like this until Gwen held out her arm.

'Careful,' she cautioned.

Along the treeline, the air shimmered like an oil spill. When they looked down at the earth, there was a small statue, spinning in the roots of a tree. A dancing fairy, with hollow hands that made strange music in the rain.

'It sounds like . . . that sinking feeling when you've gone the wrong way,' Jonas mused.

Jan put her fingers up to the shimmer and stared at them, her thick brows furrowed. She seemed both fascinated and surprised by their deduction.

'You're close, actually,' she admitted. 'They're wards. The Order has them all over the world. They come in all types. Some keep things in, some keep things out. Mostly they confuse Red Bloods, sending people back the way they came, but if some do get through, their memories and any pictures they try to take will be fuzzy. Bloom Bloods like us, though? We can push through.'

And with that, she and Thomas stepped across the singing barrier.

'Welcome to Faymore Manor,' Gwen announced, as she too vanished into the trees.

The twins followed. Immediately there was a ringing in their ears, like a sudden shift in air pressure, then a pleasant pop. But it wasn't until Astrid looked up that the magic truly revealed itself. Warm lamplights greeted them, floating miraculously like stars brought down to earth. Where there had once been the endless view of thick forests, now there was the sweet smell of hay, and the sea, and budding gardens, for they had emerged on to an entire estate.

Etched on to the cliff side, Faymore Manor belonged to the earth as much as to those who resided inside her. The grounds were home not just to the Faymore Cluster, but all manner of creatures, from stables of horses, to frog ponds and bird houses, and something far stranger.

'Look,' Astrid gasped, pointing.

In the gardens, tiny legs scurried along tree branches, leaves flickered . . . except, not leaves at all, but wings, tiny sprites just out of sight.

'Incredible,' the twins mused, and Astrid was sure that the grass around them preened at the compliment.

'They're tree spirits,' Jan told them, smiling fondly. 'A good sign that a place is rich with Bloom. I'm hoping to study them around the world when I become a Custodian.'

Astrid realized this must have been what she'd seen at the abandoned station – the mushrooms and leaves that had moved had been magic. Like her.

'Oh no,' Gwen suddenly breathed, taking a cautious step back as they approached the large manor doors. 'Brace yourselves.'

The twins paused, hearing what she did – a deep rumbling down the corridor. When the door was flung open, it was with such force, one might have believed a hurricane was blowing through the hallways.

But it was no hurricane at all; a woman stood in the doorframe, wearing a charming floral dress and a furious expression. She was tall, with dark, dewy skin and hair pinned up in intricate braids. Her voice echoed through the trees.

'Gwendolyn Chatterjee!'

Gwendolyn, Astrid thought, finding even more crevices to explore in the name.

While Jan and Thomas quickly snuck into the manor, Gwen, who was quite clearly not so thrilled by this, shrunk back on herself.

'What in the Twelve Spells were you thinking?' the woman shouted.

Charging forward into the drizzle, she pulled Gwen in with a grip so tight the twins feared she might shatter.

'C'mere to me now!' she declared, looking her over. 'Goodness gracious, have you been bathing in an ogre's swamp?' She picked a twig out of Gwen's hair. Turning her around, the woman reached into Gwen's pocket, grabbing the broken Savonnette and holding it up to Gwen's face like a warning. 'Don't you ever think of sneaking about again, do you hear me? This is not a toy.'

Gwen nodded slowly, her jaw twitching.

Carefully, the lady tucked the golden item away, the twins watching as the mysterious thing once again disappeared out of their reach. Then she turned that fearful gaze on the twins. They saw it then. At her breast was a Savonnette with a slightly different pattern from their pendants. A sword, like theirs, but from the sea, instead of resting in spirals. Hers was also new and shiny, with a winder at the bottom and a clasp at the side – a pocket watch.

At the same time, the woman's eyes spotted the shards hanging from Astrid and Jonas's necks. It was just for a second, but in that moment the twins caught that she looked . . . afraid?

She knew something.

'They didn't do anything,' Gwen insisted, her fists clenched in determination, like a child who'd found a stray dog she wanted to keep. 'They saved me. We all ended up in the station mentioned in Magnus's notebook,' she went on, fiddling with her coat sleeves. 'There was something weird in there, Lorelei, something really wrong.'

The lady – Lorelei – tutted. 'This is why young girls don't go messing with things they're not ready for.'

Gwen's face fell.

'Thank you for rescuing our Gwendolyn,' Lorelei said to the twins, her voice softening like butter in the sun. 'Let's get you all inside and cleaned up. Magnus should be back soon.' Ushering them in, she gave the twins another once-over before heading back out.

'That's Lorelei,' Gwen whispered. 'She's Magnus's research partner and Thomas's cousin. It's best to just do what she says.'

The twins nodded, not needing to be told twice.

The manor's inside was as peculiar as its outside, and absolutely massive. The twins had never seen so many rooms, and all filled with so much *stuff*. Following Gwen through the entry into a haze of sweet-smelling smoke hanging like a candied fog, Astrid had to manoeuvre herself round the comfortable disarray of colourful trinkets: horseshoes hanging like good omens, potion bottles and more musical instruments than the twins had ever seen, each beautifully crafted and well cared-for.

The twins took in every detail like they were planning a heist . . . and well, perhaps they were – they hadn't decided yet.

Escorted into a well-stocked kitchen, they found a rotund man with a frilly apron and curly auburn hair fretting about an antique pot. The twins saw that he too had a golden pocket watch.

Spread across the humongous table in front of him was an unreasonable amount of cookies – chocolate chip, maple, ginger, cranberry. The smell was heavenly.

'Oh, thank goodness.' The man sagged in relief when he saw them, pink cheeks forming apples on each side of his mouth. 'Are these your new friends?' he asked, reaching up for another set of plates and mugs.

'Elijah, this is Astrid and Jonas.' Gwen spoke for them, looking a little self-conscious.

The man glanced at the twins as they stuck themselves to the wall, and once again, just like with Lorelei, his eyes flitted over to the pendants. Astrid's heart nearly skipped a beat. They knew something, definitely, but what?

'Well, please make yourselves at home,' he said, beaming, then began to fluster himself with various kitchen tasks. 'I know it's terribly late – I mean, goodness me, the sun will probably be rising soon, but I thought you all might want some hot tea and cookies before bed.' He paused, licking some chocolate off his thumb, then added, 'Magnus is very keen to meet you.'

Thomas got busy filling up his plate, with Jan next to him vigorously stirring a sugar cube into her rosy teacup, before she did something the twins found most curious indeed. Tapping the bottom of the saucer, the tall girl began to hum, a strange, punchy melody that the twins could feel like a furnace in the pit of their bellies. The tea in her cup began to billow steam, freshly heated.

'Gwen, dear, you're filthy,' Elijah sighed, coming over to wipe at her face with a damp cloth – which Gwen immediately swatted away.

'I'm fine, Elijah,' she grumbled, stuffing a chocolate cookie in her mouth. 'Eat 'irst, 'ath 'ater.'

'At least let me patch up your scrapes,' Elijah insisted, reaching for an ornate ladle resting in a pot of creamy hot chocolate.

As if it were second nature, Gwen opened her mouth while Elijah brought the steaming contents over. Along with the rich scent of cocoa, the twins picked up a gentle ringing, much like the hum of sleep song – Bloom, Astrid realized.

When Gwen slurped it up, the melody sparkled through the room, and they watched as she winced, only for the small scrapes and bruises along her exposed skin to vanish in front of their eyes.

'Fascinating,' Jonas murmured.

Elijah quickly got back to work filling a mug for everyone, and despite all the fuss as Gwen, Thomas and Jan jostled around the table, happily digging in, everything seemed to fall into its own chaotic order.

This cosy domestic setting was so far removed from anything the twins were used to that it sent a confusing, warm feeling into their stomachs. It was a feeling they could not place and therefore made them uneasy.

When Elijah turned to hand them their own mugs, the twins were nowhere to be seen. Quiet as mice, they had snuck out.

Outside again, the world seemed to pulse around them, the sheer expanse of sky and sea and trees spinning. It wasn't raining any more. The sky was turning mauve and the sun was soon to rise. Further up the path, they could see a charming building with lights on – a wooden sign by the door read *Windyside Cottage*.

Astrid had to wonder: just how big was this estate . . .? And why weren't there more people?

'Did you see how they looked at our shards?' Jonas asked, staring up at the purple clouds like he was looking for answers.

They had waited, hidden behind a yew tree, but after a few minutes it became clear that no one was coming after them. Now they ambled along the manor's exterior, drinking in the fresh air and cool breeze on their skin.

'They seemed afraid, didn't they?' Astrid murmured, fiddling with her split pendant.

Jonas nodded. 'We can't trust these people. We don't know what they want from us.'

Astrid knew he was right, of course. They'd spent their whole lives being trapped and monitored by adults; they couldn't let it happen again.

'There's secrets in these walls,' she said, running her fingers along the vines on the brickwork.

Jonas also placed his palms flat along the creepers, the two of them feeling the rhythm of the Bloom under their skin, and deeper, to that hidden part of their matter that now lay restless, waiting to be freed again.

If only they knew how.

'Gwen said we shouldn't,' Astrid said, mischief pulling at her lips. 'But I suppose we've never been much good at doing what we're supposed to.'

Despite not knowing how to call on their Bloom, it was still there. A burn of something ancient resting at the back of their throats. They spent several minutes in strained concentration; but as hard as they tried to conjure that feeling, that formidable power that had moved the very earth, they could not.

And yet . . . Astrid didn't want to give up. She thought back, trying to work out what might have changed. There was only one thing that came to mind – something she was sure Jonas also knew, even if he wouldn't dare say it out loud.

'What if . . .' Astrid's voice trailed off, unsure. 'What if we thought of Gwen?'

'Maybe.' Jonas hesitated . . . and then his gaze landed behind Astrid and his eyes widened. 'What on earth is *that*?'

Darting a glance over her shoulder, Astrid looked back at the entrance to the manor. There, perched on the eaves, was a bird, bigger than an eagle. It had five horns sprouting from its head like a crown, and feathers so pointed they looked sure to be sharp to the touch. This creature was not from the world of Red Bloods.

As they cautiously approached, it roused itself and glided down to land in front of them. They saw that something had been tied round its throat – a cylinder.

'Good evening,' Astrid said, for she did not know the proper way to greet such an extraordinary creature.

Blinking at them with eyes black and glossy, the thing ruffled its feathers and let out a single croak. Then it began to tap at the cylinder as if to say, *Well, hurry up then!*

After a shared glance, Jonas went to very carefully reach over and undo the pack from round the bird's body. Then he popped open its lid to reveal a scroll.

'A messenger!' Astrid said, impressed.

Gently, the twins unrolled the parchment, squinting at the lettering. It wasn't a message for them after all.

It was a message *about* them.

Custodian Magnus,

Thank you for your report; it has caused quite a stir here. We have collected all documentation available on Astrid and Jonas Bunting. I'm sure you will find these documents as fascinating as I have.

Appropriate potions and spells have been put in motion to remove all traces of them from Red Blooded society, both on paper and from memory.

Their significance to our research is of tantamount importance; therefore it is by my decree that Astrid and Jonas Bunting must not be let out of our sight.

It is the verdict of the Fountains Abbey Ambassadors that they should Pledge themselves to the Order of Pendragon and be taken in at Fountains Abbey Academy as soon as possible, where they can be monitored appropriately and begin their magical education.

Sanguis Noster, Officium Nostrum

Your Magister
B. Doria

It was almost too much information to process. But one word stood out: *research*. It was so clinical, so reminiscent of all they'd been trying to escape.

Astrid glanced up at the looming manor house with all its spires and creeping ivy. A refuge, or just another cage?

One thing was certain. This time they were not going to wait to find out.

8

Ancient Magic

When Gwen came to look for the twins she was ambushed.

Muffling her yelp of surprise with his hand, Jonas pulled Gwen inside the manor and through to the reception room. Astrid grabbed her wrists and the twins towered over her against the wall, cornered prey.

'You tricked us, you naughty thing,' Astrid scolded as Gwen thrashed, causing a table of trinkets by the wall to rattle dangerously. Furious, Gwen licked the inside of Jonas's still-muck-covered palm, startling him into pulling his hand back.

'Urgh gross –' Gwen spat out the mud on her tongue, clearly regretting her action. 'Get off me!' she growled.

'Not until you tell us what *this* is about,' Jonas demanded, waving the letter in her line of sight. 'What does the Order want with us?'

Confused, Gwen's eyes flitted over the delicate script on the parchment, her brow furrowing, until her mouth fell open in shock.

'What on earth do they mean by "research"?' Gwen suddenly breathed, and although it was not the explanation the twins had been hoping for, she certainly appeared equally flummoxed.

86

'Something fishy is going on here,' Gwen huffed as Astrid and Jonas released their grip. She took the letter from them to inspect. 'For the Magister and all her Ambassadors to be so involved . . . I wonder . . . You know, when I found the Savonnette there were these photos . . .'

Gwen reached into her pocket and pulled out an old sepia image. There was a whole group of them, eight in total. One of the faces was blurry, the figure caught in motion, but the others were clear.

'That's Magnus and Elijah there in the middle, and that one there . . .' Gwen swallowed, her nose scrunching up like she was trying to scrunch up her emotions. 'That's my mum . . . But look here on the back.'

Leaning in, Jonas read over the words, his eyes narrowing.

'The Rapscallions' first mission to hunt for Ancient Magic.'

The photo was decades old, and yet Elijah hadn't looked like an old man when they met him.

'What's the average lifespan of Bloom Bloods?' Jonas asked, his mouth going a little dry.

'About one hundred and twenty years, but some have been known to live up to two hundred,' Gwen explained, entirely too casually.

'Well then,' Astrid said, trying to process it all. 'And you stole that photo?' she asked, raising an eyebrow.

Gwen looked sheepish for a second, but then shrugged. 'It has my mum in it.' She placed the photo in her pocket again.

Taking a step back, the twins weighed up all the information they had, and Jonas found he couldn't get a grip on it. Something fishy was indeed going on, and if it were true that the Order had been looking for the twins' powers, the last thing they wanted was to be kept and monitored like an experiment. Never again.

'So, what are you going to do?' Gwen asked, looking like a wounded puppy. 'Magnus will be here soon. I mean, he should be here already.'

Echoes of clinking plates and joyful chatter wafted in from the kitchen. The sounds made Jonas squirm.

'We've not decided yet,' Astrid said simply, stepping away to pace around the room, inspecting some of the instruments in the lamplight.

Then she turned back to Gwen. 'Fountains Abbey Academy. What is that?'

'It's our faction's headquarters and main instructional institution. Most of our Bloom Bloods live and work in the surrounding area of Fountains Vale.'

Astrid cut her eyes at Jonas, and he instantly took his cue.

'Why aren't you studying there?'

'That's none of your business.'

'Oh, but I think it is,' Astrid said, beaming at her, a look Jonas rarely saw her give anyone but himself. 'What's so wrong with your Bloom exactly?'

Jonas watched the exchange from the corner of the room where he'd found a little music box, his fingers absent-mindedly winding the lever while he watched his sister in the same way he might a brewing storm cloud. Teasing people together had always brought them tremendous joy, and in that moment, he could almost feel the way Astrid's stomach swooped, sensing that she was getting far more out of bothering Gwen than she ever had from anyone else.

Gwen glowered.

'You can't do it, can you?' Astrid asked, crowding the girl. 'You can't use your Bloom.'

'I – it's not like that. I . . .'

Gwen seemed to wage some kind of world-shattering internal battle with herself, eventually grunting and marching over to where a violin hung on the wall in the corner. She grabbed a bow and proceeded rather violently to rub it down with a molten lump of rosin, before snatching the instrument from the wall and forcing it into submission.

'If you want to know so badly, I'll show you. But don't say I didn't warn you.'

Standing to the side, the twins watched, utterly mesmerized, as Gwen took a centring breath, and began to glide the bow over the strings. Springing forth from her fingers, the melody she conjured was airy, light and refreshing, the music hitting the twins like a cool breeze.

Untangling each note, Jonas was surprised to find that he knew this song, in the same way he knew the age of every plant and tree – and it was not a song at all: it was a spell.

The magic grew, a wind picking up, but just as the spell should have tipped into a command, the air went oddly still – not like the quiet before a storm, but like death. Like a cold shadow. Gwen started to sweat, a small glistening sheen on her brow.

And the strangest of things happened: the more Gwen played, spilling her Bloom into the notes, the more Astrid and Jonas felt their throats and fingers burn in answer.

Something was wrong. Even as inexperienced as they were, the twins could feel it, a darkness blooming within the melody. They could see that Gwen was afraid, and their own magic was responding.

Jonas turned to his sister, and she too seemed equally perplexed, and yet, while Jonas found himself recoiling from the feeling, Astrid leaned in.

It was swelling in their heads again, a pulsing call to action.

Help her

Almost on autopilot, the twins flexed their fingers.

'*Stop.*' Astrid breathed the word, and as she did, every plant in the room sprang to life. Vases toppled over, pots cracked like eggs, anything in the vicinity with roots or buds surged forward, blanketing Gwen and holding her still before she could produce another note.

Gwen screamed, 'What the hell?'

Her playing came to a screeching halt, her bow falling.

The twins blinked, hardly believing what they'd just done. The magic slowly recoiled, setting Gwen free. She quickly scrabbled away, shaking off the loose leaves and petals sticking to her like they were venomous spiders.

'Gwen, sorry, we didn't –'

But Gwen was looking past them, to the door.

'My, that *is* impressive,' a voice said.

A man stood in the doorway, watching them like one might a science experiment. In his hand, the broken Savonnette dangled on a chain.

Jonas cleared his throat, pausing to recover from their moment of panic. 'Magnus, I suppose?' he asked.

The stranger chuckled, smooth as silk. 'You suppose correctly.'

Narrowing their eyes, the twins came to stand in front of him, scrutinizing the strange man who seemed to hold their fate in his hands.

Magnus Faymore, with his pointed eyebrows and unusual garb, was an oddity. A cane at his side, he was dressed in a cape as black as his hair, with feathered ends like a raven's wings. On his head was a rather bizarre pointed hat. He looked like a plague doctor, or perhaps a court jester.

Leaning back and looking behind him, down the hallway, Magnus held up a hand, smiling. A warning, Jonas realized, to everyone in the kitchen. Telling them to stay back.

Magnus's eyes caught on the letter now lying on the floor surrounded by dirt and petals. Carefully, he picked it up, inspecting the words with an entirely unreadable expression.

'Gwen,' Magnus said, crumpling up the paper and shoving it in his pocket as if it were nothing more than a used tissue. 'Would you do me an ever so big favour and go and ask my husband if he'll help with this mess?'

'But –'

Magnus cut her off with a smile. 'If not that, then perhaps you could clean up and prepare some fresh clothes and bedding for our guests?'

Pouting, Gwen looked down at her dirty outfit, then at the mess of broken plant pots and tipped vases. Muttering under her breath, she took one final look at the twins before slinking into the hallway.

Magnus surveyed the twins, his gaze resting briefly on the shards at their necks. Jonas took a small protective step in front of his sister.

'Now, Astrid and Jonas, was it?'

The twins nodded.

'It's terribly stuffy in here,' he complained, reaching down and gathering up a bouquet of sweet-smelling lilies from the floor that had tumbled down when a vase had tipped over. As he restored them to their container, the stems gave a trill of protest that made the twins wince.

Then he turned to them again. 'How tired are you?' he asked seriously.

The twins glanced at one another.

'We're still rather jittery from the events of the day,' Astrid confessed.

'Excellent. I was just going to visit my brother. Would you care to join me?' He hardly waited for a response, turning on his heel.

The twins found themselves scampering outside to keep up.

'He didn't look upset about the mess, did he?' Jonas muttered under his breath.

'Not at all,' Astrid agreed. 'I think he looked pleased.'

Above their heads, a grand selection of oak trees creaked in the breeze, the moonlight making shifting, dappled patterns on the ground.

Magnus's brother, it turned out, resided in a graveyard nestled at the rear of the main estate, hidden behind a thick line of hawthorn bushes.

Magnus hummed, and silvery flames flicked to life around them to lead the way.

Jonas saw the flowers first – roses, all black. Then the names on the stones – so many names.

If Bloom Bloods were built to live such long lives, what had happened to them?

'Here we are.' Magnus stopped at one of the bigger headstones, shaped in the form a strange bird of some kind, a mystical being forever guarding the body buried below.

The name on the stone read *Rupert Faymore*, and beneath it: *Amor Vincit Omnia*.

'Love conquers all,' Astrid translated, the words flat on her tongue.

'Yes, he was quite a romantic, my brother, Rupert,' Magnus said.

He arranged the flames around them, the ice-white fire floating like lanterns, and the twins could feel their gentle heat holding the night air at bay. They understood that this man used magic like an appendage, an extra limb he could wield as easily as any of his arms.

'That was quite impressive, what you did in the parlour.' Magnus turned to them again, his glance caught in a single beam of moonlight. 'The Order of Pendragon will be keen to find out what you're capable of.'

It sounded like a warning.

'Why did you bring us out here, sir?' Jonas asked.

Magnus continued to fiddle with the broken Savonnette in his palm. 'Because,' he said, holding it out towards them temptingly, 'this belonged to Rupert.'

The twins flinched. A million questions sat perched on their lips, and an outrageous thought occurred to them.

'You're not our uncle, are you?' Jonas asked seriously.

Magnus blinked at them, before breaking out in a hearty laugh. 'Heavens, no,' he sputtered, 'that's extremely unlikely, knowing my brother's history.' He wiped a tear from his eye, smiling. 'No, no, whatever you are is likely to be far more interesting. You see, this Savonnette . . . it's not like the ones issued by the Order nowadays. It's an ancient artefact made of a mysterious metal, and when Rupert left it to me before he died, he gave me one clear instruction.'

The twins cocked their heads to the side, breaths held.

'He said I must find the other piece, for the entire fate of the world depended on it.'

Jonas nearly snorted.

'Well, that's rather dramatic,' Astrid said, and both twins crossed their arms.

'Indeed,' Magnus chuckled in agreement. 'He was a romantic *and* a dramatic. But let me ask you a question. What do these words mean to you: the Order of Pendragon?'

The twins were used to being tested with trick questions by doctors and therapists, so they were reluctant to answer at first. But Magnus continued to smile, waiting for them to speak with all the patience of a sturdy old tree.

'We assume it's named after Arthur Pendragon, sir. Of the Knights of the Round Table,' Astrid said eventually.

Seeming pleased again, Magnus nodded his approval. 'Precisely that,' he said, then he put his fingers to his lips in thought. 'A funny name for our Order, really, because we are not knights or warriors. Our whole Order is built around academies. We dedicate our lives to the study and protection of magic, and magical things.' A wind was starting to pick up, the trees murmuring as Magnus looked out into the distance. 'It's hard to believe, but this land, and much of the world, was once ripe with Bloom.' He turned to them again, eyes flashing silver-blue. 'Truly, the Order of Pendragon has only just begun to scratch the surface of all the magical wonders buried by time.'

Jonas glanced at Astrid, the two picking up on a dangerous scent, and when they scrutinized Magnus more carefully, they realized his eyes were not entirely blue. There were miniscule flecks of red lining his irises, the colour glowing ever so slightly with magic.

'Something about that letter tells me the Order might consider *us* one of these magical wonders,' Jonas said gravely.

'Yes.' Magnus beamed, his hair spilling like ink over his eyes. 'You see, your existence, and the magic you can perform, is a bit of a mystery to us – a puzzle, if you like.'

'Perhaps it's Ancient Magic?'

Magnus raised an eyebrow. 'You already know about that?'

Astrid shrugged. 'We're quick learners.'

'So I've heard,' Magnus said, something sombre entering his tone.

Jonas had to wonder exactly how much information the Order had already unearthed about them.

'So, Mr Faymore,' Jonas went on, looking at him straight on, 'if the Order wants us under lock and key at their fancy academy, what do *you* want?'

This, apparently, was the right question, for Magnus smiled at them again, a glint in his eyes like a secret they were being let in on.

'I want to make a deal with you.'

Around them, the earth seemed to stir, the sea swirling over the cliffs.

'We're listening.' The twins spoke in unison.

'I have gifts for you, but they come with a price,' Magnus told them, his eyes glittering.

'Then they're not gifts, are they?' Astrid countered.

He raised an eyebrow again in response, but continued: 'The first is this Savonnette. You can do with it as you please – keep it, study it, pull it apart, whatever you desire. And we'll polish up your pieces and get them on proper chains for you.' He held the item out, and the twins felt a pull like food in front of a starving man. 'And the second gift is a promise. Everything belonging to the Faymore

Cluster is yours to use; you can live here safely and study magic to your hearts' content with no obligation to stay or join our Cluster should you change your mind.'

Astrid and Jonas exchanged a glance, one question burning a hole on their tongues:

'And what do you want in exchange?'

Magnus paused for a moment. 'I would like you to study magic with Gwen under my tutelage, and together, perhaps we will solve the mystery of Rupert's Savonnette.'

Jonas opened his mouth to ask another question, but suddenly there was a rustling in the hawthorn bushes, followed by a little yelp. All three of them glanced over at the sound, knowing exactly who it was, hidden amongst the foliage.

'Oh dear. Gwen, would you care to join us?' Magnus asked the bushes.

There was a prolonged silence in which a smile grew over Astrid's face. Then, eventually, Gwen's head popped up from the bushes.

She was furious, as usual.

'Was anyone ever going to tell me any of this?' she demanded. Jonas noticed she had a fresh set of twigs sticking to her hair now.

Magnus only shrugged. 'I wanted to speak to them first, dear.'

'Well, it's only fair I should get a say in who I study with,' Gwen huffed, dusting herself off as she sidestepped the gravestones. 'Besides, they're my . . . they're *my mystery* and I have a right to know. I found them, after all.'

Jonas winced, while Astrid giggled.

Staring up at Magnus, her hands on her hips, Gwen clearly would not back down.

Stepping forward into the silvery light, Astrid leaned towards Gwen like a moth to a flame.

'Do you want to study with us?' she asked frankly.

Suddenly flustered, Gwen took a step back. 'I don't know . . . I . . . The letter says you have to go to Fountains Abbey . . . and besides, together we'd be the worst students ever,' she grumbled, scrunching up her nose. 'You can't even play any instruments, can you? I mean, you have to be able to do that – it's how you learn to engage the magic. And I can't . . . do spells.'

'Hmm, yes.' Astrid shrugged. 'You're right, we don't have any musical training. So it seems we would be at rather a disadvantage at an elite magical school.'

Magnus nodded, with a curious smile. 'Quite a pickle indeed. I dare say you two have a lot in common with Gwen here, in that Fountains Abbey Academy simply isn't suitable for your needs.'

Gwen's face fell, and both twins' eyes flitted up to Magnus again. Jonas said, 'But . . . the letter said we're supposed to go there.'

Laughing, Magnus plucked the crumpled letter from his pocket, then did something neither twin expected. He balled it up and set the whole thing ablaze. Gwen gasped, scandalized.

'In truth,' Magnus said, smiling, 'I've never been much good at doing what I'm supposed to.'

Jonas felt a twinge of recognition. It seemed they had at least one thing in common with this odd man.

'So, do you accept my offer?' Magnus asked.

Gwen stood to the side, staring so intensely her eyes nearly burned a hole through them. It seemed she wanted them to say yes, but whether she would ever admit it out loud was another story.

Astrid and Jonas stepped away to deliberate.

'I want to know,' Astrid whispered to him, 'where do we come from? Why were we left behind?'

As she spoke, her gaze wandered over to Gwen again. There was a spark there, a fascination.

'And . . . I want to do it here,' she said. 'There is so much to figure out.' She meant Gwen, of course, and the mysterious influence she had on them – and their power.

'I do too,' Jonas admitted. 'But I just can't help feeling like Magnus is hiding something from us.'

Astrid nodded, pondering. 'That may be true, but we won't get answers if we leave. And he said we could use anything we want here . . .'

'This isn't our home,' he reminded her. 'If we become trapped, if anyone or anything tries to cage us again . . .'

Astrid looked him dead in the eyes. 'We leave.'

Jonas nodded.

'All right, Magnus,' he said, turning back to their host.

The twins spoke in unison: 'We accept your offer.'

Gwen all but squeaked in excitement, before quickly schooling her expression.

Beaming with satisfaction, Magnus tossed the Savonnette in their direction. Jonas caught it with an *oof*, the feel of it in his palm icy cool.

'It's been a pleasure doing business,' Magnus said. 'Come along, Gwen, let's go and tell the rest of our Cluster the good news.' Heading back through the gravestones, he called over his shoulder: 'Help yourself to food in the kitchen. Pick any bedroom you want. Try not to get lost. Oh, and after you've settled in, we'll head out to the cove for your first lesson.'

Gwen fell in line beside the man, a little more bounce in

her step than before as the two of them faded into the trees in animated conversation.

Astrid and Jonas remained standing in silence, surrounded by the dead as they ruminated on their decision. Was this freedom? Or something else? Strangest of all, they were out in the open, unsupervised, in the middle of the night, and no one seemed particularly upset about it.

The Savonnette rested heavily in Jonas's hand, the puckered ridges digging into his fingers like thorns.

A most baffling turn of events.

'I think we can agree our situation is somewhat improved,' Astrid finally said, the wind whipping hair across her face.

She held out her hand, grinning. Jonas took it, squeezing her fingers.

'Yes,' he agreed. 'And if they ever try to trap us . . .'

'We leave,' Astrid repeated, though her eyes strayed back to the trees.

Jonas followed her line of sight, and he noticed how her glance lingered on where Gwen had just been. And it was just for a second, for the briefest of moments, that Astrid's grip on his hand wavered.

9

Dangerous Music

When Gwen was eight years old, she'd sat in the alcove at the top of Faymore Manor, curled up small as a mouse, and watched through the window as her older sister left for Fountains Abbey. When Jan returned years later, she'd told Gwen of a secret pledging ritual and the many wondrous things that followed at the school, firing a dream in Gwen's young mind – only for that dream to be shattered.

Now, Gwen felt utterly perplexed. These curious runaways she'd found in the station had been given the opportunity to achieve all the things Gwen could not. But they had chosen to shirk their Pledge, and instead study here, with her. Did they really understand what they were giving up? And why did their choice make Gwen feel so nervous?

They'd all gone straight to bed after the impromptu meeting in the graveyard and were given the next day to recoup before officially starting their lessons. Gwen had hardly seen the twins at all in the last twenty-four hours, leaving her to wonder, who were they, really?

They with their unfathomable and unfair proficiency with Bloom, who had faced off against such a frightening monster in the underground station.

100

They who had saved her life.

Gwen kicked against the bedsheets, the dawn shedding a single beam of glorious light through the drapes.

And there were two sets of blue eyes gazing down at her.

'Good morning.'

'Queen's mercy!' Gwen flung herself back, bashing her head against the headboard. Rubbing her head, she glared at her visitors. 'What is wrong with you two? You nearly scared the life out of me!'

Astrid and Jonas were almost unrecognizable. Their newly starched clothes – a gift from Magnus – were luxurious and shiny, with matching ruffled shirts black as liquorice, and perfect ringlets of white-gold hair. Astrid had tied hers up with a velvet bow.

Gwen found herself thinking that the gothic attire suited them. One detail stood out to her in particular – or rather, two. Round their necks, freshly polished, the mirror copies of the split Savonnette lid were shiny now, and sat proudly on dainty gold chains. A mark of honour, proof that they were special.

'A peace offering,' Astrid said, presenting a glistening buttered bagel on a pretty floral saucer. 'We thought you could enlighten us about something.'

Stomach betraying her with a growl, Gwen angled herself up against the pillows to grab it from the plate.

'OK.' It only took three mouthfuls to demolish her breakfast. 'What's the problem?'

'We think it'd be easier just to show you . . .'

Pulling on some overalls and a cable-knit sweater, Gwen followed them to the rooms down the corridor from her own on the third floor. They were the same ones Gwen and her sister used to share, with identical layouts connected in the middle by an archway draped in misty gauze.

Opening the door to Astrid's side, the rooms looked nothing how Gwen remembered them. Warm light poured in through the open windows, along with the crisp scent of pine and sea. Creeping up the window frame and over the sills, an assortment of vines from outside had, overnight, found sanctuary here along these walls. Tendrils of ivy spun themselves up the posts of the beds, and wisteria grew along the ceiling, with racemes of blossoms hanging down in swathes of purple and blue, like a night sky. It was hard to tell where the inside world ended, and the outside began.

'What in the Twelve Spells did you do?' Gwen asked, her mouth falling open at the sight.

'We were hoping you could tell us,' Jonas said.

'It happened while we were sleeping,' Astrid added, twirling her fingers over some buds of preening honeysuckle.

This room was like an echo of everything that had happened the other night, a stunning display of magic. Gwen's new classmates were prodigies, the stuff of prophecy. She gulped. How could she ever match up?

'Maybe one of you had a nightmare?' Gwen offered, trying to find a lick of sense in what she was seeing. 'Jan says it's common to have Bloom spurts around our age, maybe you were singing in your sleep, or –'

Astrid cut her off. 'We weren't having a nightmare.'

We? Even overlooking the fact that the twins seemed to share dreams, Gwen floundered. 'Then what were you dreaming about?' she asked.

The twins shared a silent glance and laughed quietly. Gwen couldn't help thinking she was somehow the butt of the joke.

'Well, if you don't have any answers for us, then I think we'd better head to the cove,' Jonas announced, pulling his sister back out of the door. 'We need to be on time for our first lesson.'

'Hey, wait –' Gwen scurried out of the room after them and jogged down the stairs to keep up, all the while wondering what on earth they'd dreamed about that could be such a big secret.

Outside, the grey dawn and earlier rain had left a sweet, earthy scent in its wake. They followed a steep, treacherous path down to the beach, and Gwen found herself slipping and stumbling more than usual. Yet the twins moved through nature like silk – fluid and graceful, the salty air playing in their hair as they took their time observing each little daisy or nettle patch. Sometimes it was hard to tell if they were marvelling at the earth, or if the earth was marvelling at them.

'So,' Astrid said, her voice startling Gwen as she focused on not tripping over. 'If you're left at the house alone usually, what are your sister and the others up to?'

The question stung.

'They're at our Enchanted Quarter at Watersmeet collecting samples,' she said. 'I've never been allowed to go,' she added bitterly. 'Too dangerous.'

Both twins looked at her curiously, and Gwen was reminded once again how green they were, almost like babies. Ones she had to look after.

'Enchanted Quarters are Order-protected habitats. They're hidden all over the world. There's a big one here that the Faymore Cluster rewilded themselves. Think of them as sanctuaries where we – I mean *they* – take and tend to magical fauna and flora.' There was also some sort of ongoing research project that had been occupying them for the past few months – Order-related stuff that Gwen *'didn't need to concern herself with'*. Whatever it was, it meant there was even less chance Gwen could step a foot in the habitat.

In the companionable silence that followed, the twins seemed to be lost in their own thoughts, while Gwen too thought of her future. How a trip to an Enchanted Quarter might soon be in reach, if she could finally access the power she knew she had, and prove herself in these lessons. Magnus was giving her a chance here, one she couldn't miss.

They arrived on the narrow strip of beach, and made their way over to a makeshift dock, leaving a trail of footprints in the wet sand. A moored skiff creaked and swayed in the shallow water.

'Magnus is at the cove over there,' Gwen said, pointing. 'It's high tide, so we'll have to take a short boat trip.'

Pulling at the rope, Gwen yanked the boat in closer.

'We can't swim,' Astrid announced.

Gwen fumbled, nearly tipping into the water. 'What?'

The twins shrugged, turning back to watch the sea. But now there was something else in their expressions: caution.

'Wait, have you two even *seen* the sea before?'

'Yes,' Jonas said. 'Yesterday.'

Taking a deep breath, Gwen reminded herself once again that although the twins might be unfairly powerful they were strangers to this world, and whether she liked it or not she had become responsible for them.

'OK, well . . .' she said, steadying the boat for them. 'I'm good at rowing. We won't fall in.'

The twins shared a glance; then, hesitant as fawns, they climbed into the boat.

With Astrid sat in front and Jonas behind, Gwen took the middle with the oars, beating a path through the water, every sweep stirring up the familiar salty sea air while gulls hollered above. The sun was up in its full glory now, streaming over Gwen's back and illuminating Astrid where she sat still as a monk, her eyes glued to the waves.

'It will only take a few minutes,' Gwen said.

'Ahoy!' a voice called across the water. Magnus.

Peering over her shoulder, Gwen could see him waving from inside the cavern, like some kind of benevolent spirit with a top hat and a cane. She rowed the boat into the yawning cavern, letting it grind over the slippery pebbles at the edge to stop next to Magnus's little dinghy.

'How was your journey?' he asked, coming to assist.

The twins all but kissed the ground as they stepped off the boat.

'Thrilling,' Jonas replied, looking at the green and blue pools dotted around the cave. 'We thought we were going to die.'

Magnus smiled down at them. 'How fun.'

Clambering over rock pools, they followed their new teacher into the shadows, marvelling at the flickering reflections of water along the stone walls. Above them, the cliff spilled over, chalky sediment dripping into the pools below.

'This way,' Magnus called, humming silver flames to lead the trio further into the cavern.

Coming to a stop at a ledge, they stared down into a large pond of midnight-blue water, their reflections gazing back at them. Gwen watched the twins, how they easily picked up on the melodies of Bloom from inside the water.

Well, she thought, they were about to get the shock of their lives.

From his sleeve, Magnus pulled out his ocarina and brought forth a melody. It was one Gwen knew, unique to the Faymore Cluster, like their own set of keys.

The water began to ripple, and with each ripple an image became clearer. Melting out of view, their own faces below were replaced by a view of old desks, shelves chipped into stone, and piles upon piles of books filling a huge, cavernous space that had been completely hidden only moments before.

Gwen knew that the study in the cove, older than the manor itself, once belonged to ancient witches. It had been repurposed centuries ago by the Faymore Cluster, and Gwen had visited only a few times, to collect books with Jan and Thomas, or to watch Elijah work on potions.

She stepped down into the gaping entrance. The air wavered, and she landed gently on the floor below, as if she were an umbrella in the wind.

'Unbelievable,' the twins breathed, happily following suit.

Magnus came in last, playing another melody to close the illusion behind them as he too floated to the ground.

Most of the space was exactly how Gwen remembered it, dusty and dry, despite being hidden in a soggy cave. Candles flickered silver from sconces along the walls, charmed with powerful, singing magic so that the wax would never melt.

The twins wandered about, peering nosily at each book cover and prodding at each glittering potion bottle and ingredient.

'How old is all this stuff?' Astrid asked.

'This collection holds the instruction books and workbooks of every resident of the Faymore Cluster; some are hundreds of years old,' Magnus replied. He was busy setting himself up at a giant square apothecary table, the scents of sage and rosemary stirring up as he opened different drawers. It smelled like a lamb dinner.

'Gwen, you can grab whatever of Jan's you don't already have, and could you take Astrid and Jonas through to the back to find Rupert's old bits and bobs? They should be next to mine.'

'On it,' Gwen replied, gesturing for the twins to follow her.

Clambering around the obstacle course of book stacks and papers, the trio ducked under a doorway of dried hogweed into the back of the study.

'This place is more like a mystical storage unit,' Jonas murmured, just as Magnus dipped entirely out of sight, lost to the jumble of magical belongings.

Gwen couldn't deny it. The place *was* a mess.

After some minutes' searching through the various piles and tags, she spotted a box on a high, rickety shelf with *R. Faymore* written on it in bleeding red ink. 'That must be Rupert's study materials,' she said. 'I'll get it.'

'Perhaps you need some assistance?' Astrid asked, something mocking entering her tone that Gwen didn't like one bit.

'I can do it myself,' she insisted. Rolling up her sleeves, she stepped on to the bottom shelf, reaching up and up to curl her fingers over the books at the top. Any other Bloom Blood could have managed it easily just by humming the spells of Wind or Push or Pull to get the troublesome items down. But not Gwen.

'I'm not sure if –'

But Jonas had no chance to finish the thought; the shelf let out a furious groan.

'Oh crumbs,' Gwen muttered, just as the whole unit began to fall forward.

The twins grabbed the bookcase before it could crush her, but Gwen went tumbling to the ground anyway, with books and papers spilling around her like a snowstorm.

She really needed to stop finding herself in these situations.

Righting herself, Gwen looked up at the twins, expecting them to be ready with some rude little quip. Except, they weren't looking at her at all.

'Is everything all right back there?' Magnus called through.

'Yeah . . . all good,' Gwen called back, distracted by what the twins were doing.

Getting down on to their knees, the twins were in a state of rapture, eyes practically glowing as they took in the books around them.

'What are you –' Gwen froze, her gaze landing on the pile too.

Nestled in the middle of Rupert Faymore's grimoire – his potion book, magical botanical, monster study, all the stuff that should have been there – was something else. Something utterly peculiar. It was a deep-red book, like a bloodstain on the floor. The thing throbbed with Bloom, an eerie whispering of music hissing from its pages.

Leaning forward to inspect it more closely, Gwen saw that the thing appeared to be hand-bound in crimson scales, like the skin of some ancient beast.

'Don't –'

Gwen tried to warn them against touching it, the sound of the magic making something in her stomach coil and twist. The twins, of course, ignored her warning.

Could they not hear it?

Blinking, Gwen realized they couldn't. Only Gwen could hear that terrible discord, and the realization made her nervous.

Jonas picked it up first. He flicked through some pages, oblivious to the nauseating whispers from within, then handed it over to Astrid. She too paged through, then held it up to show Gwen . . . nothing.

There was no title page, and no words at all. It was totally blank.

'I think you should put that down,' Gwen instructed, reaching for the book herself. Her fingers brushed over the twins', and just as they did, the whispers stopped, and the book lit up like a star.

Gasping, Gwen pulled back as if she'd been burned.

She was sure, for a split second, when she'd touched the book, that she'd felt something watching her.

'Whoa!' The twins, shocked, held the book together at arm's length.

They watched, fascinated, because where light burned across the pages, words and images began to appear, until the book was full of strange, indecipherable text.

But one part Gwen did understand. The inside had a stamp – charmed letters that could be read in any language. It was a name she recognized, as it was the very headquarters of the Order: the Shadow Library. Either the book was long overdue, or, more likely, someone had stolen it.

So what was it doing here? And why had the text been hidden?

When they flipped the cover over again, there was now a gold title cut into the scales.

'*The Cursed Melodies*,' Gwen whispered, and it sent ice

down her spine – even uttering those words out loud seemed dangerous. 'We need to put this away. This is bad magic; this book shouldn't even exist.'

All Bloom Bloods knew that Cursed Melodies were forbidden by the Order. They were long-buried Ancient Magic that should stay that way.

And yet, Gwen could feel its pull, that cold shadow creeping over her. The darkness seemed to whisper, calling to her, willing her to touch the book again. It sounded exactly like when she tried to use her Bloom.

The twins, ignoring her, flicked through the pages again, oblivious to the cold dread coursing through Gwen.

'Is that . . .?' Astrid gasped.

'I think it is!' Jonas confirmed. Both twins held their pieces of the Savonnette up to the pages, and sure enough, there it was, the exact same intricate spiral pattern behind the Pendragon sword.

Rupert's artefact, the very one that now hung round the twins' necks.

'Does it say anything about it?' Astrid asked, and Jonas turned the page, searching. The problem quickly became clear. The symbols inside were indecipherable. Half the pages were missing, torn out or damaged, and those that remained were filled with mysterious etchings and runes. The more Gwen stared, the more the symbols seemed to shake and pulse, as if trying to communicate with her. She blinked it away, gasping as they turned another page.

'Wait, I've seen that!' Gwen exclaimed, leaning forward. There was a perfect sketch of rocks and water – the fairy pools. 'That's exactly where Magnus and my mum were in that photo I showed you,' she said, trying to make sense of it.

'The Rapscallions,' the twins whispered.

'Yeah, the ones hunting for Ancient Magic . . .'

Gwen immediately regretted bringing it up because the twins lit up at the words. They glanced at each other, a silent exchange, and before Gwen could say anything else, they began to put the book away in their bag.

Gwen baulked, her eyes nearly bulging out of her head.

'What are you doing?' she hissed, checking to make sure Magnus wasn't looking. 'We need to put it back!'

The twins only smirked at her, merrily collecting all of Rupert's other study materials like they were picking wildflowers.

'Part of our deal with Magnus is that anything belonging to the Faymore Cluster is ours to use,' Jonas explained, looking very pleased with himself. 'And that includes weird cursed books.'

Gwen opened her mouth to protest, but the words dried up on her tongue.

'How are you doing back there?' Magnus called through. 'Have you found what you need?'

'Yes!' the twins called back. 'We've definitely found what we need.'

They stared at Gwen, beseeching her, waiting to see if she'd tell.

She'd never had classmates before – she'd hardly even had a friend – and she was at a loss as to what to do.

'Please,' Astrid whispered.

Even now, Gwen could hear the melody of the book, a muted whispering. It sent ice-white fear through her veins; it was like the book was trying to find her.

'Excellent.' Even from a distance, Magnus sounded pleased, his voice light and airy. 'Come on through and we can start our first lessons.'

'I –' Gwen went to speak, to try and persuade the twins that taking the book was a bad idea, but she paused as something – a sound – caught her off guard. 'What was that?' she asked, her body going still as she listened. Beyond the slowly fading melody of the book, there was . . . a fluttering.

The twins hesitated, hearing it too, and as they did, the candlelight flickered, as if something had run past.

'What the –'

Another flutter, another shadow. They all froze, looking around for the source. Whatever it was, it was scampering between the books.

It seemed they were not alone in the cavern.

'We need to leave,' Gwen said, trying to calm her jack-hammering heart. It was just like the abandoned station again, except this time, if a monster appeared, there would only be stone walls, no plants or earth for the twins to call upon and save the day. They needed to get back to Magnus.

Gwen went to help the twins up – but she never made it.

Instead, she heard it again, the fluttering; only this time, it was right behind her.

She had hardly a second to process the dark mass of wings and teeth soaring towards her.

All she could do was scream.

10

Little Beast

Every cell in Astrid's body burned hot and wild. She could feel it, scorching her fingers and throat, the need to do something, to *protect*.

Gwen screamed, clawing at her face to get the beast away. Fur flew, hisses and flutters echoing through the cave. The twins lurched forward, but there were no plants, no roots at all in the underground cavern, so their magic was useless here.

'We can't . . .' Astrid panted, pleading with Jonas, but he was equally lost.

'Oh, for goodness' sake!' Gwen huffed, the irritation in her voice pulling the twins out of their panic.

It was only then that Astrid really took in the scene. And she nearly laughed out loud.

'Get off me, you stupid pest!' Gwen shouted, grabbing at the thing flapping about . . . a thing that was no bigger than a kitten, and twice as adorable.

The little beastie finally stopped bothering Gwen and frantically went about knocking over piles of books and potion bottles instead. It seemed determined to cause as much chaos as possible.

Then, from behind them, a melody began, its soothing notes like the gentle patter of rainfall in a stream. The effect was instant: the creature stilled.

Shaking itself off, it flew now into Astrid's hands. Its heartbeat slowed in her palm as it recognized the magic, and that it was safe.

When they turned back towards the doorway, Magnus was there, his ocarina at his lips spilling out the first of the Twelve Spells – the melody of Calm.

'My, my,' he mused, pulling away from his instrument. 'What do we have here?'

It had midnight-blue fur, soft as spider's silk, and the fluffy tail and fangs of a cat, but its dark eyes were round and bug-like. Two feathery antennae twitched on its head, and folded neatly on its back was a set of perfectly elegant moth wings.

'She's a felimoth,' Magnus announced, a reverie to his voice.

Still furious, Gwen marched forward, scowling suspiciously down at the little moth-thing.

'Well, what the hell is she doing down here?' she demanded.

The twins glanced up at Magnus, their heads tilting to the side, questioning.

'They're native to the Himalayas,' Magnus explained, tapping his chin thoughtfully. 'What this one's doing on the Devonshire coast is a mystery indeed.'

The twins couldn't help but coddle the thing, allowing it to rub its scent into their hands.

'You are devilishly cute,' Astrid said, chuckling. 'What frightened you so much, hmm?'

In response, the creature rubbed its cheeks against her with a smug little purr.

'You're going to spoil her rotten,' Gwen warned.

The twins glanced at each other, then back to Gwen.

'She's just like you,' they said.

Gwen let out a noise of utter indignation, turning away to cross her arms.

'And look,' Jonas added, 'she's stolen one of your buttons.'

Sure enough, when Gwen looked down, one of the buttons on her overalls was missing, and presently clasped in the creature's paws.

'Hey!'

The beastly thing only stared at Gwen like butter wouldn't melt, its tail swishing back and forth while it purred into Jonas's hand.

'I think we will call you Buttonbug.'

'No,' Gwen said, stamping her foot. 'We are not naming her.'

'Now, now,' Magnus chided them. 'We will have to try and put her away in my Savonnette for the time being, I'm afraid.'

But as he spoke, reaching to his chest to retrieve the glittering pocket watch, Buttonbug's ears fell flat, frightened. Magnus held the Savonnette out towards the creature and the response was instantaneous. The second the case clicked open and the first cog turned, Buttonbug screeched and hissed, diving into Jonas's pocket for safety.

'She's scared of your Savonnette,' Astrid said matter-of-factly.

Contemplating this, Magnus brought the pocket watch closer to the felimoth, only for it to flutter and hiss.

'Hmm, so she is,' he said. 'How very odd. Very odd indeed.' Turning away, he began to pace amongst the books, muttering to himself, until he suddenly stopped and clapped his hands.

'There's only one thing to do,' he announced. 'We shall have to take Buttonbug to our Enchanted Quarter and see if there are more felimoths active there.'

'We?' Gwen said, perking up.

Magnus chuckled, waving his hand. 'Oh, goodness no, I mean Lorelei and me, of course.'

This, the twins could not allow. They needed to go to the Enchanted Quarter too. They needed to suck dry every piece of this magical world until they had all their answers.

'We want to come along,' they said in unison, staring up at Magnus.

For a moment, he paused, considering. They could practically feel Gwen vibrating beside them. She wanted this too, more than anything.

'It would surely be an excellent learning opportunity,' Jonas chirped, smiling serenely.

Magnus looked down at the three of them, his attention then focusing on Gwen. 'I'm afraid it might be too dangerous for you, Gwen; at least, while you can't use your Bloom.'

Face falling, Gwen took a step back. It was clear she was humiliated, and Astrid couldn't help but feel bad for her.

'How about we make another deal?' Astrid said, trying to put a blanket over the tension. 'If we can prove that we can all follow orders and keep up with our studies, you'll take all three of us and Buttonbug to the Enchanted Quarter.'

'Hmm . . .' Magnus studied them, having some silent argument with himself, until eventually he sighed. Astrid already knew they'd won.

'Your education *does* require you to visit at some point,' he agreed. 'But I'll need to be able to trust you all. You can't leave my side in such a place.'

'It's a deal,' Astrid said, beaming.

'All right then,' Magnus replied. 'We'll leave in a fortnight. Now . . . did you get all the books you need?'

The twins nodded vigorously.

In all the excitement the book of Cursed Melodies had stayed hidden away in their bag. Their eyes flitted to Gwen, expecting to see some look of shock or outrage. Yet her face remained drawn, her fire dampened.

'Yeah, we got everything,' she said, staring at the ground like she hoped it might swallow her up.

Astrid looked to Jonas, but he only shrugged. Gwen's sudden shift in attitude was simply another mystery to them.

With the little moth-thing sated, they carried on with their first lessons, going through each book and making notes for potion and music practice. They headed back to the manor soon after, back across the water, with Buttonbug setting up residence on Jonas's shoulder. Two weeks. Two weeks and they would visit an Enchanted Quarter. They just had to behave.

A routine was soon formed within Faymore Manor. The twins and Gwen threw themselves into their studies, determined to prove how responsible they were. Their days were filled with music lessons, the twins singing in increasingly complicated harmonies and Gwen practising her violin, as well as riding classes and mountains of reading. The twins preferred to hide away outside in the overgrown garden between the manor and the cottage, with Buttonbug nestled in their laps. With books and notes laid out like a picnic before them, they grazed on all the tantalizing new knowledge, listening to the sweet whispers of the earth until they were stuffed full.

They'd never had so much freedom.

Together, they tried to decipher the undamaged pages in the book of Cursed Melodies, but the language was written in strange runic symbols of some unknown, ancient origin.

The reason for their split pendant and the Ancient Magic they could wield remained shrouded in shadows.

Gwen would join them occasionally after dinner, bringing treats out to the gardens or up to their rooms, but she was quieter now, so quiet in fact that on the night before their big trip, she very nearly had Astrid jumping out of her skin.

'Goodness, I didn't hear you come in!' Astrid exclaimed, then chuckled.

Jonas was in the bath, so it was just the two of them.

'I got you these,' Gwen said, placing a plate of Battenberg cakes amongst the open books. Astrid noted that there was something odd about her posture. Shy almost, uncertain.

As Astrid examined her, Gwen's own eyes scanned the text Astrid had been reading – a section from one of Rupert's old study books. It was a personal note about the Pledge, the mysterious initiation ritual of the Order.

'They certainly don't ever reveal much about the Pledge, do they?' Astrid said, rolling her eyes. 'Listen to this.' She pulled Rupert's old writing towards her and read the passage aloud: '*The covert nature of the Pledge is designed, I feel, to lure one in, but its true purpose is to examine you. Inherited from a fraught time in magical history, the ritual of the Pledge deems you worthy or unworthy, ill-intentioned or good-natured, and the secret gift one receives for participating is surely a bribe . . . and yet I too cannot resist the lure of knowing what I am made of.*'

'*Knowing what we are made of,*' Astrid mused out loud, humming as she softly fiddled with her pendant. 'That's one way of getting to the bottom of where we come from.'

Gwen scrunched up her nose. Irritated or upset? It was hard to tell.

'I guess the only way to know is to do it,' she said, something solemn in her tone that made Astrid's heart lurch unexpectedly. Strange.

'Why did you want to go to Fountains Abbey anyway?' Astrid asked, trying to lighten the mood. 'It all sounds so pompous.'

Gwen only huffed, a crumb of her usual attitude creeping in.

'My parents went there,' she muttered, as if this was answer enough. But then she sighed, a soft, sad sound. 'It's where they met. Rani and Samir.'

Astrid went very still, seeing in that moment a rare chance to get to know their new companion. And she wanted to know everything.

'Apparently they hated each other at school though,' Gwen chuckled, getting caught up in the tale. 'They were big academic rivals or something. That's what Magnus said. He was a few years above them but his little brother was best friends with my mum. They didn't actually get together until nearly a decade after they graduated. My mum went to do a placement at one of the big Order academies in India, the same one my grandpa went to, and she collided with my dad in a corridor when he was on his way to teach a potions class.' Gwen laughed then, recalling the fond memory. 'She said she caught him, that he had quite literally fallen for her.'

The story was charming – the kind of story Astrid imagined most people had about their own parents. The kind of story Astrid longed to have for herself.

'Why did they come back here?' she asked.

'They came back when my mum was pregnant with me,' Gwen explained with a small smile. 'I don't know the details, but there was some important research project they were needed for, so they ended up joining the Faymore Cluster.' Her face hardened, a determined crease in her brow. 'They were really valued and respected members of the Order.'

She sounded proud, but there was something else there. Regret? Disappointment? A whole muddle of feelings.

Astrid had to wonder, what exactly had happened to Gwen's parents? And all the other members of the Faymore Cluster? But it was clearly an emotionally loaded issue, and she didn't want to spoil the moment with Gwen.

'You're lucky,' Astrid said softly.

Gwen looked up at her, confused.

'To know so much about your parents,' she went on, a swell of yearning in her chest that she let out in a slow breath.

Gwen stared at her, something soft entering her usually tough gaze. Then, quickly clearing her throat, she gestured towards the bed covered in open pages. 'Did you find anything in that book?'

There was only one book she could be talking about.

Astrid leaned back on the covers, stretching out like a cat with a big sigh.

'Not really; we can't make heads or tails of the writing. It's all symbols we don't understand, strange flowers and weapons, and there are no other illustrations of the Savonnette . . . Although I guess there are some interesting drawings of dragons.' She laughed, flicking distractedly at some of the open books on her bed. Then she paused, looking up at Gwen again. '*Are* there dragons any more? There's no mention of them in any of the monster books.'

Crossing her arms, Gwen leaned against the bedpost, her eyes cast down. 'There haven't been, not for a long time,' she said. 'They're legends even to the Order, more like deities than magical creatures.' She paused then, gaze flitting back up. 'All beings of Ancient Magic vanished a long, long time ago.'

Astrid's breath caught for a second, her hand wandering to the split pendant at her neck.

'Except us apparently.'

Gwen stared at her, those molten brown eyes glowing like lava.

'Yeah.' She spoke softly, almost to herself. 'You two are special.'

For a second it looked like she wanted to say more. There was an almost tangible energy between them, Astrid's magic fizzing in her palms. If she wasn't careful, simply looking at Gwen might make the vines around her bed start to coil and twist.

What was this power Gwen had over her magic?

Astrid wished to see through her, to go past the delightful curve of her nose to the sharp bones under her frown, then further still into the sparkling matter of her brain where she was sure a well of secrets lay.

'Anyway . . .' Astrid said, clearing her throat. 'That's exactly why we need to find out where we come from.'

'What will you do, when you find out where you're from?'

'We'll go wherever the mystery takes us,' Astrid replied frankly.

Gwen opened her mouth, as if ready to say more, when they were suddenly interrupted.

The door on Jonas's side of the room was flung open, and Buttonbug came flapping through like a cannonball into

Astrid's arms. Jonas followed behind, all squeaky clean in his pyjamas.

'Oh, Gwen,' Jonas said, surprised to see her. 'What's going on?' he asked, looking curiously between Gwen and his sister.

'Nothing . . . we were just talking . . . Actually it's getting late,' Gwen said, inching towards the door as she swallowed whatever words had been on her tongue before Jonas appeared. 'I'm gonna head to bed too.'

Astrid didn't have a chance to say another word before she slipped out.

'What did she want?' Jonas asked, tilting his head in the direction of Gwen's hasty exit.

Astrid chewed over their conversation. She still found anyone other than Jonas confusing, and it felt like she had long since given up on understanding them. But for some reason, when it came to Gwen, she suddenly wished to try.

'I'm not entirely sure,' Astrid admitted. 'She's been in an odd mood ever since we got back from the cove.'

Jonas only shrugged, throwing himself on to his bed.

'Whatever,' he said with a big yawn. 'It's not our problem.'

Astrid looked back at the door Gwen had left through. She knew Jonas was right, in theory. So why then did Astrid find it so hard to stop thinking about the girl?

The next morning, autumn seemed to have rolled in at full force. Leaves rusted, and the light burned orange. And it was on that golden day that the three trainees were finally invited along on a journey to the mysterious Enchanted Quarter.

Riding out after breakfast, Jan, Thomas, Gwen and the twins (and Buttonbug, by way of Jonas's pocket) followed

Magnus and Lorelei down the long trail to Watersmeet. They rode past the sea cliffs, through the grassy pastures filled with cornflowers and cowslips. The journey was slow, with the twins still adjusting to their new mounts, Calliope and Merit – a bay and a strawberry roan who fussed and whinnied over their new masters, who doted on them in return.

Coming to the end of the path, down to the hidden world of the East Lyn River, Astrid noticed how pensive Gwen had become, her fingers tightening on the reins as if she were heading to war. Astrid had to wonder, what secret battle was their friend fighting?

'Past this point is our own Enchanted Quarter,' Magnus announced, gesturing to the dark mass of woodlands that beckoned them, branches waving like fingers in the wind.

Curiously, despite being so close to the swaying trees, the Bloom was muted, as though Astrid were trying to hear something from underwater. Turning to Jonas, she saw him point at the wind chimes hanging on the trees. They looked like fairy traps, but Astrid recognized them for what they were. Wards. The treeline was full of them.

'The area beyond these wards was rewilded by my great-grandparents, and is now thick with Bloom,' Magnus said. 'These protected spaces are sanctuaries for all magical beings, both benevolent and . . . complex. Therefore, we must –' he aimed his smile at Gwen – 'be cautious.'

Magnus turned his horse towards the Enchanted Quarter, glancing over his shoulder. 'Now, our mission today is to hunt for any peculiarities. Any species that might not be native to our land, or anything unusual that might frighten another creature.' Magnus gestured towards the wood. 'Is everyone ready? Then follow me.' He dug his heels into his horse's side and with a snap of the reins, set off.

Astrid's skin prickled with anticipation. Something extraordinary was waiting on the other side.

As they trotted beyond the precipice of the wards, Buttonbug twitched in Jonas's pocket, her ears pricking up, afraid. The world warped, the air seizing from the shock of magic, and just for a second, so fast Astrid thought she imagined it, a dark shadow passed over their heads.

11

I See You

Taking a deep breath, Gwen followed the rest of the procession and pushed forward into the Enchanted Quarter. After weeks of studying, spell practice and good behaviour, she was finally ready to prove her worth.

Or so she'd told herself.

If she *couldn't* prove herself, then the twins would realize they were better off leaving Gwen and studying without her at Fountains Abbey Academy. Then she'd be alone. Again.

She was not going to let that happen.

The air clutched around her like she was being squeezed from a pod; she gently stroked her horse, Willow, along the white diamond on her nose to calm her.

Instantly, everything became tranquil as a sunset – and utterly strange. Spurting from the ground like the limbs of a fallen giant, the trees were larger than reason would allow, with thick tangles of trunks and branches enveloping the path and leaves so abundant they sifted the sunlight into delicate strings.

An eerie silence washed over their group, with even the horses' hooves no more than a soft patter on the mossy ground. The streams, swollen from earlier rains, babbled along and everywhere – so much that you could run your hands through it – was the singing golden dust of Bloom.

'Look. Up there.' Magnus guided everyone's gaze to the trees, where the branches were so interwoven you could scarcely tell one tree from another. What looked to be some sort of seedling critters peeked out at the visitors from knots in the bark, and soon they were followed by a parade of mushroom-hatted creatures. 'Those are dryads, a kind of nymph that inhabits the forest, and those over there, scurrying along the twigs? Those are leaf-winged napaea – more young spirits.'

'Oh!' Astrid tilted her head back, her fingers fluttering in a gentle greeting. 'Good morning.'

The twins looked at one another with wonder and delight. From Jonas's pocket, Buttonbug reared her head. Jonas coaxed her out on to his palm, the little beast leaping up to sit upon his shoulder.

Gwen watched the twins lean into the breeze and allow the tips of their fingers to ghost over the hanging branches as they passed by, sharing glances, as if party to secrets and songs from the earth that no one else would ever know.

Seeing it all as the twins did, she wondered if she'd ever truly appreciated magic, having known it all her life.

It was a reminder of everything she'd come to realize since their first lesson. They were special, uniquely valuable to the Order, while Gwen was entirely talentless and useless. Nothing but a burden.

She'd been working all week, trying to find a way around her magical anomaly, and today she needed to make them see that she could be helpful . . . before they realized they were better off without her.

She would prove herself. She would make them stay.

Trekking further into the forest, it was not long until they reached the river.

'There should be laughter here,' Thomas said, bringing his horse, Cupid, to an abrupt halt. He glanced around, the little puffs of vitiligo on his cheeks catching in the Bloom. 'It's too quiet.'

Following suit, the others halted.

Everyone was dressed in sensible riding gear, white shirts with khaki and moss trousers and jackets, all of them blending into the thick brush like they were born from the earth.

'What does he mean by laughter?' Gwen whispered, as Magnus gestured for them to dismount.

Jan worried the ends of her plait. 'This part of the river is usually where the nymphs play,' she explained. 'I've never known it to be so silent.'

Seeing this as a good opportunity to prove herself, Gwen stepped forward. 'I'll play for them,' she said, her voice more confident than she felt as she gripped her violin case like a lifeline. 'I've been practising the Calm spell.'

Surprised, Magnus considered the suggestion, before beaming down at her, pleased.

'An excellent idea.'

'Then we'll sing with you,' the twins said in unison. 'We've been practising too.'

Gwen could very well have groaned in frustration, feeling sure the twins were intentionally vexing her.

'I –' Gwen hesitated. 'I want to play on my own.'

'Gwenny, don't be rude,' Jan scolded, the pet name immediately making Gwen's face go hot.

The twins gave each other a private look of surprise, and Jonas chuckled to himself, so Gwen had a horrible feeling that name was going to stick.

'That's OK, if that's what you want,' Astrid said, shrugging, though Gwen could see that she was disappointed.

Preparing her bow, Gwen found a comfortable spot on the bank where the ground curved over the running water, sitting herself down so that her feet dangled over the edge. Her heart beat in her chest like a war drum.

Taking a deep breath, she set about listening to the earth as she'd practised, sure that this time, in a place so ripe with Bloom, she would finally access the power she needed.

Moving her bow over the strings, the spell began.

She drew each note from her violin with a deep focus, feeling the pangs of heat in her throat and fingers, the minute tingles of Bloom waking up to the call. She thought of the babbling waters beneath her and set her intentions to the river, sending a message out through her music that all was peaceful, that she could be trusted.

Please work.

On her second turn around the spell, she felt the shift, her skin growing hot and cold at the same time.

Please, please work.

Her pulse quickened, her throat constricted, every inch of her body willing her to stop as her Bloom responded.

She should have listened.

Something was emerging from the spell, but it wasn't calm or peaceful. It was a growing discordance, a rot that had set itself into the magic. She heard and felt spindly dark fingers of dread, soon screeching in her head.

Bringing the spell to an abrupt halt, Gwen panted as she took in the world around her. There was nothing out of the ordinary, yet she felt it still. That same awful feeling whenever she tried to use her magic, only now it lingered. Just as it had the night she met the twins.

'Hey, hey, calm down,' Astrid cooed behind her, and at first Gwen thought she was talking to her.

But when Gwen turned to look, she saw that Buttonbug was hissing and growling, her fur spiked up in warning. And worst of all, the creature was staring at Gwen.

'What's the matter with you?' Jonas asked the beast, trying to placate her with soothing touches.

There was nothing to see, of course, but even as Gwen told herself this, as she searched through the trees and beyond the mossy banks, she felt that shadow of dread – as though something was watching her.

Always watching.

'Everyone on your horses, at once,' Magnus commanded.

'Come on, you heard him!' Lorelei bellowed, stomping over to pull Gwen up to her feet. 'Quickly now, the lot of you.'

Still gasping and confused, Gwen allowed herself to be assisted on to Willow, her head still spinning with the sickly pangs of something rotten, a terror that would not leave, and she was suddenly convinced that whatever it was that had taken hold, it was following her. That she needed to get out of there.

'Everyone! Follow me,' Magnus called.

With a flick of the reins, they set off – except the twins didn't move at all.

Their horses remained motionless on the track and Gwen began to panic, remembering their inexperience with riding.

On Jonas's shoulder, Buttonbug was screeching.

'What's wrong?' Gwen asked.

They didn't so much as twitch, the two of them still as the dead.

'What are you –'

Before Gwen could finish the sentence, Astrid stared back at her, eyes wide.

'Something's wrong,' she muttered. 'The trees, they're screaming.'

A chill ran through Gwen; her body knew, even before she'd seen it. She could already hear it.

It.

On the opposite riverbank, a shadow moved, a murky spectre of black flame.

No eyes. No face at all. Yet an eyeless stare.

Words spilled forth, creeping along Gwen's skin.

I see you.

Swallowing hard, Gwen found her voice. 'Magnus!' she cried. 'Magnus!'

When she glanced back, the thing – the *it* – was gone.

'Something's coming!' Astrid called, twisting Calliope back round.

Behind her, Magnus's white shire horse let out a frantic neigh, everything happening so fast that Gwen hardly knew which direction to look.

'Gwendolyn!' Magnus's voice boomed from the distance.

Swooping down from the treetops like the shadow of death, a vast creature with bloodied feathers reached out its talons, ready to feast.

Gwen knew this creature. A Strix. A huge, demonic owl-hybrid made of sharp talons and an even sharper beak. She knew that a Strix was a flock monster, that there would be more of them, ready to impale their prey upon a sharpened stump or branch, where they would delight in pecking out its eyes, lungs, heart. A Strix did not simply hunger for blood; it hungered for agony.

And she also knew that they were not supposed to exist

in this reserve – in this country – so why was one of them
here?

Diving off her horse, Gwen rolled along the ground,
knees grazing, just as the Strix closed its talons – just barely
scraping Willow's flank.

'Don't touch my horse!' Gwen screeched, pulling herself
up to confront the beast.

With its half-owl, half-human features, it squawked at
her, and Gwen reared back, ready to . . . to what? She didn't
know. But the instinct was undeniable – that same flame
and fury grew within her. A warrior drum that was always
simmering low in her belly, gaining momentum, ready to set
the world on fire. To protect those around her.

She pulled her fist back, ready to strike –

But before she could spark the flame of her power, she
saw a rope fly through the air and curl round the monstrous
bird's legs. The beast was yanked backwards with a harsh tug
from . . . Magnus!

'Run! All of you!' he called out, using the vial in his
other hand to douse the rope with a potion, to charm and
entrap the monster. 'There will be more!'

Gwen ran alongside Willow, hauling herself up on to the
horse with a strength she didn't know she had.

'This way!' Lorelei yelled, all of them flicking their reins,
taking off in a gallop.

Thomas and Jan took up the rear along with Lorelei as
they herded Gwen and the twins forward.

'Just keep squeezing your legs!' Gwen called ahead to
Astrid and Jonas, suddenly afraid they might be out of their
depth.

The twins nodded, and all of them clustered together,
thundering over root and stream, hooves pounding.

They were so close! The wards were mere moments away when another terrible squawk and shriek came from their left. Swooping in, a second Strix cut Gwen off from the others just as the rest made it over the threshold of the woodland, leaving her behind.

Cursing, Gwen nearly slammed right into an outstretched branch as her horse backed away from the Strix. In the nick of time, she grabbed it to swing off Willow once again.

'Get!' Gwen cried, sending Willow galloping to safety beyond the wards while she faced down the second Strix. She felt that fire rearing up inside her again.

As the monster flared its wings, beak falling open, it let out another screech – but this time, not of wrath. It was a cry of pain. A root had sprung up from the ground, piercing the bird through its left wing with an awful crack and splatter of blood and bone. The monster fluttered desperately, screeching, only for another root to shoot out and cut clear through the right wing.

The creature panicked and flailed, feathers flying and beak gnashing, its own cruel game mirrored as it found its own unwilling body was impaled. The roots twisted and held the desperate beast in place.

Gwen saw them then. They must have run back into the Quarter to help her. The twins, hands outstretched, bending the trees to their will.

Their intention was clear: they were going to rip the bird in half.

This was power Gwen could only dream of, an affinity with magic and nature so strong they could command the world around them. From beneath their riding hats, it looked as though their hair glowed with power.

'Stop!' Magnus's voice cut through the horror. 'Get back!'

He too appeared next to the twins, and hauled them back, their spell shattering on their lips.

He held Astrid and Jonas at arm's length, and rasped, 'The Order never deals in death.'

The twins blinked at him, breathing heavily. At first they looked frenzied, ready to bite or scratch to get back to helping Gwen. But then, they seemed to come back to themselves, seeing the plea in Magnus's eyes. They hung their heads.

'Sorry, Mr Faymore.'

'We'll speak more later. Quickly now,' Magnus said.

The trio scrambled through the ward perimeter to safety, where welcome sunlight warmed their skin. Gwen was immediately ambushed by Jan, who pulled her into a crushing embrace.

'You frightened me!'

'It's fine . . . I'm . . . fine.'

Gwen, truthfully still shaken, sought out the twins' faces, and somehow they appeared virtually unchanged, standing doll-like, not a hair out of place. Even Buttonbug was nestled away again in Jonas's pocket, as though nothing in particular had happened.

Astrid grabbed Gwen's hand and held it, palm up.

'It hurt you!'

'It only stings a bit,' Gwen insisted, pulling her hand back to her chest, the skin tingling where Astrid had touched it.

'The plants,' Jonas said, his eyes narrowing. 'Before that thing attacked, they were like alarm bells in our heads.'

Gwen realized that the twins had not seen the shadow. They had no idea at all that she had been the one who had opened a door to this evil, that she was being watched by it. For a moment, she felt obliged to tell them, the words bubbling up, only to stop short as she swallowed them back down.

'The Strix,' she lied. 'The plants were warning you about the Strix.' She didn't want them to know that not only was she weak and untalented but she was also *cursed*.

'You three!' Lorelei called over, gesturing them all back to the woods. 'You'll want to see this.'

Reluctantly, Gwen and the twins pulled themselves away from each other, and joined the rest of the group at the cusp of the Enchanted Quarter. Magnus stood opposite them, inside the magical reserve, the Strix subdued at his feet.

Hands coming together as if in prayer, the head of the Faymore Cluster looked like a saint as a calm expression devoid of any fear or anger settled over him. Even through the wards, Gwen could feel it – a great sigh of relief, the Bloom being mollified.

'Spirit, I summon you.'

His hands moved apart, and between them, spinning airbound and ringing with glorious resolve, was the golden Savonnette.

'Let this creature find comfort at my side.'

The Strix, which had once been thrashing and bloodthirsty, lay still, entrapped, the *thwip thwip thwip* of the turning watch the only sound beyond the peaceful song.

'Release them from the earth, to which they are bound.'

The effect was immediate. From the spinning hands of the pocket watch, a light grew, pure and simple, and gently reached out towards the beast.

'*Sanguis Noster, Officium Nostrum.*'

The Strix turned to golden dust, floating like seedlings into the awaiting Savonnette. The watch closed, and Magnus grabbed it from mid-air.

Then it was done. It was over.

Now there was only the pleasant ring of Bloom, in perfect harmony once more, and a warm scent, sweet and healing like ginger and honey. 'So, this is what the Order does,' Jonas whispered.

'Yep, and with enough practice,' Lorelei said, 'one day you might do it too.'

Dusting himself off and adjusting his hat, Magnus surveyed the troupe. 'This is quite a predicament,' he said, cogs turning behind the specks of red in his eyes.

'We'll have to take it to Fountains Abbey,' Lorelei said, nodding towards the Savonnette. 'It's not right for such a thing to be in our Quarter, and behaving like that? It's not natural.'

She held Magnus's gaze for a long time, and Gwen felt sure there was more going on that they dared not speak out loud. For the briefest of moments, the two of them cut their eyes at the twins.

Letting out a long sigh, Magnus attached the pocket watch back to his coat. 'I fear you're right. Now, shall we head back?'

By the time they arrived at the manor, night had taken hold, and all of them were relieved to see the welcoming glow of the manor's lights in the mullioned windows.

Gwen was more than ready to bury the mystery of the shadow in the back of her mind, at least until morning. But she could feel the secrets growing like weeds in her belly, seeking her out, even now.

As if they could hear her thoughts, the twins watched her, hawk-like.

'What do we have here?' Magnus called out as they approached the front door.

Peering down at them from his perch on the door header was a large and fat ruffled bird with a crown of horns and a single red ribbon tied to its breast – a messenger the twins recognized straight away.

The bird flew down on to Magnus's shoulder, letting out a caw as he retrieved the scroll attached to its throat.

'Well, this is certainly unusual,' he said.

It is by Order decree that, despite not being in attendance at Fountains Abbey, all new students of the Faymore Cluster are to be given the exceptional privilege of undergoing the sacred ritual of the Pledge at our Western European headquarters. In exchange for this unprecedented opportunity, they will be expected to meet with the Ambassadors prior to the ceremony so that we may thoroughly investigate their extraordinary affinity with Bloom.

A Cloud Skimmer will be sent for you on Saturday afternoon. We look forward to your attendance at this most prestigious event.

Sanguis Noster, Officium Nostrum
Ambassador H. Loupe

No, Gwen thought, reading over his shoulder. It was worse than unusual. It was her greatest dream twisted into her ultimate nightmare.

12

The Ambassadors

Astrid had learned that sometimes getting what you want is not, in fact, a blessing. Like all the seemingly lovely foster homes from their childhood that had turned out rotten, and, in this case, permission to break the Order's rules by taking their Pledge.

Yes, it was all extremely suspicious. As suspicious, in fact, as the aircraft Astrid now found herself in.

But here they were, in a Cloud Skimmer.

'This can't be safe,' Jonas said, peering through the stained-glass window into the white mass of clouds. 'There isn't even a driver. Buttonbug was right not to want to get in.'

They'd had to leave the creature behind, the clever girl avoiding the dastardly machine.

It was a strange, winged contraption, an ornate compartment just big enough for five of them and their suitcases. The vehicle had landed on the Faymore grounds that afternoon like a kite swooping down for the kill, cloth wings spreading across the meadow.

'A Cloud Skimmer is the safest and fastest way to travel,' Magnus explained. 'It takes a tremendous amount of charms and spellwork just for one journey. It's a privilege usually reserved for Ambassadors, or magisterial families.'

The twins looked at one another, unconvinced.

'Then why on earth would they send one for us?' Jonas asked.

At this, Lorelei let out a hearty laugh, patting him on the shoulder. 'I don't think you two realize quite how special your magic is.'

The twins gave each other a grave look, not liking this one bit.

Astrid clutched her cape tighter, for it was freezing inside the carriage, the cold seeping in from the grey tangle of nimbostratus clouds conjured to keep them hidden.

With wings beating on either side, the lacquered wood sang with spells, the whole Skimmer charmed to its bones with enough Bloom to leave a gentle glittering trail in their wake, like the tail of a comet.

'This whole thing is putting a bad taste in my mouth,' Jonas muttered, low enough that only Astrid could hear. 'First the Strix, and now this?'

Astrid hummed her agreement. 'We must look at this as an opportunity. This is our chance to infiltrate the Order, to get a sense of whether anyone knows anything about us, or *this*.' She pointed to her piece of the split pendant, currently shaking against her chest from the rumbles of air. 'And you never know,' Astrid added, with a cunning smile, 'maybe your precious prince will be there.'

'Please, I'm not a child.' But even as he spoke, Astrid saw him flinch, and she couldn't help but remember the way he'd scoured the water to find that silly black-heart lighter all those weeks ago.

Astrid's thoughts turned to a different problem. 'There's one other thing that's perplexing me.'

They both turned their attention to Gwen, who was presently sulking against the window, as moody as the sea.

She'd hardly said a word to them since the letter had arrived, and Astrid was quite convinced that she – like everyone else here – was hiding something.

Jonas leaned over and nudged Gwen. 'Come now, Gwenny. I thought you'd be excited to take the Pledge?'

'Don't call me that!' she hissed.

Astrid levelled her brother a withering look, but Jonas only shrugged, and then – *Crash!* – went hurtling into the aircraft's wall.

Astrid and Gwen yelped, scrambling to hang on to anyone or anything as the Skimmer turned sharply and then down.

'Here we are!' Magnus announced brightly, jutting his cane out to stop himself flying into the side of the Cloud Skimmer.

With a crescendo of melodic Bloom, the clouds suddenly cleared to reveal the most spectacular view the twins had ever seen. Even with her stomach turning, Astrid could not help but stare as the Skimmer darted towards the academy.

Spires and arches, built up like a fortress. A bastion of knowledge, of clean, gleaming white walls, like the abbey had been built from the chalk in the earth. Like it had always been there, and always would be.

Once a monastery, but long ago converted for Order use, Fountains Abbey Academy sat in the vast rolling green land of Fountains Vale. In this hidden pocket of the world the twins could spot smallholdings, farmland, gardens, ponds and glittering lakes, thatched shops and old wood-beamed residences. A whole magical society – the Order – had developed over centuries around the academy.

Jonas pointed at a thick patch of woodland quite a way out from the outermost building, howling for their attention.

'What's that?' he asked.

'That's their Enchanted Quarter,' Gwen replied. 'It's the third biggest in the world. It's where they do the Pledge ritual.'

Astrid watched Gwen then, how her whole body seemed to wilt. She was most certainly hiding something.

'Incredible, isn't it?' Lorelei breathed, interrupting Astrid's thoughts to lean a gloved hand on the glass to get a better look. 'As much as I try to avoid this place, the view is still remarkable.'

Confused, Astrid turned to her. 'Why do you try to avoid it?'

'Hmm, yes, I'm afraid I must warn you,' Magnus said, lowering his voice. 'The more pious areas of the Order . . . They do things a little differently from the Faymore Cluster.'

The Skimmer took another deep dive, torpedoing them straight towards the middle of the abbey with such speed and force Astrid was quite sure they were bound to crash.

Yet they landed with a graceful swoop in a marble-tiled hangar. The vehicle's door fell open at once as the melodies came to a halt, leaving only a gentle hum in their wake.

A group of three women greeted them, all dressed in tailored black suits with a Pendragon sigil proudly displayed on one side and a matching golden Savonnette shining insistently on the other – this was the uniform of the Order. The woman in the centre of this gathering stepped forward; she had shiny crimson hair and a thin pink smile. Her

Savonnette was a little different, made of a cooler metal than the others. Platinum, Astrid realized.

'*Sanguis Noster*, Magnus.' The woman's nasal voice carried a subtle French accent, and although she spoke to Magnus she was looking at the twins – or, more specifically, at their pendants.

'*Officium Nostrum*, Ambassador Loupe,' Magnus replied. 'You seem well.' Magnus turned back to their troupe, gesturing with an arm towards Ambassador Loupe. 'Harriet Loupe here is our faction's Ambassador for the study of potions and charms, and I believe –' he turned to her – 'she will be escorting my students?'

Ignoring Magnus's question, Ambassador Loupe made a beeline for the twins.

Grey eyes icy and calculating, she surveyed them carefully, but there was something else, given away in the briefest lick of her lips.

Avarice.

This was a look the twins were familiar with. They'd seen it before, in Doctor Harris.

Instinctively, both twins moved closer to Gwen.

'So, these are our little miracles. Astrid, Jonas and . . .?'

'Gwen,' their friend finished, filling in the blank with enough venom in her voice to be deadly.

'Oh, yes, the one who . . . *right*.' The Ambassador cleared her throat, while Gwen stared hard at the ground. 'Well, I will take them off your hands now, Custodian Faymore, and . . . Custodian Murphy, was it?'

'Just Lorelei is fine.'

'Right, well.' Ambassador Loupe snapped her fingers. Immediately, the two attendants on either side rushed to grab the students' suitcases.

'Are you not coming with us?' Gwen asked Magnus suddenly.

'I'm afraid we have research business to attend to,' he said, patting his Savonnette, where the Strix still lay dormant. 'We will see you tomorrow for your Pledge.'

The Ambassador took a step back from Magnus's pocket watch as if afraid, before quickly covering it up with another plastered-on smile.

Astrid caught Jonas's eye, and he gave the slightest of nods. Something else to add to their list of curiosities.

'Excellent. This way to the Ambassador's conservatory,' Ambassador Loupe said, and began walking briskly away.

Reluctantly, the twins and Gwen followed her, the three sharing a moment of solidarity as they glanced over their shoulders at Magnus and Lorelei.

'Don't do anything we wouldn't do!' Lorelei called after them.

The Ambassador led them away to a stairwell with a locked doorway, where she brandished a flute from her belt and spat out a melody that unlocked the door. They stepped through, out into the academy – and if Astrid had thought the view from above was enchanting, Fountains Abbey itself was a miracle. They were led past seemingly endless naves and arched windows, everything adorned with floating pumpkin lanterns and garlands of humming wheat and pine cones – ready, it seemed, for some kind of autumn festivities.

'Over there are the Pledge dormitories where you will be staying,' Ambassador Loupe explained, pointing out the pillared portico of a building on the other side of one of the many courtyards, before ushering them along again.

Every now and then, haunting choral melodies echoed down the halls like siren songs. Spells, Astrid realized, performed by entire choirs.

'And this is one of our many Pledge classrooms.'

They peeped in through a door with billows of plum-coloured smoke leaking through the hinges. Inside, they were greeted by an enclosed garden filled with students tending to mysterious vegetation – flowers with fangs, weeping petals, and stems that moved like limbs. Like a startled herd, all eyes turned to them.

'Interesting uniform,' Jonas murmured.

Indeed, all the students, who couldn't have been much older than Gwen and the twins themselves, were dressed in red cassocks and fascia. Choral attire, like some holy, musical army.

The students watched their trio, sizing them up, until one girl with two ginger plaits gasped, leaning over to a boy next to her to whisper in his ear. Like the steady patter of rain building to a storm, the whispers grew.

'*It's them.*'

'*The twins.*'

'*The ones with the weird powers.*'

Even the professor, a fully fledged Custodian, dropped the trowel he was holding with a loud clang and gaped at them like he was witnessing a miracle.

'Just popping in. We won't disturb your class any more, Custodian Warnock,' Ambassador Loupe tittered, a self-satisfied smile spreading over her thin lips as she ushered them back out of the classroom.

Even as the door shut, the twins could hear the aftermath: excited murmurs, chittering bugs.

'What in the queen's crown was all that about?' Jonas asked.

'Oh yes,' Ambassador Loupe said, still smiling. 'You two have become quite the fascinating topic here. Fresh, new Bloom Bloods with such extraordinary power? It's a delicious mystery.'

Astrid wanted to ask how anyone recognized them or knew about them at all, when she caught their reflection in a window. The three of them, in their mismatched gothic attire, and she and Jonas with their matching doll faces and white-blonde hair, being led around by an Order Ambassador . . .? OK, yes, they stood out like a red rose in snow.

She felt the pendant at her throat grow heavier, as though weighed down with a fate she didn't even understand.

'Really though?' Jonas huffed. 'All that fuss over us?'

'It's not *us*,' Gwen muttered, her nose scrunching up. 'It's you two.'

Finally, they were led into the school's lamplit gardens. Here, the whispers were thankfully replaced by the curious melodic greetings of the strange and beautiful plants growing either side of the cobblestones.

With the school towering above them, a peaceful silence cradled the twins, the late-afternoon air spilling a gentle fog into the garden. But up ahead loomed a glass-panelled conservatory, and the twins sensed that their tour was not yet over.

'And now, we will do a little test. Nothing too major, we only want to see some of your powers in action,' Ambassador Loupe announced when they at last reached the conservatory. With a grand flourish, she opened the glimmering double doors.

They were greeted by a fragrant wave of humidity and birdsong. Unusual winged creatures sang in a chorus above them, darting beneath the glass roof in flashes of purple, gold, red and blue. Exotic plants with striking flowers grew everywhere, their Bloom humming to the twins in melodies they'd never heard before. Yet, the name of each plant appeared in their minds as though they had always known it. Milk Tree, Parrot Beak, Corpse Flower. Astrid wanted to reach out and touch them all, to feel that hum of magic against her skin.

At the far end of the conservatory, clouded with mist, sat a group of figures.

Ambassador Loupe turned to Gwen. 'Perhaps it would be best if you wait here so your friends can focus,' she said, her smile so still she could have been a mannequin. The way she looked at Gwen made Astrid's blood run cold. Like she was a nuisance, a waste of time. It was unacceptable.

Is this what Gwen had always had to deal with from the Order?

Gwen clenched her fists, staring down the Ambassador with that fire that Astrid found so enticing – the one she hoped would now burn through this awful woman.

Unfortunately for Astrid, Gwen composed herself and said firmly, 'I'd like to stay with them.'

Shrugging, Ambassador Loupe gestured for them all to come further in, and then led the way to the mysterious strangers.

As they drew closer, Astrid was surprised to see that they were sitting round a garden table drinking tea and eating slices of cake – and, most peculiarly of all, Astrid recognized one of them.

'Oh, my gracious queen!' the familiar woman declared, clutching a hand to her chest. 'Is this them?'

Jonas was gawking at the woman like he couldn't quite believe his eyes.

'Let me introduce you,' Ambassador Loupe said, dipping in a curtsey to one of the seated figures. 'This is Princess Alice.'

And there she was, Queen Beatrice's wife, one of the dearly beloved royal family in the flesh.

'So it is,' Jonas said, entirely forgetting himself as he reached out a hand to shake hers.

Astrid swatted his palm away, tutting.

'Princess Alice is our Ambassador for the study of magical history,' Ambassador Loupe added.

'Pleasure to meet you,' the princess trilled.

Ambassador Loupe then indicated two men seated beside her. 'This is Abelard Klein, Ambassador for the study of magical creatures,' she said, gesturing to the older one, a burly man with a farmer's tan and eyebrows like caterpillars. 'And Polaris Pom, Ambassador for the study of instrumentation.' Ambassador Pom was a younger man with thick glasses and a delicate scar across his nose that left a strange silvery mark on his dark skin. Both twins turned to the last person at the table even as the two men held out their own palms to shake. What a fascinating sight she was: a blue horned owl sat on her shoulder as she smoked a long clay pipe, and she was very possibly the oldest woman Astrid had ever seen.

'And lastly, this is –'

'Oh, hush, Harriet! I'm perfectly capable of introducing myself.' The old woman waved a dismissive hand – immediately earning a point in the twins' good graces. 'You may call me Sister Seraphina. I am the Ambassador for the study of Ancient Magic.'

The twins suddenly stood up a bit straighter. Ancient Magic!

Seeing their excitement, Seraphina burst out in a laugh so joyful it was almost contagious. 'Yes, I thought you'd like that. Come closer, would you? You too, dear,' she said, nodding towards Gwen, which earned her another point from Astrid.

Sister Seraphina's hair, like her limbs, was long and pale, but wretched at the ends, brittle like spun sugar. When she gestured each of them forward, they saw that the skin round her wrists was almost translucent, as if she were made of moth wings.

Her eyes were almost entirely blood-red.

The twins understood now that the red came with age. It was a sign of many years of using magic. They were looking at their own future.

'You three don't talk much, do you? Or is it that Harriet hasn't let you get a word in edgeways?'

Ambassador Loupe drew in her chin, but Seraphina continued: 'You, my dear,' she cooed at Gwen, 'I see a lot of courage in you.'

Gwen tilted her head to the side. 'Have we met before?' she asked.

Seraphina smiled. 'I used to teach Magnus and your mother a long time ago,' she said, and Gwen sucked in a breath at this, looking down sharply. 'We've not met before, but I see a lot of her in you.'

The twins too paused at this information, for very different reasons. Had Seraphina taught Rupert too? Did she know about the Rapscallions?

The old woman caught their eyes for a split second, as if guessing all the questions swirling in their heads, then turned back to Gwen.

'I am very sorry our establishment has failed you,' Seraphina went on. 'I hope that taking the Pledge tomorrow will be a small consolation, and that you can one day join our academy in your rightful position.'

Gwen shrank back, making herself smaller in a way that made Astrid want to drag her out of this awful place immediately.

Alas, they had questions they needed answered.

Seraphina turned to the twins next, smiling widely. 'And you are our inexplicable new Bloom Bloods, carrying with you Rupert Faymore's broken Savonnette and wielding Ancient Magic.'

The tantalizing scent of new knowledge made the twins' pupils turn wide, like wolves on the hunt. This woman, Magnus's old teacher, she must have known so much . . . and whatever she knew, the twins wanted to learn.

'I've heard about where you've come from, and what you two can do,' she said, holding her pipe up to her mouth. 'Locked away in the Red Blooded world. Such awful things that were done to you.' She sucked in a deep breath and kept it while she held their gaze. 'We will do everything we can to put that right.' When she exhaled, blue smoke from her pipe billowed out towards them like storm clouds, smelling like the ocean at midnight.

Jonas spoke up first, cutting to the chase. 'What do you know of Rupert's broken Savonnette, or where we came from?'

None of the seated party spoke for a moment, but it was then, for just the briefest second, that they all exchanged glances – and they looked afraid.

They definitely knew something.

'This is taking far too long,' Ambassador Pom grumbled. 'We're not here to be interrogated. We need to get on with the test.'

He was changing the subject, Astrid and Jonas could see it plain as day, and it bothered them deeply. What were they all hiding? What did they know about Rupert?

'Yes, yes, come on now. Show us something of what you can do,' Ambassador Loupe ordered.

Unfortunately for the Ambassador, the twins didn't take kindly to orders. They felt themselves bristle.

'If you wouldn't mind?' Princess Alice interjected, noticing how tense their bodies had become.

Seraphina gave them an apologetic look, while Ambassador Loupe babbled on. 'The agreement was that you would show us some of your extraordinary powers, and then you and your little friend –' she cast a glance at Gwen – 'can take the Pledge tomorrow. Quick, quick!'

'Then answer our questions,' Astrid said, her voice flat.

'You're in the way, dear,' Ambassador Loupe said to Gwen, ignoring Astrid's demand. 'We need to keep this area clear for your friends' test, and you wouldn't want to get in their way, would you?'

Gwen winced at the words.

'Stay where you are, Gwen,' Astrid commanded, taking a step towards her.

'Let's not be silly. Come along!' Ambassador Loupe interrupted – and then she did something truly unforgivable. She took hold of Gwen and began to forcibly move her away, even as the girl tried to shrug off her grasp. No! They couldn't treat their friend like this!

'If we can just . . .'

'Get off me!' Gwen cried, surprising even Astrid.

'Please cooperate,' the Ambassador said, grabbing Gwen's wrists. 'Honestly, anyone would think you were raised by Red Bloods . . .'

'Astrid, wait –' Jonas tried to intervene, even as he felt the same unbearable boiling of Bloom at his fingertips. It was too late.

The memory played like an old film reel in Astrid's head – dreamy, and romantic, and filling her with fury. Gwen had been ready to fight tooth and nail against the Strix, with a courage that bordered on recklessness, with a potential in her tiny body that Astrid feared Gwen could not see in herself.

And these people had the nerve to overlook her?

Astrid began to sing, her voice emerging without warning.

The plants responded instantly, spilling over their enclosures like floodwater at just the flick of her fingers. Unstoppable, they rushed towards the enemy, furls of green closing round Harriet Loupe's wrists and flinging the dreadful woman into the garden table.

There was a terrible clattering and an indignant yelp as the adults sprang to their feet and a teapot exploded all over Ambassador Loupe. But it was the cakes that did the most damage – chunks of vanilla sponge and whipped cream went everywhere, and the Ambassador's hair and pristine Order uniform were coated in jam and pink-and-green icing.

There was hardly a sound, but for the squawking and flapping of the birds, and a single lone teacup rolling slowly off the table, then smashing on the floor next to Ambassador Loupe's quivering hand.

The others could do nothing but stare at the fallen Ambassador screeching in outrage. Princess Alice simply shifted her skirts out of the way of the mess.

'I can't believe I'm saying this, but you probably shouldn't have done that,' Jonas sighed, delicately removing a stray chunk of cake from his shoulder.

In the silence that followed, it actually looked like Gwen was about to laugh.

A *success*, *then*, Astrid told herself. She was about to say as much when a loud clapping and hooting came from beside her. Astrid looked up and saw Sister Seraphina grinning from ear to ear.

'Well,' Seraphina said, her voice hoarse with laughter. 'That was certainly extraordinary!'

13

Irrational Behaviour

'I suppose if *you* weren't going to do it, I would have,' Jonas said to his sister, checking himself in the long oak-framed mirror. 'Hopefully they'll still let us take the Pledge.'

Their clothes were being washed after the incident, and they'd both had to change into some spare Order-issued uniforms, Astrid feeling a little claustrophobic in the fitted black suit and shoulder pads. Jonas, on the other hand, was growing fond of his.

Astrid considered the aftermath of her little outburst. Naturally, Ambassador Harriet Loupe had made a terrible fuss, shouting about the Faymore Cluster and *'bad influences'*. It had all been dreadfully funny, but now the reality of what Astrid had done had begun to set in. They'd left Gwen next door in her own room to change and prepare for the evening, but still Astrid was inclined to check on her, to make sure no one else was putting their spindly fingers anywhere near her.

'It's just, Gwen . . .' she said. 'Why does she make us react like that?'

Jonas raised a brow. 'Us?'

'You know what I mean,' Astrid said.

'I don't,' Jonas said, but Astrid didn't believe him for a

minute, and she knew he didn't believe it either. She sat down on one of the beds and crossed her arms.

'You reacted that way too in the station, and with the Strix,' she said, presenting each bit of evidence as if it were a court document. 'We're only here because of Gwen. She saved us, and she's an important part of this mystery.'

Jonas ran a hand through his hair. 'Fine, yes, I admit it. Her Bloom has an inexplicable hold on us. It's as though she calls to our magic. But . . . we're rational, aren't we? And Gwen, the hold she has over us? It's not rational.' He made it sound more like a question than a statement.

Astrid lay back on the mattress, staring up at the ceiling with its thick wooden beams.

The room could not have been more different from their dorm at the convent group home, an inkling of what their lives might have been like if they'd been raised in the Bloom Blooded world. Two metal-framed beds, fresh white sheets, old, handcrafted furniture with dusty, well-loved rugs and plenty of room and desk space to practise spells and music. Like their old dorm, there was only one window, but while the one at the group home looked out over the ugly brick building opposite, this one had a daunting view of the academy with its white spires and arches. In the distance, someone was playing the cello.

Would their lives have been better if they'd been raised here instead? Astrid wondered.

But then . . . they never would have met Gwen. The very idea was unbearable.

Astrid thought of her then, how much she delighted in teasing her, the way Gwen's nose scrunched up like a rabbit's when she was in a mood. How Astrid could feel Gwen's Bloom call to them, rumbling like distant battle drums. Gwen was a force unto herself, and what Astrid found most enchanting was that she appeared to have no idea of the power she wielded over them.

'Astrid?' Jonas prompted.

'But we do act irrationally around her,' Astrid whispered. 'Whatever draws us to her – we need to know why, and why she's acting so weird.'

Jonas nodded in agreement, then joined her in lying back on the bed, the two of them staring at the ceiling.

'Whenever she's in danger, our magic reacts,' Jonas said.

'Right, and if she's anxious or upset, we can't help but feel compelled to fix it.' Astrid's fingers cradled her half of the Savonnette, clutching it against her heart. 'She's such a mystery.'

Jonas sat up and turned to her, putting his hand out for Astrid to take. The feeling of their palms together was soothing. 'Whatever happens, we have to remember that we're here to find out where we come from,' he said, his fingers tightening their grip. 'We're here to solve these mysteries, not fall for them.'

For the first time in her life, Astrid was not sure what her brother was trying to say.

'I don't know –'

'Something happened in the Enchanted Quarter,' Jonas said, cutting her off before she could finish. 'One of us needs to speak to her, find out what, and see if we can get to the bottom of whatever's troubling her –'

'– and therefore us,' Astrid finished for him. She glanced down at her pendant. 'I'll go.'

He got to his feet, pulling his hand away from hers. 'You go check on Gwen, see if you can get her to open up,' he said, grinning, as he walked towards the door. 'I'll see what other alluring things I can find . . .' He paused then, serious. 'Remember: it's me and you against the world.'

'Always.'

Alone in the Pledge dorm room with a half-eaten meal of bread and pumpkin soup, Gwen imagined herself as a real student attending Fountains Abbey. No Bloom anomaly, her magic working just as it should, surrounded by her books and plants. Feeling at home.

In her fantasy, she had just got back from a research trip investigating some astonishing creature, and in a moment she would wander down to the common room, where her friends would be waiting. They'd use spells to play games and heat up tea, then they'd practise their instruments together before heading to the library to finish their potion homework . . .

But that was not reality. Instead, Gwen paced the bare room, jumping at every clang or sound of distant laughter. Wondering how long it would be until the shadow reared its head again.

She shouldn't have come to Fountains Abbey at all. She should have made the twins go alone to Pledge. She should let them go, so they could get a proper education and reach their full potential. Without Gwen – a selfish girl who did nothing but cause problems.

Her mind spiralled in the silence.

And yet, creeping around the edges of her self-pity, she found herself thinking about what her fantasy world had been lacking. She would never have found the twins, then . . . or seen Harriet Loupe covered from head to toe in cake icing. A small bubble of laughter escaped at the memory.

'Gwen?' a voice called from beyond the door – Astrid.

Gwen was quite sure that it would take only a small amount of probing by the twins for her to spill all her secrets and concerns in a most pitiable way. They needed to leave her alone.

'What do you want?' she called back, hating herself for the hostility in her voice. What must they think of her?

But when she opened the door, she found only Astrid. It was like seeing yin without yang, and Gwen tried to remember if she'd ever seen the twins apart before.

Yes, once, when she'd caught Astrid off guard in her room. It had felt strange then too, but this time it was utterly bizarre, because Astrid was dressed in the sleek, regal uniform of an Order member. She looked incredible, like the black blazer and gold trim had been made with her in mind. Perfect and dignified, as usual, despite everything they'd been through. By contrast, Gwen felt tired to her bones, and a dowdy mess, with her plaits coming loose after a very long day.

'May I come in?' There was an urgency to Astrid's voice. 'I was hoping to see your view of the gardens.'

From the strange lilt in Astrid's voice, this sounded like an excuse to . . . what?

'Where's Jonas?' Gwen asked, glancing down the corridor.

'He's investigating,' Astrid chuckled. 'Off to find out how much trouble we're in.'

Returning Astrid's intense stare, Gwen felt the strangest sensation, like being wrapped up in a blanket of safety. Astrid looked so orderly, like a knight in shining armour. What a terribly addictive feeling it was.

With a sigh, Gwen moved to one side and opened the door wider. 'Come in.'

Astrid smiled at her, and went to sit in the alcove, propping open the window. A foggy, gentle breeze rolled in, the soft moonlight playfully dancing in her hair – silky curls drenched silver in the stars. When she leaned out to take a breath, the sight wrapped around Gwen's heart and tugged.

Suddenly overwhelmed, Gwen struggled to break the silence. 'Thanks, by the way,' she said, 'for what you did in the conservatory.'

Astrid turned back and looked at her, the smile now creasing her eyes. 'It was my pleasure.'

Heat began to gather in Gwen's cheeks. Why did the twins, especially Astrid, have this infernal effect on her?

'Come here.' Astrid patted the cushion beside her and, reluctantly, Gwen joined her. 'I have some questions for you.'

Gwen could feel the bubbles of protest building in her throat, but Astrid's next words caught her off guard.

'What do you feel?' she asked, tilting her head. 'When you see us?'

A million words came into Gwen's head wholly against her will. *Nervous, happy, shy, irritated, jealous, yearning, safe*. But instead she said stiffly, 'I don't know what you mean.'

Astrid narrowed her eyes. 'I'm trying to figure something out.'

This is it, Gwen thought. They were planning to stay at Fountains Abbey. It was obvious why Astrid was being so intense and weird . . . well, weirder than usual. The twins had been looking for a way to break it to her, as if she were a pathetic child they thought might have a tantrum if she couldn't get her way.

Well, Gwen thought, she wouldn't give them the satisfaction. 'It's fine, you know,' she said, crossing her arms. 'I don't even care.'

Astrid looked confused. 'What's fine, Gwenny?'

Ignoring the nickname, Gwen stared out of the window. 'That you're going to stay and study here, at Fountains Abbey,' she said. 'Without me.'

She swallowed down her emotions before they could spill over, waiting for the inevitable.

Instead, there was a trill of laughter.

'Gwenny, you're so funny!' Astrid's giggles were like a heavenly bell. 'You really have no idea, do you?'

Gwen was aware of how close Astrid had crept along the alcove where they sat. She could smell the sweet, earthy scent of her hair, and she wondered how she'd never noticed it before.

'I don't know what –'

'Gwen,' Astrid interrupted, coming closer to raise a hand and brush a stray hair from Gwen's face. 'Why on earth would I want to involve myself with any institution foolish enough to overlook you?'

Gwen thought of her fantasy again, seeing herself in the Pledge uniform, attending school like a good little Order member. But, looking into the blue of Astrid's eyes, that fantasy suddenly felt stale and boring.

Gwen stumbled back. 'Then why are you so keen on taking the Pledge?'

Sighing, Astrid turned back to the window, her gaze falling on the faraway woods. 'We think it might give us a clue as to where we come from.' Her simple honesty surprised Gwen. 'We can't miss this opportunity.'

The twins had no parents in this world – Gwen knew what that was like. But she and her sister had at least known theirs, and could still visit the stones where they rested. Astrid and Jonas had nothing.

'So,' Astrid began, hugging her knees to her body, 'now I've shared that, it's time for you to tell me what's had you so upset and jumpy ever since the Enchanted Quarter.'

Gwen felt her throat close up. For one glorious moment, she'd almost forgotten all about the shadow. Almost.

'Did the Strix frighten you so much?'

'I can't . . . I don't –' Gwen's words dried up when she felt Astrid's hand on her knee. The feel of the Bloom's touch, even through layers of fabric . . . it thrummed through her flesh, soothing a part of her that had always felt cleaved. 'It's not just the Strix, it's . . .' Gwen could hardly believe she was letting herself speak in this way, and yet she knew she had to. 'Do you remember when we met?'

Astrid nodded, coaxing her, the feel of her touch like a torch guiding her through the awful memory.

'Well, that thing we found in the station . . . it wasn't normal.' Gwen took a deep breath, leaning into the feel of Astrid's magic pulsing through her skin. 'I've tried to forget about it, but I just have this feeling. Ever since we went there, that . . . something is following me.'

Astrid's hand squeezed. 'What happened in the woods, Gwen?'

Swallowing, Gwen calmed herself, fighting against the heavy anchor of dread trying to stop her confession. 'There was something there,' she whispered. 'A shadow.' She shook her head. 'I can't explain it, and I'm too scared to say it out loud, in case it's real. Whenever there's a lot of Bloom, or whenever I use my magic . . . it's there. And I'm afraid that at the Pledge tomorrow, it will be there again. That it could hurt someone.' She looked up at Astrid, a single tear tumbling pathetically down her cheek. 'That it could hurt you.'

Astrid didn't flinch, her hand perfectly steady as she wiped away the tear from Gwen's face. 'Gwen . . .' She said her name like a prayer. 'You could tell me you'd been cursed by the devil himself and it could not keep me away from you.'

'But –'

'Listen to me.' Astrid's voice made Gwen shiver. 'No matter what happens, if anything or anyone ever tries to hurt you, we will rip it into pieces, and we shan't stay here without you. We wouldn't *be* here without you.'

Blinking, Gwen realized that what Astrid said was true, and the tightness in her chest released, just a bit. But as good as the twins' intentions were, and as strong as their power was, she couldn't help but doubt whether *anyone* could defeat that discordant thing waiting in the darkness, watching . . .

14

Up To No Good

Jonas could not fathom how he had ended up in such a diabolical situation. Panting behind a velvet curtain in the academy's theatre, he chanced a peek at his stalkers.

'I swear I saw him go this way!' a small girl said, frantically looking about by the big double doors at the top of the steps.

Jonas had assumed he would be free to roam the school if he could only make it out of the dormitories undetected. This hadn't been the case. He'd soon found himself flocked by inquisitive Pledges, all dressed in their various overalls, berets, robes and cassocks.

'Do you really think they're from the Red Blooded world?' another girl asked, picking through a pile of costumes.

He just had to hope Astrid was having better luck speaking to Gwen. Jonas let out a relieved breath as he saw the children finally turn back, their voices echoing backstage as they drifted away.

'My dad says they can do Ancient Magic, that their very existence is an omen,' the first girl said.

A boy's voice chimed in. 'I reckon they're changelings. That's why they look all . . . you know . . . ethereal? 'Cos they're fairies.'

Suppressing a chuckle, Jonas pondered these accusations while he waited for the coast to fully clear. How funny it was that even here, amongst the extraordinary, he and his sister were still a peculiarity.

Finally darting out of his hiding spot, Jonas ventured into the backstage gloom to find a disguise. He spotted a robe in the jumble of costumes and props, which he swiftly donned. This would help him blend in with the choral-like attire of the Order students.

Now for his mission. He had no idea where he was or what he was looking for. All he knew was that he'd recognize it when he found it. A clue, a sign . . . anything.

Ancient steps led down to the basement dressing rooms, where he found a heavy black door – locked. Thinking back, he conjured the melody that Ambassador Loupe had sung to the door in the Skimmer station. At first it didn't work, but reluctantly, he did what he had to do and thought of Gwen, remembering the boiling of Bloom in his veins when he'd seen her handled so roughly in the conservatory. The spell began to burn in his throat until on the third time the door – finally! – creaked open.

The other side was cast in shadow, and he lamented that he hadn't managed to find that black-heart lighter in the flooded station. He thought of the prince, wondering if he was there, somewhere in the academy, wearing the real lighter round his neck right now.

Shaking off the thought, Jonas remembered himself, and hummed the song of Fire until a small flame appeared in his palm, just big enough to guide him.

In the flickering light, he could just about make out the strange room, the whole space filled to the brim with what looked to be antiques. At first, Jonas thought they were props until he made his way further in and cast his flame over other items – eerie portraits draped in canvas, ancient, patinaed weapons . . . and a graveyard of musical instruments. Fiddles missing strings, tables heaped with hand-carved ocarinas and cracked flutes. And there, in the heart of the room, was a glimmering harp.

If Astrid had been there with him, he probably would have found this fun to explore, but . . . something wasn't right here. A shiver passed over his body, and he decided it would be best to leave as quickly as possible. He crossed the room to the other side, skirting past the objects as though he were dodging ghosts, and was surprised to spot an actual door up a set of steps. He pulled on the handle to find it far heavier than expected, and when it opened, there was . . . a wooden wall.

It can't be, he thought. Putting his hand against the dead end, he heard the squeak of hinges, and pushed. Then he saw it, surrounding him – the edge of a frame. It wasn't a dead end; this was the back of a painting, one that was hiding the door.

Following through, he carefully shut the door and the painting behind him and examined this new space. It was far less unnerving – a long, candle-lit corridor with a deep-red carpet.

Quietly, he took cautious steps through the hallway of paintings. Gold-framed, each depicted a person wearing plum-coloured robes. It wasn't until he got to the second-to-last one that he realized who they were. English rulers, right up to the late King Albert, and followed at the end by Queen Beatrice herself.

'Oh!' Jonas said, suddenly enlightened. He'd found his way into the magisterial quarters, and these portraits were the previous Magisters.

Then, a whisper – faint at first, but coming from the double windows where branches tapped at the glass urgently.

The earth, she was whispering to him.

But other voices could be heard as well. Human voices.

Following the soft Bloom hum, Jonas crept quietly further down the corridor, stopping suddenly at a turn, where he glanced around to find a door left open, flickering firelight spilling out across the floor, the voices building into the bitter crescendo.

An argument.

Quiet as a shadow, Jonas snuck forward until he could see through the crack in the hinges. He stifled a gasp. The scene in front of him was precisely the sort of thing he'd been looking for.

The raised voices, it turned out, belonged to the Ambassadors from the conservatory earlier, all of them assembled again, and debating furiously with . . . Magnus.

Jonas brought his eye close to the crack and watched.

'I assure you,' Magnus insisted, with an unwavering smile, 'they have never done any such thing to me.'

Ambassador Harriet Loupe paced by the fireplace, now dressed in a long white robe, her hair flowing like blood down her gown. 'They need to be controlled and studied,' she said. 'This is why they need to be here, at Fountains Abbey. This kind of power needs to be handled delicately.'

Jonas felt sick to his stomach and he bit his lip, forcing himself not to call out in protest.

Sitting in an old brown armchair, Ambassador Klein released a long puff of smoke from a pipe similar to the one Seraphina had smoked earlier. He cleared his throat with a terrible hacking sound.

'It is possible,' he grumbled, bushy eyebrows furrowing, 'that we made a mistake by inviting them to take the Pledge tomorrow.'

Polaris Pom – Ambassador of instrumentation, Jonas recalled – removed his thick glasses and stood up from where he'd been sitting at a desk and walked across the room, right into Jonas's line of sight where he could see the look of utter dismay and fear etched across Pom's face. 'No, no, no! They *must* take the Pledge. We have to know if they're an evil omen. Not to mention that girl, the one with that dreadful Bloom anomaly!'

Gwen, Jonas knew. They were talking about Gwen. Even from a distance, Jonas could see Magnus's smile waver.

'This whole thing reeks of misfortune,' Ambassador Pom continued. 'We have to test them.'

Magnus took a deep breath. 'My students are clever and good-natured,' he said, forcing a small laugh. 'For the most part . . . But if anyone is concerned, we could always ask them if they *want* to take the Pledge.'

Ambassadors Loupe and Pom looked so enraged they could start moulting feathers, but before they could utter a word they were beaten to it by Seraphina.

'Magnus is right. You are being alarmists,' she declared, tapping her foot impatiently. 'So far, we have nothing to be concerned about.'

'Well, that's not entirely true.'

Jonas angled his head to see who this soft, pondering voice belonged to – Princess Alice.

'We have multiple letters now from other factions stating that magical creatures have been showing up in the wrong places, as well as that terrible serpent woman in the station, and Magnus's discovery of a Strix, no less. All these creatures in the wrong place? We have to consider that something much bigger might be going on here.' She paused. 'We need these young people.'

Jonas blinked at this information. The twins knew the appearance of the Strix was unusual, but the Ambassadors seemed to believe that it was somehow linked to Astrid and himself? Suddenly Astrid's absence felt like a hole through his stomach, and it bothered him greatly to think of her and Gwen back at the rooms, oblivious to the strings being pulled behind the scenes.

'My suggestion would be that we continue with Magister Beatrice's plan to have them take the Pledge,' Alice went on, raising her hand for a vote. 'All who agree say aye. And when my wife returns next week from her meeting with the rest of the Grand Coterie at the Shadow Library, we will also have news for her.'

Jonas watched as the Ambassadors voted. Hand after hand rose into the air as people muttered their agreement. Only Magnus sat staring at his hands in his lap, saying nothing and casting no vote.

So they would take the Pledge, but at what cost? What was the danger here?

With no time to digest all the information, there was a sudden surge of melodic Bloom that had Jonas's skin prickling. A warning? But why?

Turning towards the source, he came to a window to the left of him. Jonas peeked out into the night, and very nearly tumbled backwards when he spotted a pair of eyes staring . . . at him?

Sister Seraphina's blue owl.

It looked like a ghostly figure in the distant trees. Jonas put his finger to his lips, hoping the owl would keep his secret.

'That's Lapis,' said a voice from behind him. 'She always gives me the creeps.'

This time Jonas very nearly shouted in surprise, but a hand covered his mouth, the mystery person pulling him back against the opposite wall, and he felt breath, hot against his ear.

'Sorry, sorry, I didn't mean to startle you,' the voice continued. 'I wasn't expecting to find anyone else using my spying spot. Let alone *you*.'

Slowly, the stranger let him go, and Jonas turned to look.

'You –' Jonas couldn't get any more words out.

The stranger stared down at him with a charismatic smile Jonas had seen many times before. In magazines and on giant screens, and plastered on bedroom walls. The figure's hair was long and dark, his bronze skin finely raised with acne scarring along his sharp jaw, and he wore a black-heart lighter round his neck, identical to the one Jonas had tried to win all those weeks ago.

No, not identical.

This was the original, because this beautiful boy who had caught him spying? It was Prince Theodore.

Shaking himself out of his stupor, a million questions began to bubble up in his throat.

'Shhh, wait.' Rather rudely, the prince held a finger to Jonas's lips, forcing him into silence.

Then he heard it too; the meeting was ending. They needed to get out of there.

'Quickly, this way.'

Stunned into compliance, Jonas could only follow along when Prince Teddy wrapped a hand round his wrist and pulled him closer. He smelled like cinnamon, the spice of abundance. Without another word, he rushed them down the corridor and through a set of double doors that he closed behind him with a soft click.

It was dark inside but for the blue moonlight filtering through a set of gauze curtains in front of three glass doors. Despite the low light, Jonas could make out the grand piano in the middle of the room, but it paled in comparison to the view – a perfect vista of the Enchanted Quarter, the very place they would be taking their Pledge come morning.

He needed to get back. He needed to tell Astrid what he'd heard.

'I have to go,' he said. 'How do I get back to the dorms?'

But the prince didn't seem to be listening. 'It's ridiculous really,' he announced, rolling his eyes. 'All the Ambassadors have been in a big panic since these magical creatures started showing up in the wrong places. You know, I heard a Rock Troll showed up on the Thai coast – can you imagine?'

Then, casually, as if he did it all the time, Prince Teddy reached for the black-heart lighter at his chest, flicked the flame to life, then sang a strange, swirling variation of the Fire spell, until the flames danced from his hand and landed on the various lanterns around the room.

Impressive, Jonas thought. And his voice, rich like coffee with cream; he wanted to hear more of it.

Shaking off the thought, Jonas reminded himself again that he really needed to leave . . .

'And you,' the prince said, something devilish entering his smile as his dark eyes narrowed on the Savonnette shard resting over Jonas's heart. 'Seems they're mighty frightened of you.'

. . . Or, perhaps he could stay a moment.

'Maybe they're right to be,' Jonas replied, his angelic face a picture of innocence.

The prince's eyes went wide, excited. 'Is that so?'

Without realizing, the prince had wandered closer to Jonas, the taller teen staring down at him with heavy lashes. Up close, Jonas could see the kiss of freckles over his nose. While Jonas was still dressed in the robe he'd stolen, the prince wasn't wearing the typical cassocks of an Order Pledge. Instead he wore the kind of clothes Jonas associated with the Red Blooded world. A black shirt and skinny jeans.

Jonas pulled his eyes away and his gaze landed on the huge painting on the wall behind him. 'What's this?' he asked, sauntering over to the canvas as if being pulled in by a lure.

Depicted in oils, the scene featured a huge lake – Geneva, Jonas recognized – and lording above it, a fortress of white towers and golden spires. The kind of building one might imagine they'd find beyond the gates of heaven. Too grand, too pure for the mortal world.

'That,' the prince declared, 'is the Shadow Library.'

Shadow Library. Jonas had heard that term.

'It's the magisterial headquarters. Bastion of magical knowledge, haven to Bloom Bloods,' the prince continued.

Jonas kept his expression neutral as he connected the dots in his head. This building in the painting was where the book of Cursed Melodies had seemingly been stolen from. Thinking of that book sent butterflies into his stomach, the taste of dangerous mysteries yet unsolved.

He couldn't pull his gaze away. 'Fascinating,' he breathed.

When Jonas turned to the prince, he was staring back at him, his dark eyes calculating; the black heart twitched at his chest in time with his heartbeat.

'Quite,' he agreed. Then he took a step back, chuckling to himself. 'I must confess, actually: I snuck into Mother's office and read all about you and your sister. You two have certainly managed to rack up a remarkable amount of disorder.'

Jonas found himself taking a step back too. He didn't like when other people thought they knew more about him than he did. Even princes.

'You're nosy, aren't you?' Jonas shot back.

The prince's lips twitched. 'Says the boy I caught spying.'

Jonas glared at him.

'What were you doing anyway?' the prince probed, trying to get close again, but Jonas moved back, keeping his distance.

'I need to head back,' he said instead. 'I've overstayed my welcome.'

Prince Teddy pouted, his eyebrows knitting together like a child about to throw a tantrum. 'Why the rush? Were you doing something *very bad*?'

Ignoring his teasing, Jonas walked to the glass doors and was relieved to find they opened easily. He had no doubt he could find his way back to the dorms; the earth would guide him. It was calling to him now, anxious for him to return to his sister.

'Oh, come on,' the prince called, chasing after him. 'Can't you stay a little longer, Cinderella?'

Jonas flinched at the nickname, slipping through the door and into the cool, blue night. 'Goodnight –'

But before Jonas could close the door behind him, the prince grabbed his wrist again, pulling him back.

'If you don't stay,' he breathed, something menacing entering his expression, 'I'll tell my mothers you were spying.'

Jonas baulked, and felt the earth respond to his emotions. The grass bristled, and when he turned to face the prince, the line of ornamental cherry trees lining the veranda creaked, roots and branches ready to strike.

At the end of the day, the only person Jonas could ever really trust was his sister.

The prince let go of Jonas's hand, having enough sense to feel the shift in Bloom. To know he was in danger. 'I was only joking,' he spluttered. 'Really, I was . . . Come on, don't be that way.'

But Jonas ignored him, setting off into the gardens as the prince shouted after him recklessly. 'I wouldn't . . . Fine, fine, I'll see you tomorrow! Goodnight!' he called, his voice following Jonas as he vanished out of sight into the bushes.

Tomorrow? Jonas laughed to himself. *Unlikely.*

Heading back to the dorms, Jonas thought only of the Pledge and all the information he needed to give Astrid. But as he approached the Pledge sleeping quarters and saw the light still on in their dorm room, he had the strangest thought – a thought he'd never had before. That perhaps he didn't need to tell Astrid about his meeting with Prince Teddy.

That maybe that was just for him.

15
The Pledge

The Pledge needed to take place just as the sun rose, when the trees burned orange and the sky blushed between light and dark. This was when magic was at its most potent and most unpredictable. The Witching Hour.

The hooded Custodians led the trio in single file, silent as the grave, along a winding path from Fountains Abbey through the vale, their footsteps echoing against the cobbles. Occasionally, the twins would glance behind at Gwen, her face hidden under her own hooded robe. A cloud of doom seemed to hang over all of them.

A shadow.

Jonas reviewed the information he and Astrid had shared with each other before they had gone to sleep. The word felt dangerous. They would have to be on high alert. With the Pledge approaching and all that Astrid had learned and what Jonas had eavesdropped on, there had been no time to mention the prince – at least, that's what Jonas told himself.

They had the Pledge to focus on now.

Astrid's gaze settled on the moon just as they left the parameters of Fountains Abbey. 'Something wicked this way comes,' she whispered.

Something wicked, indeed.

Eventually, the cobbled path turned to packed dirt, and then to open grass, until they arrived at the lip of the forest, where chipped wooden pillars dotted with runes etched the land. A single scratched sign warned them not to step further without explicit permission – and Jonas could immediately see why.

This Enchanted Quarter was nothing like the one back at Faymore Manor. The trees creaked with centuries of age, godlike, and whereas the Bloom in the forest at Watersmeet had hummed enticingly, here it screamed.

Jonas felt it like a tether, pulling him in, shrieking through his blood.

The sky was already starting to bruise with the sunrise, and the Custodians stepped between the trees without hesitation. For the twins, the hisses and whispers of the earth were dizzying, imploring them to lie down in its mossy lap until their limbs entwined with the roots.

'No matter what happens here,' Astrid whispered to Jonas as they approached the magical barrier, 'we have to protect Gwen.'

He couldn't disagree.

Although it was likely not considered proper for the ritual, Astrid held both her hands out on either side. Jonas took one, and Gwen took the other. 'Come on, then,' she said with determination. 'Let's take this Pledge.'

Stepping over the threshold felt like stepping into a whirlpool. Submerged, sucked in with a force so strong that it nearly blew their hoods off. Looking back, they saw that the wards here were so potent with Bloom that the whole treeline was warped, like an image composed of slowly drifting, glittering watercolour paint.

With little time to dwell on the eerie echoes of laughter above or the hooves pounding in the distance, they hurried to follow the string of lamps continuing ahead.

Soon, the trio came upon a strange body of water – a lake with two slivers of crescent-shaped land in the middle, like two crescent moons facing one another as if they were yin and yang. More hooded figures, in plum robes with gold sashes, stood waiting for them with lamps of their own around the bank, as if they had sprouted from the grass. Three were standing nearby – their guides for the Pledge – and another five were scattered on the north bank – witnesses.

It was here that their Custodian guides left them, silently turning to march back to the academy.

One of the three nearby guides stepped forward, and they immediately knew who it was from the flash of crimson hair under the hood.

'*Sanguis Noster*, everyone!' Ambassador Harriet Loupe announced the greeting, arms outstretched to beckon the newcomers closer to the water.

As Jonas looked out over the small crowd of witnesses across the lake, one of them held a cane he recognized. Their robe twitched, a hand extending in a thumbs-up.

Magnus, of course.

Next to him, adjusting her robes uncomfortably, must have been Lorelei.

'*Officium Nostrum*,' the small crowd called back.

Jonas was getting sick of hearing the ridiculous Order chant, and, unable to resist, he leaned over to Astrid as they approached the water's edge.

'I guess it just doesn't sound as good in English. "Our blood",' he whispered, mocking the greeting. '"Our duty".'

He could see Astrid struggling not to let her shoulders shake from her quiet chuckling.

Then, to his bafflement, a small bell of laughter came from one of the nearby purple robes, and looking over, he caught a glimpse of Prince Teddy peeking out from under his hood.

Astrid too clocked the prince, her eyes going wide, and, sensing Jonas's sudden awkward shift in mood, she turned to scrutinize him. But he quickly stared forward, avoiding her eyes, and feeling entirely ridiculous for doing so.

See you tomorrow. Jonas replayed the words in his head, feeling like a fool. They hadn't been meaningless; they'd damn well been a threat.

The third robed figure stepped up to them, the Pledge candidates now crowded right up to the edge of the lake, just as the blue twilight began to shift to gold.

'We three will be your guides through the Pledge today.' The three guides' voices spoke in unison. One of them was a rattling voice they recognized – Sister Seraphina. An odd selection for their Pledge, Jonas thought: Ambassador Loupe, Seraphina and Prince Theodore. But he supposed they always did things in peculiar ways.

'For our first order of business –' Ambassador Loupe's voice boomed across the lake – 'we must determine if our prospective Pledges be worthy. This we leave to you, oh great spirit.'

The other five hooded figures on the far side of the lake bowed, somehow causing a breeze to blow over the windless lake, rolling forward like a storm cloud. Ripples grew into waves, and the waves gathered swirls of white foam. The moving water gained momentum and took shape until hooves emerged from the crests and a form appeared, tall and noble, stampeding to the surface. A giant water horse that Jonas recognized from his brief studies at the manor – a Kelpie.

Jonas stared in awe. He'd never seen anything that radiated so much power. It was a being of pure magic.

The Kelpie's mane eddied, a constant rippling through his ethereal form. The dawning sun glanced off his liquid coat as he galloped across the water's surface.

On instinct, the twins gave a deep bow of respect.

Sister Seraphina had stepped forward, palms outstretched towards the Kelpie. 'Oh, Ferryman, great guardian of the Moon Banks, we offer you these new Pledges to fight for and uphold the order of magic on earth! May you deem them worthy to wade into the centre of the Moon Banks, or let them sink below.'

Gwen spluttered, and the twins straightened up quickly.

'Wait, what?' Gwen asked, her face contorted with worry. 'If we're not worthy, he'll drown us?'

From behind them, Ambassador Loupe began to titter. 'Oh no, don't be silly!' she said lightly, as if this was all just a game. 'The Kelpie, Ferryman here, simply creates a path in the water for those who are worthy, to allow you to wade across even the deepest part of the lake.' Her eyes narrowed. 'Those who are not worthy will sink below and have to swim back.'

Jonas felt his skin prickle with unease. His sister too had gone very still.

'Will you give us a minute?' Gwen grabbed the twins and pulled them into a huddle by a nearby tree.

'You can't swim!' she hissed, panic giving her words a sharp bite.

'Yes, this could be a problem,' Astrid agreed, staring over her at the glowing form of Ferryman. Then she turned back to Gwen. 'What do you think? Are you feeling any, you know, dark presences following you?'

Hushing them, Gwen leaned in closer, looking around suspiciously. 'Not yet.'

'Good.' Astrid set her gaze on Jonas. 'And what, exactly, is going on with you and the prince?'

Gwen's mouth dropped open as she looked between the twins.

'What? Nothing!' Jonas protested, the lie heavy on his tongue. 'I just . . . bumped into him last night.'

'And you failed to mention it?' Gwen hissed. 'Why is he even here?'

One of the guides cleared their throat impatiently.

'Can we please continue?' Ambassador Loupe called over in a shrill voice. Clearly, her patience was running thin.

Gwen threw the twins one last look and marched back.

'OK, I'll go first,' she announced, rolling up her sleeves and stomping to the water's edge. She glanced back at the twins. 'If you guys aren't worthy . . .' She turned to scowl at the Kelpie, as if daring it to suggest such a thing. He stood silently, watching them. 'Then I'll pull you back to shore,' she added, more quietly.

Letting out one of her witchy cackles, Seraphina came over and patted Jonas and Astrid on their shoulders. 'Then let us begin,' she said.

Gwen scrambled to remove her shoes and gave the twins one last nod, her face pinched and tight with determination.

Both twins found themselves unexpectedly charmed by her sudden moxie.

'Let's get this over with.'

Fists curling at her side, Gwen let out a huff of air through her nose and trudged into the water. The Kelpie dipped beneath the surface as she waded through, the water coming up and up until it was at her midriff, and then, quite abruptly, it stopped rising, her body now wading through water that reached far below her feet.

'Ah!' Gwen let out a jubilant cry of disbelief. 'It's working!'

She turned back to the twins with an unexpectedly joyful look, a smile finally breaking through the layers of disquiet. It did not escape Jonas's notice that he felt his and his sister's chests flutter at the display, as if they'd been filled to the brim with excitable butterflies. But while he found the feeling to be an utter nuisance, he could sense Astrid leaning into it.

'Your turn!' the prince announced, gesturing them forward.

Skin twitching, it didn't take long until Jonas found his sister's grip, the two coming to stand beside each other, and, hand in hand, they kicked off their shoes and waded into the lake.

Despite burning fiery colours in the dawning light, the water was near freezing, crawling up their legs like icy fingers promising to drag them under. Yet, the siblings persisted. The freezing water reached their thighs and then their hips, their bare feet sinking into the lake's sandy floor. They could see it there, a sudden drop-off – one step further and there would be no ground beneath them at all.

The twins glanced at each other.

'Now?' Astrid asked, her hand gripping tighter round his.

'Now!'

They drew big breaths, and with a *whoosh!* they took the plunge together, giving themselves up to the possibility of a watery demise. Only – their feet continued to tread, a bubbling around their legs that allowed them to wade through to the centre of the lake. A magical path created by Ferryman.

'Incredible!' Jonas mused, feeling suddenly giddy.

They arrived beside Gwen, in between the crescent islands of the Moon Banks, where the water was the deepest.

'Well, none of us drowned, at least.' Astrid smiled at Gwen, who immediately crossed her arms.

'Not yet,' she replied, but the relief on her face was undeniable.

She'd been deemed worthy – they all had.

Their guides arrived in a flurry behind them – Ambassador Loupe and the prince following an ice path sung by Sister Seraphina. The path melted behind them as they came to a stop beside the lake's central banks. Rising from the water, the Kelpie nickered and whinnied under Seraphina's gentle cooing, sending up a spray of white foam as he took off at a gallop round the Moon Bank, then dropped below the surface once again.

'Congratulations!' Ambassador Loupe applauded.

Seraphina, Ambassador Loupe and the prince hauled themselves up, dripping, on to the crescent islands while Gwen and the twins remained magically suspended, half-submerged in the deep centre. With both Ambassadors on the opposite points of one crescent and Prince Teddy in the middle of another, they made a triangle round them.

Still submerged to their stomachs, each Pledge candidate was summoned towards their respective guide. Ambassador Loupe stood over Astrid; Seraphina over Gwen; and Jonas, as fate would have it, found himself still magically standing on water, up to his waist, before Prince Teddy . . . and it seemed the young royal was in the mood for chit-chat.

'I really was joking yesterday,' the prince whispered. 'I'm not a snitch.'

Jonas turned his back and tried to stay focused on the ritual as Sister Seraphina raised her arms from where she was standing behind Gwen.

'Our guardian of the lake has deemed you worthy of this ceremony. The Bloom in your blood weighed, and declared pure and righteous.'

Behind him, the prince laughed quietly. 'I would love to see someone not be deemed worthy, just once.'

'What are you doing here?' Jonas hissed over his shoulder. He needed to concentrate, in case Gwen's mysterious shadow would suddenly reappear.

'I'm in training,' the prince explained. 'Mothers thought it would be a good opportunity to practise my duties.'

'Do you, Gwendolyn Chatterjee, Astrid Bunting and Jonas Bunting, swear to pledge your mind, body and spirit to upholding the magical order of this world?' Ambassador Loupe declared, then reached down and cupped water in her hands.

Jonas could hear the prince doing the same behind him.

'If you choose to, now declare the sacred dictum of our Order. You will pledge that with your hallowed blood comes hallowed duty.'

Together, all three guides spoke in one melodic chorus: '*Sanguis Noster, Officium Nostrum.*'

Gwen was the first to reply. '*Sanguis Noster, Officium Nostrum.*'

The twins followed after, less enthusiastically.

With the vow spoken, the cupped water was released over their heads in a christening of sorts. It fell in gentle drops – not of sorrow, but of joy. Jonas sought out the faces of both his sister and Gwen. They looked . . . happy?

'Are you going to keep ignoring me?' the prince asked,

as they shook the remaining water from their hands. In his robes, the black-heart lighter was hidden away, but Jonas could imagine it there, as much a part of him as his own flesh and blood.

'I'm certainly going to try,' Jonas hissed back.

Prince Teddy chuckled.

Did he have any idea how important the Pledge was, why the twins had gone through with it?

'Bit tense, aren't you?' the prince said.

Jonas sighed. 'Yes, actually.'

He felt the tingle of Bloom at his fingertips, and before he so much as realized what he was doing, he hummed a tune, winding a reed up through the water, and with a flick of his wrist splashed it into the prince's face.

'Hey!' Despite his protests, Prince Teddy sounded almost excited. 'So it's true what I've read. You're a terror, aren't you?' The prince came closer, leaning right up to his ear. 'If only I could have pledged with you.'

Jonas froze at the words. Not *you and your sister*, not *both of you*. Just *you*.

Why did that make him feel so odd?

'Thank goodness for small mercies,' Jonas said, gathering himself, and turned his body to make it clear the conversation was over.

From her position by the opposite Moon Bank, Astrid narrowed her eyes.

He gave a small shake of his head, telling her not to worry, to keep her focus on the ritual.

'Under the watchful eyes of our saints, Arthur, Merlin and Morgana,' both Ambassadors spoke together, hands coming up to rest over their Savonnettes, 'we welcome these new Pledges to the Order of Pendragon, and offer them this gift to bind them, hold them and entrust them to our sacred purpose.'

Taking a step back, they both bowed down, placing their palms on the water's surface as if prostrating themselves in prayer.

'Oh, oops, it's starting. Have fun,' the prince said, his voice light. Jonas saw from the corner of his eye that he followed suit, placing his palms on the water. And despite still being annoyed with him, Jonas was overcome by the melody that began to spill from Prince Teddy's lips.

A spell . . .

It pierced Jonas's skin and soul. It was the stuff that filled a heart, and made thoughts take shape. Glittering, it swelled with the rising sun, the world melting into nothing but pink-and-orange light. And the sound, like it had become the shining lake itself, dragged Jonas down beneath the surface of its melody to where the world turned gold, and all sound vanished but the soft pounding of the three Pledge candidates' heartbeats.

Just as Jonas dipped under the spell, he held a single thought.

The Prince has a beautiful voice.

'We welcome these new Pledges to the Order of Pendragon and offer them this gift to bind them, hold them and entrust them to one another.'

As the ritual's spell began, Astrid was plunged into a world bathed in golden sun, where only she, and Gwen and Jonas, existed alone. Together.

There was no feeling or taste or scent to this place, and at first Astrid believed all sound too had been drowned out by the singular pump of her own heartbeat. Then, piece by piece, she heard the melody of their rhythms uniting. Their pulses, their heartbeats, their breaths.

She followed the sounds as they sent off sparks in what felt like their own gilded palace. A melody began to form.

'*Hello?*' Astrid tried to call out, but it was not any human word that left her mouth. Instead the sound escaped her thoughts like air through a flute, dancing around them.

She sensed that Jonas recognized these sounds too, his body pulsing in time with her own – the revelation of their very own Bloom.

She began to understand. The purpose of this ritual was not to reveal her truth or her magic to the Order. It was to reveal the truth of their magic to *themselves* – a shared knowledge between the three of them.

Astrid and Jonas felt their souls laid bare. This was a melody both innocent and wise. Soon it became a steady sound, persistent like the patter of rain. They could see it, meadows overgrowing, weeds stubbornly springing up through brick and stone, the jubilant music of a wild, untamable and everlasting power.

Only, just as they felt united, their souls split apart.

Jonas's song became a melody of impish insistence, refusing to do as expected.

Astrid's became a romantic swirl, lighting up the sky with heart-pangs of yearning.

Both twins looked at one another as understanding bolted through them. They did not share the same truths. It had always been inevitable, of course. They were twins, but not the same.

For the first time, Astrid felt a sense of grief to hear her brother separate from her.

She wondered, as did Jonas, how this difference might manifest in their magic, and, more crucially, in their futures.

Gwen had listened to it all. Now, she was the next to be exposed, sharing this journey whether she liked it or not. They felt her resist at first, fidgeting as the spell unwound inside her, but the magic could not be denied. Her melody was a thrumming, certain thing, gushing around Gwen as though she'd become the centre of her own universe. A strong core, a home.

Hesitating at first, Gwen leaned into this revelation. Immediately, the melody engulfed her, a fierce, pounding beat like a war drum. It scorched through all three of them like wildfire, igniting everything in a burning glow – a holy light that made them all feel immortal.

Their truest selves were laid out in the open.

Yet Astrid felt sure that she had heard these melodies before.

Where? How? It was impossible, and yet she felt a *nostalgia* for them, like a lullaby from a childhood she'd never had.

Or a battle they'd once fought.

They reached out, trying to dissect, *feel* the melody with their fingers. But just as they felt the edges of it flutter through their fingers, just as Gwen's jubilation crested like a wave, it all came crashing down when a single, awful discordant note tore through the song.

The twins tried to cover their ears, but the noise would not relent.

'Stop!' Gwen tried to rear back, but the magic had rooted her in place.

It was as if the melody of Gwen's magic had become infected, hissing fits of anguish and fear ripping away at the notes, leaving them festering. Gwen tried again to pull away, but tendrils of dark gripped at her, a screeching, blood-dripping roar nipping at her from the ripples below – and from this sound, this jarring beat, something foul emerged.

A shadow.

The shadow.

This was it, the very thing Gwen had been so afraid of. It had torn through the melodies and begun to inhabit Gwen's shape, consuming her.

Neither twin could move as the shadow hands laid themselves over Gwen's shoulders, her face contorting in horror.

I've found you, the shadow hissed.

Gwen's mouth split open – ready to scream, but then all three of them were yanked free of the spell, their golden world of Bloom abruptly ripped away, the three of them coming to in the lake once more.

Astrid had only one thought – to protect Gwen. She'd sworn to keep her safe.

Gasping, she tried to wade through the water, but she was stuck in place like a lead weight. Jonas was struggling too, hands flailing as he tried to move his legs.

The shadow had disappeared, and on the Moon Banks there stood the Ambassadors, hoods down, watching.

'Get them out!' someone yelled from the shore – Lorelei.

Astrid looked over to her and then she saw him – the guardian of the lake, Ferryman. The Kelpie who had deemed them worthy and let them wade through on his magic now watched them with hollow eyes.

But oh, that was not all: where once his skin had rippled and dripped with clear, glimmering water, now it *oozed*.

Black and purple liquid spilled from every orifice, his eyes and mouth bubbling and spitting tar, like a poisonous infection.

The sight reminded Astrid of the first monster they'd ever seen – the serpent woman in the abandoned station. Those same eyes devoid of life, skin peeling, and the sound of its Bloom deformed.

The water creature's melody tore through the air, so terrible and discordant that the robed figures along the bank clutched at their ears.

'Astrid! Jonas!' Gwen screamed their names across the water as the Kelpie sank below the surface of the lake to . . . do what? As the terror crept across Gwen's face, all three felt the Kelpie release its magic – they could no longer float in the water.

They were being left to drown.

16

Something Wicked

'They can't swim!' Gwen breathed, panic setting in as she started frantically treading water, the twins having disappeared below the surface.

From the crescent bank, she heard Prince Teddy cry out, 'What's going on?'

'THEY CAN'T SWIM!' Gwen shouted again, louder.

'You get the girl!' Teddy called over, followed by a splash as he dived into the water. Gwen was vaguely aware of Seraphina's voice shouting commands, and the pop and zip of potions being unleashed, but she hardly registered any of this over the sound of her own limbs beating a path across the lake.

I'm coming! Hold on, Gwen pleaded silently. Tearing off her robes, she launched herself under the water towards Astrid without a second thought for herself or the demonic Kelpie swimming somewhere beneath them; instead, her mind raced with shame and self-loathing. *I shouldn't have gone through with the ritual. I shouldn't have been deemed worthy.*

Beneath the surface of the water, the lake was alive with vibrant, emerald hornwort, the plants swaying around her with every stroke. Gwen watched as a jungle of vegetation reached out towards the twins in the distance, as reeds tangled in their robes, embracing them as if trying to protect them, and in their alarm to keep them safe, began to drag them under. The pair sank down, arms outstretched helplessly towards each other, hair rippling in the murky water, as a golden ray of sunlight cut through, illuminating them.

This was bad. Very bad. The twins' Bloom was out of control, the lake's flora hearing their desperate call, and responding with the same level of panic. If Gwen couldn't get to them soon, there's no way they could make it back to the surface in time. Her heart felt ready to burst out of her chest, her lungs burning with held breath.

Even as they drowned, she thought, they were beautiful, like death itself wanted to preserve them. But this idea ignited a flame inside her so ferocious she half expected the water might begin to bubble, and she kicked harder to get to them.

Beyond the light, another figure pushed through the water – the prince.

Teddy got to Jonas first. He tore through the reeds to hook his arms under Jonas's armpits, trying and failing to pull him free of the vegetation's grip.

At the same time, Gwen stretched out to grab Astrid. Disorientated, Astrid flailed in Gwen's arms, trying to get to her brother while also trying to untangle her ankles from the reeds. Then her eyes locked on to Gwen's, the whites so wide they glowed.

Still responding to the twins' panic, the vines reached up and round them, trying to help but only getting more in the way. The plants were simply responding to the distressed Bloom, but if it didn't stop, all of them would end up in a watery grave.

Gwen could have swum away, saved herself before she too became ensnared in the lake weeds . . . but right then, nothing on earth – not herself, not the Order, not any evil shadow or Kelpie – was as important as holding on to Astrid.

Astrid could do this – Gwen knew it. She had seen what the twins were capable of. She just needed to help them gain control again. The tips of her fingers burst with Bloom, fizzing and alive. Yet she didn't understand what her body wanted from her. *What do I do? What is expected of me?*

She knew, with a terrifying certainty, that even if she started to drown, she would never abandon her friend.

The fire in Gwen simmered as their world slowed down to a rhythm all of its own. She cupped Astrid's face with one hand, and kept hold of her gaze. *Calm down. Trust me.*

Astrid blinked in acknowledgement. Astrid touched her palm to the back of Gwen's hand where it rested on her face, the forget-me-not blue of her eyes focusing as she came back to herself.

A warmth, a familiarity, sparked between them where their skin met, something that was ancient and inexplicable. Gwen's own Bloom burst to the surface of her skin.

Astrid must have felt it too, because she breathed out at last, bubbles flooding from her nose in a gentle stream, her hair a golden halo of light around her as the lake weeds felt the returning calm. Frond by gentle frond, they began to release Astrid.

Immediately, Gwen took a stronger hold of Astrid and, kicking her feet, propelled them up to the surface. Her Bloom burned through every muscle and cell of her body with a power she had never felt before.

The Bloom. It was working!

They broke through the surface, retching and gasping for air, followed soon after by another explosion of water as Teddy and Jonas fought their way up.

Turning on to their backs, Gwen and the prince swam to the Moon Bank with their trophies clutched against their bodies. There they finally crawled out of the water and flopped down on to the small crescent of land, chests heaving.

'Sweet mother Mary,' Teddy wheezed, leaning forward on his knees, while Jonas was on all fours coughing up the water that had filled his lungs.

'That's still –' Jonas paused to suck in some air – 'only one out of three.'

Gwen looked up from her panting. 'What?'

'One out of three,' Astrid repeated. 'Times you've saved us. Versus the two times we've saved you.'

Jonas turned his face towards them, water dripping from his hair – and he grinned. 'You need to keep up.'

Gwen scowled, even as a smile threatened to tug at her lips. 'I should have let you drown!' But she had never felt more relieved in her life.

Then, before any of them could say another word, the north shore of the lake burst into chaos. Robed figures cried out as the dark Kelpie sent wave after wave over the Ambassadors, trying to drag them into the water.

Ambassador Loupe threw her limited arsenal of potions and sang the melodies of Ice and Water in an attempt to control the waves, while Seraphina was doing her best to make the festering Kelpie retreat, humming spells to prompt Calm. None of it was working.

'The Kelpie is stopping anyone from getting to us,' Astrid realized. She climbed to her feet, shouldering off her sodden robe as her gaze narrowed at the scene. 'But why?'

'Where are Magnus and Lorelei?' Jonas asked, hauling himself up. He removed his own robe and threw it down on to the bank with a heavy *shlock*.

Gwen and Teddy glanced around. The four of them were stranded on the furthest Moon Bank, far from the rest of the Order.

Then the horse-shaped mass of sludge turned its attention back to their group. It started galloping towards them, pausing to rear up on its hind legs, rotten silt and weeds coating its legs.

'Well, shoot . . .' Prince Teddy nearly laughed, but his quivering lips betrayed the fear simmering beneath.

The twins stepped in front of Gwen, their palms facing down towards the grass on the bank. But Gwen pushed forward between them, to join them. She wouldn't allow them to do this alone. She needed to chase the feeling of her Bloom, the power under her skin, before it slipped away again.

'Gwen, get back!' Astrid cried.

In response, Gwen took another step forward.

The Kelpie, possessed by whatever evil had taken root inside his heart, raced across the lake's surface, hooves of white foaming water thundering towards them. Lips peeled back, it let out another roar of tainted Bloom.

But instead of being intimidated, Gwen responded in kind. She threw her head back to let out her own war cry. And in a fleeting moment, in the hollow caverns of the Kelpie's eyes, she saw a shadow. The creature that had been following her all this time was, somehow, inside this Kelpie.

With the beast only metres away, Gwen screamed, her fists curling as she brought them down on to the ground – hard.

The Bloom rang inside her mind, echoing and growing louder.

The earth in front of Gwen cracked, tearing apart under the force of her blow, and sent a wave of water so fierce it knocked the Kelpie off its course – a small tsunami of Gwen's own making.

But it wasn't just the Kelpie; all four of them fell back from the force, and Gwen couldn't help thinking, *I made that happen!*

'What was that?' the prince screeched, scrambling behind himself for purchase. 'Did the Kelpie do that?'

When Gwen looked up, the twins were staring at her, awe in their faces.

'No,' Astrid said, her voice calm as a distant storm. 'I don't think it did.'

Another furious neighing pulled them all back, and the Kelpie righted itself once more, clumps of sludge and decay dripping into the water as he shook his head.

Cogs were turning in Gwen's brain, when a shout caught her attention.

'All of you, get down!'

Magnus, at last. He was at the opposite side of the lake, rushing over to them.

Unlike the Ambassadors, Magnus didn't try to come straight towards them. *Smart*, Gwen realized. He was the only one who'd understood that the Kelpie would not let anyone cross the lake from their position at the north bank. Instead, Gwen caught sight of Lorelei and Magnus running round from the east and west sides of the lake, the two waiting for the ideal moment to cut across the middle, and that moment was now.

Rushing from both sides, Magnus and Lorelei smashed potions of Ice and hummed to the cold, calling forth a deep chill to freeze an ice path through the middle of the lake towards the Kelpie.

They glided across the surface as though they were born to the ice. To have such control over a Bloom – it was an incredible sight.

Together, they circled the beast, and while the Kelpie was still orienting itself, Lorelei threw another potion, this one releasing a punchy melody that she bolstered with her own voice. It made the creature snort steam from its nostrils, staggering back.

While it was distracted, Magnus did something Gwen never would have expected: he covered the creature in sand, and played the song of Fire.

There was an odd noise like a sparkler, then the popping of stiff joints, and as the musical charms got louder, the Kelpie began to crystallize into place.

There, in the gathering sunlight, Ferryman was soon totally immobile, gleaming even in his twisted, rotten state – because the beast had been turned to glass.

A spell like this would not last, to will something out of its natural state; no matter how well you sang of Ice, or Fire, the truth of an object's Bloom would always persevere. A *crack, crack, crack* could be heard in the places where it tried, still, to move.

'Quickly!' Ambassador Loupe called from the bank of the other crescent moon. 'We have to cleanse it!'

She was already pulling out her Savonnette, preparing the blessing to capture the Kelpie, in the hope of curing it.

Magnus raised a hand. 'You know we have to kill it.'

Silence fell on the banks as the words pierced everyone's hearts.

'He's right,' Sister Seraphina said finally, her face solemn. 'This cannot be Delivered.'

'This' from the way she spoke, was clear: *this* was not of any magic the Order could deal with.

Gwen understood now, even if she hadn't before. That thing in the station, that deformed serpent woman. It was the same now: the Kelpie was beyond saving.

What evil borne of Ancient Magic was this? And what did *Magnus* know of it?

She felt weak. Helpless, her magic now cold.

Ambassador Loupe looked at Seraphina. 'It's not . . . it can't be,' she said.

Magnus held his hand to his chest. 'I'm sorry.' Spinning out his cane, he twisted the top, revealing at the end a single point of pure, shining silver. A blade. But it couldn't be?

'*The order does not deal in death.*' That's what Gwen had always been told. She looked to the twins, and their faces were pinched and white. Whatever happened now, none of them could stop it.

Magnus lifted the cane and, in one decisive motion, stabbed it into the Kelpie's head. Gwen took in the strangely beautiful sight and then turned her head away as the once proud guardian of the lake shattered into glittering dust.

The Kelpie – the Order's ageless friend turned enemy – was gone.

17

The Grim

'Magnus is hiding something,' Gwen whispered.

She felt Astrid's own whisper against her ear: 'They're *all* hiding something.'

'Quick!' Ambassador Loupe insisted.

Ambassadors Pom and Klein had slunk off to be checked for injuries, while Magnus and Lorelei guided their charges to follow the Ambassador and Sister Seraphina through the magisterial quarters, along a corridor of paintings and down into a strange, dark room hidden behind one of the frames.

Seraphina shut the painting-door behind them with an ominous boom.

With most of the academy still slumbering, Gwen was weak on her feet, almost having been dragged through the woods and gardens back here. She saw it all in flashes. Fresh robes to warm their soaking bodies, Princess Alice insisting her son be taken to the apothecary, the other robed figures shouting:

'We're all doomed!'

'It's their fault!'

And worst of all . . .

'*They* brought this here!'

Now, Gwen concentrated on the feel of Astrid's hand in hers, her pulse underneath her fingers, still alive, still breathing. 'We should have done this sooner,' Ambassador Loupe hissed at Sister Seraphina.

'Calm yourself, Harriet,' the other Ambassador cautioned.

Lorelei and Magnus set up a hum. Songs of Fire filled the room, revealing a cavern of disused, forgotten instruments. But stranger still, Gwen realized that she knew this place – Jonas had described it to them the night before.

'Why would they bring us here?' Astrid hissed to Gwen and Jonas.

Gwen found she couldn't respond. A feeling of discord had pierced through her brain like a needle.

'I think there's something underneath us,' she whispered. 'And it sounds . . . *wrong.*'

The twins now knew that Gwen's instincts were not to be ignored, and they warily stared down at the tiled floor. What could be lurking beneath?

Seraphina and the Ambassador had settled themselves on opposite sides of a glittering white harp in the centre of the room. They began to pluck at the strings, and an odd, upsetting melody sprang forth, something that sounded less like music than a warning.

Magnus came over to them now and said, 'Don't be alarmed; you're safe here.' He was all smiles again, despite the monstrous events that had happened before, the sharp tip of his cane hidden away.

Beneath them, the ground began to shiver and groan with the melody; a silver light melted up through the floor like mercury, forming patterns over the floor and up the walls. Then, as if it had only been an illusion, the bricks on the left wall rolled away, parting with a *thud thud thud* to reveal a tunnel leading down, threaded with roots.

'Hurry, now,' Ambassador Loupe insisted.

They had no choice but to follow the adults as they descended into the abyss. Once they had passed inside, the wall behind them closed with a *thud*, leaving no way to go but further into the darkness.

Astrid sought out Gwen's and her brother's hands, and the three of them soon found that with each step a light appeared, a flickering blue flame to lead the way. To where, they could only guess.

'I don't like this! All these secrets . . .' Astrid's voice rose as barely a whisper. She was scowling, her fingers twitching. Magic ready and waiting for a command.

Magnus glanced over his shoulder with a brief smile – one that Gwen realized was wracked with guilt. Anger began to burn in her stomach, convinced now that Magnus had been hiding more from her than she could even begin to guess.

Jonas turned to Gwen and tilted his head towards Magnus. 'Perhaps it's time we started building an arsenal of secrets ourselves.'

Gwen knew what he meant with that – that Gwen should keep her mouth closed tight. The power she'd unleashed on that lake shore, the raw, unprecedented strength of her Bloom, it was unlike any magic she'd ever seen before. She had no idea how she'd done it, nor how she could do it again, but one thing she did know was that no one had really seen it except the twins and the prince, and the twins wanted her to keep it that way.

Gwen didn't have long to dwell on the predicament before a nauseating wave of sour Bloom rolled through her.

'What's wrong?' Astrid asked, feeling Gwen seize beside her.

Before Gwen could respond, the next set of blue flames lit up, revealing their cloak-and-dagger destination. Buried beneath the academy like a tomb was a cavernous space with three doors leading off, each made of iron bars like prison cells. Lining every wall was a gruesome collection of research, most of it locked away behind thick, reinforced glass: the dry bones of magical creatures, a severed unicorn horn in a warded case, preserved roses dripping rot, feathers that oozed like they'd been drenched in tar.

In the heart of the room, encased in glass and twisted iron, was a black lump of *something*. A dark organism that undulated and roiled in its confinement.

Gwen and the twins recognized it at once. Not from sight, but from sound. That same discordant Bloom that had leaked from the serpent woman and the Kelpie. The sound of Gwen's shadow.

'A laboratory,' Jonas said, giving a faint laugh. 'Of course. You've all known about this all along.'

The churning lump of black ooze hissed a song of rot and decay, and as they approached, the wretched lump began to prickle, its hissing turning to screams.

'Look, look, see? I told you!' Ambassador Loupe screeched, gesturing. 'Look how it reacts to them. We should have tested the twins long ago!'

The twins.

Gwen suddenly understood why Astrid and Jonas wanted them all to keep their cards close to their chests. Right now, the adults thought the shadow, the dark Bloom, was all to do with them.

Harriet was overlooking Gwen . . . again.

Astrid and Jonas cut their eyes at her. *Don't say a word.*

'Fascinating,' Sister Seraphina said, petting Lapis while she watched the undulating black mass.

Gwen stayed as far away from Ambassador Loupe as possible, lingering by a table full of mysterious objects. There were antique knives and mirrors and boxes, and stranger still, fossils and old stones, all of it seeming to have little to do with the organic research lining the walls.

As she stepped closer to get a better look, her skin erupted with gooseflesh, her whole body shivering from an odd chill in the air. Instinctively, she pulled her sleeves down. Except the chill was not in the air at all, but coming from inside her, creeping through her skin, and she noticed the feeling got worse the closer she came to the table.

She glared at the antiques, and something in particular caught her eye. A small silver box, something ornamental, no bigger than her palm . . . a tinder box perhaps? Whatever it was, it was calling to her, whispers crawling along her neck. She knew this feeling, and it was not the shadow; it was not the roiling blackness in the centre of the room – it was just like the whispers from the book of Cursed Melodies.

Lorelei pulled her away abruptly, lining the twins up next to her, and then she and Magnus began humming the spells of Fire and Wind until a warmth crept over the three, the cold bleeding out of them like blood out of silk.

Yet the prickles on Gwen's skin did not subside.

'What *is* that?' Astrid and Jonas asked in unison, pointing at the swirling black mass as Lorelei fussed around them.

'This,' Ambassador Loupe cried, throwing her hand out towards it, 'is the end of the world!'

Magnus took a step forward. 'Perhaps it would be best if *we* explain?'

Sister Seraphina nodded her permission.

'Go ahead, Lorelei,' Magnus prompted.

Lorelei began speaking, albeit reluctantly. 'It is an infection of sorts, an illness that can alter a creature's Bloom. It can turn the creature dark and hateful.' She rubbed at her chest as if the next words were trapped in her throat. 'We call it . . . the Grim.'

Grim. Gwen could taste it like rot on her breath – a violent little word. But more than that, it felt . . . familiar?

'Where does it come from?' Jonas asked. Gwen could see the cogs turning in the twins' eyes.

Ambassador Loupe pointed at the pendant at Jonas's neck. 'It comes from *that.*'

The twins froze, touching the split lid of the Savonnette, their eyes wide in shock.

Magnus cleared his throat, a wordless exchange passing between him and his old teacher.

'A long time ago, a ritual was performed. Dark, Ancient Magic.'

A *cursed melody*, Gwen realized, nearly gasping as she thought of the red-skinned book. She had to quickly school her expression, while the twins remained impassive, easily keeping their cool as they absorbed all the information.

'The ritual opened that antique Savonnette, the one you're wearing now. It had held something for ages, and it was believed the power inside could change the world for the better. But ever since that day, something evil has begun to grow instead.'

'The Grim,' the twins said in unison. Gwen observed how their eyes flitted to each person in the room, analysing them, like hawks watching for movement in the grass, any shred of information they could devour.

'For the past many years,' Lorelei continued, 'it has been the unique . . . how do we say?'

She cleared her throat, looking to Magnus, who offered, 'Responsibility?'

'Yes, *responsibility* of the Faymore Cluster to find cases of it popping up around the world in the hopes of finding a cure.'

'Who knows about it?' the twins asked, expressions blank.

'Well,' Magnus said, taking over, 'all the Magisters around the world, some Ambassadors, like those in our faction, and any fully fledged Custodian from the Faymore Cluster.'

Something dawned on Gwen. 'My parents.' She was unable to hide the crack in her voice.

There it was again, that guilty look in Magnus's face. 'Yes, Gwen, they were amongst the best researchers we have ever had.'

Gwen could feel all eyes in the room trained directly on her, and she dared not look at the twins for fear they could read her mind, that they would sniff out the pain. She should have guessed, of course. That she was cursed. First her broken magic, then her parents being killed, and now this. Somehow, she was linked to this terrible thing her parents had been fighting.

She thought of her magic again, how it seemed so connected to this evil, and wondered if it would be best to not only keep it a secret, but to never use it again.

'Small instances of this infection have been on the rise across the globe for the past half a century or so,' Magnus went on, as Gwen tried to clear her dark thoughts.

'Recently, it's been growing. And with magical creatures appearing in places they should not, we have no choice but to assume the evil is taking root. If we don't solve it soon, the entire landscape of magic will be altered irreversibly.'

At this, Seraphina sighed, patting Magnus on the shoulder in a tender and familiar way – an old bond between student and teacher. 'To most Order members it is just a rumour, a thing they whisper about . . .' she explained, her voice hoarse. 'But now, it has spread its tendrils into our faction's academy, and at your very own Pledge no less.'

Ambassador Loupe added, 'It's time for us to figure out once and for all what the Grim is, and how to stop it before it spreads out of control.' She stepped forward towards the twins, her deep purple robe sweeping along the floor, and she reached out to grasp Astrid's pendant in her thin fingers, turning it over in the light.

Gwen gasped at her boldness – and marvelled at the twins' restraint, not moving a muscle in protest.

She stared both twins in the eye, lips quivering. 'Rupert left these shards of the Savonnette to you two. He wanted us to find you, and it's clear to us now that you hold the answer. We need you to tell us,' she said, her face coming closer, 'what did you see inside your ritual?'

What would they say? Would they admit that it was Gwen's fault, that she brought the Grim with her wherever she cast her power?

But as Gwen watched the twins, their faces stayed calm.

'I don't remember seeing anything noteworthy,' Astrid said.

'Well, think harder!' The Ambassador's red fingernails tapped against her hip. 'You!' She turned to Gwen then. 'What did you see?'

Gwen's mind immediately filled with the murky events of the ritual, the shadow spilling out of her own soul's melody, the giddy rush of Bloom that had coursed through her fingers and sent waves across the lake.

'We . . .' Gwen swallowed, cutting a glance to the twins. 'I don't remember either.'

The Ambassador flinched, beady eyes narrowing. 'Can't you be at all useful?' she screeched, marching closer as if ready to shake Gwen. 'Don't you understand how much danger we're in, you stupid girl?'

Gwen, frankly, had had quite enough, all the rage and fear she'd been subjected to now blistering inside her, ready to burst.

'If we're in so much danger, why are you keeping it a secret?' she cried, startling the Ambassador. 'What about my sister? And Thomas?' She turned sharply on Lorelei. 'He's your cousin, don't you care?'

Lorelei looked away.

Seraphina stepped forward, and answered on their behalf. 'The rule of the Grand Coterie is that all those in the Faymore Cluster are to join this cause once and only once they become Custodians. Until then you are not to tell a soul of what you've seen.'

At last, the twins and Gwen understood. This was not a choice the Faymore Cluster had made. This was the command of the Order.

Gwen looked to Magnus. 'But Jan . . .' Her sister's name spilled from her lips like a plea. 'She has no idea. She wants to study tree spirits, for Mary's sake.'

Magnus's smile strained. 'Gwen –' he began, but this time Astrid cut him off.

'And what about the normal, Red Blooded people?'

Jonas nodded, eyes narrowing. 'These dangerous things are in their world, too.'

Ambassador Loupe scoffed, as if this was the most ridiculous thing she'd ever heard. 'Red Bloods? We have much more important things to worry about. We can just skew their memories and –'

Astrid's voice cut through like a crack through ice. 'It's not about them finding out.'

'It's about them getting hurt,' Jonas added.

Gwen could feel the twins' Bloom sparking something fierce.

'Yes, well . . .' the Ambassador muttered. 'I'm sure you two would understand better than anyone that they're far from innocent, and as far as we know it could be the Red Bloods themselves who are inciting these evil manifestations!'

And what a dreadful thing that was to say. A sourness spread through the air like poison. Even Magnus, ever unflappable, flinched at the words. But it was Sister Seraphina who stepped between the twins and the Ambassador.

'I think that's quite enough,' she said, Lapis flapping at her shoulder in warning. Seraphina held up a finger, her expression serious as a plague. 'Custodians Faymore and Murphy, may we speak with you a moment while we –' she paused to hold Loupe's gaze – 'all calm down?'

'Yes, I think that's a good idea,' Magnus agreed. 'Gwen and the twins can mull it over and tell us if they remember anything that could be of importance.'

The twins nodded politely, but Gwen still felt frozen in place, in shock at all the information stirring in her head. Magnus and Lorelei followed the Ambassadors through one of the iron doors.

Finally alone, Gwen sagged against the table behind her, aware once more that her skin was shivering.

'The way Magnus and Seraphina keep looking at each other, I feel like they're still not telling us everything,' Jonas said, tapping his chin in thought. He stopped then, both twins turning to Gwen with that scrutinizing gaze.

'What's wrong?' Astrid said.

Gwen crossed her arms in frustration. 'Are you kidding?' Her words had more bite than she'd intended. 'This whole thing has been a nightmare!'

'No, not that . . .' Rolling their eyes, the twins reached for her, each grabbing an arm and pulling the sleeve up. 'This. Your skin – it's all prickly. We saw you pulling your sleeves down earlier.'

For a moment, Gwen felt breathless. She was wearing a long robe, and yet she felt totally exposed, aware suddenly that there was nothing she could hide from Astrid and Jonas. They could see straight into her.

Lowering his voice, Jonas leaned in. 'Is it . . . you know?'

Gwen quickly shook her head, glancing over at the black convulsing orb in the middle of the room locked behind glass. 'No, I don't think so . . . It's something on the table. Whenever I go near it my skin starts pinging like a dousing rod.'

The twins shared a glance. 'What something?'

Gwen stared down at the object in question, committing it to memory. The little silver box was etched with fairy scripts and flowers, but it was not the container that was calling. It was whatever was inside. If not for the prickles it caused, the thing could almost have got lost amongst the table of showier items – splendid knives, a jewelled mirror, etched relics – but none of those made her Bloom boil like a geyser waiting to blow.

'What is it?' Astrid asked, her voice quivering with excitement.

'I don't know; it looks like a tinder box . . . I think . . .' Gwen fumbled for the words, pulling her arms back to herself and rubbing the wrists nervously. 'I think, whatever's inside, it belongs to me.'

Gwen couldn't tell, and yet she could. That item – it was hers. She was meant to find it.

'Curious, aren't they?' called out a voice as Magnus and Lorelei returned to the room through the iron door. There was no sign of the Ambassadors.

Magnus approached the table himself, turning items over. 'Most of this stuff was found at sightings of the Grim,' he explained. 'Although we have yet to understand what even half of them are, what their purposes are.'

Staring at the box, Gwen tried not to dwell on what it could mean, that she was so drawn to something that was connected to the Grim.

'Well, come on, then,' Lorelei said, indicating the painting-frame doorway.

'We're leaving?' Gwen asked, confused.

Magnus beamed. 'Yes, I think we've far overstayed our welcome, don't you think?'

Truly, Gwen could not agree more, and she was more than ready to leave, desperate to get back to the safety and comfort of Faymore Manor.

Then the iron door screeched on its hinges again, and the Ambassador's voice could be heard beyond it.

'No, no, no, we can't let them leave!' they heard Ambassador Loupe protesting. But it was Seraphina who stepped through the doorway. 'Seraphina, listen to reason, we should be keeping them here, in the lab, to be studied –'

Gwen saw Astrid and Jonas's expressions curdle. Fortunately, and rather surprisingly, Seraphina shut the door behind her, on the Ambassador, with a decisive *thud.*

'My apologies,' Seraphina sighed, rubbing at her forehead. 'Harriet is afraid. The events of today have rattled her.'

'Sorry we couldn't be more help,' Astrid said earnestly, and the look of apology was so believable even Gwen nearly fell for it herself.

'I think you're right, Ambassador,' Magnus said over his shoulder as he continued to usher them out. 'Our new Pledges need to rest. Thank you for allowing me to take them back.'

'Magnus . . .' Seraphina said his name like a warning, all five of them pausing on their way out of the lab. 'I need you to keep these Pledges safe. You too, Lorelei. I do not know what role they are to play, but we need them ready for whatever it is.' Her gaze fell on Gwen and the twins then, looking them over in a way that made Gwen shudder. 'I fear evil has set its sights on you.'

Magnus nodded, while Lorelei's grip on Gwen's shoulders tightened. Protective.

Sister Seraphina's words rang in Gwen's mind like a prophecy, and it wasn't until they were a far way back in the tunnel that she felt the heavy weight of the day's events truly settle over her shoulders. Staring at the back of the twins' heads as they walked through the corridors, she wished she could read them the same way they could read her, to know what threads they were busy unravelling.

The twins fell back in line with Gwen.

'We've done something terribly naughty,' Astrid said, a small smile tugging at her lips.

Gwen hissed under her breath, 'What have you done now?'

Both twins shared a glance, a conversation passing silently between them. Then, pulling her close, Astrid opened her robe just so, and as Gwen looked down at what was hidden there, the skin on her arms began to prickle.

Tucked neatly into the inside pocket was the mysterious tinder box that had set Gwen on edge.

'We brought you a gift.'

18

Rapscallions

Stealing the box had been the obvious choice for Astrid and Jonas. It was, after all, Gwen's. And, well, Gwen had saved Astrid's life, so naturally Astrid owed her a thank-you.

The memory of their underwater moment was bittersweet – the panic, yes, but also the feel of Gwen's warm hand against her cheek, the sound of Gwen's Bloom like a flare in the dark.

What choice did Astrid have but to repay her friend with a gift?

Unfortunately, Gwen did not agree.

'I still can't believe you did this!' Gwen squeaked, closing the door to her bedroom in Faymore Manor behind her as quietly as possible. 'Can't you at least keep it hidden?'

Rolling his eyes, Jonas propped a book up in front of the silver box. 'Better?'

From the look of boiling rage on Gwen's face – no, it was not better.

Astrid paid no mind. She was jittery in a way that was rare for her, like that excited and frustrated feeling she had right at the brink of solving a particularly difficult puzzle. It probably didn't help that there was an actual buzzing in the atmosphere. A storm perhaps? Even the earth was excited.

She'd played the events of their Pledge and the conversation in the laboratory over and over again in her head. There was something there, a titbit of information, something they were missing. Something that was being *hidden*. They just needed to find it.

'How's it looking out there?' Astrid asked.

'Coast is clear,' Gwen confirmed, pacing the room nervously. 'Everyone's gone to bed.' Then she sighed, grumbling under her breath, 'Let's get this over with.'

Only a night had passed since their Pledge ritual, the memory still raw in their minds. They'd waited, patiently, keeping their lips sealed and playing the perfect students with Magnus and the others, all the time expecting trouble the moment the Ambassadors back at Fountains Abbey Academy found one of their precious research items missing. But nothing happened. No letter. No call. So tonight, with the household heading to bed, they were going to risk studying the artefact.

Of course, there was one little resident who didn't mind their nefarious activities.

'Goodness, you're needy!' Astrid chuckled, putting down her book and making room for Buttonbug, who grumbled and fussed as she settled into Astrid's lap. She'd missed them.

'Hey!' Gwen began to object.

'Not *you*!' Astrid smirked, patting the floor beside her. Gwen joined her, sprawling on the rug, and they watched the windows above them rattle as a fierce wind picked up from the sea. Jonas was busy staring into his notebook, his fingers fiddling restlessly with his half of the split Savonnette. How odd it was that the items they'd held so dear their whole lives could have such terrible origins – a ritual item that had caged a great evil, now hanging round their necks.

Astrid could feel it again, as if the answer was on the tip of her tongue. What was she missing in all this?

Jonas glanced up. 'Ready?'

'I'm not sure.' Gwen hesitated. 'I . . . I keep thinking we should have told the Ambassadors about the shadow, and that weird surge of power I had. They should know I'm linked to the Grim . . . What if I need to be restrained, or detained, or . . . worse?'

'Absolutely not,' Jonas protested. 'Someone wanted us to take that Pledge. Someone who might have planned for this whole thing to happen.'

'Yes,' Astrid agreed, turning to Gwen. 'And until we know who or why, we are not telling anyone about you or the shadow or your powers. For the time being, we'll let them keep thinking we're the only link to the Grim.'

'But –'

'No buts, Gwen. Now, let's see if we can work out what this thing here means.'

At this, Gwen huffed, crossing her arms over her chest while the twins gave each other a knowing look.

'Fine,' she grumbled.

Jonas placed the tarnished artefact in the middle of their little circle. The three of them stared at it while the wind picked up outside the window again, howling.

'What even is it?' Frowning, Gwen stared at the box like it was diseased.

It was clear she wanted nothing to do with it all. That she'd rather hide her head in the sand.

'Hmm.' Astrid pondered. 'Why don't you touch it? Maybe it'll communicate with you like the earth does with us.'

Gwen glared at the two of them before sighing in defeat. 'All right, all right.' She grabbed it. 'But don't go crying when –'

They all froze as Gwen's fingers wrapped round the silver box, momentarily stunned when a bright silver light emanated from its etched skin, so brilliant and clear that it looked like Gwen was holding a living star. Most spectacular though was the sound – a choral harmony like the voices of angels, a perfect lull that lit up inside their souls and banished every dark thought and feeling.

'Holy –' Gwen threw the box back on the floor, shaking her hand as if she'd been burned. When she'd let it go, the song and light had faded abruptly. 'What the hell was that?'

Despite the shock, Buttonbug hardly reacted; in fact, she seemed placated by the sound, purring happily. Strange.

Astrid could barely spare the creature a glance, because something most peculiar was now happening to Gwen's box.

Trembling where it lay on the rug, the silver box burst open, and from inside, a wispy cloud of ash floated like a cloud. They all watched, hearts pounding, as the ash hissed and whispered, shifting form, until it was ash no more, but three elegant pages now floating in the air.

Pages that belonged to a very particular book.

Jonas clocked it at the same moment as Astrid, their eyes going wide. He shuffled back to the bed, searching through the books for the red-skinned cover – *The Cursed Melodies*. They held the book up, the cover turning on its own as if possessed.

Immediately, like a magnet, the strange floating pages surged towards the book, torn edges melding themselves to the spine. The book was healing itself.

They stared down at the new pages.

'What is that?' Gwen asked, her voice barely a whisper. 'What the *hell* just happened?'

She was practically panting, clutching her chest as if her heart were about to jump out. There was no denying it now. Gwen was linked to this book somehow. Her Bloom was intertwined with it.

Together, the three of them peered over the book of Cursed Melodies.

Etched into the paper were drawings of a sword, and the sea. And all round, engraved with such care it was almost like a love letter, were delicate pansies. The flowers bordered the paper, and there was even one in the hilt of the sword, a shining silver pansy where one's thumb might rest if they were to wield such a thing.

Blinking back to herself, the reality of the situation suddenly dawned on Astrid.

What were these pages of *The Cursed Melodies* doing hidden away in such a place? What did all of this have to do with the Grim? And why on earth had this book been hidden amongst the Faymores' belongings?

'*Oh.*' Breath catching in her throat, Astrid's eyes went wide, staring at Jonas as he too came to the same conclusion.

The two of them turned to look at Gwen.

Still panicked, Gwen frowned at them. 'What? What is it?'

Swallowing, Astrid considered which was the best way to explain. 'Gwen, don't you think it's odd that it's the Faymore Cluster that has been tasked with tracking the Grim?'

Gwen only continued to look at them with a confusion that bordered on irritation.

'Why has such a dreadful and dangerous task fallen to them?' Jonas prompted.

'I . . . Because . . .' Gwen stumbled over her words, getting flustered or annoyed, it was hard to tell. '. . . Because it has to be a secret? Right? Magnus and my parents and everyone, they were respected and trusted with the task because they're such valued members of the Order.'

Astrid understood that Gwen needed to believe that, that it helped her fill in the blanks.

'Do you still have that photo?' Astrid asked. 'The one of Magnus and Elijah and your mother? What did they call themselves . . . the Rapscallions?'

Hesitating, Gwen went to her bed and reached under the pillows to retrieve the old, sun-stained photo. Her fingers trembled as she passed it to Astrid.

It was as Astrid remembered: eight people – Magnus, Elijah, a young man that must have been Rupert, and Gwen's mother – the resemblance uncanny – and four others. One person at the end was half obscured, their face unclear compared to the others. Who was that, anyway? Astrid had the sudden strange thought that she recognized them, and for some reason, the thought made her shiver.

'What does any of this have to do with the Grim?' Gwen demanded, struggling to keep her voice low.

Astrid swallowed, putting Buttonbug on to the floor and pulling herself up to standing. The truth was bitter on her tongue. 'Don't you see? It was Rupert's Savonnette; he probably found it somewhere. Why did he have all the broken pieces? And this group, the Rapscallions, what if they used this book? Don't you wonder why it was here? It's highly likely they figured out how to perform some of its spells. Spells that should never have been touched.'

Gwen frowned, taking a step as she shook her head. She didn't want to hear it, but she had to.

'Gwen, what if they're responsible for releasing the Grim?' Jonas said bluntly.

'What if that's why the Faymore Cluster has to solve this?' Astrid breathed, feeling the crushing weight of it all. 'As punishment.'

Gwen stumbled, nearly tumbling over a cushion on the floor.

'No,' she said. 'No, it's not possible. Magnus . . . My mum, she wouldn't. They're respected members of the Order.'

'We have to consider it, Gwen,' Jonas demanded, ignoring the way she recoiled. 'We need to know what this ritual was and exactly what happened to everyone involved.'

A thought suddenly occurred to Astrid, something dark, something she almost dared not say out loud. She looked at the photo again, and thought of the graveyard on the property. All those stones. All those names.

Jonas sucked in a breath through his teeth. 'Rupert,' he said. 'Magnus told us he died before he could give him all the answers, but . . . died of what?'

Going to sit on the bed, Gwen looked up. 'Lorelei said that the Grim can alter any Bloom . . .'

'Magical creatures are not the only things with Bloom in their blood,' he said. 'And things that are infected with the Grim . . .'

'. . . Have to be killed.'

The horror of that possibility sat between them in the room, almost alive. A squirming, terrible revelation that made Astrid's stomach turn. She couldn't imagine what

Gwen was feeling – had her parents become infected, and been executed by the Order?

Before Astrid could say anything, the window rattled, a fierce wind shaking the foundations of the manor. Beyond the walls, the plants were humming, the atmosphere electric.

'There's a storm coming,' Jonas murmured.

Gwen sniffed, hard, forcing her emotions back under control even as her voice cracked with the effort: 'I think you both should leave now.'

Confused, Astrid tried to take a step towards her, only for Gwen to stand up, her fists balling.

'Gwen, we need to know –'

Suddenly, all the fire that had been building within Gwen was aimed at Astrid. 'Well, maybe I don't want to know!' she yelled, so loud that Buttonbug fled behind a chair. 'If all this is true about the ritual, then why are we involved? It's not fair!' Her voice was pitching higher, her emotions spilling over. 'Why should we have to fix problems we didn't cause? What does any of this have to do with me?'

Astrid tried to take a step towards her again. 'That's what we're trying to find out, Gwen.'

'Well, I don't want to find out,' she replied, the ferocity of her words alarming Astrid, reminding her of this girl's tremendous power. 'Whatever my link is to the Grim, it's a curse. Or a mistake. My parents may have *died* because of it, and if the Order finds out about me . . .'

Marching forward, Gwen kicked the silver box under her bed, the thing clinking against the wall.

Jonas went to protest, but just as he opened his mouth, another furious gust of wind rattled the window. With a *bang*, the whole thing blew open.

The bedding rippled like it was alive and Jonas climbed

up on the mattress, rushing to the window to get it shut again.

'Gwen –' Astrid tried, her fingers burning with Bloom. Her magic willing her to respond, to help her.

Gwen shook her head, having to speak louder over the wind. 'Just leave me alone . . . *please.*'

Before Astrid could try to reach out again, Jonas turned to them, his eyes wide and frenzied like he'd seen a ghost. 'There's someone out there,' he said, his voice low.

'Jonas, we –'

But Astrid couldn't get another word out because he held up his hand, silencing her.

'Shh, look!'

Astrid crept over to where Jonas was leaning out of the window, the wind whipping at his hair. A single electric pulse through Astrid's skin told her Jonas was excited . . . or nervous.

From Gwen's rooms, they had a clear view of the sprawling gardens leading up to Windyside Cottage, where Magnus, Elijah and Lorelei slept. The building looked like a doll's house, something Astrid could hold in her palm. The windows were all dark, so her attention was drawn to the swaying orange light that was winding its way through the trees.

'What is that?' Astrid whispered, squinting her eyes.

'I think it's Fire magic,' Jonas replied. 'But where would anyone be going at this hour, when there's a storm on the way?'

Leaning forward just a little more, Astrid could make out a cape and a hat in the distant figure's silhouette.

'I think . . . I think it's Magnus,' Astrid said, but Jonas was already grabbing Astrid's wrist, pulling her with him to the bedroom door.

'Where are you going?' Gwen demanded, rubbing at her eyes.

'We need to see what Magnus is doing down there,' Jonas said, gesturing for them to follow.

Gwen only scowled, staring down at the floor, dejected. 'I don't want to.'

Jonas looked ready to fire off, and from the building tension in Astrid's chest, she could tell he was growing exasperated by Gwen.

'Fine,' he said, letting out a long breath as he went to pick up the book and put it away in his bag. 'We'll go on our own.'

Torn between the two of them, Astrid felt herself split down the middle.

Yet they all needed answers. That was the whole reason they were there.

Jonas's hand curled round her wrist even tighter. 'You heard her,' he said, his voice cold. 'Let's just go, we'll do our own investigating.'

Gwen didn't even look at them, still staring down at the floor with a furious expression.

Conflicted, Astrid lingered. She'd never experienced such a thing before, a twisting sensation in her gut that made her bones feel heavy. She couldn't help but think of all the framed works lining the walls of the corridors of Faymore Manor, old photos and oil paintings depicting all its former inhabitants. This building was full of secrets and whispers. And looking at Gwen now, she saw her hurt expression, how clearly these hidden truths had injured her.

Astrid wondered if the twins were selfish to pluck at the feathers of all these mysteries, knowing she and Jonas wouldn't hesitate to leave the manor if they ever felt trapped. Members of the Faymore Cluster didn't have that luxury.

And what if they found what they were looking for . . . where they came from? Would they really just leave?

'Astrid,' Jonas prompted, 'come on.'

She wanted nothing more than to go to Gwen and comfort her, but she knew they couldn't miss this opportunity. So, she let Jonas lead her out into the hallway, Buttonbug following behind.

The door closed with a soft *thud*, with Buttonbug flying off to their room for the night, leaving them alone. The corridor was dark but for the low glow of the charmed candles on the walls. Astrid had made her choice, so why did she still feel compelled to go back to Gwen?

'OK,' Jonas said, licking his lips in nervous anticipation. 'We're going to spy on a Rapscallion.'

19

Dead and Buried

By the time the twins made it downstairs and outside on to the grass, the night had turned oddly silent, the harsh wind settling. The earth smelled like salt and energy. Astrid recognized it for what it was: the calm before the storm.

Astrid knew it in her bones, that whatever happened tonight with Magnus, there was no going back.

Silent as shadows, the twins sought out the firelight, running their fingers gently through the ivy and white dead-nettles along the path. In response came a ghostly melody of Bloom under their skin. Fitting, of course, because it seemed Magnus was heading to the graveyard.

Pushing through the overgrown hawthorn bushes, the leaves rattling like a rain maker, they hid amongst the branches. The cemetery was just as the twins had remembered, with most of the headstones blanketed in lichen and moss, mourning flowers curling up from the long grass. And Magnus, standing still as the stones themselves, his cape at his back like raven's wings.

'He's at his brother's grave,' Jonas said. *Amor Vincit Omnia*. The engraving they'd seen before.

Hidden in overgrowth, they watched as Magnus leaned down, speaking words to the gravestone that they could not hear. He looked supernatural against the moonlight, as if he were one of the spirits risen from the ground.

Then, suddenly, he raised his voice. 'And what are you two doing out here so late?'

The twins glanced at one another, then shrugged. Rustling out of the bushes, they pushed open the squeaking gate and came to join Magnus at the grave, a million questions now burning at their lips.

'We were going to ask you the same question,' Jonas said, as they came to stand either side of Magnus.

Their tutor smiled, but the smile didn't quite reach his eyes.

'I come out here when I can't sleep,' he said, staring up at the grey, undulating clouds above. 'I'm afraid tonight we received more bad news. There's been a report of a Thunderbird off the coast of Edinburgh.'

The twins had read about Thunderbirds in one of the encyclopaedias of magic. Powerful creatures – and ones that didn't belong in this country.

'Very rare and sacred beings, native to the Americas,' Magnus explained, his voice distant, like he couldn't quite believe what he was saying. 'It's deeply concerning. Misplaced creatures of such power can alter the entire ecosystem.'

The twins followed Magnus's gaze up to the roiling sky. The odd atmosphere suddenly made more sense: weather made of magic.

'There will be storms all across the country tonight,' Magnus sighed, tapping his fingers along Rupert's gravestone.

'Does it have anything to do with the Grim?' Jonas asked him bluntly.

'We have no choice but to assume so for the time being,' he replied, his eyes not straying from the sky. 'Something is changing.'

Astrid reached for Jonas's hand, both of them knowing what they were going to do. What they *had* to do.

'We know what you did,' Astrid said calmly. 'The Rapscallions.'

Magnus turned to them, the scraps of moonlight highlighting his resigned expression. He'd been waiting for this.

'You did it, didn't you?' Jonas looked at their teacher so intently they could see the red tint again in his silver-blue eyes.

Magnus didn't flinch.

'*You* performed the ritual that released the Grim into the world.'

Around them, the salty air began to swirl once more, howling like a wild beast, but Magnus was unmoved, only his cape billowing. Then, slowly, he knelt to put his hands to the cold ground and began to hum, singing life back into the mourning flowers, before standing up to face them.

'Astute, as usual,' he finally said, rubbing the soil from his hands.

'We need to know what happened at the ritual,' Jonas pressed.

'Magnus,' Astrid continued, 'what happened to your brother, and the rest of the Rapscallions?'

Magnus kept his gaze focused on the headstone. 'The truth is strictly confidential, I'm afraid ... but, well ... perhaps if you've already guessed ...'

The twins understood. He *wanted* them to solve this. They just had to say it out loud.

'You said that the Grim turns Bloom dark,' Astrid began, her heart thundering in her chest. 'That there is no cure, that it can only end in death.'

Jonas continued. 'But magical creatures are not the only things to have Bloom running through them.'

Magnus smiled – a sad, broken smile. 'So, what conclusion have you come to?'

Astrid swallowed. 'Our conclusion,' she said, keeping her voice steady and strong against the growing wind, 'is that Rupert was cursed by the Grim, and you were forced to kill him.'

'Very clever,' Magnus said at last. His smiling expression was both pleased and nearly tearful with sorrow. How long had he been waiting for them to solve this? To confront him? He sighed, as though preparing himself. 'I suppose this is long overdue.'

This is it, Astrid realized. Jonas squeezed her palm. Even the grass around them hummed with Bloom, ready and waiting, for they were about to hear a story – a terrible secret.

'There were seven of us in total,' Magnus explained, his voice firm over the growing howls of wind. 'Myself, Rupert, Elijah and Rani, we established the group, and we recruited three more – close friends of ours, Abigail, Quin and Francis.'

As he said each name, Astrid's eyes landed on the headstones. They were all there.

Abigail Bane

Francis Yonge

Quin Larkspur

'We were the Order's most promising students of Ancient Magic. Troublemakers, some called us. But our professor called us the Rapscallions.' Magnus's face softened at the name, the memory fond and warm – until it twisted, turning dark. 'Sometimes I wonder how things might have been different if that book had never fallen into our hands.'

The twins froze, schooling their expressions. Surely there was only one book he could mean. The very one currently hiding in Jonas's bag.

The question was, did he know they had it? And if he did, why had he let them keep it?

'Not to worry, it's been hidden for many years now; Rupert took care of it, said it was never meant for us to find.'

Astrid swallowed the information hard, wondering then if there was someone who was *meant* to find it.

Had Rupert charmed the book? Had it been waiting for someone in particular all this time?

She thought of when they'd found it, when they'd touched it and brought it to life. Except . . . it *wasn't* them. Thinking it over, Astrid remembered it clearly. The book had not begun to change until Gwen had touched it. *Gwen*, not them.

'Back then, before we knew better, it led Rupert to that Savonnette you're wearing now,' Magnus explained.

Astrid reached up to touch the broken shard at her neck, her fingers trembling.

'There was something ageless trapped inside. We would hear it, whispering to us. We thought we were doing a good thing, unleashing a magic that could change the world. The spell was supposed to give us the power to change hearts. With magic like that, we thought we could make a kinder world, that we could stop all hatred and evil. So, one night, after months of heated discussion and then preparation, we got together to perform the ritual.' As Magnus told the story, they could almost feel it, the magic they must have used, the power and thrill of their discoveries. 'But, when the Savonnette opened, it shattered, releasing a force so powerful it shook the earth to its core.'

'What was inside?' Jonas asked, his voice hoarse.

'Nothing, at first,' Magnus said, surprising them. 'There was nothing but a whisper of magic. We heard a horrible sound for just a moment, a heart-shattering hiss of words in a language long forgotten . . . and then it vanished. And that was it. We kept what we had done secret for many years, thinking whatever had been inside had simply . . . faded away. That's what we had hoped, at least. But then we heard reports of strange and twisted magical creatures . . .' Magnus winced, the memory painful. 'We went to investigate, and we heard it again, the whispers from the ritual, that dreadful, Bloom-curdling sound.'

The twins spoke as one: 'The Grim.'

Magnus nodded. 'We spent years hunting any trace of the infection, trying to identify its source before it was too late, before anyone could learn of what we had done, but the Order worked it out. My husband, my brother and I – we took responsibility.'

Astrid sucked in a breath. 'So you had to be punished,' she said.

This time, Magnus looked regretful, an age-old guilt souring his expression. 'The Order declared that the Faymore Cluster would dedicate their lives, and the lives of every generation to follow, to finding out what the Grim is and curing it. It is the most important assignment in the world . . . and for many of us, a death sentence.'

Astrid found herself breathless. They'd guessed as much, but hearing the truth out loud was like poison in her ears.

'What happened to Rupert?' she asked, almost scared to speak such a painful question.

Magnus let out a soft breath, sparing a fond glance at the gravestone.

'It was the very same day Gwen was born,' he told them, the fact surprising the twins, but before they could dissect the detail, Magnus went on. 'He completely disappeared. He claimed he'd found something that could save the world. We were to meet that night, once he had his answers. But when he arrived at the manor, he was not himself.' Magnus gently ran his fingers over the stone. 'Whatever he found, it put the Grim inside him.'

Astrid found herself squeezing Jonas's hand, wondering how Magnus could possibly have endured the loss of his brother. She wanted to tell him to stop, feeling cruel for making him recount the tale, but they needed this. They needed to know.

'He had one final moment of clarity before he died, when he was himself again. He thanked me, and with his last breath, he gave me that Savonnette, the one we thought had shattered and disappeared, and he told me to find . . .' He paused. 'Well, I suppose he told me to find you two.'

Glancing at Jonas, Astrid suddenly saw themselves through Magnus's eyes. They were not just a mystery that needed solving – they were his last link to Rupert. A chance for redemption.

'And this is why the Magisters don't want people to know,' Jonas said, keeping his voice steady even as Astrid could feel him trembling with unease. 'Because the Grim could be anywhere. Even amongst their friends and colleagues.'

Magnus nodded, his expression grave.

But there was one thing they still didn't understand.

'That book you spoke of . . .' Astrid began, swallowing. 'What exactly did Rupert do with it?'

Magnus chuckled, staring down at his brother's grave. 'I have asked myself that very same question.' He smiled at them, a knowing glint in his eye. 'All I know is that my brother set many things in motion before he died, and all we can do is trust his plans, and hope that he knew who could be trusted to obtain such knowledge.'

There was something unspoken in the words.

'So, if Rupert wanted you to find us,' Jonas said, looking to Astrid for reassurance as he tapped the pendant at his neck, 'what, exactly, are we meant to be doing?'

'Perhaps that is for you to figure out,' Magnus said, looking away.

Astrid felt the answer like a seed sprouting from her chest. It was the same feeling she'd had when they sang to the earth and it had answered.

Gwen.

It was all to do with Gwen.

Jonas sighed, frowning even as the truth bled into him. He'd reached the same conclusion.

Shrugging, Magnus looked to the skies, as though there might be an answer lurking beyond the undulating clouds, just out of reach.

'All I know is that you must listen to your Bloom,' he said gently. 'Whatever this connection is you feel towards Gwen, trust it. Our hearts rarely lead us astray.'

Astrid gasped. 'How do you know about our connection to Gwen?'

He chuckled at this, a warm sound.

'I might be old, but I'm quite observant, you know.' He smiled then, something private, as he looked down at his brother's grave once more.

Perhaps, Astrid thought, Magnus knew far, far more than they could ever begin to guess.

'Whatever this is, I can't face this for you, but I will always be here, no matter what secrets you wish to keep.' He looked back up at them. 'Or what you wish to confide in me.'

As he spoke, the wind picked up suddenly, howling through Astrid's hair and sending their coats whipping about them.

Magnus stepped away from the grave, his cape flaring in the gust. 'Now, I think we should get inside.'

Something worrying crept over his features as he looked up towards Gwen's bedroom. A deeper knowledge.

'I have a feeling the weather is about to turn.'

20

The Storm

Gwen curled up tightly in her purple blankets with a terrible stomach-ache, overwhelmed. It was the witching hour, and she couldn't sleep a wink.

After the twins had left, she'd wallowed on her own in bed, staring at the photograph of her mother and the Rapscallions, thinking of that damn ritual. It couldn't be true . . .

Could it be that her parents had been possessed by the Grim, like those dead-eyed creatures oozing black goo and shrieking discordant, twisted Bloom? And if her dad had never been in the Rapscallions, how had he been dragged into all this? Just because he had loved her mother?

It was such a dreadful thought. How much you can hurt someone just by letting them get close to you.

Gwen turned over in the bed and shut her eyes tightly.

But . . . could her parents have infected her? Is that why her Bloom was being stalked by the shadow?

Or perhaps . . . it was she who had infected them?

The wind screamed at her window – a storm, just as the twins had promised. There was no doubt in Gwen's mind that this was an omen, a reminder that everyone around her was in danger.

'Please, please,' she pleaded, willing the night to stay still and clear.

Flitting behind her eyelids, she kept seeing it, the pages forming from the ash in the box. And she hadn't just seen it; she'd *heard* it. Magic beyond her understanding, yet it recognized her, an old acquaintance. And what a terrible thought that was, that this book that may have caused so much grief, that could very well have brought about the downfall of her parents . . . That it had been waiting for her.

'Please leave me alone,' she muttered, opening her eyes to stave off the visions.

Her gaze locked on the corner of her room. The shadows seemed off somehow – as though someone . . . or some*thing* was there.

Startling, Gwen sat upright, sheets tangled round her ankles.

There was a low hum of discord. Whatever it was, it wasn't good.

Gwen ground her teeth, that fire simmering inside her. She was sick – not just from fear, but of all these secrets. Of not knowing what was going on, or why. As rain began to tap at her window, Gwen dared to lean forward.

'What are you?' she called into the dark.

There was nothing but silence, so she tried again.

'What do you want from me?'

Now, she could not be sure – the witching hours play tricks on the mind – but for a split second Gwen thought she saw the darkness smile.

A flash of lightning lit up the room, and Gwen nearly jumped out of her skin, grabbing the bed sheets closer. But there was nothing there, only her mess of books and trinkets.

Then came a growl of thunder. The storm had arrived.

'No,' Gwen pleaded, scrambling over the bed to peek beyond the curtains.

The rain and wind picked up, the storm drawing closer.

'You're fine,' Gwen hissed. 'You can handle this. You're not a child.'

Except, when the next bolt of lightning illuminated her room and the ferocious boom of thunder followed only a second behind, Gwen threw the blanket over her head, holding it tight round her while she slid pathetically down to the floor, furious at herself for behaving like a wretched worm. There was nothing she hated more than to feel helpless.

The wind and rain became relentless, frantically thrashing at her window. Gwen crawled towards her wardrobe, then opened the doors and tucked herself inside, making a space for herself amongst old garments and spare bedspreads.

Under no circumstances could she ever let anyone know about her fears. She would ride this out. She would survive on her own, like she always did.

Astrid wasn't sure what had woken her at such an early hour – the storm, or the flowers.

Eyes snapping open, she could hear the taut, high-strung whispers of Bloom, every leaf of every vine in the room shaking with alarm while the rain battered at her window. All was not right here.

'Jonas?'

There was a brief rustle of sheets. 'Yes?'

She could feel each root and stem like veins through the house, pumping hard and growing fast in panic. 'Do you feel that?'

Sitting up, Jonas hummed thoughtfully. 'Something's wrong.'

The storm raged harder and the windows began to shake, furious fists of wind pounding at the glass.

Growing up in the care of Doctor Harris, storms had been considered too high-energy, too affecting for their fanciful minds, so they had never been allowed to sit and watch them through their windows. Now, Astrid could. She stared, captivated, at a bolt of molten light that shattered the sky. And even though she'd had only limited experience with storms before, she somehow understood that this one was different. This was what happened when the earth burst with magic.

Below the rocky crags, the sea frothed like a potion, each foaming wave crashing in a fury of light and sound, the air electric. The feral beauty and power of it reminded Astrid of their Pledge ritual, the sound of their souls, of Gwen's magic.

Gwen.

The name felt different now somehow.

'Do you remember in Gwen's room last night,' Astrid whispered, stepping over to Jonas's side of the room, 'the way Gwen got so upset when we mentioned a storm?'

Jonas gave a grim smile, pushing the hair out of his face. 'You're terribly observant when it comes to her.'

Astrid faltered; she couldn't deny it, even if she wouldn't say it out loud. 'Shush!' She dragged her brother out of his bed. 'You heard what Magnus said. We need to trust our instincts and right now they're telling me –'

'That we need to go to Gwen,' Jonas finished for her, rolling his eyes. 'Yes, yes. I feel it too, you know.' His tone made it clear he still viewed their mysterious connection to Gwen as a nuisance, rather than an intriguing puzzle.

Astrid just had to hope he would come around.

They slipped out of their room, crept down the corridor, and arrived outside Gwen's door. There was a sign that read, *Knock first.*

Obviously they weren't going to do that.

The door's creaking hinges were drowned out by the storm's symphony. Gwen's bed had been left in disarray, her stack of books and papers knocked over.

Astrid could feel the prickles of concern growing, not just on her own skin, but on Jonas's too. It was impossible to ignore the feeling of alarm that sent shockwaves of Bloom vibrating through them like a tuning fork.

She's not here.

Outside, the storm had turned violent, a flash and bang so fast and close it rattled the building.

And then they heard it. A gentle thud, and soft, babyish whimpering. Astrid thought that she was hearing a small animal – a puppy perhaps?

'It can't be?' Jonas whispered, but they already knew.

This wasn't a puppy. Coming from the wardrobe was a rhythmic murmuring.

When Astrid leaned her head against the antique wood, she could hear it more clearly. Gloomy words of affirmation.

'You're not a child. It's just rain; you're fine. It's just rain.'

'Gwenny,' Astrid hummed against the wood panel.

With a little hiccup, the whimpering on the other side stopped.

'Open the door,' Astrid coaxed. 'We're here.'

There was a furious rattle of the storm at the window. As Astrid reached for the wardrobe's handle, a crack of lightning split the sky in half, the ensuing thunder like the roar of an ancient beast. With it, the wardrobe doors flew open, and

Gwen, white-robed and murky-eyed, flung herself into Astrid's arms, the two of them tumbling to the floor.

'It's OK,' Astrid whispered. 'I've got you.'

Clinging on, Gwen's skin was hot with emotion, her face wet and snotty.

Astrid breathed a sigh of relief, and she had the oddest sensation that she was in a memory, as though she'd dreamed this all long ago. As though she was meant to be here.

She turned her face over Gwen's shoulder to look at her brother. His eyes remained hooded, considering.

'I hate storms,' Gwen muttered against Astrid's shoulder. 'Foul!'

'They should be hanged for their crimes,' Jonas agreed, walking over to close the curtains.

'A certified menace,' Astrid added, stroking Gwen's plaited hair.

There was another *flash, bang!* This one a little further away. The storm was retreating. Yet Gwen still jumped, clinging on to Astrid's nightgown.

'It's not just the storm,' Gwen said, her voice muffled.

'I know,' Astrid replied, and she did. All three of them were starting to feel the pressure, trapped under the thumb of the Order and their expectations, under the constant threat of something evil and unknown lying in wait for its next chance to attack.

Astrid's pendant felt tighter round her neck as she replayed Sister Seraphina's words in her mind: *'Evil has set its sights on you.'*

'I know . . .' Astrid repeated, squeezing Gwen tighter.

'I feel humiliated,' Gwen moaned, daring to pull herself away.

Jonas went to the bed and flicked on the bedside light, dropping himself down on the mattress.

'It's not that bad, Gwen,' he sighed, and from the seasick feeling in Astrid's gut, she could tell he was debating whether to speak his next words aloud. 'At least you didn't smack the heir to the royal throne in the face with a wet reed.'

'Is *that* what happened?' Gasping, Gwen turned to face him, her skin glowing in the rosy lamplight, lashes wet with tears.

Jonas crossed his arms. 'The prince, it turns out, is an extremely irksome individual.'

Catching her brother's eye, Astrid couldn't help a sly smile. 'So you're not a fan any more?'

Shrugging, Jonas rubbed his chin in thought. 'Well, not of his personality, at least.' He shrugged. 'The rest –'

Astrid rolled her eyes. 'You're intolerable.'

At this, Gwen laughed – a real, truthful laugh.

Astrid climbed to her feet, helping Gwen to stand. For a moment, the storm outside was all but forgotten.

'Thanks for . . . Well,' Gwen sniffed, looking down at the floor – in frustration or embarrassment, Astrid couldn't tell. 'For not making fun of me. I know you probably found it very hard.'

Jonas made a pained sound that Astrid could feel in her gut.

'Almost unbearably so,' they said in unison.

'Shut up,' Gwen scowled at them, but her lips twitched with the threat of a smile.

Jonas rolled himself off the bed and sauntered to the door, holding it open for the other two, that impish glint in his eye. 'Come on,' he demanded. 'I expect Elijah made a fresh batch of Tranquillitea yesterday, and I consider it our duty to steal some.'

'Oh, absolutely,' Astrid concurred, and was delighted when Gwen nodded her agreement.

All three of them tiptoed out to the stairwell, thankful for the plush runner along the boards to mask the sound of their footsteps.

They were almost at the kitchen when Astrid noticed Gwen was shivering.

'I'll get a blanket,' she said quickly, heading back upstairs.

Coming back round the banister, Astrid paused at the bottom of the second-floor stairs to find a lanky figure creeping up.

Jan.

'Hi,' Astrid said.

Jan looked up startled, loose strands of hair flailing about her face. She placed a hand over her chest. 'Mother Mary, you scared me! I was just going to find Gwen. She, well . . .'

'It's OK,' Astrid assured her. 'We found her in the wardrobe. She's downstairs with Jonas having some tea. I was just going to fetch a blanket.'

'Oh,' Jan blinked. 'That's . . . Wait. You calmed her down?'

Astrid nodded, moving to the side to let Jan past.

'Wow. Thank you.' She sounded genuinely amazed, as if Astrid had performed some small miracle.

There was a brief pause.

'Is there a . . . reason?' Astrid asked carefully. 'Why Gwen is so afraid of storms?'

Jan sighed. 'Our parents,' she said, her voice cracking. 'They were . . . Well. We lost them in a storm.' A million conflicting feelings passed over Jan's face.

Astrid saw that it must have been hard for Jan to always be the older, responsible sibling. When it came to Jonas, they had always been the same, always equal.

Jan sighed, and it looked for a second like she might not elaborate, but then she said, 'It happened the same day Gwen used her Bloom for the first time.'

Astrid gasped softly.

'It was just the four of us in the manor – everyone else was out – and Gwen was only tiny,' Jan explained. 'There was a huge storm. It nearly blew the manor down, a real tempest. I barely remember what happened myself, but I remember Gwen was at the kitchen table, and she did this incredible spell – it split the whole door in half. We were all so excited . . . but then our parents had to go out for some reason, a serious emergency, and . . . well, they never came back.' Jan swallowed her emotion. 'I think she always blamed the storm . . . and herself.'

Astrid pictured a younger Gwen, a ferocious little thing, shouting at storms and hiding in cupboards. She saw her scraped knees and knotty hair, muddy hems and angry tears – a lonely little girl.

But then Astrid had a terrible thought, one that made her nearly falter on the stairs. 'What exactly happened to your parents?' she asked, sweat building on her brow.

Jan shrugged. 'I don't know . . . I – they never found them . . .' she confessed, rubbing her arms as if she were cold. 'There's one thing I do remember, though; it was really bizarre.' She laughed nervously, like she was embarrassed to be saying it out loud. 'I mean, I must have imagined it or misheard, because when Mum left the house, the very last thing she told me was to keep the shadows away from Gwen . . . Isn't that strange?'

Astrid had to school her expression, the revelation making her nearly breathless. They had already guessed that Gwen's parents died saving her from the Grim. But the question was, just how long had this evil been following Gwen? And why? What had her parents known about her? And why hadn't they told the rest of the Order?

The door to Jan's bedroom creaked open. 'What's going on out here?' said a voice.

Jan froze in the doorway as Thomas emerged from her bedroom, with a big stretch and yawn, his brown curls falling in little ringlets over his cheeks. Rubbing the sleep from his eyes, Thomas was dressed in pyjama trousers, the faded shimmer of matching scars on his chest like little lines of moonlight.

Astrid raised an eyebrow at the older girl, who could probably have turned water to steam right then with the sheer heat of her embarrassment.

So, Jan and Thomas. Interesting.

'We were up late studying,' Jan offered, suddenly fiddling with the end of her extremely long plait.

'Oh, Astrid. Hi.' Thomas yawned, oblivious. 'Crazy storm, huh?'

'We couldn't sleep. We're going to steal some of Elijah's tea, if you wanted to join us?' Astrid offered.

Just then, the ground beneath them rumbled. It was a strange sensation, as if the manor was lurching in surprise. Had the storm returned, or was it something else?

Frowning, Astrid and Jan both leaned into the sounds of Bloom. It was a high-pitched keening, as though the vines surrounding the manor were squeezing tighter, protective. But what were they trying to protect them from?

'Something's wrong,' Jan said quickly.

'We need to wake up the others!' Thomas cried. 'I'll go to the cottage and –' But he didn't have time to finish, because the manor shook and rumbled again, accompanied by a cacophony of screeches from the floor below.

Piercing cries that Astrid recognized all too well.

It was the sound of a Strix . . . one infected with the Grim.

21

A Precious Possession

Astrid made it to the kitchen just in time to see the windows shatter.

Shards of glass fell across the tiles, and in their wake was the curdled screech of the bloodthirsty Strix. Clawing its way through the window's opening, the beast's teeth dripped decay with each spluttered croak. Wet, oozing wings beat a stench like death into the air.

'What the hell is that doing here?' Thomas yelled from the doorway as the creature opened its beak again, leaning its crooked body over the mantel, where it conjured a sound so rotten with discord that everyone recoiled.

Jan fell against the wall. 'What's wrong with it?'

Thomas hurried over to her, his eyes never leaving the beast.

Astrid knew the sound, the rotten tang of it. It was the Grim.

There was no time to explain. Gritting her teeth, Astrid focused on her Bloom, seeking it out like she had at the Pledge ritual. She found the chiming vines along the building. She could feel them like the thrum of her own heartbeat. A war drum.

Then she spotted Jonas and Gwen, crouched down on the floor by the Aga. Jonas was sheltering Gwen as best he could against the kitchen cabinets, while the creature prowled above them. They held themselves perfectly still; if the Strix so much as glanced down, it would see an easy feast.

Somehow, Astrid had to get the creature away from them. 'Look at me!' she cried out.

The Strix's head whipped round unnaturally, and Astrid could see right into its dark, cavernous eyes. *The Grim.* Clear as day. Astrid nodded to her brother. Counting to three, she took a deep breath – and ran out of the doorway.

The fetid creature threw itself across the kitchen, chasing at her heels as she sprinted down the corridor.

She could see the flora light up like flares inside her head, every vine clasping the manor, each leaf and root pulsating, willing her to use their power.

Clutching the finial at the bottom of the stairs, Astrid flung herself round the corner, while the Strix, unable to quell its momentum, went crashing into the wall, feathers flying. Scrambling and screeching, its talons tore paintings in half, wings sending ornaments smashing, more black sludge oozing to the floor.

Astrid scarpered through the door to the parlour, the infected creature hacking and shrieking behind her. She didn't look back, imagining only the pain that might follow should she miss a step.

'Astrid!' she heard Jonas yell from behind, his panic like a hot poker on her spine.

Diving over the sofa, Astrid turned just in time to witness the Strix flay the upholstery, antique fabric exploding under its talons.

Then, somehow, two sets of hands grappled with Astrid's arms, and her body recognized the grips of Jonas and Gwen. They dragged her out of the way into the corridor again, her legs scrambling.

Voices cried out from a distant corridor. Jan and Thomas screaming at them to move.

Whizzing past Astrid's head with a soft *thwip*, a curved bottle made direct contact with the Strix, shattering in a pink cloud. The melody it released was cloying, sickly sweet, and heavy like syrup. Before Astrid's eyes the pink smoke bubbled, thickening under the music, while the beast screamed and writhed in confusion. Astrid was confused too; it looked like the Strix was trapped in syrup, or gum.

'What kind of potion is *that?*' Astrid asked.

'It's all we had in the kitchen!' Gwen retorted, grabbing both twins by their hands as Thomas and Jan shoved them into the kitchen again and slammed the arched doors shut.

They tumbled across the tiles before scrambling right back to help Jan and Thomas hold the door shut – just as the heavy mass of the monster's body thudded against it.

'All good?' Jonas muttered, pushing his back against the rattling wood.

Astrid wheezed, 'Been better.'

'What on earth is that thing?' Jan looked about ready to combust. 'Why does it . . .' she winced. 'Why does it sound like that?'

Another bodily *thud* at the door sent them juddering, but it held.

'It's the Grim,' Gwen explained. 'An infection.' Astrid saw that the scared girl from the storm was entirely gone.

'What – argh!' Thomas grunted.

A particularly violent blow threw them a few steps away from the door, but they gathered again, leaning their shoulders against the weight.

'Whatever it is,' Thomas panted, 'it's going to get through.' His eyes were wide and wild. 'We need a plan. Now!'

'We don't have any potions,' Jan said, 'or our instruments, let alone our Savonnettes. We're in our pyjamas, for Mary's sake!'

'Deliverance won't work anyway,' Jonas said, quickly.

'Then what *do* we have?'

There were only herbs in the kitchen, but below and all around them, there were vines, roots, branches. Astrid felt them like the veins under her skin, a melody of power waiting to be unleashed. If they could just get close enough.

'We'll keep holding the door!' Thomas rasped. 'Gwen, you climb out of the window and run as fast as you can to the main house to get Magnus.'

Then, with a furious shriek, the Strix stuck its talons through the wood of the door, the sharp points barely missing Thomas's face. Their hold on the door faltered, and it was just enough give for the beast to send them all flying.

The twins scrambled and grabbed Gwen, hauling her to the side and out of the way of the rampaging beast. Splinters of glass from the broken window were still scattered across the floor, digging into their hands as they crawled, drops of blood blossoming along the tiles.

'Everyone! Out of the window!' Thomas screamed.

They made for the shattered windowpane, their only escape.

Thomas reached for the only thing available – a bread knife.

'You can't!' Jan gasped as Thomas raised the knife towards the monster scrabbling towards them. 'We need to help it!'

Astrid winced. Jan didn't know. She didn't know this thing could not be saved.

When Thomas lunged, the Strix stood up on its haunches, revealing its true, monstrous size. It whipped one of its powerful wings forward, smacking Thomas and sending him flying into the wall as if he were nothing more than a plaything.

The whole time, its gaze was trained solely on Gwen.

Screaming, Jan ran to Thomas's side, but they'd all heard it – a single crack, the unmistakable sound of breaking bone.

Thomas wheezed, clutching his arm close to his stomach.

'Get him out of here!' Astrid hissed. 'Run for help!'

Blinking back tears, Jan cradled Thomas, helping him run out of the nearest doorway.

They were alone with the monster.

'No one make any sudden moves,' Jonas said softly.

A skulking mass of feathers and rot, the Strix staggered towards Gwen. Astrid could feel her heart in her chest pounding so hard she thought she might burst.

Outside, the vines were still screaming to be used, but they were still too far away, roots just out of reach.

Slowly, the trio backed up, until they were pushed against the kitchen counter with nowhere else to run. Yet, the creature did not charge at them the way Astrid had expected. It watched, edging ever closer, rotten feathers moulting. Her grip tightened on Gwen, their chests heaving.

It was the most peculiar thing, because now that the monster had them in its sights, cavernous eyes oily with the Grim, Astrid could sense that there was something else there, something lurking beyond.

'What's it doing?' Gwen breathed.

The Strix prowled forward, curious, but it did not attack. It was watching them.

'Strange . . .' Astrid breathed. Scouring her memories, she thought back to the abandoned station, the Kelpie and, most of all, that dark, evil thing that had appeared in their Pledge ritual.

Why, she suddenly wondered, did these demonic creatures always seem so intent on Gwen? Even as a child, the first time she'd used her magic – the Grim had always been seeking her out.

The beast leaned forward, sniffing the air around Gwen.

'Why's it looking at me like that?' Gwen's voice was hoarse with fear.

Astrid could only watch as the Strix carefully, almost gently, raised its talons towards Gwen.

The realization hit Astrid so quickly she felt it like an explosion in her head. All the pieces lighting up, clear and bright, and terrible.

'It wants to take you!' Astrid hissed, her eyes blown wide.

Hot black sludge spilled out from between the Strix's razor-sharp teeth. A drop landed on Gwen's cheek, bubbling a line down her skin as she winced. They heard it then, sizzling words made of Bloom, like it was coming from inside their own heads. A deadly whisper.

I've found you.

'It's the shadow!' Astrid cried. 'The Strix, it's not just infected, it's . . .'

Jonas's eyes lit up in recognition. 'Possessed.'

Astrid felt dizzy with it, seeing the beast now for what it was, not sick, not cursed, but controlled.

It was being puppeteered by something else, some greater evil. A greater evil that was watching them.

An evil that wanted Gwen.

Well, Astrid thought, *they'll have to go through me first.*

'What –' Before Gwen could even finish, Astrid and Jonas flung themselves on to the counter, pushing back as hard as they could, ignoring the shouts of pain from their palms where the glass shards from the window dug in.

'Argh!' Gwen cried as the creature clutched her shoulders, flailing like a captured animal. 'Get off me!'

Spreading its wings wide, the beast unleashed a torturous scream from its pocked mouth, sending spit like tar across the twins' skin.

It pulled back its head, its razor-sharp beak ready to strike.

Just as it lunged forward, Astrid felt it in her bones, rattling through the marrow.

Whatever this evil was, she would never let it touch Gwen.

Shoving their hands against the exterior wall, Astrid and Jonas breathed in, deep and slow, sinking into the melodies of the earth, listening to the exact shift in tone that told them they'd made the connection. Astrid thought of Gwen, of how it would feel to have her ripped away, until the sound became a primal thing, every cell of every plant around them vibrating with the bloodiest of screams.

'Now!' Astrid barked.

Green clouded the edges of her vision, and both twins flicked their wrists, and opened their mouths.

The earth answered.

With a euphoric rush, every plant and seed anywhere close to the manor answered their call. Flooding in from the broken window, coils of ivy and rose stem, weed and clover, all rolling in like a tempest.

The surge of power . . . it had nothing to do with their own survival.

No, this was for Gwen, and Gwen alone.

Suddenly, the screeching of the Strix was cut off, yelping as the stems cut through its wings, thorns pressing into its oozing arms as each vine tightened and pulled.

Gwen began violently kicking at the thing, scratching at its limbs while the beast gasped, its feathers ruffled, its wings becoming more useless with each piercing vine. And yet, the Strix would not let go, even wrapped in crushing vines, with thorns spilling Grim from its flesh.

'We have to kill it!' Jonas cried.

Nodding, Astrid raised her voice to the sky.

But, then –

A blade appeared through the centre of the Strix's chest. Black ooze spattered from the cavity and the blade retreated, only to pull back again and swipe around, under the beast's throat and then – *swipe!* – the beast's head toppled off.

There was a dull beat of silence.

Gasping, Gwen fell from its clutches, scrambling on the floor towards the twins. Jonas faltered, but Astrid rushed to cradle her friend, holding her palms out, checking for injuries.

'Is everyone all right?' Magnus's voice boomed through the room, a sword dripping ooze at his side. From behind him, Lorelei ran to them.

Astrid couldn't answer, as she checked Gwen over again and again. She looked up at Jonas, whose eyes were wide and frenzied.

'Your arm!' he sputtered.

Almost as he said the words, Astrid felt the drip down her elbow, and then glanced down at the trail of thick, warm . . .

Blood.

22

Out in the Open

'So, let me see if I understand this . . . Ouch!' Thomas sucked in a breath as Elijah continued to bandage his arm.

'Sorry,' Elijah apologized. 'Just need to tie it off.'

'It's all right. Where was I? Oh yes, so it's like an infection?' Thomas asked, reaching for a cup of Elijah's healing tea with his other arm. 'And our Cluster has been tasked with looking for the cure?'

Astrid's own shoulder all but screamed in protest where Elijah had sewn the skin together with some charmed thread. When she took a sip of her own healing tea, her head rang with curative Bloom and another sneaky shard of glass pushed its way out of her palm. She was a mess.

'And we're all sworn to secrecy.' Jonas's voice rang cold. They were the first words Jonas had spoken in a while, and there was something oddly chilling to Astrid in his tone, a bitterness she wasn't used to hearing. She could feel as well as see that her injury had alarmed him. Astrid had joked that if anyone asked about the four-inch laceration down her left shoulder blade, she would tell them it's where one of her angel wings had been cut off, but Jonas was not amused.

On the sofa by the fire, Gwen frowned at her own palm.

'Don't,' Astrid had whispered to her earlier. 'Don't say a word.' The last thing they needed right now was for any of this information about Gwen's link to the Grim to get out. Astrid and Jonas had dealt with untrustworthy adults their whole lives; if the Order knew, they'd swoop Gwen up in their own talons and use the girl as bait. Besides, if Gwen's parents had known the truth and kept it secret, they must have had a good reason.

Right now, Gwen could hardly look Astrid in the eye. The whole ordeal had deeply disturbed her.

'So why hasn't it infected us?' Thomas asked, staring at his own injury.

Lorelei huffed, shaking her head. All business, she had her braids neatly tied on her head, and she was dressed in a dirty apron and thick gloves that were both covered in the leftover sinew and black blood of the fallen Strix. 'It's unclear how the infection works. We know it's not transferred through blood or exposure, but we'll have to watch you all carefully regardless.'

As Lorelei spoke, Astrid's injury throbbed. She didn't feel any different. She didn't feel *possessed*. But what, she wondered, did possession even feel like?

Would they be able to tell if a person was possessed?

Staring into the flames, Magnus seemed to be having a similar internal battle, his body hunkered over against the orange glow.

'What alarms me the most,' Jan began, stroking Buttonbug, 'is the amount of damage it caused so quickly.'

She was not wrong; regardless of the myriad injuries, and even with magic, it had taken a whole day for the manor to come back to itself. No spell was spared to get everything, and everyone, whole again. Elijah had used bottles of Bind and vials of Heal to sing Thomas's bone back into place. Magnus and Lorelei had set about tackling the debris, pushing their Bloom through melodies to mend and remake. The Grim was the most difficult to remove, puddles of the black gunk melting against the tiles, paintings and panelling on the walls tarred with jagged splatters like a warning. Even with the withered body of the Strix removed, the discord of the Grim left the air tainted.

Gwen suddenly looked up. 'How did it get out of the Enchanted Quarter?' she asked, her voice gravelly with lack of sleep.

Lorelei's expression turned grave, her hands fidgeting in her skirts. 'I'll ride out to check the wards.' She looked out of the window. 'If that's even where it came from.'

The room filled with an awkward silence.

Eventually, Magnus sighed heavily. 'I think it's time we took a long overdue trip to Windsor.'

Gwen's face scrunched up. 'Sorry. What?'

'We need to tell the queen about this.'

'I'll get a raven ready,' Elijah offered, climbing to his feet.

'I'll prepare a horse to ride down to Watersmeet,' Lorelei added. 'And you . . .' She pointed at Thomas and Jan. 'You need to rest.'

That just left Gwen and the twins.

Before they could be given their own instructions, Jonas leaned into Astrid's ear and whispered, 'We need to talk.' Then he looked up at Magnus and said, 'We're going outside for a second. We need some fresh air.'

He grabbed Astrid's hand and led her away to the gardens, where the grass was still on edge and the grounds still wary after the storm. He stopped abruptly under an oak tree at the bottom of the garden, beneath its coppery leaves.

'OK,' he began, grabbing her good shoulder, and looking around suspiciously as if checking the coast was clear. 'We have to leave.'

The flowers around them practically screamed in protest.

'What? Why?' she asked, unnerved by how rattled he was.

'I've come to my senses,' he hissed. 'Because this? It's madness, Astrid. Your shoulder? I . . .' He took a deep breath. 'It's not normal. We shouldn't be worrying about protecting Gwen when we should be protecting each other.'

Putting her palm to his cheek, Astrid willed him to relax, and trust her. 'I'm fine, Jonas, see?' She rolled her shoulder, suppressing a wince when the muscle twinged. 'We knew this was a possibility when we agreed to guard her. I thought you understood this . . .' She searched his face. 'She's important, Jonas. Not just to help us solve where we come from, but perhaps important to the entire world.'

Jonas narrowed his eyes. 'I don't care,' he said, drawing away from her hand. 'I don't care about *the world*. I care about you. I couldn't bear to see you injured.' He crossed his arms. 'This was never meant to be our battle. We agreed to leave if anything or anyone tried to cage us again. You heard Ambassador Loupe's rambling: the Order wants us under their control, just like the Faymore Cluster does.' He glared at his twin, daring her to disagree.

'We're not trapped, and I am perfectly fine,' Astrid insisted. 'And we still have questions that need answering.'

Jonas sighed, a disappointed sound. 'How can my genius sister be so deluded?'

Astrid opened her mouth to protest, but Jonas cut her off. 'Don't you see? You're falling for her.'

'I'm . . . what?' All her words caught in her throat, making it impossible to say anything else. But the thoughts still came, flashing through her mind: Gwen with a Bloom that burned brighter than the sun. Gwen and her mercurial moods, changing like a rolling tide. Gwen, whom Astrid would rip the very earth in half for . . . even if it meant tearing herself apart too.

Hadn't Jonas felt the same link with Gwen? Was it only she who felt this way?

Oh.

Oh god, she realized – *he's right.*

Clearing her throat, she found words again. 'Yes, I see that,' she said calmly. 'I'll deal with it.'

His body sagging in relief, Jonas wrapped his arms round her, careful of her injury. She could sense that he thought this would be the end of her feelings – now that she'd recognized them, she could destroy them.

As though anyone could do that.

'But . . .' Astrid added, carefully removing his arms. 'Whatever the case may be, we're not trapped . . . yet. There's no need to panic.'

'But your arm –'

She cut him off. 'I'm *fine*, Jonas. You need to get a hold of yourself.'

'Fine, fine. You're fine, I get it.' He ran his hands through his hair before holding out his palms for Astrid to take. 'But you have to swear to me: no matter what your feelings for Gwen, and no matter this pull we have towards her, or this duty you think we're fated for – if for a second we sense a cage coming down round us, we leave.' He held her gaze. 'You promised.'

Yes, she had promised, and they'd lived in a cage before. He was right: they couldn't do it again. No matter what was at stake, it was them against the world, and they had their own mission to focus on.

Astrid took his hands, their palms stinging from the cuts. 'I promise.'

Jonas's smile began to appear, only to swiftly vanish when Astrid spoke again.

'Her parents *knew*. Gwen's parents knew she was linked to the Grim, but for some reason they wanted to keep it a secret, even from Magnus.'

Despite his irritation, Jonas couldn't help but lean into the mystery, the cogs turning behind his eyes.

'You think . . . they were worried about someone in particular finding out?'

Astrid nodded. The question was, who?

'I keep thinking about that photo of the Rapscallions,' Astrid said, picturing all those smiling faces in her mind, as well as the one they couldn't make out. 'Magnus said there were seven of them, but there were eight people in the photo. Who was that eighth person, and what were they doing there?'

Jonas's eyes narrowed, a whip-fast surge of exhilaration fluttering over his back. 'Maybe –'

But before he could get another word out, the earth trilled – a greeting, because someone had arrived.

'What are you two doing out here? Astrid, you should be resting.' It was Gwen, rustling through the wet bushes.

The twins turned sharply, dropping the conversation, and each other's hands.

'We were hoping for some privacy?' Jonas said.

Astrid swiftly nudged him in the ribs. 'What's the matter?' she asked, noticing the anxiety etched across Gwen's face – something was wrong. She had to force herself not to immediately run to her side. How ridiculous that she'd never recognized the strength of her emotions before.

'Magnus says that we need to find appropriate clothes for tomorrow morning,' Gwen answered. Her glance darted to one side, as though she couldn't bear to see the expressions on their faces. 'Apparently, we're going with him to the palace.'

23

The Palace

A horse-drawn carriage picked them up from the north-east tower of the palace as the sky grew black and heavy. The driver at the front merely grunted in welcome as they climbed in. Then, with a crack of his whip, the carriage jerked forward and they set off through the great stone wall and into the heart of the palace.

'It's been a long time since I've come through this entrance,' Magnus mused, the four of them squished into the little coach with Gwen beside him, pulling at the collar of the prim white dress she'd been forced into for the occasion.

Jonas would have told her to stop fidgeting – if he weren't doing the very same thing, fretfully tapping his fingers on his grey wool trousers while he ruminated on what might be awaiting them at the palace. Or, rather, *who* might be awaiting them.

He could think of one person in particular, and couldn't tell if he was excited or aghast at the idea he might be seeing the prince with the black heart at his chest.

Whether they liked it or not, Magnus and the Ambassadors had decided it was important that the Magister finally meet the twins in person. Why, though? Jonas had to wonder. Did the Order think them dangerous? Did they not trust their progress? They just had to hope Magnus was right to bring them.

'Have you come here often?' Astrid asked politely. She was unfairly composed. She sat with one leg crossed over the other, wearing a black angora cape tied at the front with a red bow that matched Jonas's shirt and scarf, and a book in her lap on ancient monsters.

'Oh, yes, we were very close with Beatrice's parents.' A wistful look came over their mentor's face. 'They were good friends of the family.'

'What?' Gwen cried. 'Why didn't I know this?'

They reached the upper ward, the carriage coming to a stop at the lawn beneath the keep – the most protected part of the palace, where no one could get in, or, in rare cases, out.

Gwen whistled, taking in the wide expanse as she hopped out of the coach. The twins, on the other hand, felt their stomachs squirm at the expanse of immaculate lawn and neatly trimmed hedges, everything snipped into submission. For Jonas, this was precisely what he feared could be done to them.

'I have a terrible feeling about all this,' he whispered to Astrid.

She nodded in silent agreement, looking out over the tidy rows of snapdragons. 'Do you feel that?'

Jonas leaned into whatever melodies his sister was picking up on. At first, they were barely audible, more like the memory of a sound. But then, hidden under the tamed garden rows, came something pulsing, hard and wild, like a slumbering beast.

'Odd,' Jonas murmured. Maybe everything here wasn't so tame, after all.

Three attendants in hefty wool coats and hats escorted them across the grounds. There was not a Savonnette or Pendragon sigil in sight, a fact that suggested to the twins that most of the palace was likely operated by regular Red Bloods.

When the heavy doors of the building opened to allow entry, Jonas truly began to feel the weight of their situation. Inside was a maze of gilded hallways, where velvet drapes dripped blood-red over plush carpets. The stairwells hung with tapestries and portraits surrounded by panels of gold leaf. All of it was too pretty, too perfect.

Upstairs, they were led to a door along a corridor where the air smelled like roses, and empty suits of armour watched like prison guards.

'We have prepared this room for your stay,' the tallest of the three men announced, opening the door.

'Who's staying?' Gwen said, hands on her hips, refusing to enter.

The attendant continued to stand as still as a mannequin, not even making eye contact. 'The wards of Mr Faymore are to wait here until given further instructions.'

Jonas did not like this, not one bit.

'I would rather they came with me,' Magnus said, his fingers twitching against his cane.

'These are our orders,' the attendant said.

An alarm went off inside Jonas's body. It was too orderly, too militant. It reminded him of the ward at the Saint Peter Institute, of doctors, and medicine, and no escape.

When the twins looked at Magnus, he paused a moment in thought, then turned to them and smiled. 'I will be right back.'

Cutting his eyes at Astrid, Jonas realized that she felt the same as he did – on edge, nervous, distrusting. They'd been separated from Magnus before at Fountains Abbey, and the consequences had been disastrous. And yet, it appeared they once again had no choice.

'Very well,' Astrid sighed, leading the way into the plush, expansive living room. Their temporary, if rather beautiful, prison cell.

The whole room seemed designed for lounging, featuring feather-soft sofas, chaises, butter-yellow leather armchairs and footstools. Even the carpet felt like spring grass under their shoes.

But there were no plants, not even a vase of flowers.

Grey light poured in from a set of bay windows that gifted them a view of the painstakingly manicured gardens, although Jonas couldn't help noticing how the curve of the windowpanes reminded him awfully of a bird cage. A gate-leg table with teapots and elegant, colourful cakes sat in offering like an altar.

'Bribes,' Jonas muttered.

Behind them, the door shut with a menacing *thud*.

'This is ridiculous,' Gwen grumbled.

Jonas stared out of the window. 'Why would they bring us all the way here, just to make us wait?'

Astrid hummed in agreement, falling back into an armchair by Gwen. 'Suspicious.'

Frowning, Gwen stared at her own hands, swallowing down whatever else she might have been about to say.

'What's the matter?' Astrid asked.

Jonas watched them uneasily, the way their bodies moved towards one another. And Gwen, as usual, was entirely oblivious to the influence she had on his sister.

'Tell us,' Astrid pressed.

Pulling at one of her plaits, Gwen bit her lip before asking, 'What if the queen comes to the same conclusion as Ambassador Loupe? What if they decide you two need to be put in their custody? Or they find out about –' she covered her mouth to whisper – 'the Grim being a . . . *possession* . . .? And that some other evil is controlling it all, watching us?'

Astrid gave a thin smile. 'Then we'll burn the whole palace down.'

Jonas knew that there was truth to Astrid's jesting. If they stayed near Gwen, they could not help but follow her every whim – helpless to her powers, even to the detriment of themselves.

He needed to think.

Going to the window, he tried to feel out the Bloom in the gardens beyond, wondering if he might catch another chord of that odd pulsing they'd felt from the earth. He listened intently for a welcome rush of magic, only to find everything muted, out of reach – only trimmed roses and hedges clipped into obedience.

It felt like being blindfolded.

'Someone's coming!' Astrid suddenly announced, and they heard a shuffling and then a knock at the door.

A voice came from the other side of the door: 'Hello?'

Oh god.

The door opened.

'Ah, you *are* here.'

Dressed in a long red button-down and billowing, pleated trousers, Prince Teddy was just as fiendishly beautiful as Jonas had remembered. Only this time, his hair was as scruffy as a family dog, his eyes bleary, as if he'd just woken up.

'What are you doing here?' Jonas cried, rushing over.

'Do you always greet visitors like that?' the Prince replied. 'I wanted you to know that I've been on leave from Fountains Abbey since your little Pledge incident. Over-protective parents and all that – you know how it is.' He paused, taking in their expressions. 'Oh, wait. I guess you don't.' He chuckled awkwardly.

'What do you want?' Astrid asked, her eyes narrowing.

The prince strode into the room, looking around from face to face. 'Actually, I was hoping you three might help me with something. Something . . . mischievous,' he said. 'I know how much you love to get up to no good.' He cut his eyes at Jonas, a smirk playing over his lips.

Wary, the twins and Gwen moved towards one another.

'We're not really allowed to perform any magic around here, you see,' the prince went on, something electric entering his eyes. He was excited. 'But there's a room under the castle I've never been allowed into where my mothers go for any Order- or Bloom-related work. Naturally it's always guarded; no one's allowed in without permission – you can imagine the deal . . . But with you three here, I thought we might devise a plan to sneak in and see what's there.'

Astrid let out a huff, and Jonas knew what she was thinking, because he was thinking it too: if there was any secret room to do with the Order, they had to know what was in there. It could provide clues – or even answers – to the numerous mysteries surrounding Gwen and themselves.

'You're not really considering it, are you?' Gwen said, noticing the look on Jonas's face.

His only reply was to hold out his hand to Astrid, helping her up with her good arm so they could get the whole thing over with.

Astrid turned to Gwen. 'Come with us. We'll look out for each other.'

Gwen deliberated for a moment, tugging at her plaits, but then her shoulders slumped in defeat. 'Fine,' she said flatly.

'Excellent news,' the prince said, grinning from ear to ear. 'This way.' He darted a glance out into the hallway, checking, then led them back through those same opulent corridors, their footsteps creaking on every floorboard.

Luckily, the guards they had seen before had vanished.

Outside, the black clouds in the sky had grown thicker, threatening to burst at any moment. Prince Teddy ushered them in near silence through paths of red roses, beneath trellises, and down steps towards hidden trails between the palace walls. Slowly but surely, the garden began to come undone.

It started with weeds – dandelion stem and thistle, little pockets of unkempt ground that welcomed the twins with a chime of Bloom – but it wasn't until they reached the palace's rear walls, by the overgrown grass beneath the northern tower, that the twins truly heard it at last: that pulsing they'd heard when they'd first arrived. It appeared again, breaking through the surface of trimmed Bloom. With each beat, it whispered:

Follow me, follow me.

'What is that?' Jonas asked, his interest sparking.

'You two *are* special, aren't you?' the prince said, sauntering to a stone wall. He gestured them to crouch, covering his mouth with his index finger as he whispered, 'What you're hearing? It's Ancient Magic.'

He pulled back the lattice-work of vines and buddleia that covered the wall to reveal an entrance to a dark tunnel that seemed to go underneath the palace.

Astrid turned on the prince, suspicion prickling along her shoulders. 'I thought you said it was always guarded?'

Prince Teddy nodded, seeming equally perplexed. 'It usually is . . .' Together, they all stared down the steps, an odd hum of Bloom coaxing them down.

'One of us will have to stay here,' Astrid announced. 'To keep watch.'

'I'll stay,' Gwen offered up quickly. 'This place gives me the creeps.'

Both twins turned to her in unison. Gwen was their compass for all things involving the Grim, the centre of this whole mystery. She couldn't stay behind.

'No, you have to go,' Astrid insisted.

Gwen scrunched up her nose.

'How about I stay?' the prince offered instead.

They all stared at him now.

'But I thought you wanted to see what was in there?' Astrid questioned.

Jonas agreed – it was certainly suspicious.

'I just want to know what's down there.' Prince Teddy rolled his eyes as if they were all being extremely difficult. 'OK, here's what we'll do. You two go.' He pointed to Astrid and Gwen. 'And Jonas and I will stand guard.'

The twins exchanged a glance – they weren't entirely convinced by this plan, but, like the prince, they needed to know what was down there. The Bloom was calling them.

'Does that work for you all?' the prince asked expectantly.

'I'm not sure –' But Jonas was interrupted.

'I think that's an excellent idea.' Astrid chuckled, something devilish playing across her face, which she aimed at Jonas. Next to her, Gwen snickered.

Scowling at his sister and Gwen, Jonas crossed his arms. He was going to murder them both.

'Fine,' he conceded. 'You two go ahead, we'll stay here.'

The prince grinned, an utterly diabolical expression. 'Off you go, then. Let me know what you find.'

This was it, then.

Hesitating, Jonas grabbed Astrid's hand before she went down, pulling her closer. 'We need to find answers,' Jonas whispered, nodding at Gwen. 'No matter what they are.'

Astrid squeezed his hand. 'I know.' Without another word, she dropped her grip, then she and Gwen shared a final glance before stepping down into the hidden depths of the palace, leaving Jonas alone with his troubled mood, and an equally troublesome prince.

24

Closing In

The tunnel was much like the one under Fountains Abbey – cold and dark. Astrid could only hope that they wouldn't find anything on the other side as awful as the laboratory had been.

Unlike the abbey, the walls of this tunnel weren't bare. They were decorated with jagged mosaics and gems that peered at them like curious eyes, illuminated only by the fire that Astrid cradled in her hands – summoned with her own Bloom.

'This place makes me uneasy,' Gwen muttered as the daylight receded behind them.

Astrid turned, a roguish smile playing on her lips. 'I can protect you, remember.'

Gwen stared back at her, and Astrid's breath caught, seeing the glittering molten brown of Gwen's eyes in the firelight.

'How are you always so confident?' she asked Astrid, in a rare moment of honesty.

It was the first time Astrid had been alone with Gwen since their night at Fountains Abbey and to her, Gwen was still a precious thing, someone to protect, a purpose given to her by the earth – only now that calling was clearer, a polished diamond.

'The earth guides me,' Astrid said.

Gwen scrunched up her nose. 'But how can you trust it? When so many bad things keep happening?'

Astrid could imagine exactly what her friend was thinking of – the Kelpie, the Strix, Astrid's blood spilling from her injured shoulder.

'Because it led me to you.'

She didn't give Gwen a chance to reply.

'We're here.'

As they approached the end of the tunnel, the air was cold enough to ice their breath. Before them was the entrance to some sort of hall lit by blue light.

Holding their breath, Astrid and Gwen peered through at the large room, the thumping magic of this ancient space cresting like the rising call of a battalion, the Bloom here so potent as to be dizzying. Drenched in the milky-blue flame of several torches, statues were carved into the hall's walls. They looked like ancient rulers, deities. Astrid recognized some of them – Empress Matilda with rubies for eyes, and there, facing the door, King Arthur himself, a sword resting beneath his hip.

'It's a temple,' Astrid said, eyes wide as she let the flame burn out in her hand. 'These vines . . .' She ran her hands along a wall. 'They're older than the palace bricks.'

Blood-red ivy and green moss blanketed each wall and monument, sighing dream clouds into the air.

'What does this mean?' Gwen asked, her voice hushed.

'It means this place is old,' Astrid explained. 'Older than history.'

She knew, because she could hear it, a growing chorus of

murmurs and whispers. It tugged at her soul, pulling her further into the room, voices from a distant past.

'I feel weird,' Gwen said, her voice shaking. 'My arms!' She stumbled back as she stared at her skin.

Astrid's eyes lit up. It was just as she'd seen in the lab under Fountains Abbey when they'd found the silver box that contained the missing pages. Gwen's skin was covered in gooseflesh.

'It's OK,' Astrid said. 'It's the Bloom. It's trying to show us something.'

What though?

'Listen to it,' Astrid purred, keeping her voice calm. 'Where is it leading you?'

Swallowing, Gwen answered slowly, pointing towards an altar on the other side of the room. Astrid approached the platform, the whole aged thing shimmering with silver. She crouched, tracing her fingers over the engravings hidden beneath mountains of ivy – a story carved into precious metal.

'Come over here,' she said to Gwen, but she could sense her hesitating.

'Astrid, I don't like this.' Her voice sounded small.

'Come on, Gwen.' Turning, Astrid held her friend's gaze. 'You have to face this.'

Reluctantly, Gwen came to her side, and the two of them looked over the etchings. One section caught Astrid's attention.

'It's a dragon,' Gwen said, noticing it at the same time. Her fingertips traced the grooves.

It was an evil thing, with snarling jaws and malevolent eyes. Beneath its claws were the severed bodies of men. Astrid was sure she had seen this dragon before. She'd seen it in the book of Cursed Melodies.

She heard the whispers grow again, voices of the earth that felt as ancient as the stars. She wanted to reach out, to compel the ivy to move so she might see more of this strange tale – except it wasn't *her* they wanted.

'Touch it,' Astrid told Gwen, her voice breathy with Bloom.

Gwen let out a long breath, her body going still.

'OK,' she said, all the wavers in her voice gone now. 'I'm going to do what you do. I'm going to let the earth guide me.'

Ever so carefully, she placed her hands amongst the ivy.

The sensation in Astrid was immediate, the hiss of Bloom now a chorus of murmurs, of ancient, indecipherable words rising to that unyielding power that lay buried inside Gwen – a power she could not even see in herself.

As Gwen caressed the crimson body of ivy, as the murmurs grew into a choir, the leaves shook and rustled, snaking away to reveal the story beneath.

The story they'd come here for.

The dragon did not stand alone. There was a man at his side, a crown glowing above his head. In his hand was a sword, one that pierced the dragon straight through, blood spilling. And the sword – they knew it. They'd seen it before. A silver pansy was carved into the hilt – just like the one in the book of Cursed Melodies. From the very pages Gwen's magic had brought back to life.

Only, it didn't stop there. The vines kept moving.

'Oh no.' Astrid spun round, seeing what she'd missed in being so entranced by the engravings. The moss, the ivy, the roots – they were spreading out over every inch of the temple, covering the door and any path out. They were being caged.

'Stop!' Astrid called out, flexing her hands, but the earth would not listen. Instead, the Bloom seemed to *hiss*, like a feral creature, or . . . Astrid leaned in, listening. The sound was urgent and fiery, like a mother protecting her young.

But what was it protecting?

'What's going on? *Argh!*' Gwen shouted, panicking as a vine snaked over her feet.

With hardly a moment to think, Astrid grabbed Gwen's hand and ran to the doorway, except there was hardly a doorway left, the roots knitting themselves together to block their path.

'Why is it doing this?' Gwen shouted, desperately pulling at the thicket.

But Astrid had no answer. Instead, all she could hear was the alarm call of Bloom rising again, warning her that something was coming.

No, not something – someone.

'It can't be,' Gwen gasped, her face dropping at the sound.

Eyes darting around the room, Astrid wondered if perhaps the vines had been trying to hide them. To protect them from what was currently approaching.

There was a quick shout and call from the tunnel beyond, and Astrid had only a split second to push Gwen out of the way, the two of them tumbling to the floor just as the vines covering the door were set alight in a blaze of blue-and-green flame.

'What have you done?' a voice screeched through the hall. A voice they recognized.

Lifting her head, Astrid saw them all on the other side of the flame-lined doorway, the vines hissing and screaming as they burned to the floor under each new spell.

Charred and dying, the earth recoiled, leaving the doorway open again. And there they were – Magnus Faymore and a stampede of Ambassadors, each of them staring, wide-eyed and gaping at the frenzy of vines and moss and roots that had taken over the temple.

'This . . .' came the shrill voice of Ambassador Loupe, her face twisted as though she'd sucked on a lemon as she gestured to the mess of leaves that now covered every inch of the temple. 'This is precisely why they need to be locked away!'

Jonas had been in many unpleasant situations in his life – therapy sessions with patronizing counsellors, being locked up in a room away from the world, not to mention fighting monsters and nearly drowning. But he truly believed he'd never been in a situation as horribly awkward as the one he was in now.

Sitting cross-legged on the damp grass, Prince Teddy stared up at the sky, singing. Worst of all, his voice sounded utterly beautiful.

'Would you stop that?' Jonas muttered. 'I'm trying to listen out for any warnings from the earth.'

The prince lit up at this, staring at Jonas. 'You can do that?'

Jonas blocked him out, trying again to hear the wild Bloom, and trying his best to ignore the near unbearable pull from the tunnel beneath them.

Something was going on down there – something that the earth wanted him to see. But instead, he was stuck babysitting the prince.

With the sun setting low, the palace cast long shadows over the overgrown trellises and weed-tangled gates.

Through the gap in the fencing Jonas could see the lamps in the main garden coming to life.

'You know,' Prince Teddy began, leaning back in the grass. 'All the Pledges at Fountains Abbey heard about what you two did to Loupe.'

'Sorry to disappoint,' Jonas said, pulling up the memory, 'but that was all Astrid.'

'Was it?' Prince Teddy's smile faltered, but then he pushed on. 'Either way, it's terribly exciting what you two can do.'

Huffing, Jonas turned away to put his focus back on the melodic Bloom, only to hear Prince Teddy laughing again – and the sound was mocking this time.

'Why are you so annoyed by me?' the prince asked.

Jonas knew he shouldn't answer. He had far more important details to consider – his sister down in the tunnel, and the fate of the world for that matter. Yet, like an itch under the skin, there was something about the prince that made him impossible to ignore.

'If you must know,' he began, 'I find you arrogant, meddlesome and untrustworthy.'

The prince grinned. 'Is that all?'

Singing to himself again, Prince Teddy reached for the front of his shirt, and began to flick his black-heart lighter.

'It's funny, actually, I was so delighted when I found you spying,' he mused, the little heart clinking over and over in his hand. 'It was thrilling. Coming face-to-face with the greatest mystery the Bloom Blooded world had seen in centuries.' Jonas found his body stilling. The prince sounded as though he was conjuring a fond memory. 'Finding you up to no good like that – I knew immediately you were everything I'd dreamed you'd be.'

Dreamed I'd be? There it was again. He wasn't talking about Astrid, not them as twins, just Jonas. On his own.

Jonas opened his mouth, but before he could get a word out, Prince Teddy jumped to his feet, coming right up to Jonas, the lighter still in his hand. He waved it about teasingly.

'I see you staring at this, you know,' he said, something devious entering his dark eyes.

'Excuse me?'

'My lighter. There's a reason I bring it everywhere,' the prince reiterated. 'It's special.'

Jonas found himself leaning forward for a better look. 'How so?'

'I knew that would catch your interest.' The prince laughed, eyes sparkling as he carefully unclasped the lighter from round his neck. 'Come here, I'll show you.'

In one fluid motion, he grabbed Jonas's wrist, spinning him round until the prince stood behind his back.

'Hey, what are you –'

'Oh hush, just trust me.'

Jonas most certainly did not trust him, and did not like being told what to do, and yet, when the prince's fingers delicately placed the black heart in Jonas's hand, and when those same hands unwrapped the scarf from round Jonas's neck and tied it over his eyes. Jonas, for reasons he could not fathom, let him.

'OK,' the prince said, leaves rustling as he stepped away. Jonas felt alone and compromised. 'Now you're going to hold the lighter out, and walk towards wherever I am.' His voice darted around Jonas; the prince was moving from place to place.

It wasn't much of a game though, because Jonas could just ask . . .

'And you can't ask the grass,' the prince called. 'That's cheating.'

'Well then how am I supposed to . . .?'

'Just try it! It's a game, that's all!'

Not much of one. But what could he do? Refuse and annoy the prince, making him leave – possibly alerting the palace to the fact that Astrid and Gwen were down there somewhere, trying to find out the Order's secrets? Maybe he needed to be more like Astrid. Maybe he needed to trust more. What if . . . what if he could trust the prince?

Then he felt it.

No, he heard it.

A gentle push and pull like waves on the shore. Except there was no shore here.

He followed it, taking one step, and then another. The lighter in his hand, his own instincts, they knew exactly where to take him. And on the tenth step, he bumped right into his target.

Strong hands came out to steady his shoulders, then slowly, like waking into a dream, the prince removed his blindfold. He was staring right down at him, heavy lashes over charcoal eyes.

'That's incredible,' Jonas breathed, his hand coming to Teddy's to give his black heart back. 'How did you do it?'

Prince Teddy smiled again, a real smile this time, as rare and electrifying as an eclipse.

'I spent a whole year working on this charm,' he said. 'It's a mix of the Push, Pull and Bind melodies, and took an unreasonable amount of steeping in moonlight and sea tides.'

Charmed by this, Jonas leaned forward ever so slightly, the black heart now resting between their hands.

'It's tied to whoever possesses it, so . . .' A spark of mischief entered the prince's eyes again. 'Jonas, I gift it to you.'

Entranced, Jonas could hardly move as the prince leaned over him and began to clasp the chain round his neck.

As Teddy worked, Jonas took in every inch of him up close, how the acne scarring on his jaw made little constellations, the shifting colours of his skin catching the light, and the scent of his cologne.

'Good lord,' Jonas breathed, nearly laughing to himself. 'You really are as charming as they say.'

Jonas wondered what he should do next, reluctant to pull away, except, as he looked up into Teddy's eyes, something else passed over them, something that quickly pulled him out of the fantasy – because Prince Teddy looked guilty.

'Jonas,' he stumbled, 'I should have told you . . .'

Face contorting into a scowl, Jonas felt the Bloom from the earth begin to hiss, and it was only then he realized he'd been entirely ignoring the earth around him in his distraction.

'What have you done?' Jonas growled, pulling away.

But the prince did not need to answer, because Jonas heard it, voices closing in on them, the grass around him shrieking a warning.

'Custodian Faymore, would you please calm down!' he heard someone shout, and then five silhouettes charged round the side of the palace.

It was Ambassador Loupe with an attendant, Princess Alice, Sister Seraphina and finally – at the head of the charge – Magnus Faymore.

'Jonas! Where are your sister and Gwen?' he demanded, his voice firm. 'We're cutting this trip short.'

'Magnus, please listen to us,' Princess Alice insisted, holding her skirts and trotting to keep up. 'Perhaps Harriet is right.'

The game was up. There was nothing Jonas could do but gesture towards the entrance to the tunnel under the castle. 'This way, sir.'

The prince tried to reach for him, but instinctively Jonas pulled away.

With the rest of them trailing behind, Magnus led them down under the palace, Harriet following behind, calling out to them to stop.

'Magnus, for goodness' sake, you must be reasonable!'

Jonas walked through the dark tunnel speedily, trying to keep up with the rest of Magnus's entourage.

'What on earth?' Jonas paused in his footing, listening to the strange hisses of Bloom, the earth poised, fearful and protective.

Then they saw it, in the distance, a wriggling mass of vines and moss, undulating over a huge doorway. They were being blocked out.

'Mother Mary!' Princess Alice gasped, her mouth falling open at the sight, the endless, towering wall of earth.

Magnus and the Ambassadors stood for a moment, astonished. Then, collecting herself, Ambassador Loupe marched forward and sang a furious melody of Fire, the spell blasting out in a fireball that set alight the whole earthen barricade.

Jonas could only watch, mesmerized, as the charred remains of the vines fell away to reveal behind them an underground temple room – and there, in the centre of it, hunkered on the floor, were Astrid and Gwen.

'This . . .' Ambassador Loupe shrieked, her red hair

poking out of its bun in sharp points. 'This is precisely why they need to be locked away!'

Looking around the temple, it was clear something utterly strange had occurred. Every inch of the space was covered in moss and vines, all of it still moving, still pulsing like a heartbeat.

Sister Seraphina was the only one who remained calm in the face of it all, loitering at the doorway, analysing every leaf and root.

'What happened here?' Magnus asked them calmly, his voice low and measured as he helped Gwen and Astrid to their feet.

'This temple . . .' Astrid whispered, her eyes flitting about the hall like she was trying to solve a puzzle. Her gaze landed on Gwen. 'It was protecting something.'

'What's going on?' Gwen demanded, staring down the wall of Ambassadors.

'I think we've been deceived,' Jonas said, scowling at the prince as he came in at the end of the troupe.

The prince faltered at the doorway, gasping at the sight in front of him, the utter chaos Astrid had apparently unleashed.

Standing in front of them and holding out her arms, Princess Alice made them stop near the entrance to the temple.

'After careful consideration, and . . . the unusual current events . . .' Her voice wavered, gaze flitting nervously around the temple at all the vines still wriggling in the corners of their vision. 'Harriet has suggested that it is in the best interests of the young Pledges to be quarantined here at the palace where we may study and assist you until we understand what is causing the Grim, and why you seem to be a beacon for it.'

That, to Jonas, was simply unacceptable.

'You!' Jonas turned on the prince. 'You were trying to distract us.' The prince hadn't wanted them to find out the Order's secrets at all. He'd just been keeping them hidden away from Magnus.

Furious, Jonas could hardly believe how foolish he'd been when it was all so plainly obvious. The prince's perfectly timed arrival, the lack of guards at the palace and the tunnel entrance, none of it had been a coincidence.

'I was only told to keep you entertained and far away from them,' he tried to reason, and Jonas felt extreme satisfaction at seeing him so flustered. 'I didn't know that's what they were discussing.'

Jonas simply turned away, hardly able to look him in the face, the black heart now heavy against his chest. This was the reminder he'd needed, that he could not trust anyone but Astrid. It was them against the world, forever.

Ambassador Loupe cleared her throat. 'Magnus.' She made his name sound like poison. 'These children are the most valuable clues we've ever had to what is happening with the Grim. Rupert left them that part of the Savonnette for a reason and their power is unprecedented . . . and frightening. We cannot let an asset like that be compromised.'

Magnus shouted out his reply: 'They are not *assets*!'

Harriet stumbled back from the force of his response.

'They are talented individuals who have been thrown into this against their will and have just as much of a right to their freedom as everyone else.'

At last. At last someone was talking some sense. But before anyone could respond, there was a sound from above and Lapis, Sister Seraphina's blue horned owl, circled the temple, before swooping to land on Seraphina's shoulder. It must have followed her down here.

'Now, if everyone will calm down,' Seraphina croaked. 'I'd like to remind you all that we cannot keep these young people here without direct clearance from the Magister – who, it appears, is not here because she has once again been called away to the Shadow Library due to another magical creature disturbance.' She stared around the temple, daring anyone to contradict her.

'I trust Magnus, as I have known him for many, many years. So, as a compromise, I suggest we allow these two Pledges to go back with Magnus. I suggest we instigate a territorial lockdown for their own benefit.'

Lockdown. The twins felt the word like a death sentence.

'The lockdown in question will require the twins to be quarantined inside Faymore Manor at all times. After seven days, when the Magister returns, if no major progress has been made in solving their link to the Grim, or the cause of all these magical anomalies, then we shall have to consider other measures. Are we all in agreement?'

Jonas felt his throat closing up. Seven days? It wasn't enough time.

Magnus looked to Astrid and Jonas, and gave a small nod. It was time for them to decide. At least they were given that privilege.

Jonas leaned over to whisper in his sister's ear.

'You promised.'

She nodded, her expression blank, even as he knew she must be in turmoil . . .

They would not be trapped again. They knew what they had to do.

'We agree to your terms,' Astrid began, her voice clear and decisive. 'I think we'd all gladly take such deplorable measures over spending another second here.'

'They are Pledges to the Order!' Ambassador Loupe cried, all but flapping like a bird. 'They should follow *our* commands.'

'Then, for the time being, it's agreed,' Princess Alice announced, stepping to the side to allow them all to leave. 'We will bring the matter to the Magister once she returns.'

Magnus placed a hand over his chest, dipping his head in clear relief. Then he turned to the trio.

'I am sorry. Now –' he faced the rest of the group – 'we're going home.'

With quiet dignity, the four of them left the ancient temple, and Jonas found his mind to be suddenly troubled. It was not the verdict that troubled him, nor was it the growing mystery. No, Jonas had become fixated on a word Magnus had spoken; this passing utterance could not be true – or more so, he thought, it *must* not be true.

Faymore Manor was not their home, and it was time for them to leave.

25
Cages

The rules were put into practice that very same night, with new wards pitted into the grounds of Faymore Manor, forming the parameters of their prison. The twins locked themselves away in their room, not even coming down for breakfast or lunch the next day, leaving Gwen to wonder how, if at all, she could fix this.

'So the plants tried to trap you?' Jan asked, stirring a spoonful of charmed honey into a cup with long, well-manicured fingers. She was standing at the kitchen table, assisting Elijah with various bottles and cakes and tea, all enchanted with Bloom to help with the next stage of healing Thomas's broken bones. 'I can't stand the thought of it,' she added, worrying a loose thread on her knitted sweater.

'And they think the twins caused it?' Thomas offered, wincing as he took a sip of the tea, his bones mending themselves with magic.

Slumped against the table like a wilting flower, Gwen listened passively. She couldn't get it out of her head – that unbearable pull of Bloom as Astrid had led her to the metal engraving with its heroic scene. She saw the dragon again in her mind, its twisted face a vision of incomprehensible evil, a thing of discord and mayhem.

And just as Gwen had thought that was all, the room had tried to trap them inside – but why? What were the vines trying to protect?

The hairs on her arms stood on end.

'I do hope they know they're not in trouble.' Elijah pushed a tray across the table, filled with bread and cheese and chopped fruit. He was smiling, big cheeks round as peaches, but even through his glasses Gwen could see he was worried. 'We missed them at lunch, and breakfast, actually . . .' His voice trailed off. 'Hopefully, we will hear from the Magister soon. Or . . . make some miraculous discovery before it's too late.'

'Still though . . .' Jan swallowed, distracting herself by grabbing a knife to cut up some cake. 'So many scary things have happened since they arrived.'

A spark of anger had Gwen jolting upright, hardly believing her sister's words. 'You can't say things like that,' she demanded, a fire burning in her throat. 'You have no idea what you're talking about.'

As if to make a point, Jan filled Thomas's teacup with more healing tea, drawing Gwen's eyes back to the sling round his shoulders.

'We're just saying,' Thomas said, pushing a curl out of his eyes, 'maybe they really are dangerous.'

Gaping like a fish, Gwen couldn't find any words. Everything was upside down.

They had it all wrong. It wasn't the twins. All of this was *her* fault, and the twins were taking the blame.

'Gwenny,' Jan sighed, reaching out to stroke one of Gwen's plaits like she used to when they were kids. 'We just don't want anyone else getting hurt.'

Gwen's heart thudded painfully in her chest, and she

swallowed hard. Suddenly her blouse felt too tight, and she was sure that the house had begun to shrink around her, the air growing thick and stale.

Jan was right: people were getting hurt. Everyone was getting hurt because of her.

'Now, now, you lot,' Elijah interrupted. 'Gwen, would you take these up to the twins?'

Now it was Gwen's turn to wince. 'It's not their fault,' she grumbled under her breath, grabbing the tray and storming off. *It's mine*.

Marching up the stairs, she paused, juggling the tray in one hand, with the other in a fist at the twins' door. They'd put up a holly wreath, the little red berries watching her like beady eyes, and beyond, she could hear whispering and – worst of all – the sound of her own name.

Gwen held the tray with both hands and kicked the door open.

'What are you –' Gwen froze, nearly dropping the whole tea set, because sprawled over every inch of the room were books. They were everywhere. Dangling from the ceiling, held open by vines, plastered to the wall by moss, and the twins themselves straddled a trapeze of ivy, gazing up at one book in particular, held open against the ceiling.

It flooded her mind with memories of what they could do, how deadly they could be with the flick of their wrists and, most of all, how they so often wielded that power for her sake.

Gwen glanced up at the book on the celling, guessing the title before she even saw it. *The Cursed Melodies*.

'You know you're really supposed to knock first,' Astrid said, craning to look down at Gwen so that her hair, as if made of silk, spilled over her shoulder. She looked like an angel.

282

Gwen tiptoed over the mess of flora, nearly tripping when Buttonbug darted out from under Astrid's bed to coil round her ankles.

'What are you two doing?' She swept away a pile of leaves to lay down the tray. 'Everyone's worrying about you.'

'We're reading,' Astrid said.

Jonas rolled his eyes. 'Obviously.'

With the window open, the grey dusk drenched their hair silver. Gwen's eyes lingered on Astrid as she settled like a falling leaf on to the floor in front of Gwen. She was reminded of when Astrid had led her into the palace's underground temple, the feel of Astrid, cool skin against hers, and that devotion in her eyes.

She swallowed the thought back by stealing a slice of cake.

'What are you looking for?'

Sitting on the windowsill, Jonas chuckled to himself.

'We're not sure you'll approve, but we've been trying to find out about the images on the engraving in the temple.'

Gwen did not approve, but not for the reasons they thought. Once again, they were throwing themselves into the mystery, researching stuff that they didn't need to concern themselves with . . . all for Gwen's sake.

With a brief whistle, Jonas had one of the plants bring the book of Cursed Melodies to Gwen. She heard the whispers then, louder now, reaching towards her, those dark fingers of melody hissing from the paper as the open pages were deposited in her lap.

It almost sighed as it settled. Like a lost pet that had been searching for its master.

From the floor, Buttonbug sneezed, shaking her fluffy head and whiskers before running back under the bed. It seemed she too would rather be far away from the book, and yet Gwen found she couldn't pull her eyes from the pages.

There it was, the sword they'd seen etched on the altar in the temple, the silver pansy on the hilt. But it wasn't the sword that alarmed Gwen, it was the illustrations surrounding it. Most of the pages were torn or missing, but what remained showed strange and terrible monsters. Some in particular that took her breath away.

Dragons.

Looking at the things set a festering lump of dread into her belly, and Gwen quickly pushed the book away.

'Why would the Grim have anything to do with a bunch of old dragons?' she huffed, trying to swallow her fear.

'One dragon, specifically,' Jonas corrected, pointing at the same swirls of dragon scales that she and Gwen had seen etched into the temple.

Astrid sighed, a dreamy sound. 'We've looked through mountains of books on ancient monsters and deities,' she said, twirling her fingers through a vine. 'Almost every monster drawn in the book of Cursed Melodies can be found mentioned in an encyclopaedia or essay, but not that one. That dragon. There's nothing at all.'

Jonas frowned at the books. 'It's as if someone has buried the information. Or hidden it.'

'Who would even have the power to do that?' Gwen demanded, trying to ignore the feeling of dread bubbling up in her throat. 'This is . . . this is all too much.'

Astrid frowned. 'We just think it could be important information for you to know. As far as the Order goes, you can't trust anyone.' Her eyes almost seemed pleading for a moment. 'We're just trying to help.'

Gwen's lips twitched. 'Well, I don't want your help.'

'But –'

'No, no *buts*; none of this makes a difference.' She felt sick. None of it made sense. How could she be so important when she had always been so insignificant? Untalented. Cursed. 'I can't do this!' she spat out. 'You two, you're prodigies!' She threw her arms out to the room. 'Look at all of this! You can summon the Bloom whenever you want, but I'm just . . . I'm just . . . cursed.' She hid her face in her hands. 'My magic does nothing but cause problems for everyone. So, whatever all this is, just stop it. I don't want you helping me. I don't . . .' Her eyes burned. She thought of Thomas's injury, of Astrid's bleeding back, of her parents, and Rupert, and everyone who'd suffered because of this thing she was connected to. 'I don't . . . I just don't want to bring anyone any more trouble.'

'Gwen, we –'

But she wouldn't let Astrid finish.

'I don't want it.' Her voice cracked, and for one frustrating moment she worried she was going to cry. 'Please.'

A voice called up the stairs.

'Gwen, Astrid, Jonas?' It was Elijah. 'Magnus has news. Come down to the parlour, please.'

Turning on her heel before they could say another word, Gwen stormed out, knowing deep down that if it came to it, she would have to tell the Order it was always her. Even if that meant being locked away forever.

The door slammed shut again, the ensuing silence loud enough to ring in Astrid's ears. Once her breath had evened out, she turned to her brother.

'Do you think she noticed?'

Jonas shook his head, then checked beneath the bed.

'Doubtful.'

There, hidden away, were two large camping packs full of things they'd stolen: clothes, food supplies, money, sleeping bags and trinkets to sell. Everything they would need.

'I'm sorry it all turned out like this,' Jonas said, fiddling with the split pendant at his throat. There was something else there too, a new piece of jewellery hidden under his white shirt. It was odd, but Astrid had other things to focus on right then. Like how they would never solve the mystery of Gwen and the Grim. And of course, there was the matter of Astrid's feelings for their friend.

'You're still not sure?' he asked, prompting her towards the truth.

Astrid knew he could feel her dread as though it was his own, and when he came to lie back with her on the bed, the two nestled together staring up at the ceiling as they used to in their bunk.

'This isn't our home,' Jonas said.

The Bloom around them shimmered in protest.

Twisting her hands through a vine, Astrid hummed until it curled through her fingers, caressing the leaves.

'This power. All of this,' she said, voice measured. 'We would know nothing of it if not for her.'

Astrid could feel the prickle of Jonas's words before he even spoke them. 'We would have found it some other way. Eventually.'

Astrid turned to face him on the pillow just as he turned to look back at her. A near perfect reflection. The same blonde hair and delicate complexion, same glacial eyes now darkened in the same frown.

And yet, for the first time in their lives, they were finding details that didn't match.

'Why would you deny it?' she whispered. 'Since when do you turn away from the truth?'

Now Jonas sat up, curling his knees to his chest. 'Because our freedom is at stake.' He'd said it before, and he'd say it again. He'd been saying it all this time. They were prisoners. 'The Faymore Cluster might do things differently from the rest of the Order, but they're still under their thumb. This was never our home. It was an escape, but one that's working against us now. We can't stay here.'

The flora bristled at his words. It seemed, Astrid realized, that everyone was in a bad mood.

'I know, this was always the plan,' Astrid said, leaning into his shoulder. 'If we ever felt trapped again, we would leave.' She took a deep breath before continuing, knowing that Jonas would not like it. 'I just think it's worth considering that if we are so tortured by our protective instincts for Gwen, so wound up in the mystery of her, then we should . . . take her with us.'

Jonas's body turned rigid. 'You heard her,' he said eventually. 'She doesn't want it. Not her destiny, not our help, not anything. We'd be doing her a favour if we left.'

'But would we be doing a favour to ourselves,' she said, her voice serious now. 'I had a realization in that temple.' She held the memory like a light in the dark. 'When I saw Gwen in the temple . . . The way she looked at everything. She does care, Jonas. She does. But she's too scared to admit it. We could help.' Gwen meant something. Something bigger than the two of them. 'I think we've had it wrong this whole time, Jonas,' she said, lifting her head to look into his eyes. 'We're not here to protect her, but to help her unlock her destiny. We're meant to serve her.'

Jonas's eyes went wide, the revelation sparking inside

him, and Astrid knew that deep down he felt it too – the truth, as undeniable as the turning of the seasons. This was their purpose.

'Jonas,' she hummed, 'she's in this cage just as much as we are.'

This, unfortunately, was the wrong thing to say. He turned so fast that Astrid nearly toppled over, only for him to grab her by the shoulders.

'Don't you get it?' He was frantic, almost afraid. 'She *is* the cage.'

'Jonas, I –'

He refused to let her finish; the floodgates now opened. 'This effect she has on us, the pull she has on our power, we're trapped by it,' he hissed, his voice but a whisper, like he was scared by the truth of it. 'But we can't let anything jeopardize our freedom.' He stopped to gently trace his fingers along her still healing shoulder. 'Or our safety. This is how it's always been. Forget our fate, or this ridiculous calling: it's me and you against the world.' Beseeching her, Jonas held out his hand for her to hold, the way they always had, but now his fingers trembled.

'You promised.'

That she had. Sighing, Astrid put her palm in his, warm and familiar, and squeezed. The relief that flooded over him was enough to set her mind at ease, if just for a moment. 'Come on,' she said, pulling him up. 'We should head downstairs before anyone gets suspicious.'

Together, they made their way to the door, the two of them lingering under the trellis over the frame where the pearl succulents hung like a string of tears. The Bloom was still ringing in protest, to which Jonas crossed his arms and glowered.

'Yeah, yeah,' he mumbled.

As they headed down the stairs, Astrid could not help thinking that he was behaving an awful lot like Gwen.

When they reached the parlour, Elijah was so busy making sure Thomas, Jan and Gwen all had a warm drink and a comfortable seat near the fire that he hadn't noticed their tardiness.

'Oh wonderful, you're here,' he said, practically falling over himself to welcome them, pushing his glasses back up his nose where they'd drifted down. 'Please have a seat; I've got blankets and tea, and, well, we'll be having cottage pie for dinner after, if you want to join?'

Behind Elijah, sitting with her arms crossed and her sights trained on the darkness outside, Gwen did not so much as look at them – although it appeared that it was taking all her willpower not to.

'Thank you, Elijah,' Astrid said. 'We're OK for now.' Frankly, the whole domestic scene was making Astrid squirm, this time not from the novelty but from the thick sludge of guilt that threatened to choke her.

Magnus, thankfully, chose that moment to arrive, sweeping into the room with Lorelei, both of them in thick cloaks and their hair a little glossy from the growing mist outside. 'Thank you for all joining us.'

Jonas and Astrid squirmed in their seats, feeling that the words were directed at them.

'What's going on?' Jan asked, unable to hide her nerves.

'A letter has arrived with important news.' Magnus helped himself to some tea, smiling and relaxed as usual. 'The Magister has returned, and she's requested our immediate presence, to reassess the situation.'

'That's good, right?' Thomas offered, smiling encouragingly.

From the doorway, Lorelei let out a thick laugh, earning a scowl from her cousin. She said, 'Well, to put it this way, Magnus and I think it would be best if we went up on our own.'

'In case they might want to keep us there.' Jonas said the words to Magnus, but he was looking at Astrid, his point abundantly clear.

'Quite,' Magnus agreed, taking a small bite of cake. 'We will be leaving now, and likely won't be back until tomorrow night.'

'What?' Gwen squawked from her corner. 'Now?'

While the room turned to Gwen, Jonas ever so subtly squeezed Astrid's hand.

Fate was funny like that, Astrid thought, in that it so often loved to make decisions for you. With Magnus and Lorelei gone, this would be their perfect opportunity to slink away unnoticed.

'We'll be back as fast as we can,' Magnus reassured Gwen.

Lorelei nodded, already dusting herself off in preparation to head out into the night once more. 'While we're gone, none of you is to take a single step outside the new wards I've placed around the grounds,' she instructed, making room for Magnus as he headed to the door. 'Is that understood?'

They all nodded, but Astrid could not help noticing how Gwen seemed to shrink in on herself. In truth, she could hardly stand to look at Gwen, as even the shape of her silhouette was a hypnotic tether that threatened to bind Astrid to her side. The entire situation was becoming unbearable, yet Astrid was sure of one thing: the twins had never felt this way when they'd run away before.

'We'll see you all tomorrow,' Magnus said, smiling with great affection at them. Pausing to give his husband a brief kiss on the forehead, he then made his way back out to the front door, where he hummed a quick melody to a lantern until it burned to life in his hand.

The twins watched them through the window, Astrid swallowing down every thought bubbling up inside her.

Magnus carried the lantern out into the woods, he and Lorelei heading down and down the dark trail, the little orange light flickering smaller and smaller.

Astrid held on to it for as long as she could, finding great discomfort in the realization that this would be the last time she'd ever see Magnus Faymore.

26

Spirited Away

Scritch, scritch, scritch.

Gwen awoke abruptly, emerging from the throes of a bad dream. Someone or some*thing* was scratching.

'Wha–'

Gwen's breath caught short.

Throwing off her quilt, she marched over to her bedroom door, pushing the hair out of her eyes.

'What are you doing here?' she hissed at Buttonbug, who promptly flew right into her arms, flapping wildly. 'Hey, stop that! Did the twins kick you out?'

Buttonbug gave a panicked chirp and set off down the stairs. She was clearly distraught – something was wrong.

Her pulse pounding, Gwen ran to follow the little cat creature.

Buttonbug hovered beside the main door to the stable house, little claws performing the same frantic scratching they had done on Gwen's bedroom door. Gwen's hand moved towards the doorknob, and she peered out at the midnight world through the little glass window. Everything was drenched in black, other than the amber clouds that drifted idly past a bloated moon.

'Wait a second,' Gwen whispered, running to the boot room to quickly don some shoes and a coat, then she returned and slowly opened the door.

Outside, the air was thick with haze, wisps of fog curling yellow in the slow flashes of moonlight. Gwen looked down, the wards along the parameters of the woods taunting her.

Buttonbug bolted past her and into the mist, vanishing beyond the boundary.

'Wait!' Gwen hissed, her voice melting against the distant crash of waves. Gripping the cuffs of her coat, she looked back over her shoulder at the stable house, hopping from foot to foot from the cold and nerves.

Why, she wondered, did everything always seem to happen to her?

On second thoughts, she decided that she absolutely did not want to answer such a question.

'Damn it.' Gwen ignored the way her heart jackhammered as she took off after Buttonbug. Her lungs squeezed as she crossed the wards. She was exposed.

She followed the path down to the stables, muttering into the silence, everything so eerily quiet that her own breath and the grass beneath her feet sounded out an entire symphony.

'Buttonbug!' she called softly. 'What –'

Stopping abruptly, Gwen listened out as a horse began to neigh and whinny from inside the stables. She hunkered down, shuffling closer to the wet scent of muck and hay before quickly ducking behind the swinging door where a pool of lamplight flickered and the sound of voices began to grow. Someone was inside.

Not just someone – the twins.

'Go back home, you silly thing,' she heard Astrid's voice

say, and for a split second, Gwen thought they were talking to her.

'Buttonbug, for goodness' sake!' Jonas snapped. 'You can't come with us.'

Come with us? Gwen frowned at the words.

'We won't be coming back, and you can't blame us when you get homesick.'

The words swam in Gwen's head, alongside a cold, empty feeling in her chest. She couldn't believe it. No, she didn't want to believe it: the twins were running away.

Without a second thought, she kicked the door further open. 'You hypocrites!'

The twins spun round to the door, faces white with shock. Their horses startled, Calliope nickering as Merit began trotting on the spot. Astrid and Jonas held on to the reins, soothing them.

They were in their riding gear, a bag slung over each of their shoulders. Buttonbug was trying to burrow inside a scarf at Astrid's throat.

Gwen stared them down, her skin prickling with Bloom. 'Here I was, worrying about you both, thinking about how I can put this right, and you're what? You're just leaving? After everything? All the dangers, all the mysteries you insisted on pulling me into, *you're* the ones who are running away?'

'You couldn't possibly understand,' Jonas said, settling his horse. 'You're oblivious to everything. You have no idea what it's like to be trapped the way we have been. We're not doing it again.'

'I was willing to turn myself in for you two!' Gwen shouted, refusing to back down. 'I won't let the Order take you.'

'So what?' Jonas scowled. Gwen had never seen him so venomous. 'We can't trust you, or anyone.'

'Jonas!' Astrid said, her voice low with warning. 'Gwen hasn't done anything wrong.'

Jonas snorted. 'Of course you're defending her, but look what she's doing to us.'

'*She's* not the one making you behave like a fool.'

'No, clearly she saves that power for you.'

Gwen couldn't believe it: the twins were actually bickering. A sight she never thought she'd see.

'Would you two just shut up for one second?' Gwen interrupted.

They looked back over at her, as if surprised to see her there.

'You want me to admit it?' Gwen began, cutting them off before they could interrupt. 'Yes, OK, something's wrong with me.' She sighed, the weight of the confession sitting heavy on her tongue. 'I don't know if evil really has set its sights on us, but whatever is happening with the Grim, the three of us, whether I like it or not, are clearly caught in the middle of it.' She paused, taking a deep breath. 'We might not have caused this, and it's completely unfair, but somehow, for some reason, it's up to us to solve it, and I won't turn my back on it any more.'

Fire churned inside her as she stared each of them down. 'So if you think for one second that I'm letting you abandon me to whatever cruel fate this is, then you can think again. Now get back in the house.'

Jonas's response was to place a foot in his silver stirrup and launch himself up on his horse's back, looking down at her.

'No.'

Marching over, Gwen grabbed Jonas's leg, Merit trotting in little circles to try and avoid her while Buttonbug fluttered and hissed around them.

'I'm not letting you two go. I don't care if you can't stand me, and I'm useless and frustrating, but I promise I'll fix this. If all this really is linked to me, then I'm going to put it right. I won't let you leave.'

'Urgh,' Jonas groaned, kicking her off. 'Why don't you get it? You have absolutely no idea.' He scowled down at her, a well of emotions appearing on his usually indifferent face, until his sight drifted over Gwen's head to his sister, and slowly he took on a look of . . . defeat?

'We stayed *because* of you, Gwen.'

Gwen gasped, turning to find that Astrid had crept up on her. Shocked, she stumbled backwards until she was trapped against the empty stable door. When Gwen looked up into those glacial eyes, a chill ran through her that had nothing to do with the cold.

'This is what you don't understand,' Astrid said, her voice thick with melancholy that mirrored the ache in Gwen's own chest. 'It's been so hard for us. Gwen, everything about us seems to exist for you. Even our own magic.' She looked at Gwen as though she was the greatest mystery in the world. 'All of our lives something was missing, a question hanging over us with nothing but an empty echo in return, until finally we found our answer, and it was you.' Her eyes skittered around Gwen's face. 'You have no idea of the power you have over me.'

A simple word that pierced Gwen. *Me.*

She was not speaking on behalf of her and her brother; this was between the two of them alone.

Gwen swallowed, her skin heating up, that tingle of

Bloom that felt like burning at her fingertips spreading up through her palms, waiting for her to do something, but what?

Voice cracking, she tried to speak. 'I didn't know you –'

But suddenly, Astrid put a finger to her lips, her eyes wide and alert. 'Wait, shh.'

'Hey!' Gwen tried to push her hand away. 'You can't just . . . mph–'

'Quiet!' Astrid insisted, covering her mouth.

On top of his horse, Jonas was straining forward in the saddle, his head to one side as he listened.

'What is that?' Jonas whispered.

Astrid's eyes flicked from left to right in concentration, while Gwen went very still to try and hear what they were hearing.

'There,' Astrid breathed, and Gwen heard it too, her brows furrowing. A gentle tune, meandering up and down, it seemed to switch between a gentle hum and sharp whistling.

Very quietly, so as not to alert the source of the sound, Jonas climbed off his horse, and crept to join them at the stable door.

Gwen could see his alarm, but she certainly could not have predicted the words he mouthed to them.

'It's Elijah.'

Confused, Astrid and Gwen peeked round the door.

At first, Gwen thought the figure in its white-and-purple robe was a ghostly vision, but sure enough, as she focused on the silhouette heading towards the coastal trail, it could only have been Elijah.

'Where could he be going at this hour?' Astrid asked.

Another mystery.

'We have to follow him,' Gwen said. 'Come on.'

But the twins stayed frozen to the spot. Gwen stared from face to face, realization dawning over her. 'You're kidding, right?' Gwen had to take a deep breath to calm herself down. 'Well, I'm going after him and you two have a choice.' She stood with her hands on her hips. 'I have to fix this. I'm not going to run away from it any more. So you have a choice. You can quit on solving this mystery, on me, on the whole world for all I care. Or you can admit that you're part of this, and . . .' She exhaled, holding out her hand. 'Help me.'

The only reply was the quiet of the night.

Astrid looked to her brother, a silent question etched across her face.

He gazed back at her for a long while, then something seemed to break and he suddenly raised his hands, the hint of a smile playing across his lips. 'Fine, you know what?' he sighed. 'You win.'

'You agree?' Astrid said. 'I need to know that you genuinely agree.'

'I fear our fates were decided for us a long time ago.' He shrugged. 'We can't fight it any more.'

Confused, Gwen watched as both twins came to stand in front of her, mischievous smiles spreading over their faces as they looked her dead in the eye, and bowed.

'We're here to serve you.'

Gwen stepped back, suddenly embarrassed. It was ridiculous . . . and yet, having them here, teasing her again, it felt right. She wouldn't have it any other way.

Shaking off the thought, she stared at the ground, flustered.

'Yeah, yeah,' she mumbled, turning away as her cheeks grew hot. 'Let's go and solve this.'

They tracked Elijah to the meadow, Gwen and the twins watching as he veered off towards the cliff edge, his body swaying.

As damp grass licked at their ankles, they followed him to the crag, keeping low and quiet to peer over the cliff edge where Elijah, still humming in the distance, began the dangerous descent down the slimy, jagged stones of the shore path.

'What's he doing?' Gwen hissed, nervous now, not just for Elijah's motive but his safety too.

Ahead of them, something screeched along the beach. It sounded like a siren's call, and a black writhing responded.

'Bats,' Astrid whispered, recognizing their distinctive movement.

Jonas leaned forward over the cliff edge. 'Startled.'

Elijah stood at the edge of the ocean, ignoring the writhing mass above him.

'Come on,' Gwen ordered, 'we need to help him.'

'I'm not so sure,' Astrid considered, holding her back. 'We need to assess the situation first. That screech down there . . .'

Gwen looked at her, seeing the cogs turning behind her eyes.

'What are you thinking?'

Astrid swallowed, scouring the beach.

'It's just . . . Do you remember that photo you found of the Rapscallions?'

Gwen nodded.

'Well, Magnus said there were seven of them in total, but in that photo, there were eight figures.'

Gwen tried to make sense of what she was saying, thinking back to the photo with the blurry face she couldn't decipher, and yet had somehow felt so familiar.

'Maybe there really is someone trying to cover this all up,' Astrid said, nearly breathless. 'Someone who's been pulling strings behind the scenes. Who knows about the ritual Magnus and Rupert and your mother did all those years ago?'

Gwen blinked, a dreadful realization creeping over her. Someone who had taught Magnus and her mother, someone she'd thought she'd recognized but couldn't say why. Someone who could have set everyone on this wicked path a long, long time ago.

Someone who'd suggested the twins be locked up in Faymore Manor. It was never a compromise: it had all been part of their wicked plan.

Gwen thought again of the vines enclosing them in the temple. It hadn't been to trap them at all: it was a warning. They'd been trying to protect them from one person in particular.

'Oh god,' Gwen breathed, her voice catching as she tried not to panic.

They watched, helpless, as Elijah reached into the pocket of his robe to reveal a book.

Gwen knew it immediately. Not just from sight, but from the way it made her blood scream with Bloom. In Elijah's hand was the book of Cursed Melodies.

'What the —'

'Quiet!' Astrid warned.

It took a second for Gwen to see what the twins had already noticed. The shadows from the caves along the shore extended and a black-robed figure appeared, drifting along the beach towards Elijah. The hooded spectre came right up to him and plucked the book from his waiting hands.

Gwen had to supress a moan at the spike of horror that tore through her heart, an unexpected thought shocking her. *No, not the book. It's mine.*

'We need to get back to the wards,' Jonas said, his voice trembling.

Astrid nodded, but as they reached for Gwen, the robed figure turned sharply, and, even hidden beneath the hood, they saw the eyes looking directly at them. The figure snapped its fingers, and Elijah fell to the sand. His use had been served. There was no helping him.

'Run!' Astrid cried.

Gwen felt hands at her back, the twins hauling her up as they prepared to sprint back across the meadow to the wooded trail.

That same screeching sounded above them. It was the sound Astrid had recognized.

Descending on them, blood dripping from its beak, was a blue horned owl.

It swooped down so fast the twins had little time to react. All they could do was throw Gwen to safety, trying to protect her with their own bodies, but this sent her ricocheting towards the cliff edge.

'Gwen!' the twins screamed in unison, using their magic to summon a set of roots from the earth to cradle her body.

A dizzying shriek of discord rattled through Gwen's bones, and as she teetered on the cliff edge, she was able to see below. From one of the caves emerged what looked like decaying bodies.

Five Strix, all infected by the Grim.

As if commanded, one of them grabbed the robed figure in its talons and took off, hauling them up to the grassy meadow where the twins and Gwen had come together, warily crouched in a defensive stance.

The other four Strix followed, descending like a storm. Oozing Grim from their feathers and teeth, the five monstrous creatures hissed and shrieked, circling and closing in on the three teens.

The figure came forward, the shadowy mass slinking towards them with the book gripped in their hand.

'Hold them,' the voice demanded, and moving lightning-quick, the Strix swept forward, grabbing all three of them with their oozing talons, holding their limbs wide and their mouths shut, their magic trapped in their throats.

Gwen thrashed, trying desperately to pull herself free, sure that if she could just tap into that war drum of her Bloom, she could rip the hideous bird apart.

The figure simply cackled, a thick, croaking sound. 'You might be strong, but you cannot win this fight.' As she spoke, the blue-feathered body of Lapis came to rest on her shoulders, and her hood fell back to reveal ... horror. Translucent skin, a spindly skeleton, teeth exposed in a wicked smile and a small smudge of black at the corners of her mouth.

Sister Seraphina, possessed by the Grim.

'You know,' she mused, black liquid spitting from her lips. 'Let this be a lesson to you three not to steal my things.'

Gwen tried to scream, or hit, or kick, or anything at all, but they were all of them utterly powerless as Seraphina pulled a potion from her pocket and hummed them all to sleep.

27

Evil Takes Form

'*Wake up.*'

Head throbbing, Astrid became aware of a rhythmic dripping nearby, and something that sounded like an angel's voice.

'*Your king needs you.*'

Astrid's eyes fluttered open.

There was no angel, of course, and they were certainly not in heaven. She was in a dark cavern. Groaning against the pulsing inside her brain, Astrid tried to focus on the glowing white orbs staring down at her.

'Wake up. I need you.'

She knew that voice. She'd know it in every life.

'Gwen . . .' Astrid stirred. 'Where are we? Where's Jonas?'

'I'm sorry, I'm sorry.' The words tumbled out of Gwen. 'This is all my fault. I should have let you leave.'

'Stop that.' Astrid wouldn't hear it, and was frustrated that Gwen still did not understand. 'We're here to serve you; it's the very purpose of our magic.'

Swallowing, Gwen nodded.

They were alone but not restrained – not that it mattered, for Astrid could not sense a single living thing around them. They were surrounded by cold, dripping

303

stone, a cavern of sorts, but it was nothing like the warm, book-filled study in the cove – this place was empty and bleak. More like a tomb.

Beside her, a body shifted against the rocks.

'I'm here,' Jonas said, his voice thick. 'What's that sound?'

Eyes adjusting, the twins helped each other up, as that odd wavering light surged again.

'I think the more pressing question is . . .' Gwen swallowed, her voice trembling. 'What is that?'

As she spoke, their eyes landed on *that*, the strange source of light, throbbing in time with the discord in their heads. There, in the middle of the cavern, was a giant egg sitting on a granite throne.

Astrid finally realized what the dripping was. Black ooze was leaking from the egg through lightning-shaped cracks along its mottled shell, creating pools. This was the screeching sludge of the Grim.

Moaning, Gwen brought her hand to her head.

'What do you feel?' Astrid asked.

Gwen sucked in a breath. 'Evil.'

'Someone's coming,' Jonas warned.

Astrid heard it too: a distant squawking, and the soft clicking of boots on stone.

'Seraphina,' she breathed, the name tasting like poison.

What a rare and unpleasant new sensation it was for the twins, to discover they had been bested so thoroughly. How glaringly obvious it all seemed now; she'd been the one to defend them in the matter of their Pledge, and she'd ordered their lockdown in the guise of a kind alternative, but now they saw all her niceties for what they really were – nothing but clever tricks.

The Ambassador for Ancient Magic, she'd been Magnus's

tutor. There, right from the start, to nurture and guide this whole mess. The Faymore Cluster had held themselves responsible, but it seemed someone else had been pulling the strings.

But what, exactly, was her end goal?

In her mind, Astrid began to run through every spell they'd learned that could possibly be of any use. Fire? No, they could only make small flames so far. Wind? They could maybe cause a whirlwind, but Seraphina could likely counter it. Beside her, Astrid could tell Jonas was running through a similar list, and she was about to ask him his thoughts when something odd happened – her scarf began to move.

'What?'

Before she could get out another word, a furry face appeared through the fabric.

'Buttonbug, you little fool!' Astrid hissed, Gwen and her brother turning to her in alarm as the footsteps slowly got louder. 'You've been hiding here all this time!'

Jonas's eyes began to flit around the cavern, an idea tickling Astrid's brain at the same time. Her twin reached into his shirt and pulled out . . . a black-heart lighter, just like the prince's, like the one they'd tried to win all those weeks ago – except this one had a delightfully unique twinkle of Bloom.

'What are you doing?' Gwen asked.

'The prince gave it to me,' Jonas explained, busying his hands to wrap the chain round their fluffy companion. 'It's charmed.'

Astrid narrowed her eyes. 'Excuse me, he gave it to you, when?'

'Shh! Is that important now?' he asked, pouting. 'The gist of it is, it can always make its way back to me. Helpful, yes?'

Yes. Extremely.

'Buttonbug, you need to find a way out of here and fly back to Faymore Manor,' Astrid said, her voice low and her heart beating as fast as a bee's wings. 'You need to find someone there and give them this lighter, do you understand?'

The little thing chittered, fur standing up, then with a little shake flew up high to the cave's roof and out of sight.

They just had to hope that maybe she would make it out, and that maybe they hadn't been taken too far away to make any difference. Too many maybes to count.

'Stay calm, Gwen,' Astrid said, reaching out her hand.

Orange light flickered from a gap in the rocks and they could hear screeching, and see looming shadows of wings stretching along the walls. Their host was arriving, and she wasn't alone.

They saw the Strix first. Three of them skulking in on their rotting talons. Then came Seraphina, a flame in her hands, her eyes black as coal.

'It seems you're awake,' she croaked, coming to set her torches on the sconces dotted around the cave walls. 'Good, good.'

She flicked her wrists, and all three Strix came careening towards them. Gasping, both twins reached for a melody – any melody – Astrid summoning Fire, while Jonas went for Push, but they hardly had a note out before the birds had knocked all three of them to the ground.

'You're sick, Seraphina!' Astrid called. 'The Grim has got its claws in you.'

Cackling, the Ambassador walked up to the giant mottled egg, her brittle fingers caressing the shell. 'This is not a sickness. It's a gift. One that I chose a long time ago.'

Even with her body pressed to the stone floor, Astrid's eyes narrowed. 'The egg,' she said, the puzzle pieces slotting together. 'The Grim comes from the egg.'

Beside her, Jonas grimaced. 'And what hatches out of an egg?'

Gwen frowned. 'A dragon.'

No, not just a dragon, *the* dragon, the very one from the altar in the temple at the palace. Whatever it was, it was pulsing evil, and Astrid most certainly did not want to see it hatch.

'What did you do, Seraphina?' Astrid demanded. She wanted answers; she wanted to know what really happened all those years ago when the Grim was released into the world.

'Magnus, Rupert and your mother, Rani, they really were some of the best students I've ever had.'

Astrid saw Gwen flinch at the words, a fury of unmatched fire burning behind her eyes.

'I knew about their little group, studying things they were not supposed to. Things the Order deemed dangerous, and evil.' She recounted the story with fondness, as if it were all a happy memory. 'I encouraged them, of course. See, it's our job as Bloom Bloods to fix this world, and I found a cure for all its wretched problems. Problems like Red Blooded humans, and the messes they make. Yes, the world was much better before, when magic ruled, and regular humans knew to fear it.'

Seeing the pure hatred flash in Seraphina's eyes made Astrid's blood go cold.

'I led them along, helped them to find the ritual and the Savonnette, but I had no idea what it really was,' Seraphina went on, circling the egg on the throne. 'The most amusing part is that I let them believe that *they* persuaded *me* to help them perform the ritual. They all felt so guilty, not realizing what a good thing they'd done. That I'd had them do.

'What came from that ritual was not just the Grim; I was given knowledge, shown the truth. Unfortunately, the others were not chosen. They did not see the beauty in it. But their foolish mission to *turn back progress* ends here, tonight.'

Astrid cut her eyes at Jonas. Whatever Seraphina was planning, they couldn't let it come to fruition. They owed this to the Faymore Cluster; they wouldn't let all their sacrifices be for nothing.

'You see, the Grim is a blessing. It led us here, to this lost cave. We chosen few have been tasked with tending to him, so we may share this blessing with the world.' Seraphina looked up at them, smiling. 'Then once and for all we can end this plague that is humanity.'

The information swam around in Astrid's head. The fate of the world. How many people had Seraphina already infected? Who in the Order could be trusted? Who was this *him*?

She stared at the egg again as it pulsed. *Him.*

'I have been waiting all these years for the key to wake him, and at last, it is here.' Her voice was filled with jubilation, and once more she came to stroke the egg like it was her own child. 'I just had to keep the rest of the Order occupied so they couldn't get to you first.'

'It was you,' Astrid suddenly spat out, the realization like a splash of cold water on her face. 'You've been moving magical creatures around the world to create distractions for the Order to deal with.'

That's why the Magister was always occupied, why the Nure-onna had been in the station, the Strix in the woods, the Thunderbirds . . . How much chaos had Seraphina caused?

Seraphina paused then, eyes flitting over the twins. 'So clever, as always. Perhaps I should give you a demonstration. I imagine your curious minds are desperate to know how the Grim takes hold of people, what it feels like,' she said, cracking her knuckles and looking at them hungrily. 'I believe there is hope for you two yet.'

Jonas swallowed. 'What do you mean?'

Humming to herself a tune of rot and decay, Seraphina strolled casually in front of Jonas and cupped his chin in her hand. Astrid had to resist the urge not to scream as the melody increased. The sound burned through them, igniting every cell like they'd been set on fire.

This was an evil sound, a *cursed melody*.

They couldn't escape the tune as it wound through their ears and mouths, like someone was pouring hot tar through their airways. Drowning them in shadows.

As Seraphina came closer, Astrid saw how her teeth had turned grey and jagged with the Grim, and Astrid had to wonder how many charms and potions she had needed to keep her true appearance hidden – and how easy it might be for others to do the same.

'You've lived in the Red Blooded world,' Seraphina continued. 'You've seen how awful they are. What they do to nature.' She leaned in. 'What they did to you, locking you away.'

Each of her words lodged inside the twins. The discord flooded through their minds. Their isolation, all the adults who had failed them, how the world had treated them, the pain of being shunned, the years of mental torture under

Doctor Harris, every family that had ever rejected them . . .
It all hurt.

Seraphina smiled. The melody was doing this, bringing
forth every dark memory. Rubbing salt into the wounds.

'You do not need the Grim to show you what humans
really are. You never did. You have already lived it.'

Biting her tongue, Astrid fought the melody in her head,
the sound needling through her brain, looking for any
painful thought to shine its darkness upon. She could see it
now, what this evil really was, how it worked. These were
the chords of disharmony that existed in everyone –
loneliness, cruelty, hatred. The Grim didn't infect you with
them, it simply brought them to the surface.

'Don't listen to her!'

Astrid startled at the sound – Gwen's voice, piercing
through the darkness.

'You've never let anyone tell you what to do. I'll never
forgive you if you start now – *argh!*' Gwen let out a cry of
pain as the Strix tightened its talons round her arm.
Immediately, Astrid felt her own Bloom surge in response.

'She's wrong! This is how you're supposed to feel,'
Seraphina snapped back. 'Let it possess you.'

'Jonas, I think she's trying to convert us,' Astrid said,
fighting through the black sludge swirling in her head. 'But
there's something she doesn't realize.'

Jonas sucked in a sharp breath, coughing through a laugh
as they both grinned up at Seraphina.

'We've never been much good at doing what we're
supposed to,' he said.

Sighing, Seraphina let go of Jonas. 'You know, I must
admit . . . I've grown fond of you two. I was hoping I could
offer you up as a gift.' She rubbed her chin in thought as she

had the Strix lift them up, dragging them across the floor towards the egg. 'I've spent so much time watching you through Lapis's eye.'

Astrid glared at the bird. The evil little spy.

'But for all the sneaking about, and getting up to no good, you were always just a few steps behind the answers you've been searching for.' Seraphina cackled, withered skin held taut round her veins. 'You two could never guess what you really are or where you come from.'

Jonas stared daggers at their captor. 'What do you know about us?' he demanded.

Astrid could feel it too, that desperation, answers out of their grasp.

With a cruel smile, Seraphina moved her attention to Gwen.

'What do you know about what we are?' Jonas shouted, trying again.

'Enough fun now,' Seraphina said, a speck of black drool running down her chin. 'We have work to do.'

Astrid and Jonas felt an electric surge of Bloom in their blood, their magic screaming for an outlet as Seraphina had the Strix move Gwen over to the pulsing egg. Desperate, Astrid reached for her Wind melody but was scarcely able to summon a breeze when the Strix covered her mouth, silencing her and her magic.

The twins watched in morbid fascination as Seraphina grabbed Gwen's hand and held it against the book.

It was only then the twins realized the book had turned blank again under Seraphina's grip. The pages empty once more thanks to Rupert Faymore's magic.

'Get off!' Gwen growled, but the Strix only tightened its grip.

As it had before, the book of Cursed Melodies came to life at Gwen's touch, and Seraphina's eyes lit up, joyful and blood-thirsty.

'Yes, yes, finally.' Seraphina cackled as the book glowed, words etching back into the pages. 'All this time, the power of the book has been locked away, but you –' her fingers squeezed tighter round Gwen's wrist – 'you were the key all along.' At this she let out another awful cackle. 'Oh, Rupert, you thought you could hide it from me? Thought you could best me?' Seraphina spat, cursing the name as she found a loophole in whatever charm the book was under. 'I have waited so long to find you again.' She sighed, caressing the pages of the book as they sprang to life once more.

Gwen roared, trying desperately to pull away. Flinching each time Seraphina touched the paper.

'Calm down now,' Seraphina ordered, reaching into her robe. 'This will all be over soon.'

Eyes wide, Astrid saw the glint of metal in the firelight before she truly registered what Seraphina was holding. A knife, one she now slowly lifted to the light.

'You know it was very clever of you all,' Seraphina hummed, wiping the blade along her robe. 'Tricking us into thinking that you two were the answer, when the real truth was right here all along.' She inspected Gwen's palm then, pulling the skin taut. 'Who would have thought that someone so seemingly useless could be the key to changing the world?'

She hummed then, and the book held itself open in front of her on a page she scrutinized.

Then, with no word of warning, she began to sing whatever it was she was reading.

Wincing, the twins recoiled, the melody utterly rattling.

It was not the voice of an old woman. It was a dark, guttural thing, as if some ancient demonic voice had possessed her. It sounded like fire and brimstone, and the silence at the end of the world.

As the spell finally came to an end, Seraphina drew back the knife and, in one quick motion, sliced across Gwen's tender skin.

Gwen screamed, a sound as furious and desperate as Astrid's Bloom. Her blood welled in her palm and dripped on to the egg.

Everything after that seemed to happen in slow motion. A loud crack echoed through the stone like a thunderclap – then another! – followed swiftly by a scorching, malevolent melody. It was so loud and frightening that the possessed Strix dropped the twins, who fell to their knees and then scrabbled away from the egg.

The sound seemed ancient, like some strange nightmare they'd long forgotten, but it was a melody they knew. This was the sound from which all the Grim was born.

'Rise, my lord!' Seraphina hissed, stepping back as the shell began to fall away.

They saw the claws first, sharp, cruel things. Then the tail whipping out, spiked like a deadly weapon. When the whole beast finally uncurled itself, rising into the air, none of them could look away.

Evil, it turned out, was not black and rotten. No, evil shone like gold.

Mesmerized, Astrid and Jonas watched the dragon uncurl, its scales bleeding a near holy white light. But it was still weak, wings like moth-bitten fabric, and teeth not quite sharp.

Seraphina fell to her knees, presenting to the beast the book she'd stolen from Gwen.

'I've brought you the book, and the girl,' Seraphina intoned, face cast down in supplication.

The dragon's eyelids flickered and gazed around the tomb. Then he stared out at them, his radiant pupils full of hatred, pure and powerful. He grasped the book in his claws and a low rumble built in his chest, a sound of cruelty vibrating through Astrid's skull. He was laughing.

'Thank you, Seraphina.' When he spoke, it sounded like ice cracking. 'You have served your purpose.'

The Ambassador looked up, confused. With a razor-sharp talon, the beast sliced her throat, then proceeded to stretch his jaws wide, teeth shining like knives, as he consumed her in a frenzy of splitting bone and cartilage.

The twins could hardly catch their breath; instead, petrified on the spot, they squeezed their eyes closed at the dreadful sound of Seraphina being eaten alive.

When they dared to open them again, the dragon's wings extended while its white-gold body rippled with muscle, the beast growing bigger and stronger until he could have swallowed a human whole.

He let out a roar and turned his unfeeling eyes on the twins as hot air steamed from his nostrils.

'Really now,' he sighed, throat rumbling. 'After all this time, is this the welcome I get?'

28

The Shadowling

Blood dripped from his teeth – Seraphina's blood. It left smudges of red across the dragon's shimmering scales. Gwen watched as those jaws now careened towards the twins.

Gwen's Bloom chased across her fingertips, calling for her to *Do something! Anything!*

But every time she tried to focus on it, the Grim and her own terror stifled her. Why her? Why this?

Stalking forward, the dragon's body rippled, his forked tail flicking back and forth like a pendulum of death. He reeked of evil, hatred pooling from every scale.

And yet, the twins did not sway. They stood firm, their silhouettes flickering in the orange torchlight. Their eyes did not move from the dragon's, their backs turned to Gwen.

They were protecting her.

No, not protecting, that was not the word they used. They were serving her.

'What are you?' Astrid spoke up.

Both twins had edged towards each other, their forms blending together in the low light.

The dragon seemed surprised by the question, stopping to consider, and then laughed again, in that low rumble that sounded like an earthquake. His claws scraped the stone floor in front of the twins – those same claws that had torn through Seraphina as though she were made of butter.

'I've had many names. The Wretched Wyrm, Sun Blotter and some I've not heard since I took this form.' Then he paused, edging ever closer to Astrid and Jonas. 'But I suppose you might call me the Shadowling.'

Gwen flinched. The name sent heat along her skin, as if it had struck a match against her Bloom. The shadow – the one that had always chased her, that lingered in the murk of her magic. She recognized it now. It was this creature, the Shadowling.

'And do you know what we are?' Jonas said, his voice barely wavering.

Gwen felt her fingers twitch again. *Do something! Do something!*

'Yes, I think I do,' the Shadowling murmured, scales shimmering. His snout lowered further until he was breathing threads of smoke over the twins. They didn't flinch. 'And two of you . . .' He looked from face to face. 'How fascinating.' Eyes narrowing over their broken pendants, there was a flash of terrifying anger as he leaned ever closer. 'You have come to taunt me with this?' His voice rumbled, a deep, dark fury simmering there.

The twins only shrugged.

'Not intentionally.' Jonas said.

At this, the dragon reared back ever so slightly, and Gwen nearly screamed, convinced he was about to bite Jonas's head off, when instead, he chuckled. The sound was a dreadful, blistering thing that made Gwen's skin prickle.

Nostrils flaring, the Shadowling's jaws stretched back in a devilish grin as he leaned forward again, his nose mere inches from Astrid's neck.

'Ah, that scent.' He breathed them in, and sighed. 'How I've missed this.'

Raising his claws, he brought them slowly up to Jonas, and Gwen felt her Bloom scream.

Finally, Gwen's fear crystallized into rage. 'Hey!' she shouted, shocking even herself. 'Don't touch them.'

They all froze, Gwen's voice booming off the stone.

Gwen didn't know where her bravery had suddenly come from, but the twins had said they were going to serve her, and if they insisted on such a ridiculous thing, then she had just as much duty to them as they did to her. It was her turn to protect them; she just had to figure out how. She needed to get that simmering Bloom inside her to rise again. But how? What was the trigger?

'You, on the other hand,' the Shadowling droned, 'are here to ruin my fun, I presume?'

But Gwen would not back down. She had to get his attention away from the twins. 'You're my shadow,' she said, fists clenching at her side to stop the tremors. 'You've been following me.'

This finally seemed to do the trick. The dragon turned to stare at her, those wicked shining eyes nearly sucking her into their whirlpool depths. 'Slow as always,' he said, prowling over.

Holding her breath, Gwen looked up and up at the looming beast that now towered over her. One move and he could slice her in two.

'How must it feel,' he cooed, his smile cruel, 'to know that the thing you hated so much has been brought back into the world by your own blood?'

The question nearly knocked her over. The realization of what Seraphina had been looking for, why Gwen had been so important. She was not just linked to this terrible creature; she was the key he'd needed to awaken.

She didn't know how or why, but somehow she knew that she had brought this on the world. And it was her responsibility to fix it.

Across the room, the twins were staring at her, their eyes pleading with her not to do anything rash, yet Gwen felt uncontainable. Swirling like vipers in her stomach, her fury was growing, her Bloom pounding at her skin.

Do something! Do something!

What did it want from her?

She thought back to when she'd felt it before, when the twins had been drowning. Astrid and Jonas were at their strongest when they were protecting Gwen. They'd told her that their magic was tied to her.

So what was Gwen's magic tied to? If theirs existed to serve her, what was she meant to serve?

'Now, what to do with you all?' the Shadowling pondered, oblivious to the fire blazing inside Gwen's head.

Gwen had done this; she'd released the dragon from its egg, and if it got out of this cavern, it could destroy the world. All her life she'd wanted to prove herself, to show how strong she was, but what was the use of any of it if she couldn't save anyone?

Her Bloom thundered at the thought. She was so close.

'I might eat you alive,' the dragon continued to drawl. 'Although that might be a problem if I need you later.' He laughed again, his breath tickling Gwen's neck as he sniffed along her shoulders. 'How wonderful it will feel, to snuff out your light at last, and with it, all of humanity too.'

Oh.

Gwen nearly laughed, the clouds parting over her Bloom, until she could hear it clearly, those shining rays of immortal power that scorched through her mind like a battle cry. She could pull it apart clearly now, the dark shadows from the light, like picking weeds.

It tingled through her entire body, a near euphoric surge of magic. There was no fear. There was nothing to be afraid of at all.

Her magic was not a curse, not a thing to hide away from. All this time, she had been the other half of this beast. And if this terrible thing existed to end humanity, then Gwen existed to protect humanity.

Her Bloom did not exist for her.

It existed for this.

'Thank you,' Gwen said, her fists closing like weapons at her side. 'I get it now.'

If this was her shadow, then she was the light that would destroy it.

She pulled her fist back, and punched the dragon in the snout.

Immediately, the twins flung themselves across the floor, Jonas grabbing at the book as it went flying from the Shadowling's grip, while Astrid pulled Gwen to her side.

The three of them huddled together, watching as the Shadowling shook his snout, eyes rolling back in his head.

'What did you do?' Astrid breathed, her eyes near bulging in shock. 'You . . . you punched him.'

'I did what you said,' Gwen panted, her skin still fizzing with power. 'I listened to my Bloom.'

The Shadowling staggered back to its feet, wings splaying out – the very picture of hatred – and turned on them.

'You!' he growled, those cold, glimmering eyes locking on to Gwen again. There was something terrifyingly familiar in the look.

Throwing back his head, he roared. The sound echoed off the ceiling and shook the walls. Trickles of dust fell around them.

When the dragon charged forward, they summoned their Wind spell, catching the beast's wings like a sail and slowing him down. Then, while he stopped to try and streamline his body against the tug of wind, Jonas and Astrid sang again, holding his wings out, trapping him.

Gwen grabbed the moment and ran forward, punching the beast under its jaw, smashing his teeth together.

Growling, the Shadowling quickly swiped back, but the twins were prepared. They shifted the songs to the Bind and Pull melodies, the spells wrapping round Gwen's wrists and snatching her out of the way just in time.

There, another opportunity: Gwen summoned her own Bloom, feeling the swells of power, her duty to the earth. A light pooled round her fists, bright as the sun, and burst like an exploding star as it made contact with the beast.

The bone underneath her shuddered, knocking the dragon off-kilter.

The three of them were seamless, a perfect orchestration, as if they'd done this before, a dance they knew all the steps to.

'Enough!' the Shadowling roared.

Gwen was readying another blow when the twins grabbed her and pulled her into the tunnel Seraphina had come through. There, they found what looked like a catacomb in the wall – a place carved out long ago for people to be buried. They hauled themselves inside it, limbs close. They were just in time, for the Shadowling made an earth-shattering sound and let forth from his jaws a tidal wave of flame.

Burning gold and red, the fire licked across the stone, scorching everything in its path. Above them, screeching, were the Strix, caught in the flames in the Shadowling's fury.

'You cannot defeat me!' the Shadowling roared. 'I will possess every creature on this wretched planet so they will all see the hateful ways of humanity. Your vile, filthy species will be scorched from the earth!'

Pounding and scraping against the packed dirt with each step, the dragon stalked towards their hiding spot.

'So, dragons really do breathe fire . . .' Jonas said, trying for a smile.

The twins and Gwen shared a glance. They were out of ideas, with nowhere to run.

'Bloom Bloods, Red Bloods, they're all the same, a plague on this land, one I must cleanse.' The Shadowling's voice rumbled through the stones, echoing like a prophecy.

Gwen felt the creature's hatred like fire in her bones. She had to do something, but what? Blinking through the dark she looked around inside their hiding space, and sensed . . . something. She knocked her knuckles against the far wall of the catacomb, and it echoed, as though there was an empty space behind it. Yes!

She felt the Bloom's power flood through her again, and smashed into the wall. A tumble of stones fell down over them, cocooning them deeper into their pocket just as the dragon turned round the corner.

'Hiding, are you?' the Shadowling laughed.

From the other side of their crawl-space, they could hear the dragon's throat roil and burn with fresh flames, ready to be unleashed.

Gwen sensed the grip on her Bloom wavering. She felt so small suddenly beneath the sound of the Shadowling lumbering over them, the crackling in his throat as he prepared to strike again. What good was her strength against fire and brimstone? How could she protect everyone against a hatred so powerful?

Outside their tomb, the Shadowling let loose another deep rumble. There was the sound of his claws digging into the ground. Far too close.

'We're with you, Gwen,' Astrid whispered through the dark like a single flickering flame.

Jonas's voice joined hers. 'Always, until the very end.'

Swallowing her fears, Gwen closed her fists around the twins' hands, letting their Bloom connect, now and forever, in a destiny that was beyond their control – a destiny Gwen must take furiously by the reins.

She felt it then, a pulse, like a flash of dream-memory, their magic flowing through one another. Despite the imminent danger, she clutched the feeling, gasping in cold-water shock. They'd lived this before, she was sure of it, this destiny they shared. If she could just bring it to light, hold this thought under the sun.

'We're not going to die here,' Gwen said furiously. She had a responsibility now, to the world, to the twins . . . to Astrid. She had to know what it all meant.

She had to kill this evil.

There was a final roar from the dragon and fire exploded through the rubble to expose the terrible shining form of the Shadowling towering over them. Flames coiled around his muscular body, ready to send them off to some fresh new hell.

One they weren't prepared to go to.

Until, quite suddenly, the flames stopped.

In front of their eyes, the dragon tumbled sideways, and voices shouted down from the tunnel – voices they knew.

The Shadowling roared again, turning his attention down the tunnel.

Shooting through the darkness, melodic firebolts and songs of lightning shot towards the dragon, forcing him back. One caught on the wall, blowing a hole through the tomb, a single glorious ray of light breaking through.

'No!' the Shadowling shouted, blood like oil dripping from his scales.

Gwen was grabbed once more by the twins, who pulled her further back into the catacomb, but she peered out and saw them, running closer: Magnus, Elijah, Lorelei and Harriet Loupe.

Never in her life had Gwen thought she would be so relieved to see Ambassador Loupe's blood-red mane of hair.

As the dragon stumbled back, the group wielded their magic with terrifying precision. Loupe threw a potion that exploded with a clanging melody, while Magnus conjured Flames, the mixture exploding into molten metal that cut through the dragon.

Lorelei tossed charmed rope that hummed with Bind and Pull, while Elijah unleashed spells of Wind and Push, until the rope wrapped tight round the Shadowling's jaws.

The beast snarled, slashing at the next potion, sending it back. It exploded in mid-air, a heady, whispering song that dissipated into a cloud of smoke, blocking everyone's vision for a moment.

Furious, the Shadowling hissed flames through his teeth, the rope catching and setting his face alight as it burned the bindings. 'Enough!' he growled at them, stumbling back into the tomb where the shattered egg lay on the throne. He whipped his tail around, knocking Harriet so that she flew, painfully, back into the troupe.

'Gwen, twins!' Magnus called. 'Run!'

But they had nowhere to go.

Jaws wide, the Shadowling stared at the tunnel opening, snapping his teeth.

He turned to Gwen where they were pushed against the wall, his black eyes boring into her own.

'You cannot escape me,' he hissed. 'I will regain my full strength, and I will be back to end this once and for all.'

For a moment, it seemed he was going to tear her to pieces.

Instead, he slinked back, laughter rumbling from his throat. Then, before anyone could conjure another spell, he beat his wings, flying up to the gap above in the stone, and began clawing his way out of the tomb.

The rocks fell hard and fast, but Gwen felt herself possessed. Fists balling, she ran to chase after him, only once again the twins grabbed her, pulling her to safety just as a huge slab of stone threatened to flatten them all.

'We can't let him get away!' Gwen screamed, trying to break free. 'I have to stop him!'

More hands came to grab her, followed by murmurs and cooing as she was lifted away.

'It's OK, Gwen.' Magnus's voice echoed in her ear. 'You've done enough.'

Tears pricking her eyes, Gwen could do nothing but watch as the shining scales of evil tore through the sky and vanished into the clouds.

29

Lost and Found

They had arrived back at the manor in a blur – the earth rejoicing upon their arrival, Jan and Thomas rushing to greet them, all of them being hurried to the parlour to be tended to.

Ambassador Loupe had been frantic for answers, wanting to know everything about Gwen's link to the Grim, and why they had kept it secret. If not for Magnus insisting they were not in any shape to be questioned yet, she may very well have whisked them off to Fountains Abbey straight out of the tomb.

Everything was out in the open now. There was no going back.

Having attempted to run away, Astrid and Jonas found the familiar comforts of Faymore Manor to be dream-like, even the sound of everyone's voices fawning over them, humming healing melodies and offering calming potions. They filled the twins with feelings they were most certainly not accustomed to. Comfort. Belonging.

'Here you go,' Elijah said, handing them each a steaming mug.

Astrid glanced at her brother, both of them wracked with an almost unbearably heavy guilt.

After hours of checks and treatment for their various scrapes and bruises and burns, they were now cross-legged on the floor of the parlour, a thick medicinal haze billowing from the various potions and spellwork Elijah had used. Astrid watched Gwen where she lay on the chaise, glaring at her bandaged hand.

'You punched it in the *face?*' Jan was beside herself, fretting about Gwen like a mother goose. 'An ancient evil dragon, and you punched it. I can't believe it.'

Both twins held the cup of steaming bone broth Elijah had handed them, a gentle twinkling emanating from each sip, the soup charmed by his ladle. Jan and Lorelei paced around them, distributing tinctures and bandages, blankets and extra pillows.

Not one of them had mentioned the twins' escape attempt. The stolen bags and money had been in the hallway when they'd arrived back. An elephant in the room.

'I'm fine, really. I've been fine since Elijah healed me hours ago,' Gwen insisted while Jan propped another cushion behind her.

Astrid had gone over the circumstances of their rescue again and again, analysing every detail, wondering what might have happened if they'd managed to run away before Gwen had found them.

The fate they had nearly left Gwen to was too painful to think about.

When Magnus and Lorelei had arrived at Fountains Abbey, they'd been informed that the Magister had not yet returned, and that the letter was a forgery. Ambassador Loupe had been the one to piece it all together. She'd suspected someone close was using magical creatures to intentionally cause chaos across the factions and distract the Magisters. She'd wrongly assumed it had been Magnus.

The only Ambassador not accounted for was Seraphina, so Ambassador Loupe had insisted on accompanying the Faymore Cluster back to the manor, and on taking a Cloud Skimmer for haste.

Poor Elijah had woken up in his robe and pyjamas on the beach, thankfully unharmed, not remembering anything that had happened or how he'd got there. Sister Seraphina had used an Ancient and evil spell to control the man in his sleep, and had spared him seemingly in the hopes of framing him for all her misdeeds. When Magnus finally arrived back at Faymore Manor, it was to find Jan, Thomas and Elijah desperately searching for Gwen and the twins, with only their backpacks left in the stables giving them any clue to their whereabouts.

All had seemed hopeless until Buttonbug came crashing through the kitchen window. Magnus caught the felimoth, and immediately recognized the musical signature on the lighter as a makeshift homing charm. They set off in a boat at once.

The tomb was frighteningly close. They found them just across the channel in Wales, in a cavern near the coast, hidden by Ancient Magic – a place Seraphina had investigated many years prior and deemed '*unimportant to Order research*'. The tomb would now be quarantined by the Order of Pendragon for investigation.

Magnus's expression had remained unreadable, hardly a wince as the twins recounted what Seraphina had done in the cave. How did it feel, Astrid wondered, to discover that the woman he'd trusted had been working against him?

That his old tutor had been searching for the book his brother had hidden?

Astrid wondered if he had suspected anything at all, all this time.

Ambassador Loupe, meanwhile, had been openly mortified by the whole ordeal, not only from Seraphina's betrayal, but that so many things had been hiding right under her nose: the book of Cursed Melodies, Gwen's powers, and whoever else in the Order of Pendragon was infected with the Grim. Demands for 'Truth Trials' run by the Grand Coterie had spewed from her mouth – trials, the twins had learned, that were designed to find more traitors.

What a dreadful thought that was indeed, that there were more like Seraphina, snakes lurking in the grass. And all Astrid and Jonas could think about was how they'd been planning to leave Gwen, and the whole Faymore Cluster.

A soft rap came against the door, Thomas appearing sheepishly through the crack.

'Magnus is done with the paperwork for Ambassador Loupe,' he told them. 'He's hoping Astrid and Jonas will come and see him in his office up at the cottage – oh, and I think I have someone who's rather anxious to say hello.'

The door flew open, and Buttonbug came charging in, flapping her wings and grumbling as she went flying to Jonas, who let out a little *oof* at the impact.

'You little menace,' Jonas cooed. 'You saved our lives.'

Buttonbug purred happily at the attention.

Astrid leaned over to her brother. 'Don't you mean, *Prince Teddy* and his black heart saved our lives?'

'Only by accident,' he insisted, refusing to look her in the eye. The lighter in question was now safely back in his pocket, having redeemed itself as a literal lucky charm.

'OK, everyone,' Elijah said, clapping his hands. 'Let's allow Gwen and the twins to have some peace. We have supper to prepare.'

Lingering too, Jonas glanced at his sister and Gwen, before letting out a world-weary sigh and scooping up Buttonbug. 'Why don't you two have a talk,' he whispered to his sister. 'I need to make sure I've washed all of Seraphina's blood out of my hair,' he added with a wince, before making his way out.

Astrid was left alone with Gwen.

'Astrid . . .'

'Gwen?'

Astrid took a moment to commit the sight of Gwen to memory. Her hair had come loose during the fight, a small strand at the front singed shorter. The twin plaits now spilled down over her back like black ink – Astrid wanted to reach over and stain her hands in it, to keep a piece of Gwen that would never fade.

Mostly, she wanted to burn the dragon alive for harming a single hair on her head.

'I should have killed him!' Gwen blurted. 'I wasn't strong enough. It's my fault it's even here.'

'No. We're the ones who weren't strong enough.' Astrid reached for Gwen's hand. 'Somehow, Gwen, you have become terribly important to me, and I protect the people I care for. I expect them to take care of themselves too.' She locked eyes with her. 'Do you understand?'

Gwen faltered, her pupils blown wide until there was only a sliver of molten brown at the edges.

'I understand, I think, I just . . . I don't know what to say.' She stumbled over the words. 'I've never . . . Everyone who's ever cared about me has ended up hurt, or . . . worse.'

Astrid squeezed Gwen's hand tighter, holding her gaze. 'Then I suppose I must prove to you that I'm indestructible.'

Gwen stared down at the blanket covering her legs.

It was undeniable to Astrid now, the way she felt for Gwen. She'd been unfathomably foolish to think she could ever leave her side. Even if Gwen didn't feel the same way about her. Like Jonas, and the pendant round her neck, Gwen was hers whether she knew it or not, and all Astrid wanted was to keep her close, and keep her safe.

'So, does this mean you're not going to try and run away again?' Gwen suddenly said, a smile teasing her lips. 'Even though I just raised an ancient evil?'

Astrid laughed, her eyes going soft. 'If anything, it's only endeared you to me more.'

Gwen scrunched up her nose, and in another time, Astrid imagined she would have become angry at the compliment, but now she took it. She trusted her.

'I get it now,' Gwen said. 'That drive you and Jonas have always had – to find answers. If we're going to defeat it . . . him, the Shadowling. Whatever he is! We have to know what our link to all this is.'

Astrid nodded.

'Do you think I can actually do it, Astrid? Whatever the earth wants from me – from us?'

Astrid looked over Gwen once more, the object of her obsessions. Then she leaned forward, until her hair trickled over Gwen's legs, their faces just close enough that Astrid could smell her – bonfires and sea salt.

'All I know for certain is that I'll do anything to protect you and Jonas. Both of you.'

A sound from the door caught their attention before Gwen could respond. Jonas was back. He poked his head through the doorway.

'I'm going to find Magnus. Coming with?' he asked Astrid.

'I'll see you at dinner,' Astrid said to Gwen, standing up and moving to join her brother in the hallway.

'Sorry I'm back so early . . . how'd it go?' he asked, nudging her with an elbow.

'We need to be prepared,' she said solemnly. 'The Shadowling . . . he recognized something in us. Gwen too.' She lowered her voice. 'If he has more people on his side like Seraphina, then they have a huge advantage over us.'

On their way past the kitchen as they headed outside, they could hear pots and pans clanking, the scent of Elijah's cooking creeping through the manor.

'OK, that's not what I was talking about, but yes, I see your point,' Jonas said, passing a coat to Astrid as they stepped outside and closed the door behind them.

Under the stars, everything was peaceful now, and they both took in all the overgrown buds and trees on the path up to Windyside Cottage. They listened to their gentle melodies and ran their fingers along each soft petal and misunderstood thorn, which trilled in turn, happy to have them back.

'Without any plants in that tomb, we were too weak,' Jonas said, a bitter note creeping into his voice as they approached the cottage. There was a light on in Magnus's office.

'We have to get stronger. We have to master all the spells. Not just rely on Ancient Magic.' Astrid let her eyes wander back to the manor, thinking of the rest of the

Faymore Cluster down there in the kitchen. 'Not just for Gwen.'

Jonas nodded slowly. 'No, not just for Gwen any more. I'm . . .' Jonas stared at the floor, his fists balling. For a moment, Astrid thought he was doing an impression of Gwen, when he suddenly lurched forward, wrapping his arms round her. 'I'm sorry, OK? You were right.'

Shocked for a moment, Astrid slowly enveloped her arms around him too, holding him close. 'I know,' she whispered back.

The feeling was familiar, their earthen scent mingling with the wild outdoors. Whole and complete.

No matter what happened, Jonas would always understand her. Deep down, they'd always share the same sparks. And for the first time in their lives, it wasn't just them against the world, but a whole manor house of people they felt obligated to protect.

Whether they liked it or not, their world was expanding. But Jonas would always be her home.

When they arrived at Magnus's office door, it stood ajar, a glow leaking out over the floorboards. The two of them were greeted by the scent of old books, and an ungodly mess of papers and documents.

Magnus turned to them from his spot at the window, a notebook open in his hands and an inquisitive glint in his eyes. Seeing him there, his black hair shining in the warm autumn moonlight, Astrid remembered how she'd felt when she saw him leave the night before, and she felt very lucky indeed that it had not, in fact, been the last time she'd set eyes on him.

Jonas must have felt it too. He looked away, a sudden shyness etched across his features.

'Elijah mended you up nicely,' Magnus said cheerily. 'How are my Pledges feeling?' It was as though nothing had happened at all.

The twins hesitated, and Magnus's smile wavered. 'You're right! Silly question.' He snapped his book shut.

Astrid entered the hallowed office. They saw it immediately, sitting on the desk, the writing once again gone. *The Cursed Melodies*. Back to its charmed state, waiting for Gwen to wake it up.

'A team from the Shadow Library will be coming to collect this tomorrow. They will have questions for Gwen, as it seems to have imprinted on her,' Magnus explained, following Astrid's line of sight.

'It won't work without her,' Astrid said, recalling the terrible events. 'Seraphina couldn't access its power without Gwen. It will only respond to her . . . and us, we think. We can't let anyone use Gwen like that again.'

Magnus hummed thoughtfully, his fingers tapping the red skin cover. There was caution in his eyes . . . and regret.

'We stole something from Fountains Abbey too – a little silver box,' Astrid confessed, looking down sheepishly. 'Inside were lost pages from the book, ones with a sword – an ancient weapon.'

Jonas cleared his throat, continuing before they could change their minds.

'We need to find it. It might be integral to destroying the Shadowling . . . hopefully before he has time to reach his full powers and amass more followers.'

'A frightening thought,' Magnus mused, hovering over

the desk. 'So the book allows you to read it, but it is Gwen who awakens it?'

Jonas nodded. They wished they could go back, to tell themselves to trust Magnus from the start. Then maybe all this could have been avoided.

'Seraphina. She seemed to know something about what we are, and where we come from. So, we were wondering, actually, what theories you might have about us and these pendants, and what you think Rupert might have found before he died. What he was hoping we might find in this book? We need to know everything, so we can keep you and Gwen and everyone here safe.'

It was the least they could do. They needed to prove how sorry they were for trying to run away. Hoping Magnus would not give up on them, as so many people had before.

When Magnus looked up at the twins, he smiled – a sweet smile, so soft Astrid thought she could lie down in it like a meadow.

Magnus rubbed his chin in thought. 'As much as I would love to, I'm afraid I cannot answer these questions for you, but I do know one thing. You two have done a tremendous thing today. You kept Gwen safe, even when all odds were against you.' He leaned down then, just enough that they could see the red tint in his eyes, and the warmth that rested there. 'And I think you deserve an evening off from all this, and a home-cooked dinner.'

The twins felt tears prick at their eyes. They each took a shuddering breath.

'If that's what you think best,' Astrid said, keeping her voice as level as she could.

'Then I suppose we can't disagree with you,' Jonas finished.

Magnus Faymore gazed at them fondly.

'Astrid, Jonas . . . The Faymore Cluster will always be here for you, and I am so happy you have decided to stay.'

This place they'd tried so hard to escape. They realized now what it was . . . home.

Their mentor turned to the door, gesturing them to follow.

Back at the manor, they found a feast laid out, prepared by Elijah. Jan was helping, as usual, passing out napkins, while Thomas and Lorelei carved the roast meat and plated up the sparkling collection of buttered vegetables. Taking a seat by Elijah, Magnus leaned over to give his husband a peck on his forehead, before helping himself to a large portion of mashed potatoes.

There were two seats left next to Gwen, who had Buttonbug curled in her lap.

'Will you come eat with us?' she asked as they lingered by the door, a hopeful look about her.

Astrid glanced at her brother, and he too looked back at her.

'Shall we?' he said.

She beamed back at him.

Astrid and Jonas entered society in much the way they meant to carry on – together, and as peculiarly as possible. But, secretly, all their lives they'd wondered if they might discover a place for peculiar people like them.

Now, for the first time ever, they wondered if perhaps it didn't matter where they came from. Hand in hand, they sat down at the table, thinking that what *did* matter was that they might, just possibly, have found where they belonged.

After the Storm . . . an Olive Branch Arrives

My dearest Jonas,

I thought you should hear it from me first. Consider this my apology, one I sincerely hope you will accept, for your sake and mine.

My mothers are thunderstruck. It's as if the world is ending. Perhaps it is, but I am simply too hurt by our last encounter to muster the energy for it all.

The Magisters in the Grand Coterie have been talking. They want you three guarded and the Faymore Cluster watched closely while the Order work on their plan against this mysterious evil.

Not to worry, though. I have helped them reach an agreement, one that I believe is beneficial for everyone involved and can put an end to your little quarrel with me.

I look forward to seeing you soon and putting all this horrible business behind us, for I, Prince Theodore, will be joining your Cluster for the foreseeable future as a guest.

You're welcome.

x

Acknowledgements

This book and all of my work could not exist without the constant patience and support of some truly amazing people. I am grateful every day to have such an incredible network of friends and colleagues. You all know who you are, but some of you got lucky and are getting a special mention.

As always, thank you to my agent, Richard, and manager, Mark, the coolest manager in the world.

Thank you, Mum and Dad, for everything ever.

Thank you, Sparkles* for the melodies.

A huge thank you to Linas, Sarah, Bella, Ruth, Jessica, and all the Penguin team. Working with you all is such fun, and I always know my stories are in safe hands.

Thank you, Tazmyn and Rowan, Lovey-Dovey and Captain Cookie.

Thank you, Prince of Cats, I love you.

And a huge thank you to every kid who gave me their time and let me be a part of their adolescence. I hope this book could reawaken that wide-eyed child in you.

**Read on for a bonus short story about
the Rapscallions years before . . .**

That Fateful Night

There's nothing quite as annoying as when you're up to no good and find out someone else has beaten you to it.

Not just someone – the very bane of Rani's existence.

Rupert Faymore, and his irksome little gang of boys. Troublemakers and scoundrels. Or, as Rani called them in her head, rapscallions.

There were five of them – always together, and always up to something. Francis Yonge was the tallest, with dirty blonde hair and a crooked smile. He was funny, apparently – that's what all the girls said. Then there was Quin Larkspur, a thoughtful, quiet boy with sunken grey eyes who somehow gave the impression that he knew all your secrets. He always held his flute like a weapon, like he was brandishing a knife. Next there was Elijah Ackerman, the shortest of the bunch; Rani had spell practice with him on Wednesday mornings, and he always seemed too sweet to be in a gang, with his curly crop of auburn hair and half-moon glasses.

Finally, there were the ringleaders: the Faymore brothers. They were, for lack of a better word, weird. Rani would see them around the Pledge dorms, dressed in old fluffy hats or heeled boots, or sometimes even sweaters with slogans, bought from shops in a Red Blooded city. Both had dark, unruly hair, and when they looked at you, they were like ravens with their hackles up. Rupert was in her year, a bothersome boy to say the least. He never seemed to study and yet he was always threatening her spot on the academy's leader board. Magnus, on the other hand, was an enigma; you could never tell what he was thinking. Like he was always wearing a mask.

And now, Rani was watching them all in the moonlight as they cut each other with a knife in the Fountains Abbey Enchanted Quarter.

'What the hell are they doing?' Abigail hissed.

She was furious; they both were. This was meant to be their secret spot.

The two girls sat hidden in the undergrowth, ducked low behind swollen roots that erupted out of the ground like barricades. It had been wet the past few days and the girls' dark robes were hemmed with mud and their fingernails filthy from pulling star roots out of the ground.

Rani and Abigail had waited all day for this – showing up early to morning choir, sitting prettily through their charms class, helping the new Pledges find their way around the echoing halls of Fountains Abbey. They were model Bloom Blooded students, as far as their teachers were concerned. But they also had a secret routine. Every other month during the gibbous moon – when the star root grew – they'd sneak out of their dorm at the witching hour and make the journey beyond the school bounds to the Enchanted Quarter. They'd collect exactly twelve bushels of star root to be used in the time-consuming process of making dream powder.

Then, precisely three days later, they would slip the powder into the librarian's tea, wait until she fell asleep, and sneak into the Custodian section.

Rani couldn't exactly stay top of her class if she wasn't permitted to read ahead now, could she? She was determined to read every book in that whole library until she sucked dry every bit of information about magic, even those restricted books about the old magic, which had been long lost. She had to be the best. She *was* the best.

And now these damn boys were going to ruin it.

'They're doing a ritual,' Rani whispered, narrowing her eyes.

The two girls had heard them approaching, the sounds of a snapping twig and boyish banter wafting into the clearing where they had been collecting star root. They'd had to dive into the foliage to avoid being seen, and that's where they were now stuck, crouching in the pungent mud, waiting for these troublesome boys to leave.

The group were still in their Pledge uniforms, cassocks and bands, and they were standing in the small clearing not too far from the west entrance. At least they had the sense not to wander too far into the woods. Blue flames floated around them, lighting up their work – a small pile of old toys and mixed herbs, which they were now each dripping blood onto from their palms. Every drop created a harmony, the melodic Bloom of the ritual building.

Rani watched Rupert specifically as he pulled an ocarina out of his sleeve, with a look of solemn determination that flickered in and out of view from the warbling shadows. He had a calm poise not usually seen in sixteen-year-old boys. As he raised the instrument to his lips, she almost believed he might complete the spell.

But Rani knew this ritual. She knew the music that he would play. This was magic that no one, especially not a Pledge, should have any knowledge of. And she knew it wouldn't work.

Except . . . Rani could feel the pressure change, a shift, the woods going quiet, like the Bloom was waiting to hear this boy's spell. And now, she was waiting too.

'Wait, there are only four,' Abigail suddenly said, grabbing Rani's arm. 'Weren't there five of them a second ago?'

'Huh?' Rani replied senselessly, blinking away the mysterious charms of Rupert Faymore to discover that, yes, one of the boys was missing. The one with the flute and the knowing grey eyes: Quin.

Rani turned around too late. She couldn't even cry out, only gasp as she saw him standing behind them, silent as a shadow in human form. He smiled, then threw charmed ropes humming with Bind.

'Hey!' Abigail started to shout as the ropes tightened around their ankles and wrists, but then evidently remembered where she was. This was an Enchanted Quarter, a place they were not allowed to be in, and the only thing worse than getting caught by a teacher here would be disturbing a monstrous creature.

'Got them!' Quin announced, dragging both girls into the clearing as they squirmed, entirely undignified.

The boys made quick work of tying them to a tree, staring down at the girls like hunters admiring their catch. All except Elijah, who was wringing his hands nervously.

Magnus was the first to speak, tapping his chin in thought. 'Now, what should we do to make sure you two don't snitch on us?'

Rani scoffed, unimpressed.

But Abigail spoke up. 'Oh, please. We've been coming here long before you clowns. How do we know *you* won't snitch on *us*?'

Her belligerent reply seemed to catch them off guard.

Francis blinked at them. 'Didn't you follow us in, to spy on us?'

Abigail rolled her eyes. She never did have patience for pretty boys. 'Don't flatter yourself.'

'Then why are you here?' asked Magnus.

'We come here to collect star root, for –'

'Reasons,' cut in Rani. 'If anything, you're encroaching on *our* turf, Rapscallion.'

'What did you just call me?' Rupert spluttered, bemused by the insult.

'I've got some more names for you, if you'd like?'

'Wait, I know you,' Rupert declared suddenly. 'You're in my Ancient Magic class with Sister Seraphina. You got the highest grade on our last exam.' Now when he looked down at them, it wasn't like a hunter; it was like a collector. Like he'd seen something he wanted. 'Interesting,' he mused.

The brothers glanced at each other – a wordless conversation.

'Lads, leave us alone for a moment, would you?' Rupert commanded. Without hesitation, everyone but the brothers slinked back. Standing together, the two of them were as they always were, with dark fluffy hair that stuck out like raven feathers and eyes you felt you could fall into.

Magnus whistled, and the ropes fell loose. Rupert held out his hand to help Rani up, which she promptly rejected. She could get up just fine on her own.

'I know what you were doing,' she said slowly.

'Yes?' Magnus said, one eyebrow arched.

'You were trying to speak to the dead.'

Rupert began, 'We –'

'It doesn't work, you know. All the information on Ancient and forbidden magic? None of it works.'

Rupert smiled, his eyes narrowing. 'It almost sounds like you know this from experience.'

Rani shook her head. 'The magic is lost.'

The brothers glanced at each other again, a look sharp as a knife.

They spoke as one. 'Then perhaps we just need to look harder.'

Rani couldn't help the small laugh that escaped her. She could appreciate their stubbornness. She was about to tell them as much when the other boys returned, and they looked afraid.

'We need to run, now!' Francis hissed, and began sprinting towards the west entrance.

Quin didn't give the girls a second glance, just grabbed Rupert's hand and started pulling him away protectively.

'Run, run!' Elijah panted, pushing them all forward to keep pace.

'What's going on?' Abigail choked, nearly tripping over a root.

And then they heard it: a thud of hooves and the sound of a furious bull ready to charge. No, not a bull.

A minotaur.

'OK, yes, run!' Rani squealed.

They crashed through the tangled undergrowth, lungs burning, branches whipping at their faces. The ground pulsed faintly, roots shifting beneath their boots as if the forest itself was trying to avoid the charge of this terrifying beast. Behind them, the minotaur bellowed, a sound that rattled the trees and sent tree spirits scattering into the starglazed sky.

'Faster!' one of the boys shouted, but they didn't need the reminder. Their feet struck the mossy earth in a ragged rhythm. It was terrifying. *Exhilarating.*

Rani and Abigail knew this part of the woods well, committing it to memory every time they made the journey to collect star root. They dodged every rock and ducked under every branch, quick as shadows.

Soon they overtook the boys. Not more than a few paces ahead, the whirring watercolour of magic signalled their way out: the wall of Bloom where the wards barred entry – and exit – to the forest.

'There!' Francis cried.

The roar came closer – hooves pounding. Rani was sure if she turned around the monster would be right there, breathing down her back. Heart hammering, sweat slick on her palms, she grabbed Abigail's hand and together they surged through the watery wall of magic.

Just behind them, the boys dived through and all seven of them rolled down the ditch on the other side, ears popping and stomachs roiling at the intense pressure of passing through the magic. Looking up, Rani had never been so relieved to see the glorious towers of the academy.

'Holy mother . . . We're alive!' Elijah chuckled, the sound turning almost into sobs of relief.

Flopping over on to her front, Rani panted, her heart refusing to still. She looked up to see Rupert standing over her again with his hand outstretched. This time, she took it.

'You two run fast,' he said, pleased. 'Good to know. Now, how about we all agree to keep each other's little secrets, huh?'

Rani nodded, unable to help the small smile tugging at her lips.

Perhaps she'd got these boys all wrong. And part of her couldn't help but still want to hear it. The music Rupert was going to make.

'Deal,' she said.

The lot of them began the journey back to the Pledge dorms. Back within the boundaries of Fountains Abbey, they were greeted by the ever-present hum of magic. In the distance, even at this hour, a lone inhabitant of the academy was practising spells on a violin.

Somehow, through all of it, Rani had managed to hold on to her satchel, only half filled with star root. She'd have to wait until next month to get more.

After sneaking back into their dorm room, the girls tiptoed to the dresser to get out of their filthy robes, careful to avoid their piles of inked notes and ingredients all over the floor. The air smelled faintly of candle wax and dried flowers from endless potion practice – a scent that seemed to follow Rani around wherever she went.

As they drifted off to sleep, Abigail turned in her bed, grinning over her purple duvet with orange stars, the girls' two favourite colours.

'They were fun.'

Rani snorted, and yet . . . she couldn't disagree.

Rupert and Magnus. She closed her eyes and thought of them, the mysterious Faymore brothers, that undeniable anticipation when Rupert had been about to play his ocarina. She'd wanted to hear it. His music. His power. And she wondered if maybe, just maybe, they really would be able to bring back the lost magic.

When the bell awakened them the next morning, a stream of sunlight lit up a folded piece of paper on the floor. Someone had slipped it under their door.

Fingers steady, Rani opened it with Abigail leaning over her shoulder. Rani chuckled as she read it. It seemed like her nickname was going to stick.

If you girls ever fancy doing more things you're not supposed to do, you know where to find me.
Your favourite Rapscallion